"Heartfelt and hilarious, Judy Smith's debut novel, *The Golden Years Glitch* is a true delight. Readers will not only fall for Andi and her unexpected golden years plight, but root for her to find her way into the most glorious of comebacks. A perfect book club book for any age, Smith is a writer to watch!"

—Donna Freitas, author of *The Nine Lives of Rose Napolitano*

"A unique story of marital infidelity, broken dreams, and the shattered life of a woman of 70, *The Golden Years Glitch* is also the story of love rediscovered, new dreams created, and the joy of life recovered. Judy Smith demonstrates an impressively distinctive and reader engaging storytelling style. Original, deftly crafted, emotionally engaging, and all the more remarkable considering that it's Judy's debut as a novelist. *The Golden Years Glitch* is one of those unique stories of later-in-life romance that will linger in the mind and memory of the reader long after the book is finished and set back upon the shelf."

—Midwest Book Review

"I wish Andi Parker lived nearby. She's just the kind of person I'd love to hang out with—Best Effin' Grandma to her grandchildren, loyal friend, astute businesswoman, and up for everything from sliding through mud to deep sea fishing. In *The Golden Years Glitch*, Smith reminds us that you're never too old to live life to the fullest, and it's never too late to start over. This is a sparkling, sexy debut with a lot of heart and humor."

— Suzanne Kamata, author of *Cinnamon Beach*

"Judy Smith is a fantastic writer. I thoroughly enjoyed *The Golden Years Glitch*—I could relate to so many different feelings! I loved how strong the protagonist, Andi, was—she did what she needed to do for herself. Fabulous book."

—Susan Noles, contestant, ABC's "The Golden Bachelor"

"...ably depicts Andi's empowering self-actualization in the wake of devastation as she spends more time with the women in her life doing new activities like a mud run, deep sea fishing, and talking frankly about their sex lives. In addition, realistic internal dialog about decision-making adds a layer of authenticity to this unique spin on a coming-of-age story. A big-hearted novel about finding fulfillment in the third act."

—KIRKUS REVIEWS

"Judy Smith's portrayal of the cheating husband is excellent. His cold detachment, as he treats his beloved like an experimental subject, places this character in the classic narcissistic villain camp."

— Stella Fosse, author of *Write & Sell a Well-Seasoned Romance* and *Brilliant Charming Bastard*

"*The Golden Years Glitch* was a delightful read. I liked the camaraderie of the girlfriends, and the fact Andi worked in a resale shop and was still dressing with style. It's light, heartwarming, and funny!"

—TheVintageContessa.blog

"Hats off to Judy Smith for doing an excellent job in creating such a satisfying read. I highly recommend!"

—Joy Ross Davis, author of *The Goddess of Weaver Street*

"This was a book I found hard to put down. Loved it. I laughed out loud."

—Karen Kibler, author of *The Second Chasm*

THE
GOLDEN
YEARS
GLITCH

a novel

JUDY SMITH

Wyatt-MacKenzie Publishing
DEADWOOD, OREGON

The Golden Years Glitch
Judy Smith

ISBN: 978-1-954332-62-1
Library of Congress Control Number on file.

Wyatt-MacKenzie Publishing, Inc.
www.WyattMacKenzie.com
Contact us: info@wyattmackenzie.com

DEDICATION

To Jamie and Mike, my lights, my loves, my forevers.
It's an honor to be the mother of two such
remarkable human beings.

To Ellen, the world's greatest BFF. Your leaf will always be
one of the greatist gifts I've ever received.

Him – I would love to take you out sometime.

Him – Let's get together for a drink.

Him – I'm not married or in a relationship.

Him – Wow, you are so beautiful.

Him – I've been thinking about you.

Him – When can we get together?

Him – No pressure, I just want to see you.

Him – I will be away for two weeks, but I want to see you as soon as I return.

"I can't duck down any further. Jed can't see us anyway." I looked over at Ellen from the passenger seat of Tim's car, ready for our evening of surveillance. "This isn't the way to Steve's," I added angrily. "It's also not the way to Renee's house."

Ellen grimaced. She lifted her sunglasses that we had donned along with baseball hats for our surveillance. "And, just how do you know where Renee lives?"

"I did a little bit of spying on her Facebook page, found out her last name, and where she lives."

Ellen pursed her lips together with a "hmmm" sound. "And, what else did you find out?"

"She has big boobs, two children, works at the restaurant where Jed golfs, and is ten years younger than me. Did I mention she has big boobs? Wait, he's pulling into that shopping center."

Ellen drove closer to Jed's car. "Look, he's parking in front of that little restaurant off to the side. And I'll bet he's meeting Renee there."

"Well, we can't exactly go inside to check it out, and have him see us."

Ellen removed her baseball hat and let down her long auburn hair that held only a few streaks of gray. "Well, let's just sit in the car and wait for him to come out with her."

CHAPTER ONE

WE WERE SO BUSY IN THE SHOP that I ignored the numerous text messages and calls coming from the phone buried at the bottom of my purse.

"I'm looking for a sleeveless black dress for my nephew's engagement party next month," a prematurely gray-haired young woman said as she approached the front counter. "I wear a size 10-12, depending on the style and designer."

"We have a selection of black dresses over here," I said as I guided her through the tight maze of clothing racks. A heavy waft of her Christian Dior's J'Adore Perfume floated in the air as I pointed to a sign above the section of black dresses that Melanie had titled *LBD*. "Our dressing rooms are in the back. Let me know if you need anything else." I suspected she was more a size 12-14. "Take your time and try on as many as you like."

Sweet Repeats, the store I co-own in our charming water-front town in Southern Maryland with two friends, Jeannie and Melanie, had only been open for six months, and we hadn't anticipated its early success. Jeannie's idea to open an upscale consignment shop in quaint Mathews Island was generously received by our neighbors, but it also came with very long hours—hours I didn't have, given that I was in the process of turning over to my sons the advertising business I had started 37 years ago.

Jeannie motioned to me as she cradled the phone to her ear and rang up a sale for a customer. "Can you check the appointment book to see if we have any available slots for a consignment review this Friday?"

I pulled the book out from the end of the counter and checked the schedule. "Ask her if she can come in around 2:30."

Jeannie gave me a thumbs-up as she continued her conversation, giving me one of her magnetic smiles.

I stayed at the counter after I saw Melanie walk up with another customer and an armful of clothes to check out.

As I helped Melanie remove tags and fold the clothes for the new order, I tilted one of the strategically placed, free-standing fans. The combination of a sweltering hot July day combined with a malfunctioning air conditioner had all the makings of a difficult afternoon at the store.

We'd been continually busy with customers and trying to ignore the uncomfortable heat, so it was easy to push away thoughts of answering my phone even as it continued to ring. I assumed it was my best friend, Ellen, who often became incessant when she had something she "just had to tell me."

But I couldn't ignore my 19-year-old granddaughter, Brooke. Just as I was handing Melanie's customer her packages, I saw her walk through the door.

She had a pissed-off grimace on her flawless face and gave an angry tossing of her long, unbleached blonde hair. "Grandma, why aren't you answering your phone?"

I was immediately convinced that someone had been injured. I grabbed Brooke's arm. "What happened?"

"Everyone is okay," she muttered through tightly clenched teeth. But then she began guiding me toward the back of the shop.

"Take over for me," I said to Jeannie and let myself be led by my adorable granddaughter. Brooke looked out of place in her tight skirt and exposed midriff among the 40 to 75-year-old women going through the racks of mainly Chico's and Talbot's clothing. I could see the shoppers looking at Brooke, remembering the days from long ago when they, too, could wear youthful clothes without thoughts of loose skin or varicose veiny legs.

I nearly knocked down a jewelry display as Brooke dragged me along and pushed us through the backroom door, the place where Jeannie, Melanie, and I sorted through the massive amounts of donated and consigned clothes. Brooke opened up her Facebook app and showed me a series of messages. There were 22 in total, that were posted on my beloved husband

Jed's Facebook page because yes, I counted.

Jed is the man I love, by the way. The man I have been married to for 25 years. The same man who I had waited so long to be with. Jed and I had spent the past two years planning the excursions and time together we would enjoy during our "golden years." Right now, that thought was fluttering through my head along with the image of his bony golden ass as I kicked him out of our home.

I dropped Brooke's phone after I read what was on the screen and then l looked at her in disbelief.

My husband was an idiot. Jed thought he was privately messaging a woman named Renee, evident with his words that were now stinging in my belly. How or why he had posted these messages directly for the world to see was probably enhanced by the alcohol he consumes nightly.

It took me a moment before I could speak. I tried to gather my strength and be the grandmother I should be, not a heartbroken teenager, which is how I felt. I hugged Brooke tightly. "I love you, sweetheart. Don't worry, I'll be fine."

I was far from fine.

I walked Brooke to the door and gave her another reassuring hug.

After Brooke left, Jeannie and Melanie looked at me with concern. I ignored their questioning faces and turned around.

I gathered my purse from behind the counter, hearing the phone ring yet again. "I'm sorry, I have to leave for a family situation, but everything is okay," I told them—unconvincingly, I'm sure.

Between the phone's incessant ringing, the 60s background music playing in the shop, the whirling of the fans, and the chimes we'd installed over the entrance door signaling yet another customer arriving, it was just too much noise and activity for me to handle right now. I needed to escape everything. As I tossed a wave to Jeannie and Melanie, "Build Me Up Buttercup" came through the speakers, and I couldn't get out fast enough.

I felt a twinge of guilt for leaving my friends on a busy Saturday, but this was far outweighed by my anger at Jed.

Before I started my car, I closed my eyes, sighed heavily, and took several long breaths. Finally, I allowed my eyes to open and I read just a few of the texts on my phone and scanned the list of missed calls from my daughter, my sons, my daughter-in-law, and several friends.

I didn't bother to listen to them, though.

Now I knew why they were calling.

CHAPTER TWO

THE RIDE TO MY HOME AT 150 Henry David Drive was too short, and I needed time to absorb this massive bomb to my marriage. I cranked the A/C to maximum, trying to cool down the oppressive air and my internal heat, and drove my pearl-gray Mercedes the long way back to my neighborhood, doubling the usual time before I saw the welcome sign for "The Villas of Walden's Pond." The Pond, its abbreviated name, was just as the brochure proclaimed: a scenic, 55+ community filled with amenities to love and the peace and privacy everyone supposedly deserves. It was only five streets clustered around a small manufactured pond complete with a resplendent bubbling fountain in its center. Jed and I had loved it immediately, despite, or perhaps because of, the "Stepford-like" premise.

How excited we were when we moved here ten years ago. At first, I was against the idea, but Jed won the argument. "Honey," he'd said, "You will hopefully be fully retired in a few years, and we will have time to enjoy activities and meet new people. We've worked hard and saved enough money to afford this lifestyle."

I'd stopped myself from saying to him, "You mean I've worked hard and made the majority of the money." There were times, many of them, when I quashed the utterances I held inside about his freedom to pursue his interests (golf and incessant guy outings) while I kept us afloat in the custom we had come to enjoy so much.

Jed was right, though. Even though I was initially opposed to living among identically structured quad houses on perfectly manicured postage-stamp-sized lawns, we could and would enjoy the peaceful, carefree lifestyle that The Pond promised. I was eventually won over by the luscious, luminous landscaping, the promise of a no-maintenance lifestyle, and the allure of exciting "senior" activities. Jed had dreams of buying a boat and sailing along the Chesapeake Bay. We soon immersed ourselves in this eclectic group of 520 active over-55ers, adults who were downsizing and welcoming their golden years like us. Shortly after moving in, I met Melanie and Jeannie, the two wonderful women who have become my dear friends and business partners.

As I pulled my car into the community, I waved solemnly to the annoying and varying dog walkers and hand-holding couples and hoped Jed was already home from his golf game. Was he really golfing, or was he out with Renee? As I pushed the garage door opener on my visor, I saw his canary yellow Corvette Convertible with its JEDSC8 vanity plate. The Corvette was Jed's first gift to himself upon his retirement. Did he have thoughts of driving Renee around and impressing her? Would she have trouble scooping herself down and plopping onto the bucket seat? Would she have to hold onto the side of the window just to get herself out of the car like I do? Or was she petite compared to my almost six-foot frame and could easily maneuver her less-fat ass into the necessary positioning?

I got out of my car and stormed into the house. I found Jed in the bedroom as he changed out of his golf clothes.

Without saying hello, I belted out, "What the fuck Jed, what the *actual* fuck?"

Then I opened my phone to his Facebook page, tapping my manicured peach fingernail on the words he wrote to Renee on the screen.

Jed stared at the evidence of his illicit behavior for a few seconds before looking at me. Then he reached up, bringing both hands to his head. His voice was steady and measured as if he had rehearsed the words. With a calm air of disbelief, he said, "Andi, Renee is just an old friend, someone I haven't seen in over 30 years, and I was just saying hello."

"You just wanted to say hello? That's why you made it clear to this Renee that you weren't married? You do realize you ARE married, don't you?"

I took several deep breaths. "Stop ignoring me. How can you do this to me?" I grabbed his arm and turned him around.

"It was just an innocent flirtation."

With a ridiculous neatness, Jed put his golf shirt into the hamper. Then, without looking at me, he walked slowly into the kitchen with continued calmness.

Then Jed reached into the cabinet, grabbed a glass, and proceeded to make himself a White Russian, his drink of choice as if nothing was happening. I watched as he poured vodka and liqueur into the glass, adding ice and a hefty dose of heavy cream. As if serving the drink to someone else, he gently stirred the cocktail and topped it off with a cherry. Caffeine, fat, alcohol, and sugar; all the ingredients needed to make this conversation turn even uglier.

Jed took a large gulp, and then he turned to me. "You've got to believe me, honey; I want no one but you." He narrowed his eyes at me playfully, urging me to lighten my mood.

Jed closed the space between us, turning on the charm that has always worked in the past. "I'm sorry, Andi. This is just a misunderstanding."

My eyes locked with Jed's. I could see the Asian vase with its minor crack sitting on my shiny black granite countertop behind him. I had brought it home from the shop, hoping Jed could epoxy glue the tiny crack. He had already repaired numerous donated items for the shop. The man could fix things, that's for sure. He could make a 20-year-old dishwasher behave like new, rewire just about any appliance, keep them running years past their expiration date, unclog a drain, and even put on a new roof.

I'd give him this much; whatever I wanted repaired, remodeled, or mended, he did it for me. To avoid additional builder costs for our new home, Jed put up the kitchen backsplash and the crown molding and even created a porch around the concrete slab provided to the residents. Jed had also been a huge help at Sweet Repeats, setting up the shelving and racks, putting in a new linoleum floor, and many repairs.

But I wasn't in the mood to revisit any of Jed's attributes. I envisioned picking up the vase and smashing it over his head, but then I realized I would be the one cleaning up the bloody mess. Still, I allowed myself a few minutes to revel in my vision of repeatedly plunging the vase onto his head.

Jed started rambling. "I never meant to hurt you. I don't want this to change anything between us. I'm sorry, it was a stupid mistake, and I would have never gone through with any-thing. I guess I drank too much and didn't realize what I was doing. In fact, I don't really remember writing those things to her." Jed walked into the family room and stared out the win-dow, once again turning his back on me.

I began shouting louder than I intended. "You told Renee that you would be gone for two weeks and would contact her when you returned. Well, let her know that you will no longer be going on the two-week cruise with your wife and that you can see her now. Oh wait, that's right, first you have to tell her that you do in fact have a wife. Perhaps you can see if she wants to go on the cruise with you."

Jed and I had never taken more than a week off because of my work and were anticipating the river cruise to France, Germany, and the Czech Republic. When he convinced me that my business and Sweet Repeats would survive without me for two weeks, I gladly acquiesced, and our planning began. We were supposed to leave in three days. My bags were already packed with gorgeous new sundresses and practical, comfort-able bejeweled sandals. I had helped Jed pack and coordinate his polo shirts to match my attire. This was one of the adorable (now nauseating) things Jed and I were known for—wearing matching coordinated colored clothing. So many of our cher-ished pictures were of Jed and me looking like we were posing for a magazine with our conforming outfits. Our standard pose was evident in the photos, with Jed's right arm embracing my left shoulder and my right hand placed softly around his mid-dle.

The thought of missing the trip was nearly unbearable, but I couldn't envision being able to enjoy two weeks alone with Jed after knowing about his indiscretion.

Jed quickly finished his drink, returned to the kitchen, and made himself another. I followed him with increasing anger, took the drink out of his hand, placed it on the counter, and demanded he see the severity of the situation.

I narrowed my eyes, feeling intense anger burning inside. "Do you realize you made your provocative requests visible to my children and our friends? Brooke came to the shop to show me your posts. I even received a text from Brynn, YOUR granddaughter, wanting to know what had happened. Why don't you give her a call and tell her what you did? Explain to Brynn that her grandfather only 'flirted' with another woman when he told her he wasn't married and wanted to date her."

Jed retrieved his drink and slightly tipped the glass to me in a toast before he swallowed more of the mocha-colored liquid. "What can I do to make you realize I would never jeopardize our relationship?" Then, in typical Jed fashion, he turned the situation around, trying to make himself seem like the victim, that this was about his hurt and his feelings. "You are blowing this out of proportion. How can you possibly think I would want anyone but you? Am I not always attentive to you? I'm always there for you. I can't stand it when you are so irrational."

By the roll of my eyes, Jed could tell I wasn't falling for his bullshit.

Seeing my disgust at his self-oriented behavior, he tried again. "I'm so sorry I hurt you; that was never my intention."

"Well, of course, it wasn't your intention. You wanted to get away with this." I was shouting at him.

Jed let out a huff. "Stop it, Andi. Seriously, this is ridiculous."

"Pack a bag." I looked intently into his eyes, then turned around and walked into our bedroom, where I could see the matching luggage awaiting our trip. I reached for his empty Patagonia duffel bag and threw it at him. "Go now, and leave me alone."

Jed went into his closet and then the bathroom. He gathered a few items and folded them carefully before placing them into the bag. His lack of distress infuriated me. At one point, he glanced up. "I'll come back tomorrow when you have calmed down, and we can talk this through," he said. "I love you, Andi.

Don't make this out to be more than it is. Going on the cruise and getting away will benefit us both. It will be a perfect time for us to reconnect."

"Reconnect?" I nearly spat the words out. "I didn't know anything was wrong with our connection. I was happy. I thought you were happy. Why do you want to destroy this? Do you know how much I looked forward to going away with you?"

With an annoying look, Jed said, "I told you to stop being so irrational. All I meant was that I wanted to have a romantic time with my wife."

"So NOW I'm your wife? When you were messaging another woman, you didn't have a wife." I reminded him. "Has our entire relationship been a lie? How many times have you cheated on me before?"

"I've never been unfaithful to you. I never have, I never will."

"How would I know that?" I caught myself knowing full well that he was capable of cheating. I just didn't know if he would cheat on *me.*

He glanced at me, and I knew he was thinking the same thing.

Let me interject that I am 69, and Jed is 74. This kind of thing shouldn't be happening at our age. It most definitely should not be happening amid this new chapter in our lives, especially not since I am near full retirement. I was in a good place, a reward for all the years of struggle and hard work. My three children and five grandchildren were all healthy, thriving, and a significant part of my life. I had believed, incorrectly, that Jed was also happy.

Jed, on the other hand, retired when he was 62. His body had become worn out from the handyman work he'd done since he was a teenager. At 40, he had started his own contracting business, which never quite received the success he wanted (or the success he claimed to others). Shortly after we married, my business was flourishing. While this helped us to achieve a lifestyle we both enjoyed, I was overworked, overtired, and often irritated that I was the prominent source of income. He continued to do easy, small contracting jobs on the side. While he did maintain most of the responsibilities in our home, he also spent a great deal of time golfing, kayaking, learning to sail, and riding around in his cheery little Corvette.

I became further annoyed with the exasperated sigh Jed expelled while carrying his bag from the bedroom.

Jed moved the bag from one shoulder to the other. "Please settle down and know that I love you, and I hope you will reconsider going on the cruise."

I didn't respond. There was still this confusing part of me that wanted the life back that I had had just a few hours ago. My anger took over, and I held my tears inside.

I followed Jed into the living room to make sure he was leaving. Then, once he was gone, I returned to the bedroom and slammed the door for unnecessary effect.

It had been only two hours since Brooke arrived at Sweet Repeats, and I was drained and full of anger and confusion. I should be closing up the shop with Melanie and Jeannie right now. We would be toasting and congratulating each other on another successful sales day. I would go home to my husband for an enjoyable dinner and once the heat died down, an evening walk through our community. Or, perhaps we would take a dip in the pool that was less than 50 yards from our home.

I leaned against the bedroom door and dropped onto our luscious champagne-colored carpet. I let the tears flow for the first time as my fingers traced the diamond pattern on the rug. I loved this carpet and its nouveau riche texture, which solidified the cosmopolitan feel of our bedroom. I gently wove my fingers through the strands like pushing a tiny rake through the white sand on a Zen Garden.

So many questions swirled through my head. Was I overreacting? Did I want to lose Jed? Should I try and make things better? Should I apologize for my outburst? Jed had sounded so sincere that it was just a flirtation, and I wanted to believe him. But how could I justify him writing to another woman, "I would love to take you out sometime," or "I'm not married"?

I moved myself to the bed and pummeled my fists into a pillow and cried until my anger dissipated into disbelief, and I was drained of emotion.

Jed had been a liar and had cheated before. I knew that all too well, didn't I?

When Jed and I met, he was married at the time. Just as Jed had been unfaithful to me, I had had an affair with him before he left his wife. But he and I ended up together, validating our illicit betrayal, so in my mind, it was an affair easy to justify. When our relationship started, Jed and his wife, Kathleen, were separated while still living together. But I found out later that Kathleen and Jed had reunited while he and I were seeing each other. I had immediately ended our relationship.

They stayed together for another five years before divorcing. He was always on my mind, and I still hoped we would end up together. He often said he was staying with his wife until his children were older. When they divorced, I was thrilled. I was going to be with the man of my dreams.

Oh, what an idiot I was. Once a cheater, always a cheater. Even at 74.

There were so many red flags, too. Like the golfing weekends where Jed went with his "buddies" from his golf league. Buddies that I didn't know, not any of our close friends. Or the times when he went on contracting "estimates."

I recall one time when Jed came out of the bedroom wearing his yellow vee-neck sweater, my favorite, and smelling strongly of his Aramis cologne. I nuzzled up to him, burying my neck into his, and told him how sexy he looked. I was thrown for a loop when he said, "I have an estimate to go on. I will be back in a few hours." I looked at him quizzically and asked, "Why do you smell so good for an estimate?" With that shitty-ass but adoring look in his eye, he walked away, looking over his shoulder, and said, "I wanted to smell good for you, Babe. Wait up for me."

My phone had still been incessantly ringing with calls and text messages. Before I turned it off, I started to delete every photo of Jed from my carefully organized "Jed & Andi" images file.

One by one, I pounded on the delete button with rage. Well, not every picture. I kept the photo from New Year's Eve two years ago, where I looked spectacular in my figure-hugging crimson red floor-length dress. I was sure I could figure out how to Photoshop Jed out of the picture. This had been possibly the last time I wore anything sleeveless. Now, I wouldn't dare expose the ever-increasing flab that hangs so unflatteringly from my upper arms that made its appearance well-known on the day I turned 65. The flab that my youngest granddaughter, Kendall, likes to swing back and forth.

Was that what made Jed message this woman? My arm flabbiness and the extra 20 pounds I'd put on in the past 25 years?

Of course, Renee must be younger than me. I was sure she was blonde, petite, and perky.

Realizing she must be one of Jed's Facebook friends, I grabbed my laptop nearby and started searching.

There she was.

At 58, Renee was 11 years younger than me and 16 years younger than Jed.

How classic. I went from being the younger woman to the "old" wife. She was, in fact, blonde (not natural, of course) with a toothy over-zealous smile and massive streaked curly hair. She wasn't gorgeous, but she was pretty. She wore heavy makeup with smoky cat eyes and long dangling earrings. A dragonfly tattoo was visible on her upper arm, with several silver bangles on her wrist. One of her "likes" was "Metro Lazer." Curious, I looked it up to find out it was a salon offering "Cool Sculpting." Apparently, this fat-freezing method aimed to rid stubborn fat from certain body parts. I immediately tossed the flab on my arms, wondering if it would work on me.

As I scanned Renee's page, I could see that she was single, a mother of two adult children, lived in a nearby town, and enjoyed posting photos of herself with her ample bosom prominently featured. She had a golden blend chihuahua, Butterscotch, that seemed to prefer snuggling his nose into her breasts. Those boobs would certainly have caressed the car window of Jed's convertible as he opened the door for her.

I scrutinized her photos and noticed how she tended to lean forward, exposing as much as possible. No pictures showed any evidence of a boyfriend. However, from the looks of Renee's seductive photos, I assume she was hoping to entice a few prospects. I wondered how Jed had met her. Obviously, she wasn't an "old friend," as he proclaimed.

Checking her "About" section, there it was.

Renee was a bartender for the Patuxent Valley Country Club restaurant, where Jed golfed several times a week. Boom. Old friend, my ass. While I scanned her page, I saw that Jed had "liked" some of her posts and had even included a few "kiss" emojis.

Well, Jed may not be currently having an affair with Renee, but he certainly wanted to start one. How many other women had there been?

I grabbed my phone and waited for it to boot up, knowing there would be a barrage of missed texts and calls. I quickly texted my daughter, Nicole.

I wanted to ensure that she and my sons wouldn't rush over here. *I don't feel like talking right now, honey, but I'm okay*, I wrote to her. *I will call you tomorrow. Please tell Nathan and Josh not to worry.*

Within seconds, Nicole responded furiously, *MOM, I HOPE YOU KICKED HIM OUT OF THE HOUSE. HE ISN'T WORTH IT!!!*

How many of our friends and family had seen Jed's messages on Facebook?

Oh no, maybe our neighbors, too.

I decided not to leave the house for fear of enduring people's pathetic, sympathetic faces. If just one person in our community saw Jed's post, I knew the gossip would spread through The Pond like wildfire. I could just imagine my next-door neighbor, Elise, power-walking from quad to quad, anxiously spewing gossip about the "tall" couple's marital woes.

I refused to be the victim of a polarizing scandal. Jeannie and Melanie would find out soon enough, and I needed to tell them before the chatter began.

I fed our cat, grateful for the addition of another heartbeat existing in my home.

Coco Chanel was our annoying oversized tabby for whom I truly felt little affinity. Coco was a gift from Brooke for my 65th birthday. My oldest grandchild apparently felt my home needed the presence of a massive feline, shedding fur and dander on the carpet, furniture, and clothing.

In the kitchen again, I glanced over to the countertop. I saw the vase and picked it up, allowing the heavy weight of the vintage Rose Medallion to rest in my hand. I ran my finger along the crack and realized it was too large to repair. Jed wouldn't be able to fix the vase. He wouldn't be able to fix us, either.

CHAPTER THREE

LATER THAT EVENING, I knew I would have to respond to my family and friends.

Taking the phone off mute, I sent a quick group text to everyone who had tried to reach me. *Hello all, thank you for your kind concern. As you can imagine, I need some alone time for a few days. I'm doing fine despite the unexpected shock.*

Nathan, my eldest, loudest, and most strong-willed child, immediately responded. *Thanks for the group text, Mom, but how the hell are you really doing?*

I could hear his sarcastic voice in the words of his message. Nathan would not stop until he knew exactly how I would proceed and would be the most vocal advocate for kicking Jed out of the house and onto the street.

I called him immediately, hoping to reassure and calm him, concerned that he would confront Jed. "Sweetheart, I'm okay. I asked Jed to leave. I just want to try and get some sleep."

"Okay, Mom," Nathan acquiesced. "But I'm coming over tomorrow, and we are going to pack up his shit."

Just then, Nathan's wife, Emily, grabbed the phone. "Andi, please tell me you are not going to take him back."

In the background, I could hear Madison and Kendall, their young daughters. I didn't want my sweet grandchildren to listen to their parent's anger. "I love you both," I replied calmly. "And we can talk more tomorrow. Right now, I'm drained and exhausted."

I knew sleep would be my enemy as I prepared for a difficult night.

I collapsed onto our comfortable California King Bed and tossed aside the seven throw pillows Jed had meticulously placed onto our nautical-themed blue and beige comforter. Jed was the one who made the bed since I typically arose two hours before him. I tossed through the night, tangled in the satin sheets, trying not to touch his side.

His Facebook messages to Renee blasted through my mind:
You looked so hot today. I couldn't stop staring at you.
No pressure, let's just meet for a drink.
I really want to get to know you.

Tears and torment lasted for hours until exhaustion finally allowed relief. I awoke when it was still dark and was disoriented, dry-mouthed, and hungry.

I wondered where and with whom Jed stayed last night. I'd turned off my phone, so I didn't know if he had tried to call me. I wanted him to have tried. I wanted more apologies and to hear it in his voice.

An hour later, showered and fed, I sat with my phone, determined to make some calls. My first call had to be to Ellen, my oldest and dearest friend. She didn't use Facebook, so I assumed she wasn't aware of the situation.

Ellen and I have known each other since grade school. We'd seen each other through childhood traumas, first loves, marriages, our parents' deaths, our children's births, and everything in between. Ellen married Tim, her high school sweetheart, shortly after they graduated. I'd dated Tim first. When we broke up, I suggested he date Ellen. Once they started seeing each other, they were rarely apart. But it never changed our relationship. We had always been there for each other. We became pregnant at the same time with our first children. If anyone could help me through this, it was Ellen.

With my head in my hands, I waited for Ellen to answer. When I heard Ellen's breathless "Hello?" all I said was, "I need you. Can you meet me at The Sea Breeze?"

Without hesitation, Ellen replied, "Of course. I was just putting out the inflatable pool for the kids." She didn't ask any questions; she just agreed to meet in 30 minutes.

The barista at our favorite coffee shop was an overly friendly young girl in her early 20s with a nose ring and painted eyebrows. As she took my order for an extra-large, vanilla, frozen latte and iced lemon cake, I noticed her name tag said "Reenie."

Too close to Renee. I grumbled a thank you without leaving a tip.

Waiting for Ellen, I tore apart my lemon pound cake, suddenly ravenous. As I finished my last bite, she walked in wearing her signature black capris and sleeveless black tunic with a long amethyst necklace.

"Sweetie, what's wrong? You sounded horrible."

"Jed wants to fuck another woman," I said.

Ellen's gaze narrowed suspiciously. "Wants to?"

I pushed aside the plate littered with crumbs, momentarily unable to speak. Once I started telling Ellen the story, I couldn't stop. I ran through the sordid details while Ellen nodded, her face distorting from shock to anger to sympathy.

She put down her drink and got up to hug me. "We should be drinking something stronger," she said.

I looked at my empty plate. "Or, at least, eating more comfort food."

At this, my hunger returned, and I went to the counter, asking Reenie for two vanilla biscotti.

Between mouthfuls of my crumbling biscuit, I told Ellen how shocked I was that this was happening and that I planned on canceling the cruise. And then I told her the details I'd already obtained about Renee.

Ellen leaned toward me with a raised eyebrow. "Do you remember those Dateline shows where the woman plots to kill her husband? They often poison their spouses with anti-freeze. It's odorless and tasteless, and you can pour it into his White Russian." The corners of her mouth upturned as she tried to distract me from the pain with humor.

After more tears, some bitter laughter, and sincere hugs, I told Ellen to go home to rescue her husband from the grandchildren and that I had to talk with my business partners before they heard the news from someone.

As we left Sea Breeze, Reenie called out, "Have a sweet day, ladies."

With my heart lightened by my dear friend and my stomach temporarily satiated, I buckled into my car and texted Melanie and Jeannie. They both agreed to meet me at the shop later that evening.

But first, I needed to release more anger on Jed.

When can you come to the house? I texted.

His response arrived when I pulled into the driveway and saw he was already there.

Without greeting one another, we sat in our standard positions at the kitchen table with the cracked vase in clear view.

Jed's cheeks were sun-kissed from his various outdoor activities, and his hair was slightly disheveled, which was my favorite look on him. He folded his rough hands on the table and looked me in the eyes, ready to take his punishment. "Look, Andi, I'm sorry, truly sorry, but I really think you have taken this too harshly. I flirted and was wrong, but I would have never gone through with anything."

"Even if it was just drunken flirting, you've always made me uncomfortable with how you are around women," I told him. "Do you remember when we went to Cove Point last month and we took a walk on the beach?"

"What the hell did I do wrong that time?" he wanted to know.

"You blatantly stared at every scantily clad woman we passed. Even when I told you it bothered me, you couldn't stop ogling other women. You made me feel invisible."

"Is that why you are making such a big deal out of this?"

I pushed back my chair with emphasis, grabbed my purse, and handed him a printout of the 22 messages he had sent Renee. "It's all here, Jed, in your own words. You can't deny this. Your intentions were obvious. So don't feed me your *innocent flirtation* bullshit."

Jed's face lit up in anger as he pushed his drink aside and stood. "Of course, you printed it out. Do you intend to put it up on the refrigerator with a magnet as a constant reminder of my being a jerk?"

I shoved the printed evidence back into my purse. "Let's cut the crap and have an honest conversation. I thought we were happy. I was happy."

"Babe, I'm happy, but I *have* been feeling neglected."

Before he could go on, I couldn't help but interrupt, "You've been neglected? How did I neglect you, Jed? Is it our sex life?"

"Yes—and no," Jed spoke softly as my voice increased.

"What is that supposed to mean?"

Jed paced the kitchen, stopping to touch the cracked vase. "I gave you an honest response, Andi. Isn't that what you wanted—honesty? It's not the sex itself; it's the affection I miss."

"What the hell are you talking about? You miss affection? You sound like a pathetic child who's not getting enough attention."

"You are so busy with the kids and still involved with your business that you barely have time for me. I assumed you and I would do more things together when you cut back your time at the agency."

I rolled my eyes and raised my right lip, annoyed by his childlike words. "What about all the time you spend with your friends. Do you ever hear me complain?"

Jed blew a puff of air. "Why did you have to open the shop? You never even discussed with me how it would affect us. You've always put your career first."

I took a large breath and tried to release the tension in my shoulders. "First of all, Jed, I worked long, hard hours for all those years to give us the lifestyle *we* now enjoy. And I started the shop with Melanie and Jeannie to keep myself active. It makes me feel good knowing that Sweet Repeats will donate much of the profits to women in need. We have only been open for six months, and my hours are already substantially reduced."

Jed raised his hands in anger, his face growing red. "You never miss a chance to bring up that you were the major breadwinner, do you? I get it, Andi. You made more money than me, but give me some credit. I worked, too. Maybe I didn't make as much as you, but I contributed and certainly took care of things around the house."

Trying to calm Jed, I lowered my voice, sat back in my chair, and pointed to his spot for him to do the same, "Obviously, these are issues we should have discussed before, but none of that takes away from the fact that you were willing to jeopardize what we have to be with someone else."

Jed sat in his chair and shook his leg in impatience. "Will you please stop that. How many times do I have to tell you that I was NEVER going to pursue anything?" Jed pushed back his chair, and I knew what he would do. He made a White Russian, filling the glass to the brim. Handing me a bottled water, he resumed his pathetic reasoning. "Yes, I know it was wrong, and I shouldn't have reached out to Renee, and I will NOT contact her again."

I took a sip of the offered water, wishing it was wine. But I wanted to show constraint and that I didn't need to turn to alcohol.

Jed raised his glass to his lips every few minutes and finished the entire thing quickly.

Not wanting him to drink anymore, I spoke more softly than I felt. "We aren't going to accomplish anything by loud accusations. I need time, Jed."

"So I assume that means you won't consider going on the cruise?"

I shook my head emphatically. "No, I canceled it this morning."

Jed sighed heavily and stood, exceeding my height by five inches, and I raised my eyes to him almost obediently. This was a trait I implemented when Jed was drinking. I acquiesced to him to avoid the wrath that came with his excessive alcohol usage.

Walking down the hallway toward the bedroom, Jed looked back as I once again found myself staring at the cracked vase. "Hope you don't mind, but I need a few more things if you are kicking me out of OUR house. I'm staying at Eve's in case you care."

Jed never got along with his sister, Eve, and I was surprised he chose to stay with her. I followed Jed to the front door, resisting the temptation to throw myself into his arms and pretend the last 24 hours had never occurred.

As Jed left, I watched his car pull away and stop at the end of the driveway, where he was having a conversation with our neighbor, Sam. Does Sam know, too? More than likely, Jed is talking to him without any indication of the storm happening inside our home.

I knew I had to pull myself together and get ready to meet Melanie and Jeannie. This wouldn't be an easy conversation, but I once again resisted the urge for wine and settled on a pint of rocky road.

CHAPTER FOUR

I ARRIVED AT THE SHOP right before closing. When I opened the door, I could smell the subtle sense of lavender sprigs that we had dispersed throughout the shop. I almost choked on the Thoreau quote above the entrance as I closed the door. "Never look back unless you are planning to live that way."

Since Thoreau was the namesake of the Villas of Walden's Pond, Jeannie felt it was endearing to include his spirit at Sweet Repeats.

Jeannie, Melanie, and I met at a Getting to Know You Brunch at The Pond shortly after moving in. We had an immediate connection. I was drawn to both of them. Melanie's flowing, brazen hair and absurd fashion style were just part of her gregarious and wild side. She was artistic, creative, and flamboyant. A heavy waft of pot with a sloppily disguised attempt at perfume frequently lingered in the air whenever she was present.

On the other hand, Jeannie was timid, mild, and sweet. She was also one of the most gorgeous women I had ever known. She was polished and coiffed at all times. Jeannie was a well-respected actuary, served on many corporate boards, and had traveled the world with her expertise. I remember how she introduced herself at the brunch. "I am a widow without children, searching for more meaning in my life."

What a bold statement coming from someone so demure.

The three of us formed a quick friendship. Like me, Melanie and Jeannie were looking to expand their lives in new directions. Soon, the three of us were meeting for lunch, taking walks, and spending time together.

Jeannie set up her laptop during one of our lunches and introduced us to her sister's website. Her sister, Jodi, owns a consignment shop in Florida. "Our area doesn't have anything like this," she said as we scrolled through the information on the screen. "I can really see a need for an upscale consignment shop in our area."

Melanie pushed aside her plate of crab salad and took a closer look at the website on Jeannie's laptop.

"None of us has any experience in retail, though. How would we start?" Melanie asked.

"I like the idea," I said with increasing interest. "What do you think about giving a portion of the proceeds to a charity benefiting women?"

We spent several months researching consignment shops online and the equipment needed and spoke to owners of similar shops in neighboring towns. Jeannie's sister guided us through the process from the beginning.

From that initial conversation, Sweet Repeats blossomed. We found a shop in the center of town that was for rent. Jack, Melanie's husband, and Jed spent many hours helping with the painting, cabinetry, and assembling display cases and racks.

I adored Jack. He was the opposite of Melanie. Jack was refined, and Melanie was edgy. He was calm, and she was demonstrative. Jack spoke softly and slowly with no fanfare or wild gestures. He had a slow, measured walk and a very kind smile. His typical beige shorts and white polo shirt directly contrasted Melanie's splashes of colors. Together, they were an amazing, supportive team.

Jed was always reluctant to spend time with Melanie and Jack, though. He resisted nearly every time I suggested the four of us get together. Jed said he had nothing in common with Jack and found him boring.

Prior to opening, we sent out an email blast to the residents of The Pond and several other over-55 communities. We were inundated with interest and a substantial following. Many of our items had been and continued to be donated, which helped our charity tremendously. Now, six months later, we had outgrown our little shop.

When the last customer of the day left, I ushered Melanie and Jeannie to the backroom. We sat at the table without extending any pleasantries, pushing aside hangers, pins, and tags.

I tried not to disturb the carefully mounted piles of clothing sorted by style: casual, evening, and sportswear.

Melanie and Jeannie wore their Sweet Repeats tee shirts today and had concerned looks on their faces. I couldn't take my eyes off the logo Melanie had created in pink and yellow. With her artistic flair, she carried the same color scheme throughout the shop. On one of the walls, she'd painted sunflowers behind a pink fence. Above the fence, Jed had put up shelving units for accessory displays.

Neither Jeannie nor Melanie gave any indication that they were aware of Jed's Facebook posting. I was certain that Jeannie would not have a Facebook account. I couldn't imagine her having any interest in social media. After seeing a Mathematical Equations magazine at her house once, I didn't see her spending time on networking platforms. Jeannie had lived her life in a perfunctory manner that didn't include frivolities of any type.

Then I realized that, of course, Melanie was on Facebook daily as she handled Sweet Repeats posts and updates. In fact, her expertise had already received several hundred "likes" and numerous comments. But I was certain she would have reached out to me if she had seen Jed's post.

With my heart in my throat, I started the uncomfortable conversation. "Have you heard or seen anything personal on Facebook?"

Jeannie shook her head, stiff and silent.

But Melanie seemed worried. "Is there something on the shop website that you are upset about? I thought you said it was a family issue you were having?"

I took a deep, uncomfortable breath. "No, no, it is a family situation," I confirmed. "Yesterday, when Brooke came to the shop, it was to tell me that Jed had unknowingly posted a public message on Facebook to another woman where he expressed interest in being with her."

I went on to tell them the whole ugly story, but I left out the content of his messages. I wanted to save myself a tiny bit of dignity. These were my friends, but talking to Ellen about my anger and disgust was much easier.

I finished by telling Melanie and Jeannie I was doing okay and trying to deal with the situation.

"What the hell was he thinking?" Melanie gasped once she was sure that I had finished speaking. "You're so kind, strong, and beautiful. I've never entirely fallen for Jed's well-known charm. You are so much better than him."

Her comments made me a bit defensive and yet pleased.

Jeannie sat quiet and still as she tucked an errant hair behind her ear, allowing her simple pearl stud to show through. Her typical sweet expression turned sad. "I'm so sorry, Andi. I always thought you and Jed were the perfect couple."

I touched Jeannie's hand as I watched tears appear in her eyes. "So did I," I admitted. "I'm so furious and hurt, and yet, I miss him already."

Melanie's hands were tucked inside the pockets of her white capri jeans as if shielding herself from the coldness of the conversation. I recognized the look of empathy and pity, the same look that often covered my face after listening to my sister talk about the struggles with her drug-addicted daughter.

"Do you think there is still a chance?" Jeannie pressed, her voice soft and calming. "Do you want things to work out?"

I didn't know how to answer. "No." I said, trying to match her softness. Then, "Maybe," I added tearfully with a shrug. I nodded at them and looked down at the linoleum, relieved when neither one chose to ask more questions, and they accepted my presumed need for solitude.

The tender feelings I'd always had for Melanie and Jeannie welled inside me as I tried to assure them that I would indeed be okay. I cleared my throat, hugged them with gratitude, and led them out of the backroom door, promising to take tomorrow off from the shop.

As I went to shut off the lights, I could hear the beginnings of a storm in the distance. Threatening clouds moved across the dark sky as I gathered my things. Then I straightened a display of scarves and prominently placed several Louis Vuitton and Gucci delights more visibly out front.

By the time I locked up, the clouds were gathering along

with the darkness and the promise of a downpour. I stood still on the sidewalk and felt one raindrop after another. I waited while the wind released its angry torrent. The storm was too small to whirl away the newness of my reality, but it felt somehow comforting and hid the new batch of tears.

I was wearing a light tee shirt that was now attached to my skin. I tugged and pulled it away from my body as I ran half-laughing to my car.

Once again, I wished the drive home was longer as both my hands tightly gripped the wheel. The tears now flowed freely and abundantly. It was easier to clear my head while squinting between the rapid movement of the windshield wipers as they pushed away the crystalline rain.

When I entered the door of my dark, empty home, I reached for the wall switch to turn on the lights, nearly tripping over Coco Chanel, who had neglected to meow her presence.

I didn't want to talk to anyone else today, so I sent another mass text to my family and Ellen.

I'm okay. I will be in touch tomorrow. Love you all.

Sitting alone for a few hours with Ben and Jerry's and Chardonnay was not conducive to my health and well-being, so I headed to the shower with a silent prayer that the thundering skies would guide me through my agony and a hopeful couple of hours of much-needed sleep.

Afterward, I dropped onto my unmade bed, certain of another night filled with denial, discomfort, and agony. This bed I normally shared with Jed now seemed so uncomfortably large.

The rain and the storm increased in intensity. I pulled the comforter over my head and listened to the loud claps of thunder. It was like suspense music playing in my head. Each booming sound was matched only by the lightning bolts now visible through the bedroom window. When the light I had left on in the bathroom flickered on and off, I reached over to the flashlight in my nightstand drawer. I got up and went into the kitchen, where my phone was charging. I brought it to the bedroom so I could hear any severe weather warnings. I lay in bed for another hour, flashlight in hand, waiting for midnight when the next Wordle would become available.

An exhausted wave of defeat washed over my body as I threw my back against the multitude of pillows. I'd been so foolish, so blind. My anger had become physical as if my muscles ached for peace.

I dreamt I was swinging on a rope over a deep, dark cavern. As I propelled myself to one side of the canyon, in my view were rows and rows of brightly colored flowers. Monarch butterflies were swooping up and down, kissing the peonies and roses. White doves flew in and around multiple rainbows, casting their glow. Filled with a sedate serenity, I swung my body towards the other side of the canyon, anxious to see more glory. But instead, there was only darkness and barren trees. Ugly sounds emanated in the cold, dank air. Immediately, my body tensed and shivered with nausea, replacing my peacefulness.

I woke with a start and wrapped my arms around my legs, rocking back and forth. I tried to rid myself of the painful darkness and guided my mind back to the beauty of the other side of the canyon. I shook myself out of my strange dream and thought of my day ahead.

Oh no, it's Monday. Ping Pong.

Jed and I played ping pong every Monday and Friday morning with Rosemary and Bill in the clubhouse at 9:00 a.m., and it was already 8:15. I quickly texted Rosemary. *Jed and I can't play today. I look forward to seeing you on Friday.* Why did I say that? Did I expect things to change within a few days, and we could resume our couples' activities?

"Hold on to the memory of the beauty on the peaceful side of the canyon," I parentally told myself as I got out of bed and went to my closet. "Get yourself together and figure out the next step."

I stepped into my white shorts and tried to button them. Had two days of feeding my sadness already affected my waistline? Instead, I chose what I knew was a flattering look for me: my blue and white capris, short-sleeved blue-laced top, and two-inch white strappy sandals. I topped it off with youthful earrings and heavier-than-normal makeup. I took great care with my unruly hair, using the electric curlers that had been collecting dust in the back of the linen closet.

Day three of my saga was going to be better.

I called Jed and asked him to come over in the afternoon so we could talk again.

"I can't come till later in the day," he told me over the phone. "Sam and I are playing golf."

I stared at the phone incredulously. "You're golfing? I'm barely functioning, and you can golf?"

"I can't sit around and wait for you to decide how things will be. I need to keep busy, or I will fall apart." Jed said this with such conviction that I almost believed him. "Andi," Jed continued, taking me out of the scenario in my head, which was Jed and our neighbor, Sam, casually discussing golf when his marriage was falling apart. "I want to continue talking. Do you want me to pick up something for dinner?"

"No, Jed. Stop acting like the world hasn't been upside down for me. You go ahead and enjoy your 18 holes." Then, in a jolt, I remembered that Renee worked at the club restaurant, so with sarcasm, I added, "I'm sure you can enjoy dinner at the club afterwards. You must meet a lot of interesting people there."

With that, I pressed the off button on my phone with exhaustion, feeling like it was midnight, and yet my day had just begun.

Not knowing if I would see Jed later in the evening, I quickly made my plan for the morning. First, I had to reassure my three children that I was okay.

I wanted to avoid being in the house, with all the reminders of my life with Jed, so I asked Nicole to meet me at Becky's Café, a charming new restaurant, only two doors down from Sweet Repeats; it was convenient since I wanted to stop at the shop.

Knowing my daughter was irritatingly early for everything, I pushed through the cafe door five minutes before our agreed meeting time. The door was dutifully held by an elderly gentleman who enthusiastically wished me to "have a glorious day." I nearly laughed at the irony but managed to upturn my lips into a half-smile, mouthing an insincere, "Thank you."

Becky's was a small restaurant boasting a striped awning and bench outside with two tables, complete with white lace tablecloths. Between the tables was a water bowl for the plentiful thirsty dogs in town. The café was just as warm and inviting as the elderly gentleman who held the door for me. Becky's had an old-fashioned, relaxed atmosphere. It was cute and charming with its mismatched furniture and the menu chalked on the wall. Small vases with single-stem flowers sat atop white doilies. The café opened just last month and should do very well with this ideal location.

Nicole had chosen a table in the back, close to the kitchen and as far away from other tables as possible. She stood as I joined her at the table. "Oh, Mom, are you okay? I've been so worried about you."

Even with Nicole standing while I took my seat, she was still so petite next to me. Nicole inherited her father's stature and barely made it to 5'3. I was amazed I could have given birth to such a tiny little thing. My daughter was beautiful with long, straight, light brown hair, large aquamarine eyes, and a sweet smile. She was a doting daughter, wife, and mother. She was also opinionated and expressive.

Not giving me an opportunity to speak, Nicole rushed through an apparent memorized beginning to our conversation. Nicole pushed herself down into her chair and crossed her arms in the same manner she did as a petulant child.

"Please don't tell me you plan to take Jed back."

"Nicole, I don't know what I want right now," I told her.

"Are you serious? How can you even think about being with a man who obviously doesn't care what he does?"

"Honey, I didn't say we are getting back together. I just need time and don't want to make any irrational decisions."

I was grateful to be interrupted by the waitress. Nicole ordered the asparagus quiche and side salad. I still needed to feed my empty insides, so I ordered a Reuben, French fries, and a large root beer. Calories be damned, food was satisfying me right now. I had already turned the menu over to the desserts and contemplated the selections.

Nicole looked at me with sadness, "Mom, I don't feel right about this, but Eric and I have been planning a trip to New England to get away. We've agreed to leave Brooke in charge of Kelli, and we've already booked a B&B for three days."

"Oh sweetheart, go, enjoy yourself." And then I said the phrase I'd begun to detest. "I'll be fine."

I tried keeping the conversation on my granddaughters, Brooke and Kelli, to no avail, as Nicole kept turning things back to her anger with Jed.

"Mom, Jed's an asshole."

I opened my mouth to respond, but her unkind words silenced me.

Nicole looked at me with an incredulous look. "He's never been a father figure to me. I know you had hoped Nathan, Josh, and I would benefit from having Jed around after Daddy died, but frankly, you're too good for him. Maybe Josh liked being with Jed, but Nathan and I never understood why you married him."

I looked at my daughter, surprised at her feelings. "Nicole, I knew Nathan disapproved of Jed, but I always thought you were close to him. In fact, you seemed to encourage our relationship."

Nicole pushed her plate aside and looked at me sternly. "Mom, just stop. I liked Jed in the beginning. He was charming and attentive. And you seemed so happy. You both were happy. But didn't you ever notice that you catered to him? Everything had to be about him. I never understood how a woman as strong as you could be so easily controlled."

"That's not true, Nicole." With those words, the waitress came, took away our plates, and asked if we wanted anything further. Feeling full but wanting more, I selected my dessert. Without looking at Nicole or the waitress, I said, "I'll take the lemon meringue pie."

I knew Nicole had more questions and comments she wanted to make, but we continued with small talk about her upcoming trip.

Finished with the pie and the conversation, I walked Nicole

to her car and hugged her tightly, with promises that I wouldn't make any rushed decisions.

One child down, two to go.

But first, I had to stop by the shop. I wanted to tell Melanie and Jeannie I needed to take some time off.

At Sweet Repeats, Jeannie was answering questions from the only two customers in the shop. Seeing me, she nodded with a sympathetic smile and pointed to the backroom.

I reciprocated her smile and walked back to where Melanie was examining a new consignment batch, obviously disappointed with the quality of some of the items. She put them in the "can't sell" pile. Our consignment customers had the option of picking up the things we couldn't sell in the shop or allowing us to donate them to a women's shelter, who would be delighted to receive the "less than perfect" clothes. We offered the same option to our customers for any items that had yet to sell within 90 days.

Melanie sprang up, her hair and jewelry swaying, and greeted me with a warm hug. "I'm so happy to see you. How are you? I wanted to call but decided to wait until I heard from you."

I offered my standard, "I'm doing fine."

Looking at the merchandise on the table allowed me to avoid further discussion on the status of my crumbling marriage. "Do you think it would be a good idea to put some unwanted clothes in front of the shop, offering them for free?"

"Yeah, that's a cool idea. We could do it once a week. It would probably bring in some new customers. I will let Jeannie know, and we will keep a section here for the free items. If no one takes them, we can still donate them."

The door chimes indicated the entrance of another customer.

"Hey, I'll take care of it," I said to Melanie as she started to stand up.

"Hello, ladies," I said to the two women who had just entered the shop.

The older woman in her 60s smiled hopefully. "We heard

about Sweet Repeats from the waitress at the Café. My daughter, Delia, has a job interview next week and is looking for something appropriate to wear."

In her late 30s, Delia was visibly uncomfortable and showed little interest in our wares. Her eyes quickly scanned the clothing racks and decided nothing was worth a further look.

"Tell me about the company you are interviewing with, and we can select a few items for you," I said, drawing her attention.

Delia brightened a little and turned her gaze to me. "They are a new start-up SEO company in town."

I looked intently into her deep eyes. "Oh, that sounds intriguing."

"They're seeking someone to update their web design and handle social media. It's been several years since I've been in the workforce, but now that my children are older, I want to return to work. I've freelanced as a designer for nearly ten years."

"If they are a start-up company, I assume they may be young and free-spirited?" I asked.

Delia warmed up to the conversation. "Yes, I know the company is run by two young guys originally from New York."

"I think you should go with something a bit edgy," I told Delia, who was now quite attentive to the conversation.

While we talked, Delia's mother worked her way around the racks and gathered what she thought were appropriate items for her daughter.

As I walked towards the backroom, I told her, "I have just the person to help you out. I will be right back." I went to find Melanie. "I need your help with a customer," I said, leading her out to the front. Then, I briefly explained Delia's upcoming interview and introduced Melanie and Delia.

Melanie took Delia's arm and moved her away from the rack of unqualified Ann Taylor dresses.

Delia softened after seeing Melanie in her green and white striped jumpsuit and long circles of gold earrings.

After hearing our conversation, Delia's mother returned

J U D Y   S M I T H

her armful of standard dresses to their rightful locations. "I think I will look for a few things for myself," she said with a generous smile of gratitude.

In less than 30 minutes, Delia walked out of the dressing room with the perfect outfit: white gauze palazzo pants and an olive camisole under a short-sleeved multi-colored Henley sweater. We added silver hoop earrings and strappy sandals to top things off. She looked fantastic.

Delia's mother looked at her daughter's messy bun, "You should cut your hair, maybe something chin length," she said.

"Actually, I think you would look great with a high, sleek ponytail," Jeannie offered.

Delia warmed to the idea and thanked Jeannie for her suggestion.

Then Delia and her mother, both very pleased with their purchases, walked out of Sweet Repeats. Delia promised to inform us about her interview.

After they left, I realized we had eight customers in the store, and both dressing rooms were full. Another customer was waiting to try on the long red formal dress I had donated. She was tall like me, and I told her it would look fabulous on her. I wanted to tell her to wear it often before the arm flab arrives.

It felt good to be useful and to be around the energy of the shop.

After several more hours at Sweet Repeats, I asked Melanie and Jeannie, "Do you mind if I take the rest of the week off? I promise to come back on Saturday for the town event." Our quaint little town held a summer festival with music, food vendors, and activities.

Melanie touched my arm, "Of course not, just take care of yourself. Gail and Bonnie will be here all week. Don't even worry about Saturday."

Jeannie was ringing up the last customer as I was getting ready to leave. She held up her manicured index finger, tossed her blonde highlighted hair, and indicated she wanted me to wait for her. I nodded that I would.

34

"I've been thinking about you," Jeannie said. "Tell me how you are."

Tired of giving my customary response, I switched it up. "I'm talking to Jed a little and trying to be less angry."

"I hope you two can work things out."

Add Jeannie to "Team Jed," which consisted of just her and most certainly my younger son, Josh. Everyone else was obviously opposed to any thoughts of me staying with my husband.

I checked the time on our 1950s vintage multi-colored Atomic Clock on the wall. 4:30 pm. It was too late, and I was too tired to meet the boys at the office.

I sent off a few texts before I headed home.

Nathan and Josh: *I will stop by and see you both tomorrow.*

Nicole: *Thank you for today. Please don't worry about me.*

Jed: *I have plans for this evening. I will call you tomorrow.*

I did have plans, too: an evening of Dateline and Kendall Jackson Chardonnay.

CHAPTER FIVE

I TEXTED JED EARLY IN THE MORNING. *If you aren't golfing or sailing today, let's talk later in the afternoon.* The sarcasm was sure to piss Jed off, but it brought a smile to my face.

He quickly answered, ignoring my golf innuendo. *Sure, how about if I bring dinner over around 5:00? Shrimp in Lobster Sauce from Golden Palace?*

Okay. I wrote back, keeping it short and non-confrontational.

I called the office to let Nathan and Josh know I would stop by later today. I preferred to speak with my sons together and hoped Josh's passivity would calm Nathan's gregarious nature. Or, at least, tone down his reactions.

I started The Parker Group when I was thirty-five. Nathan and Josh had worked with me since high school. They both postponed going to college to join me there.

When I heard Krista, our receptionist for the past ten years, answer the phone with her customary, "Good Afternoon, The Parker Group," I had a touch of nostalgia, missing the fast-paced life of marketing and advertising that I had come to know so well. What had started in a small section of my home basement, with one of the original Texas Instruments computers and a phoneline, had burgeoned into a 3,500 square-foot office with twelve employees and part ownership of a printing company.

I asked Krista to let the boys know I would arrive by 1:00 p.m. and hoped they could set aside some time for me. Clearly, Krista had already heard the news. "Of course, Andi," she replied swiftly. "I will surely tell them. I know they are anxious to talk with you." Krista knew everything that happened within the company and our family—often before anyone else.

After getting off the phone with Krista, I answered a few emails. There was a reminder from The Pond Activities

Committee about the remote-controlled boat race being held in our manufactured lake. I was saddened thinking about how much Jed and I would have enjoyed participating. I already missed our ping pong games, the potluck dinners, and simply walking around The Pond with Jed. We'd made many friends in our community and participated in numerous activities.

As I left my driveway to head to the agency office, I did not look over at the boat race or listen to the laughter from the lake.

I'D WALKED THROUGH THE DOORS of The Parker Group more than a thousand times, and when I still worked here full-time, I'd almost always been the first one to arrive in the morning and was often the last to leave.

Krista, wearing a short skirt much better suited for Brooke or Kelli, greeted me. "It's great to see you, Andi. Nathan and Josh are waiting for you in your office." It occurred to me that I really didn't need the office anymore. I rarely came in and could accomplish anything I needed to do for the Agency at home.

I wondered how the boys would decide who would take over my office space. My descent into full retirement was occurring rapidly, and the announcement had already been made to our clients that I was stepping down. With his easy-going nature, Josh was an ideal fit for the Agency in customer management and employee interaction. And Nathan was the ultimate salesman: charming, affable, and outgoing.

Running a family-owned business was challenging, but it worked nicely for us. Both boys understood their placement in the company and seemed to handle disputes diplomatically. But sometimes, I felt that Emily, Nathan's wife, and Lisa, Josh's wife, created issues between their husbands. Emily worked part-time at the Agency and often aggressively commented on how she felt the company should run. She easily intimidated Lisa, who would have preferred a different career for her husband. Perhaps Lisa was right. Maybe Josh would have been better suited to a less stressful environment.

I breathed deeply as I walked into my office and tried to ignore Nathan's piercing gaze. Unlike Josh, who was passive and unassertive, he was naturally persistent and authoritative. Josh's only text to me in the past three days had been, *Mom, I hope you are okay. I love you.*

Josh was only eleven when Jed and I married. They had an immediate bond, and Jed was active in Josh's life. He attended every little league game, arriving early to warm up Josh's pitching arm. Jed would often attend the sporting events solo when I was busy at work. When Josh and Lisa purchased an older home, Jed spent many hours helping with repairs and teaching him the skills his biological father was not around to provide.

I have always been grateful to Jed for being a father figure to my children. Before my recent conversation with Nicole, I'd assumed Jed had also provided her with paternal love and attention. Nathan has always resented Jed's presence, and Jed showed little understanding towards him. Their strained relationship was a continued obstacle in our marriage.

But in every way, Jed treated Josh like a son. Jed had two daughters, Rachel and Chloe, and even they resented the closeness between Jed and Josh. We never became a happy, blended family. There was always tension among our children. However, it became easier as they matured and started families of their own. Everyone behaved well at family functions, but typically under false pretenses.

Nathan responded to an incoming text to his phone while he walked to the window as if studying the weather. He looked cool and sophisticated in starched white shorts and a blue button-down shirt. Once Nathan completed his text, he intently walked closer to me.

I murmured to Nathan, avoiding his eyes, trying to calm his flaring anger. "Nathan, I'm here to talk with both of you. I'm not here to be lectured or told what to do. I am obviously deeply hurt and furious with Jed, and I'm not saying whether I will take him back. I need time to take it all in and figure out what's best for me."

Nathan set his phone firmly on the desk in aggravation.

"Take it all in? Are you serious? The man wants to cheat on you. He probably already has with other women, and you are too blind to see it. You have to stop ignoring his bullshit."

I chose to ignore Nathan's atypical foul language. I continued, "Jed and I have been together for a long time, and I owe him some consideration."

Josh walked over to his brother. "Hey, Nathan, give Mom a break," he said in an attempt to calm down his brother.

Nathan turned away from Josh. "I will, as long as she doesn't give Jed a break."

Josh paid little attention to Nathan's statement and directed his comment to me. "Mom, we both just want you to be happy. Take the time you need. While you are here, can you look at the quote from Mail Masters? I emailed it to you this morning."

"Also, Mom," Nathan began, "I emailed you the contract for the press maintenance. It seems high to me. Can you check it out?"

I looked at both boys and nodded. "Sure, I will look at them before I leave."

Just then, Krista knocked softly on the door, entering without waiting for permission. I'm sure Krista hoped she would be privy to our private conversation.

"Josh, John Fenkner is on the phone and requested he speak to you now. He said he needs to change the wording on their promotion before it's released."

With apologies and hugs, Josh left the room to attend to his client, leaving me with Nathan and his fury.

I kissed Nathan on the cheek and returned to my desk to check the emails. "I love you very much and need you to have faith in me," I said simply.

Nathan rubbed his hands on his white shorts in frustration. "I'm trying, Mom, but please don't be an idiot and take the jackass back."

Well, that went as expected.

I reviewed and responded to my emails. I shrugged and pushed myself out of my desk chair. Exhausted from the heartfelt and difficult conversations with my grown children, I headed home for comfort food and alcohol.

It was already 4 p.m. Jed would be at the house in an hour, and I was a mess. Once again, I took extra time and care with my appearance. I changed my clothes and put on a slim, deep blue silk blouse and cream capris, leaving an extra button open to expose a hint of cleavage. I added violet eyeshadow and heavy mascara and took several minutes plucking and shaping my eyebrows. Selecting deep plum lipstick, I smacked my lips together, pleased with the outcome. I wanted to make it clear to Jed that I was still attractive and desirable to other men.

Since acknowledgment of Jed's betrayal, I've felt like a discarded woman to whatever extent that may have been. It only added to the insecurity I'd been feeling for some time about the changes in my body as I aged.

I had barely finished dressing when I heard the door open and smelled the Chinese food Jed had picked up.

He set the food on the counter and retrieved the square blue Pier One plates we used exclusively for Chinese food. He began putting the containers and plates on the kitchen table and drew in a long-exaggerated, breath when he looked at me. "Wow, you look great. Did you have a meeting today?"

"Yes," I lied. "I met a prospective client at the office." I hoped Jed would get the image of me sitting across from an attractive gentleman while showing an ever-so-slight glimpse of my chest. He didn't need to know that it had actually been an exhausting and emotional day with Nathan and Josh.

Jed must have had the same thoughts with his choice of clothes this evening. Damn him, he was wearing the outfit I've told him numerous times turned me on: jeans and a white untucked button-down shirt. I knew it was intentional, just like mine. The weather had cooled down slightly but it was still prohibitively hot for jeans.

I let Jed dish out my Shrimp in Lobster Sauce and his Chicken Fried Rice while I gave myself a good pour of Pinot Grigio. I positioned myself, elbows in, tightening myself to casually expose my cramped-in cleavage.

Jed started the conversation between bites with, "Andi, I want to come home. I can't stand staying with Eve. She smokes inside the house, talks non-stop about her political viewpoints, knowing they differ from mine, and has asked me several times how long I intend to stay with her."

Jed's voice was barely audible as if he was uncertain what to do, no longer his usual self-assured cocky persona. He put his chopsticks down, reached over, and stroked my cheek. "This has been so hard for me."

"You could have at least started with an apology instead of your discomfort of staying with Eve."

But, in true Jed fashion, he attempted to twist the narrative.

"You are the one who made me leave OUR home! Do you think it was fun packing a bag and staying with Eve? She thinks it's insane that you kicked me out." This time, his voice rose, and his typical confidence resumed.

I got up and topped off my glass of wine. "Well, I didn't know Eve had a say in our marriage," I said.

Jed pushed back his chair and stood up now, too. He put his arms up in the air and walked back and forth. "Stop it. You took this way out of proportion, typical Andi style. Let me repeat this. I'm sorry, I had too much to drink and innocently flirted with someone."

I stopped myself from looking at the tiny cleft I adored on his chin. "I can't deal with this right now, Jed. I'm hurt, I'm angry, and I'm confused. Just give me more time."

Jed walked over to his glass and finished it in one gulp. He put his arm around me in a reluctant hug. "Let me move back in until we figure out what to do. At least think about it."

I pulled away from him so fast that I almost fell over. "I can't talk anymore," I said. "My back hurts, my head hurts, and my heart hurts."

"Geez, Andi, why do you have to be so melodramatic? I'm going to grab a few more things, and I will call you tomorrow."

I wrapped my hands around my beckoning glass of wine, feeling the chill seep through my fingers. I took a sip and allowed a few moments to compose myself.

I needed him to be more sorrowful and not act like he was the wounded one.

Jed walked into the bedroom without another word or waiting for my reply, huffing loudly. On his way to the front door, he stopped, hesitated as if he wanted to say more, then changed his mind. With a quick movement, he was heading through the door without looking back.

I wanted to curl my hand into a fist and hit him.

I wanted to throw myself into his arms and feel his lips.

I swallowed hard, trying to diffuse my instant wanting of both feelings.

Instead, I simply closed the door behind him. I returned to the kitchen, sitting nonplussed, and finished my meal and Jed's.

CHAPTER SIX

I FAILED TO EXIST IN THE STRENGTH I had projected to my family and friends. I spent the next few days in the comfort of my bed. When I finally found the power to leave the sanctity of the bedroom, I wandered aimlessly from room to room in the now quiet hours, seeking relief from the changes in my life. My heart was crushed, my husband was gone, and food and alcohol were my only fulfillment.

Tomorrow was the town festival. I needed to get my head out of my turmoil and the constant questions of why Jed chose to jeopardize our relationship. In the evening, I took a long, uninterrupted bath without my phone, just a glass of bourbon and my thoughts.

As I felt the Epsom salt and inhaled the scent of eucalyptus, I succumbed to the cleansing power of the water. While I soaked, I listened to the lonely sounds of the night and sipped the heady liquid. I remained motionless, allowing myself to soothe my internal and external aches.

With a promise that I would soon discontinue using a sleeping aid, alcohol, and comfort food, I indulged once more in all three and hoped for a decent night's sleep. As I lay in bed waiting the half hour for the sleep sedative to take effect, I searched for the TV remote and hoped for some distraction. Successfully, I found a 20/20 special about a woman suspected of killing her husband. After I watched the complete episode, I did, indeed, enjoy a good night's slumber.

IT WAS A PERFECT SATURDAY, ideal for the town's summer festival. My children and grandchildren would all be attending the event, and it would assuredly be a profitable sales day for Sweet Repeats. I forced myself out of bed with a strong intention of making it a good day.

I sat at my vanity table and looked at my face in the magnified mirror. I didn't like the image of the woman looking back at me. My eyes were puffy and distant, my mouth was in a constant downturn, and all essence of the woman I once was had been removed. I looked at every imperfection on my face, and there were plenty. Short lashes that only multiple mascara applications could lengthen, thinning lips, and mysterious new brown spots on my nose. No amount of cosmetics could bring back my youthful, unwrinkled face and resilient body.

But that woman looking back at me was who I am, faults and all. The same woman who Jed no longer wanted. Well, that's not entirely true. He still wanted me and our life, but he also wanted a younger, more nubile woman. And what did I want? I just wanted my life back. The life I had worked so hard to obtain.

I used the miracle of makeup, put my hair up, pulled on a cheery, flowered sundress, and inspected myself in a full-length mirror. Not bad, I told myself. It didn't make me ten years younger, but I was semi-satisfied with the look. I've always had every intention of aging gracefully and accepting it with dignity. Now, it was challenging knowing Jed was seeking the attention of a younger woman.

I decided to walk the mile and a half to the shop, hoping it would help clear my mind. I wished away my anger with each step of my flat cherry-colored sandals. Tension ran down my legs as I pounded my feet until my legs ached from the abusive force. My arms began swinging wildly as I silently cursed Jed for what he had done to my life and our marriage.

I stopped stomping as I neared the shop. It felt cathartic and not smothering like the comforter I'd been burying myself beneath. The clean air I breathed helped calm my frayed nerves. I adjusted my attitude and welcomed the festival that had sprung up in front of me.

Main Street of Mathews Island was alive and bustling with vendors as they settled their tents and the retail shops prepared for sidewalk sales. Pots of geraniums and marigolds lined the streets, and the flurry of activity was satisfying as I reached Sweet Repeats.

Melanie was already outside arranging two racks of clothing

next to a large table with jewelry and accessories. "You didn't have to come today," she said. Melanie was dressed for the festival in a short denim skirt, a peace tee shirt, and a headband with a crown of artificial flowers.

"I need to keep busy," I told her. "It's not doing me any good to sulk in my bed and eat ice cream."

When I entered the shop, I knew Jeannie was there as I inhaled the scent of her Chanel No. 5.

She set aside her iced vanilla latte and greeted me with her customary sweet hug, "Hi, Andi, so glad you came today. I was just putting out some new things from yesterday."

I assisted Jeannie with last-minute touches getting the shop ready.

Ellen stopped by the shop shortly after I'd arrived. Her husband, Tim, owns Waldron Hardware, initially started by his great-grandfather, Josiah, in 1869. The store, also located on Main Street, boasts wooden floors and 19th-century fixtures, and is one of the country's few remaining iconic original hardware stores.

Waldron's has an old southern mom-and-pop feel, like much of Mathews Island. A major motion picture studio even came to our historic downtown area and filmed several scenes in the hardware store, the marine museum, and our lighthouse.

Ellen put a box of scones onto our counter. "I've come bearing gifts. I made cookies for the customers at Waldron's and scones for you ladies."

"Did you also make your clotted cream?" I asked Ellen.

"Just the way you like it," Ellen said with a wink.

Melanie took a full mouth of the lemon poppyseed scone. "Damn, Ellen, these are incredible."

I winked at Ellen with pleasure. "Maybe you can convince her to sell them. I've been trying to for years."

"Now that I'm not babysitting the grandchildren as much, I've actually thought about opening a tearoom," Ellen said while offering some lemon curd for the scones.

Jeannie reached for a napkin and a peach cardamon scone.

"A tearoom would do so well in Mathews Island."

I took a bite of my scone and said, "*Grandma Ellen's Tea Room.* You have to do this, Ellen. It would be so much fun."

Ellen moved her head from side to side. "I'm going to give it some serious thought. I haven't mentioned it to Tim yet. Speaking of which, I've got to get back to the store. I promised to help him today."

Within an hour, our first customers arrived. We had extra help in the shop, which enabled Melanie, Jeannie, and me to take turns walking around the festival.

I stopped at Becky's Café for a latte and was again greeted by the kind older gentleman.

He moved slowly and opened the door for me. "Hello, lovely lady. I hope you are enjoying the festival."

"Yes, I am, and the weather is perfect. Do you come to the café often?"

"This is my granddaughter Becky's little restaurant, and I come several times a week under the pretense of helping her around the café. By the way, my name is Alex."

"It's a pleasure to meet you. Please call me Andi."

After our brief introduction, another handsome, chocolate-eyed gentleman walked in behind me. "Hey, Pop," he said to the friendly door greeter, and I couldn't help noticing his wavy salt and pepper hair and olive complexion. I assumed he was Alex's son from the "Pop."

"Hi Niko, the café has been busy all day. Becky hasn't had a moment to sit."

As I ordered my latte, I tried not to be obviously curious as I glanced at the man who Alex had called Niko. The young, ponytail-haired girl at the counter handed me my decaf caramel latte. As I left, I turned around just in time to see Niko looking back at me.

A slight glance from a man I'd never met before brought a lilt to my step and a smile to my lips. Two seniors simply smiling at each other. Is that what AARP flirting is like? It'd been so many years since I'd flirted with a man who wasn't my husband. But Jed found it easy, so maybe I would, too.

Activity was everywhere in the town. There was face painting, balloon artists, and a bouncy house for the kids. An antique
auto show was set up at the Marine Museum parking lot, and
vendor spaces were along both sides of the streets. Shoppers
braved the heat and enjoyed the bright sun and lemonade offered throughout the festival.

I decided to see if Ellen wanted to walk around the festival
with me. I headed up the three wooden steps to Waldron's
Hardware. The minute I entered I could smell Ellen's cookies.

Tim was behind the counter, glasses perched on the tip of
his nose, as he assisted a customer. He lifted his sturdy, kind
face to me and pointed to the basement.

The stairs to the basement were old and uneven. Typically,
I would ask Jed to fix the stairs, but I didn't dare ask him to do
anything for me, and Ellen certainly would not accept his help
now.

Ellen was already on her way up, carrying several water
bottles, just as I took my first step. "Did you come by for a
cookie?" she asked.

"No, right now, I prefer something without fat, cholesterol,
sodium, or alcohol."

Ellen handed me a bottle of water. "We've been busy. How
about Sweet Repeats?"

"Yes, doing really well. I'm taking a break now. I'm going to
walk around and check things out. Can you join me?"

"I can't at the moment. But make sure you check out the
fortune teller further down the street. Several of our customers
have given her rave reviews."

I PASSED THE TENT WITH A *Tarot Card Reading by Madame Angelique*
sign and considered stopping. I could see a woman inside the
tent with long gray hair and bulky necklaces giving a reading
to a Sweet Repeats customer. From the long line of customers
waiting to see Angelique, I ascertained I wasn't the only one
looking for advice. I asked Angelique's assistant, sitting on a
flowered lawn chair in front of the tent, how long the wait
would be for a reading.

She clanked her multiple gold bracelets and handed me a colorful clipboard. "You can sign up now and return in two hours," she said.

Impulsively, I took her red pen, put my name on the list, and continued on my walk.

I was almost at the end of town when I noticed an art gallery I had never visited. I was intrigued by the two paintings in the window and decided to check them out. A sophisticated young woman with a jet-black pixie haircut handed me a brochure. Today's showing was titled *Phases of a Woman*.

"Welcome, I'm Lilliana, owner of the gallery. Thank you for stopping in."

I couldn't determine Lilliana's accent, perhaps Eastern European. I looked around the shop containing portraits of women of varying ages.

"Hello, I'm Andi. My friends and I own Sweet Repeats at the other end of the street. I've never been in your gallery before."

"I'm glad you stopped by. We are honoring women in the arts this month. All the paintings we are showing are about women and created by women. Seventy-five percent of galleries represent more men than women. We do not consider ourselves a feminist gallery, but want to show the many dimensions of a woman as seen by a woman."

I looked at each painting with awe. There was a black and white portrait of a naked woman towards the end of her pregnancy. A pair of arms that were not her own were wrapped around her breasts. Only the arms of the other person were visible. Next to that picture was a painting of a young girl with pink ribbon-tied pigtails and golden curls. The girl was holding one single sunflower with a copy of *Little Women* on her lap.

There were paintings of women in all stages of life. One showed an old woman in a rocking chair holding a glass of wine in one hand and a cigar in the other. Some paintings showed older women looking pained and worn out, while others depicted older women engaged in spirit-filled activities. Several showed young women with large smiles holding a baby or frolicking with young children. Others showed tired, worn-out expressions on the faces of younger women, too.

Some were in bold, brilliant colors, and others were in shades of gray.

I could see myself in each painting.

I could hear the swishing of Lilliana's tight skirt as she walked up behind me. "The artists have each expressed the natural cycle of development and decline of women in all forms of femininity, aging, and the loss of physical beauty. And this is one of my favorites," Lilliana said as we both looked at a portrait of just the faces of four women on a black background. Each face held a different emotion: joy, pain, excitement, and loss.

This was how I felt: like looking through a kaleidoscope toy, changing the scenery with each turn of my wrist.

As I walked back to the shop, I thought of the paintings and how much emotion was portrayed in each of them, in the stories of their lives. When I looked at the paintings of the young girls, I felt free, youthful, and uninhibited. The ones of young mothers made me feel nurturing and complete. And the paintings of older women reminded me of my own wrinkles and newly discovered arthritis. But I wasn't there yet, was I? I was between chapters.

I NEARED BECKY'S CAFÉ and spotted Niko outside talking with a young couple and their two children. I gave him a slight smile as I passed by.

He held my gaze without hesitation.

Then I was jolted out of my moment of flirtation when I heard my favorite sound. *Grandma.*

My sweet young granddaughters, Madison and Kendall, ran up to me, their little faces painted into cats and their hands tightly clutched around pink cotton candy. My son Nathan and his wife, Emily, were not far behind them.

"It's bubble gum flavor," Kendall said with sticky fingers and mouth. "Do you want to try?"

"I sure do," I said to Kendall and picked off a piece of what most definitely was bubble gum flavored. "Can I have some of yours, too, Madison?" I said, bending to give her a hug.

"Yessssss." Madison answered, pushing the pink cone to me until it stuck to my cheek.

"Hey, Mom," Nathan said with a side hug, avoiding my now gluey fingers and lips. "You look good. I wasn't sure if you would be here today."

"I am good," I said, assuring him and his wife, Emily. "Come inside the shop. It's getting too hot for me."

As I ushered Nathan and his family into Sweet Repeats, I was able to innocently glance over to see if Niko was still visible.

There he was, all delicious six feet of him, looking right at me.

Soon we were joined in the store by Josh, Lisa, and my only grandson, Andrew.

Lisa called to Madison and Kendall as they sat on the floor and finished their gooey mess. "Be careful, girls, don't let Andrew touch the cotton candy."

Kendall stood up and walked over to her aunt. "I only gave him a little bite," she said while she tried to retrieve the bits of pink cotton candy from his hand.

Lisa glanced at Josh sideways as she bent over to pick up Andrew. "Andi, can I wash him up in the bathroom? He has it all over his face and hands."

I looked at Andrew, who had only small traces of the cotton candy on him. "Of course, let me know if you need anything."

As Lisa escorted Andrew, she looked over her shoulder at Josh. "I think we should leave soon. Andrew needs to take a nap."

Madison walked over to her aunt and little cousin. "Can't Andrew come to the bouncy house with us?"

Lisa took Andrew's hand and walked quickly toward the back. "No, sweetie, Andrew is too little for the bouncy house."

I tried to ignore the curious exchanges between Nathan and Emily.

"Do you think I would be allowed to go in the bouncy house?" I asked Kendall.

"Uh, sure, but remember what happened when you went on our trampoline, Grandma?"

I put my finger to my lips and shook my head, but it was too late.

Kendall let out a loud giggle. "You peed your pants. Remember?"

Emily gathered up the girls and mouthed, "I'm sorry," as she looked at the customers who overheard Madison tell everyone in the store that I had peed my pants while jumping on a trampoline.

After I said goodbye to my boisterous crew, I looked at the time on my phone. I hurried to Madame Angelique's tent and prepared for my reading. Her assistant led me inside, where patchouli was burning, and tie-dyed scarves were placed on the interior walls.

"Welcome. Have you ever had a reading before?" Angelique asked me.

I positioned myself as comfortably as possible on the hard wooden chair. "No, this is my first time."

Angelique handed over a pile of Tarot cards as she looked at me with piercing green eyes. "Shuffle the cards and make three piles. The Tarot aids in coming in contact with your Higher Self. This should be used as a guide to help you as you enter a new phase in life. I want you to concentrate on something for which you seek guidance."

Okay, I thought to myself, I will go along with this. I could use a lot of guidance right now. Isn't that why I signed up for the reading?

She placed the cards in what she called a Celtic Cross Spread.

As she pointed to the circle and cross-section, Angelique said, "This represents what is currently happening in your life."

Angelique placed her hand over the top of the card in the middle. "There is much activity in your life and in your mind. There is a powerful force blocking you from moving forward. You have a tremendous unresolved issue, like a large stop sign appearing each time you take a step. This is dangerous, and you must find a way to remove the stumbling block."

I looked intently at the cards, trying to determine how she derived this message.

Madame Angelique continued the reading without looking up at me. "The second card, which is crossing the first one, represents your challenges."

I shifted in my chair and wanted to ask her questions, but I waited for her to go on.

"Take a look at the card that is covering you. It is the Eight of Swords. Do you see how it shows a woman blindfolded and surrounded by swords?"

I looked at the card closely and viewed a woman who looked bound and staked. Yup, I sort of felt blindfolded and stabbed lately.

Angelique continued as I studied the card. "Yes, I can see it in your eyes that you do not know which way to move in your life. The bondage in the card shows you are in crisis."

I still wasn't sure if I should speak, so I nodded. Part of me wanted to cry in acknowledgment of the crisis in my life, and the other part of me wanted to laugh that I was sitting in a tent with a strange woman telling me that my life sucked.

She looked at the third card. "You have the Lovers card, and this indicates your past."

Hmmm, I thought to myself. The Lovers card must be good. It would show the love that Jed and I have had for many years. Maybe this will be an indication that we can reunite and move on? "That's a good card, right?" I finally said to Angelique.

"Not really."

Okay, that's not what I wanted to hear. My love life was in the past.

Angelique didn't appear to notice my displeasure as she continued, "Since the card is in a reversed position, it has a different meaning. This shows you have been in a marriage or relationship that has always been on the verge of breaking up. It shows the possibility of a wrong choice."

I became frustrated and sat up straight and looked intently at Angelique. "I have been in a good, loving marriage for 25 years."

My indignant comment had little effect on her. "I can only tell you what the card shows," she said. "Let's move on to the next card."

I folded my hands across my chest like a moody child. I would have preferred the bouncy house to sitting here, even if it meant losing bladder control.

Madame Angelique ignored my behavior and continued. "The card in this position shows what will likely occur in the next few weeks or months." She tapped the card, which looked like a man juggling two stars.

This card was also in the reversed position.

Angelique stopped tapping the card. Her fingertips, chipped and unmanicured, started to trace the image of the stars on the card. "This is the Two of Pentacles, and this indicates you will have difficulty handling two situations, both of which are in opposition."

Well, I'm not enjoying this $50 reading at all.

Sensing my apprehension, Angelique continued, "Let's go on to the fifth card. This represents what is above you and how you should work towards resolving the issue. You have the Four of Cups, which shows a disconnect with your surroundings. It also shows your hesitancy to embark on a new venture."

I drew out a lengthy breath and wished my twenty minutes were up.

"Ahh, here we have the last card of the cross," she said. "This shows what is driving you in your current situation. You have the Judgment card, and this is very good. It is the awakening, a change of position, and a renewal."

I sat up straighter now, a little happier with Madame Angelique, but she still wasn't getting a tip. Then I watched as she moved her right hand intently over to what she called the staff section of the card layout.

Angelique pointed to the first card in the staff position. "The seventh card shows how you see yourself right now. The Five of Clubs shows you have regret, loss, and emotional upheaval." She moved her hand to the eighth card. "This card shows how others see you. The Two of Swords is reversed, showing how others see you moving in the wrong direction. People in your life see that you may be creating rather than cutting through obstacles by not accepting what matters most."

With each card explanation, I leaned in closer to Angelique. I wasn't putting all my faith into her reading, but it had me curious, and I was suddenly repentant and unfolded my arms.

As her hand covered the ninth card, her face became serious. "This is one of the most difficult positions to interpret during a reading. The card in the ninth position shows what we hope for but may also indicate what you fear. Keep in mind that hopes and fears are closely intertwined."

I nodded at her as I thought of my hopes, which most definitely came with fears. One part of me hoped to salvage my relationship with Jed, and another sincerely feared that choice.

"Your card is a reversed Five of Pentacles. The meaning shows your desire for success in love, good companionship, and increased spiritual matters."

I sighed with relief. "Now, that's a good card, right?" I asked Angelique with a hopeful lilt.

Angelique inhaled a long breath. "Yes, it can be. But, be careful that what you desire or who you desire is right for you." She continued to look at me while pointing to the next card. "Your last card is your final outcome. This is where your situation is headed." This time, Angelique placed her hand over my own, not the card. "Now, *this* is a good card," she said. "Your card is Strength. Spiritual power overcomes material power. This is the triumph of love over hate. You have the strength to overcome the pain and disappointment. Reach deep inside and let it out."

Angelique stared at me with an intensity that was suddenly making me uncomfortable.

As I thanked Angelique for the reading, she reached to a side table and handed me a small card. The card contained a woman's face with a crown of flowers on her head and a colorful aura that changed to all-white on the top.

"This is for you to keep. To help you find the Goddess within."

Later, I walked home from a long, successful day, my feet pounding less on the payment than they had in the morning, and I wondered about my inner Goddess. When I stepped into my home, I headed for the refrigerator. Before I could reach the kitchen, I changed my mind, showered, and went to bed with pleasant thoughts of a man named Niko.

CHAPTER SEVEN

I WOKE UP FROM ANOTHER RESTLESS NIGHT; my mind soared with thoughts of Jed, my children's concerns, my retirement, and Sweet Repeats. I seemed to recall parts of another eerie canyon dream.

I longed to bring the brilliant side of the canyon dream into my reality and banish the dark side to a nightmarish trip. Was Jed the dark side and my freedom the light and peacefulness? Or am I overacting, as Jed so frequently points out to me?

I played the words from Madame Angelique through my mind. *Be careful what and who you desire, and make sure it is right for you.* Was she right? Was I creating more obstacles by not facing reality?

I banished thoughts of Jed, trying not to allow the pain I felt about him to dominate my morning. I picked up the remote to turn on the TV. I could see my reflection on the dark screen, and I realized how depressed I looked. I put the remote down and left the bedroom, looking for an escape.

Nothing was pressing on my agenda for the day. I knew that if I didn't force myself out of my slump, I would end up watching Dateline shows about murdering husbands while eating the entire box of Ring Dings I knew were in the freezer.

I opened the patio door to witness the sun beginning to rise above the pool. I had yet to use the pool once this summer, so I decided to pull out a bathing suit and swim before the numerous residents occupied the space, sitting under the 25 umbrellas, sipping cool drinks and chatting. I assumed I would be the only one swimming at this early hour.

When I entered the clubhouse, I walked quickly past the card room where women were gathered playing an early game of Scrabble.

The pool was empty and inviting. As I sunk into the warm water, I tugged at my skirted, unflattering, two-piece

Grandmother-style swimsuit. I turned on my back and floated, looking up at the clear, cloudless sky with the first rays of sunlight reaching down onto my face.

The alluring atmosphere brought some clarity to my mind. I forbade thoughts of Jed to infect the peacefulness. I basked in the water's purity and the distracting sounds of early morning birds until Phyllis and Elaine, my neighbors and acquaintances, came to the pool.

Phyllis, showing off her slender, toned legs in her black and white tankini, smiled, and greeted me, "Oh, hi Andi, it's so nice to see you." I was certain her pleasantries were condescending.

"I've never seen you at the pool before. How are you, dear?" The tone of Elaine's sympathetic voice was as unappealing as her bulging stomach protruding from her hideous tropical suit with a mismatched pair of striped shorts.

They know. I know they know. I could tell by the expressions on their faces.

"Hello, ladies, I was just getting out," I said as I made my way to the stairs and avoided any further mundane conversation. "I hope to see you at Sweet Repeats soon." Bullshit, I hoped to never see them again.

I walked quickly into the changing room. I struggled as I removed my skirt and put on my little gym shorts. Not bothering to take off the top, I put on a tee shirt, enduring the wetness underneath.

Once I entered my home, I could tell by the dings coming from the kitchen table that I had left my phone at home. Amongst the several missed messages were two from Nathan.

Mom, do you need help getting Jed's things out of the house?

I emailed you a copy of the Breslin proposal. Can you take a look at it?

The Parker Group had been trying to get the Breslin account for several years. An opportunity arose last month when they requested a proposal for a new direct mail promotion. Josh and Nathan were still unsteady when making final decisions and presentations and relied on me for assistance.

Our company underwent a complete makeover about twenty years ago when the internet changed the marketing world. Social media and online algorithms altered the way companies marketed their services and products. The majority of our business came from creating, designing, printing and mailing promotions. I had to quickly shift into this new world and drop my old-school methods. Nathan and Josh could adapt to the changes with much greater ease.

I replied to Nathan, *I will be there in an hour. Make sure both you and Josh are available.*

After a quick shower, I headed to the office.

I SAID HELLO TO KRISTA, walked straight to my office, and closed the door. I removed pictures and personal items from the office and piled them on my beloved desk. This was where I had spent so many years strategizing and growing the agency. I ran my hand across the oak grain with thoughtful memories. I took down the *We Go Postal, So You Don't Have To* poster that had become a part of the Parker Group's original promotional material.

Both boys walked in as I was going through the large, matching oak filing cabinet behind my desk. I had so many unnecessary files from back in those easy days before things became digitized.

I pointed for them to sit in the chairs in front of my desk before they could speak. "Decide which of you will be taking my office. You don't need me to come in anymore, and I'm sure you can use the space."

Nathan's eyes grew wide. "Mom, that's great, but what are your plans?"

"Don't interrupt me, Nathan. I have more I want to say. Regarding the agency, you both are more than capable of handling everything yourselves. What you don't know, you will figure out the same way I did when I started the company. Obviously, if you need anything, I will be here for you. I'm sure you did a great job on the Breslin proposal; no need for me to review anything."

This time, Josh opened his mouth, attempting to interject, but I put my hand up to stop him.

"I have faith in you boys and know you can do it. I have been standing over you for too long and have not allowed you to make any decisions independently. You don't need me here anymore, and I don't need to be here." I swept my arm across my desk. "I've been holding on to all of this, thinking I couldn't possibly exist without it and that you couldn't without me. But, we can and now I put it in your very capable hands."

Nathan and Josh looked at each other in sincere surprise, their faces a combination of doubt and hopefulness.

But Nathan's face contorted in annoyance. "Does this have anything to do with Jed? Has he convinced you that the problem in your marriage is that you work too much?"

"I'm so proud of both of you, and I love you and your sister dearly. This has nothing to do with Jed. I know you don't understand, but allow me to figure this out on my own." I rolled up my sleeves, scanning my numerous personal items. I cradled the desk nameplate that Nicole had given me many years ago: Andrea Parker, Number One Mom. I wiped away a few tears. "Now, get me some boxes so I can pack up my stuff."

Josh stood next to Nathan and put his arm around his taller and older brother. "Mom, we can do this."

As they walked out, Josh pointed to my name on the office door and said, "Nathan, you can have Mom's office. I prefer being in the back where all the action is." Turning back to me with a wink, Josh's smile took away any remaining trepidations I had about leaving the company.

Nathan's domineering side often intimidated Josh, and I have always worried Josh would not stand up for himself at work or with his wife, Lisa. But now it was up to the two of them to figure it out, and I had full confidence they would.

The boys loaded the boxes into my car, and I looked up at the sign for "The Parker Group" with pride and without a twinge of sadness. I momentarily reveled in the successful business I had created and the deep pride for my sons, who were now in control. With huge hugs and three pairs of water-filled eyes, I told them I would be in touch within a few days.

My car's back seat and trunk were full of more than 30 years of advertising awards and pictures, from the beginning when we had just one office to the impressive building we now own. A flood of memories from the past three decades floated through my mind. Jed had been supportive throughout all of it. I know he benefitted financially, but he had also encouraged me and took over many household details in my absence.

I sat in the car a few minutes before I started it and realized there was much truth in my words to Nathan and Josh. I had been holding onto the company. I wasn't willing to let go of the power it gave me and the hours it took up in my life. I had been concerned with how I would fill my days. If I didn't have my career, what did I have? Who would I become? I couldn't picture myself playing pickleball or attending ladies' luncheons. I couldn't imagine myself becoming an active senior by joining in on social functions. I wanted to do those things, but I also needed something else. I reveled in hard work. It kept me young and gave me value. I wasn't convinced that Sweet Repeats would fulfill my needs. I still felt a yearning for more of a purpose.

If I didn't have the career I'd built or Jed in my life, there would be too many lonely, empty hours. I had my family, but they had their own hectic lives.

Just as I was ready to pull my car out of the parking lot, I read a text from Jed. *I'm having dinner with Steve tonight and will be home right after.*

Home. It still is his home.

I hesitated over how to respond. *Okay.* I didn't feel the need to say anything further.

Steve was Jed's Ellen. His confidante, his BFF. Like Melanie's husband, Jack, Steve was the opposite of Jed, with undeniable, unconditional love for his wife. He was quiet, subdued, and always put his wife first.

I drove home listening to my favorite oldies playlist and let the last few hours sink in. I sang along with Aretha Franklin's strong words.

Once home, I prepared my mind for more confrontation

with Jed, walked around the house, and rehearsed what I would say.

With less fanfare and care for my appearance this time, I changed out of my linen capris into a pair of casual shorts and a white tee shirt. Just as I had finished changing, I heard the garage door open and met Jed in the kitchen. His arms were loaded with flowers, Godiva chocolates, and his overnight bag dangling from his shoulder.

I pointed to his bag, annoyed with his presumptuousness. "What are you doing, Jed? We never agreed you would stay tonight. I told you I needed time."

"I can't stay with Eve anymore." Jed shook his head in disgust. "The only way we can repair our marriage is if we work on it, and the only way we can work on it is if we live together."

"You know, just a few days ago, I didn't think we had a marriage that needed repairing."

"Ahh, Andi. You're the one making this something that needs to be worked on. For the 100th time, I'm sorry. It was nothing."

"That's pathetic that you think asking another woman out was nothing."

Jed dropped his bag with a loud thump and took a step closer to me. "Let it go. I was wrong. I drank too much. I didn't mean it."

I was invaded by the creeping thoughts that if I just let it go and believed him, I could have my old life back. The life before Jed fucked it up.

Grabbing hold of my temporary silence, he pointed to the garage. "Hey, what are in all those boxes in your car?"

"Thirty-eight years of my life. There are more boxes in the trunk. Can you take them out and just leave them in the garage?"

He handed me the flowers and chocolates. "You really did it? You're out of the company?" Jed said over his shoulder without looking back at me.

When Jed returned to the kitchen, he put his hand on my shoulder and said, "I miss you, Babe, and I want our life back.

I'm sorry, truly sorry."

The same old apology hung in the air for a long minute before I could respond. With a churning in my stomach, magnified by my exhaustion, I acquiesced. "You can stay in the guest room. But I'm not promising anything."

As Jed tightened his grip on my shoulder, he breathed in relief. "Just give me a chance. I can't imagine my life without you."

I wriggled away from his hand and turned my eyes from his gaze with disappointment for Jed, sure, but with more disappointment for myself. "I have some things to do," I said as I continued to the privacy of the master bedroom with no intention of seeing him for the rest of the evening.

I quickly showered and donned one of my less-than-flattering nightgowns. I grabbed my phone to text the kids, this time including Ellen. *I just want you to know that Jed is staying here. It doesn't mean anything, but he needs a place to stay. I love you, and I will be in touch with you tomorrow.* I ended the text with my new tagline. *I'm doing fine.*

In rapid succession, the reply texts came in. As expected, Nathan was the first to respond. *Are you out of your mind, Mom? Why are you continuing to let Jed manipulate you? What is going on with you?*

Followed by a message from Nicole. *I agree with Nathan. You always do everything for him and let him take advantage of you.*

Oh, Andi, why? You told him you needed time. Why can't he respect your needs? I'm coming over tomorrow. I was grateful for Ellen's message. Ellen was the only one I wanted to be around right now.

Then, there was a text from Josh, who didn't "reply all" and whose sweet message was just to me. *I just want you to be happy, Mom. Jed called me yesterday, and he really wants things to work.*

Of course, Jed reached out to Josh, his biggest ally. And Josh, in all his passivity, only wants to see the good side of everyone.

Ready to release into sleep, I felt my mouth tighten and realized I'd started grinding my teeth again, so I jumped up to retrieve my mouthguard. When I walked out of the bathroom,

Jed had let himself into our bedroom. Dressed in only his Ravens boxers, he was sitting on my side of the bed. He reached out both hands and pulled me next to him. I knew what he wanted from the familiar look in his eyes and gentle fingertips flittering on my back. I wanted it, too.

As Jed got up and turned around to escort Coco out of the bedroom, I looked at the triangle-shaped brown speckled birthmark I had kissed on his lower back hundreds of times.

I was hungry to feel desired. I craved his touch and needed to show him, and myself, that I was still desirable. I assured myself that I could control the situation and enjoy the sex. I puffed up my hair, tossed the mouthguard on my nightstand, and took off my unflattering nightgown.

Seeing the hunger in my eyes, Jed laid back on the bed and allowed me to take the lead. Our lovemaking was always good, although, in the past years, it had subsided in quantity and intensity. But now, unfathomably, I wanted him more than ever. I didn't want him back in my life or my heart, but I wanted control over him.

I wouldn't let him kiss me while I basked in the intense heat rising from him. I wanted him inside me but not near my mouth, the gateway to my heart. His hands cupped my face as he gently tried to brush my lips with his. I shook my head but pushed my pelvis into him, giving him all the invitation he needed. I enjoyed showing him who was in control. I was doing this for my pleasure, not because of love. I hoped I was letting him know this by refusing his kiss whenever his mouth neared mine.

Once I was satisfied, I widened the distance between us.

Jed looked at his upper arm with a shit-eating grin. "That's going to leave a nice bruise." He acted like it was a statement of his sexual prowess when, in fact, the bruising was due to the Coumadin he takes for AFIB.

I was satiated like never before but irritated that he viewed this as his own success. I wanted to let him know I was still the master in the situation. I told him, "This doesn't mean anything, Jed. It was sex for sex, nothing else."

He nodded and sighed heavily, showing his confusion while a smile remained on his lips.

At that, I removed his arm, which was draped territorially around my waist, and went into the bathroom. I don't typically shower after sex, but I longed to remove his breath and the touch of his hands to resume my power. I was acutely aware that I needed to wash off all the intimate places where Jed's hands and mouth had been. I wasn't sure what I felt at first—disappointment again in myself or momentarily sexually satisfied.

Returning to our bed, I quickly feigned sleep and rolled away from Jed, burying myself in my pillow. What had I done?

The following day, in the very early hours before dawn, I looked over at Jed, peacefully purring in a deep sleep. My anger and disgust resumed. At myself, at him. And then a realization occurred to me. Jed had obviously anticipated the sex and had taken his little blue pill before coming into the bedroom. I couldn't decide if this angered or pleased me.

CHAPTER EIGHT

I TOOK ANOTHER SHOWER in the morning in an attempt to remove any lingering evidence of my sexual encounter with Jed. I sniffed deeply and inhaled the scent of herbs and garlic emanating from down the hall.

I walked into the kitchen to the sight of Jed as he expertly flipped an herbal cheese omelet. "Hey babe, how did you sleep?"

"You don't have to make me breakfast," I said. "I need you to understand that nothing has changed. I still need time."

Jed handed me a cup of coffee, my favorite roast, with a dash of cinnamon. "It's just breakfast, so sit down. It will be ready in a minute."

I reluctantly went to my seat and enjoyed my coffee.

The sound of the phone brought me out of my unsettledness, and seeing it was Ellen was an automatic pick-me-up. I answered with as jovial a sound as I could muster, "Hey girl, what's up? How did you and Tim do at the festival on Saturday?" I stood up and walked into the family room so Jed couldn't hear the conversation.

"What's up?" Ellen sounded outraged. "How about the fact that your husband is a lying, cheating bastard, and you're letting him stay with you."

I moved even further away from Jed. "I can't talk about it right now."

"You've got to be kidding. He's with you, isn't he?"

"Yes, can we get together for coffee today?"

"Okay, but you know what I am going to say to you, don't you?" With an exasperated sigh, she added, "You aren't taking him back, right?"

I spoke softly yet firmly. "I will talk with you later."

I said goodbye to Ellen and followed the enticing smells back to the kitchen.

Jed motioned for me to sit where he had placed my French

omelette, roasted red peppers, and freshly squeezed orange juice on one of our good China plates, along with a cloth napkin.

"Everything okay with Ellen?" Jed asked me with a raised eyebrow.

"Yes, we're meeting later at The Sea Breeze Cafe."

I hungrily attacked my breakfast and mentally prepared myself for Ellen's lecture.

Do I tell Ellen? Do I not tell Ellen?

I finally settled on no. I should *not* tell her I had sex with Jed. As much as Ellen and I confided in each other, there were some parts of my life that I just couldn't share, not even with my BFF.

I noticed Ellen's unmistakable car in the parking lot. Her white SUV was easily discernible from the other hundreds of white SUVs in town. The rear window was embellished with ten stick figure decals, one each for all her family members. A sticker for her and Tim, two children and their spouses, three grandchildren, and one for Tyson, their drooling boxer dog.

I went inside The Sea Breeze and joined Ellen, who had my latte and cranberry croissant waiting for me at her table.

"Okay, spill it," Ellen said, looking at me intently. "What's going on? Have you seriously taken Jed back?"

"No, but I am letting him stay at the house. It only seems fair. Everyone seems to forget that it is Jed's house, too."

Ellen flashed a quick but comforting smile. "And you seem to forget what he did."

I turned away from Ellen as a few tears trickled from the corner of my eyes, "Oh, Ellen, you're not going to believe this, but I slept with Jed last night." So much for not telling her.

"What? Are you serious? How could you—"

I stopped her before she could say anything further. "Look, it gave me some perverse power. It wasn't lovemaking. It was me taking charge. And, it felt good, the sex *and* the power."

Ellen put her elbows on the table and emphatically drew closer to me, "You are the strongest woman I know. Create a new life for yourself. You DON'T need him."

"I got a reading from Madame Angelique at the festival, and she sort of told me the same thing."

"You went to the fortune teller?"

I looked at Ellen and cocked my head in sarcasm. "Yes, I am now trying to reach my inner Goddess." Seeing three more ladies enter the coffee shop, I lowered my voice. "Look, I appreciate your concern for me, but I don't feel like talking about Jed anymore. Let's talk about something less emotional."

"Well, as a matter of fact, I want to talk with you about the tearoom." Ellen's face lit up as she moved her latte from one hand to the other. "I want your honest opinion."

"Of course, I'm here for you. Always."

As Ellen leaned back in her seat, she continued as if in emphasis. "Other than helping Tim at the hardware store, I haven't had a real job in 30 years. I've been feeling displaced recently. You know how much I love my grandchildren, and spending time with them is fabulous. But now I want something else, something more. Do you truly feel that a tearoom would do well here? And, more importantly, am I not too old to do this?"

"Too old? Is there an age limit on starting a business? And, I wouldn't encourage you if I didn't think it would work. I can help you start looking for a place. You can do this, Ellen, I promise."

Ellen's eyes sparked with enthusiasm. I remembered the thrill of opening the Agency and then, years later, Sweet Repeats. "Can you, Melanie, and Jeannie come to my house for a real tea party so I can test it out?" she asked.

"Absolutely, that sounds like fun. I will coordinate a good day for everyone."

We lingered for another hour, grateful for our friendship.

I was delighted for Ellen but disappointed to feel the emptiness return in my stomach and heart as I walked to my car. I considered driving to a fast-food restaurant but opted not to indulge in junk food. I turned around and decided to walk the two blocks to Sweet Repeats. I knew Melanie and Jeannie would be there this afternoon, and I wanted to see when they would be available for Ellen's tea party. The summer heat had subsided, and the cooler hint of air touched my arms and legs with a slight breeze that sent a tingling sensation through me.

I was buoyed by thoughts of Ellen, her new adventure, and a sense of freedom with Nathan and Josh taking over the Agency. I smiled and waved at many of the store owners I had come to know. Many town residents were also out walking and shopping on this glorious day. I looked at the other stores. A Victorian Tearoom would do very well in town.

As I walked past Becky's Café, Alex stood outside by the door. "Hello, it's nice to see you again. I hope you are enjoying the beauty of the day," he said.

I turned around at the sound of a car approaching the curb nearby. I immediately recognized Niko's wavy, thick hair and broad, effortless sensuality.

"Hey, Dad, you ready to go?" he said, greeting his father. As he looked at me, Niko gave me a smile that lingered for a few seconds.

I moved away from them, more slowly than necessary. "Hello, gentlemen," I said with a surprised nervousness. When I reached Sweet Repeats, I turned around for another look at the captivating father and son. I giggled, knowing Niko was looking at me as he helped his father into the car.

"Andi, I'm so glad you are here," Jeannie said while walking with me to the counter where Melanie and another woman were talking.

"This is Lyla, and she stopped in to show us some of the jewelry she makes," Melanie said. Then she held up a magnificent pair of two-inch earrings in varying hues of green.

Lyla held out her long, slender arm and beautifully manicured hands, adorned with a bracelet of light shades of gray and vintage rose crystals. "It's nice to meet you," she said.

Jeannie lifted another bracelet that seemed to change the tint as she moved it. "Lyla hoped we could bring some of her pieces into the shop."

"We don't typically sell new items at Sweet Repeats, but the jewelry would only take up a small space," Melanie said.

"Do you think we could make room on the counter?" I

asked Jeannie.

Jeannie looked at me with a smile. "Yes, we could start with a few pieces and see how they do with our customer base."

I took a bracelet out of the case. "Is this a type of quartz?" I asked Lyla.

Lyla held the bracelet up, allowing the sunlight to show through the crystals. "Yes, it's labradorite crackle quartz. I primarily use crystals and gemstones that have healing power," Lyla said with pride. "This particular gemstone shows a rainbow of hues when it is placed in the light and taps into our personal energy."

After looking at several more pieces, we agreed to try out 20 items, a mix of bracelets, necklaces, and earrings.

"Let's sit outside and grab some sun before it turns hot again," I told Melanie and Jeannie after we had set up the pricing with Lyla. We gave her a generous percentage of all the sales for her jewelry.

We sat on the bench Jed had put out for us. He'd found the bench badly in need of repairs, in the back of the building. He painted it in the color scheme Melanie chose for our logo. Melanie stenciled the bench with a Thoreau quote: *There is no remedy for love but to love more.*

"Do you think we should start looking for a larger location for Sweet Repeats?" Jeannie asked.

I generously lifted my face to the rays of the afternoon sun. "We have a month-to-month lease, but we have put so much into making this building work for us."

"We could use another 500 feet, but I would like to stay in town," Melanie said.

"Why don't we see what is available?" I offered. "We don't have to do anything right away. "

Jeannie and Melanie closed their eyes and embraced the sun along with me. We must have looked like three old ladies taking a nap on the bench. We stayed silent for at least ten minutes, enjoying the warm air and our friendship.

The jingle of the bells from our shop door snapped us out of our peaceful moment.

I remembered my conversation with Ellen and turned to

Melanie and Jeannie as we returned to the shop. "By the way, Ellen is seriously considering opening a tearoom. She wants to have us over to her house for an official tea party. Let me know a few dates and times you are available, and I will coordinate with her."

Looking delighted, Melanie said, "That's a fabulous idea. Her scones are amazing."

We didn't close the shop until close to 6:00, an hour later than our scheduled closing on Tuesdays. I had neglected to check my phone for several hours, and along with several unimportant missed calls, I read a text from Jed.

I'm making dinner for us. It will be ready soon.

After my pleasant day, I stood tall with continuing serenity, a reprieve from the tightness I had been feeling. I walked into the house, heard the sound of the Orioles in the background, and smelled the scent of Jed's cooking. Having become accustomed to him often making meals while I was working late hours, he was rather adept and creative with his culinary skills, amongst his other talents.

"Where do you want me to put all the boxes you brought home yesterday?" he asked. "They're still in the garage."

"I'm not sure where I'm going to put them. Just leave them there for now."

"I'll move them all to the side until you decide." Jed handed me a wooden spoon. "Here, stir the risotto while I rearrange them."

I remembered Jed's detail that whenever he made risotto he had to continue stirring the pot until all the liquid evaporated.

When Jed returned to the kitchen a few minutes later, he added more chicken stock to the risotto and resumed the delicate stirring process.

"How long before dinner? I have a few emails and texts to send." I didn't, but I wanted to continue to emphasize to him that I had a life without him.

"Twenty minutes. Go ahead. I will call you when it's ready."

I went to our room and sat on the bed, stroking Coco's

fur, and thinking about Jed's contributions to my success. I felt myself soften towards him and looked forward to the simplicity of having a meal together. I put on a fresh coat of lipstick and felt some of the heaviness dissipate.

Dinner was ready. I took my seat at the table and thanked him.

"You know I've always liked cooking for you," Jed commented with a smile.

And then, nonstop, Jed controlled the conversation, taking away my momentary calm.

"Eve is obsessing with her latest conspiracy theory about the COVID vaccines. She is convinced that everyone vaccinated was implanted with tracking devices. She complains about my living with her temporarily, I hope, but she doesn't object to giving me a list of repairs for her house. I've done so much for her already. It's just never enough for her."

Without pausing, Jed continued with one unfocused sentence after the other. "I made an appointment with the chiropractor; my sciatica has been acting up again, but it doesn't seem to affect my golf game. The guys at golf were razzing me that I still had a full head of hair."

His hair? Did he not realize he was developing a silver-dollar bald spot in the back of his head?

When he was done talking about himself, I said, "I don't want to interrupt this lovely conversation about things in your life, but I need to ask you a few questions."

Jed stiffened as he rose to clear the dishes, a habit usually dedicated to me. He strengthened his stature as if his standing posture would intimidatingly take away my words. "Look, Andi, can't we just forget everything and move forward?"

I placed my hands on the table, pushed away my chair, and glared into his eyes. "Nope, Jed, that's not how we are proceeding. I need some answers." I held my shoulders high and stood my ground.

Jed turned dramatically to look out the window as he avoided me. "I thought after last night, which was incredible, that we were moving past this misunderstanding."

"No, Jed. How was this a misunderstanding? You let Renee know you were interested in her and wanted to be with her. And my entire family and friends were made aware of your intention."

Jed was a skilled liar who knew how to use his good looks and charm. His quick mind enabled him to conjure up variations and twists. But now, I needed to be in control.

His thick lips presented a pleading, hopeful smile when he met my gaze again. "Go ahead, honey. Get it all out."

I stood up with the intention of getting a glass of wine, then changed my mind and settled on iced tea. "Why would you risk our marriage for what you refer to as an *innocent flirtation*? Do I have to remind you what you wrote to Renee? You were lusting after her, and it disgusted me." I already knew the answer but wanted to see how he would lie his way around the truth. I sat back down in my chair.

"Andi, I told you, she's an old friend. I haven't seen her in more than thirty years and just wanted to catch up. I was drunk when I messaged her, and I shouldn't have. I haven't seen her, nor do I intend to see her."

Unable to stay still, I rose again. This time, I headed for the wine. "But you jeopardized our marriage, and on top of that, you posted it on Facebook for the whole world to see."

"I didn't realize I wasn't private messaging her. Doesn't that show you how drunk I was?"

"No, it shows me what a lying ass you are."

Jed rubbed his hands over his chin in aggravation. "I didn't, I wasn't. I'm *not*. But ...."

"Jed, but *what*?"

Jed's anger increased, and he walked from the kitchen to the family room and back again. "Okay, Andi, let me give you some honesty. I inappropriately flirted. But maybe that's because I needed to feel good about myself. You have never treated me like your equal. You were always working late and throwing out reminders that you had to work hard because of our lifestyle. You worked even more after your so-called semi-retirement. You never asked me how I felt about you opening the shop. I felt unappreciated, and maybe that's why I flirted, but I didn't have an affair and would never have pursued anything."

I raised my voice emphatically. "And that's your justification?"

"You never bothered to see how difficult it was for me with your long hours."

"You're unbelievable," I breathed. "Do you believe in your own crap?" I wanted to keep him talking. I wanted to hear the words and the acknowledgment.

Jed nearly laughed. "You aren't listening to anything I'm trying to say. You dismiss my feelings so easily."

I walked away from him towards the kitchen window and closed the shutters tightly as if concerned about intruders. I turned abruptly to his piercing eyes. "Jed, are you telling me that you innocently flirted while drunk because I work too much?"

He looked me in the face, walked past me, brushed my shoulder with his, and opened his bottle of vodka to make another drink. He ignored my question as if it didn't deserve a response.

Taking several good swallows, he turned back to me and said with a smirk and grin, "So what the hell was last night when you couldn't get enough of me? I'm not complaining, babe. I loved your assertiveness, but I'm thoroughly confused."

"Jed, last night doesn't change anything. You can live here for now, in the guest room, but I still need time to figure out how I want to proceed."

Jed stepped closer. The muscles on his face tightened as he cupped his hands to the back of his head. "We love each other too much to let this go."

The memory of our lustful evening made my head hurt. How could I have allowed that to happen? I didn't want Jed to assume it was a permanent invitation back to our marital bed. I still needed answers.

I ignored him for a few more minutes before I responded. He was only an arm's length away. I wanted to step forward, feel his arms around me, and take in his scent. Being near him made me quiver with the remembrance of our passion last evening.

But then I reminded myself of his betrayal. With exhaustion, I decided to end the conversation.

When I didn't respond, without looking at me, Jed made himself another drink and retreated to the guest room at the opposite end of the house. I could hear the annoying sound of the ice clinking in the glass as he walked away.

An hour later, as I crept out of the bedroom, I could hear Jed's unmistakable sleep sounds coming from the guest bedroom. Filled with more disgust, I remembered the vengeance of one of the women in the Dateline show I had watched recently. Tiptoeing into the garage, I spotted Jed's golf bag beside his car.

Opening the bag, I took out the nine-iron I had given him for his birthday. No, I wasn't planning on attacking him in his sleep, although the thought gave me a shiver of pleasure. I tucked it behind the shelving unit, strategically placing his tools to obscure the golf club. Jed had always claimed that his golf game improved by several strokes due to the nine-iron. A vengeful sense of triumph swept over me.

Giving an invisible pat on my back, I congratulated myself on my cunningness and couldn't wait to tell Ellen.

CHAPTER NINE

HELLO ALL. *Jed is still at the house for the time being. Greg mentioned his cabin at the lake is unoccupied, so I'm heading there for some reflection.*

I sent the message to Nicole, Nathan, Josh, and Ellen, and, this time, I included Greg, my brother. Forgetting to add the ever-present end to my texts these days, I sent another. *I am fine.*

I went into the bedroom to retrieve the bag I had already packed, and as I was walking out, I heard Jed.

"Hey, Andi, do you want to take a walk along the boat launch and pier? The weather looks pretty good right now. We could go to the Tiki Bar afterward for the raw bar and mojitos."

His offer was tempting, but I stayed with my plan for much-needed solace.

Jed followed me as I walked from room to room gathering some more things. "I'm going away for a while. I need some time alone. Please don't contact me. Water the plants and take care of the cat."

Jed looked curious as he positioned himself with arms folded across his chest. "Are you at least going to tell me where you are going?

"No, and my phone will be off," I said.

Jed appeared sincere as he loosened his posture. "Okay, have a good time."

I knew he would undoubtedly contact Josh and get the information out of him. But I made my point by leaving abruptly and without explanation.

With my emotional state of mind, I couldn't trust my ability to have pleasant conversations with anyone. The silence at the lake house would be soothing and calm the constricting of my leaping heart. I was saddened that I missed going on the river cruise with my husband, and I needed a distraction.

Jed was right. It was a beautiful, warm, crisp day, and it would be an easy, pleasant drive. I clicked my belt and turned the Sirius radio to light jazz music. I took a long, expansive breath and set out on my journey. It felt like an indulgence with no agenda, just the purity of air leading to a peaceful destination. I gave myself a moment, tapping my fingers on the wheel along with the smooth sounds of John Coltrane's saxophone. I looked forward to a few days of losing myself and just being in the moment to stop obsessing about the painful state of my life.

I patted the inspirational book on the passenger seat with a solemn vow to read it and embrace its wisdom. I promised myself not to sit around and watch TV while I was there. I opened the sunroof and let the wind whip through my hair as I drove.

I also allowed Madame Angelique's words to stay with me. *You have the strength to overcome pain and disappointment.*

Greg's house at the lake was more than a cabin. It was a contemporary home with large, paned windows looking out of place amongst the log cabins, small craftsman, and A-frame houses. But that was Greg. He always wanted to stand out, and I loved him dearly. His daughter had seen Jed's original Facebook post, and he had contacted me immediately to ask if I needed anything. I appreciated how Greg accepted that I didn't want to discuss my husband's infidelity and offered his cabin for respite.

I quickly unpacked my clothing, food, and wine, then settled on the patio, admiring his slightly obstructed lake view and reveling in the crispness of the air. The air at home never smelled like it does at the cabin, fresh and unencumbered. I took in the sounds of several boats on the water, the laughter of children, the wind blowing carefree from the abundant trees, and the occasional bird.

The world here was rich, alive, and pure.

Night came quickly and crisply. I tried to suck in as much of the clear atmosphere as possible into my lungs, requesting the chill to take away the heat in my stomach that begged to be filled. I couldn't remember the last time I had sat outside with the sole intention of watching the stars appear. Just the beauty and magic of our earth. For that matter, when was the last time I relaxed so thoroughly and succumbed to peace?

I had so much to figure out, but that night was for the soft breezes surrounding me.

I was surprised to find many diversified and inspirational books in Greg's vast collection. From classics like *The Great Gatsby* to Kahlil Gibran and everything in between. I was scanning the shelves when I came across *America the Beautiful, In the Words of Henry David Thoreau*.

I spent the next two blissful days primarily on the back porch, serenely wrapped in a light blanket on the eucalyptus rocking chair and reading Thoreau.

Strange that so few ever come to the woods to see how the pine lives and grows and spires, lifting its evergreen arms to the light—to see its perfect success.

I want to go soon and live away by the pond, where I shall hear only the wind whispering among the reeds. It will be a success if I shall have left myself behind. But my friends ask what I will do when I get there. Will it not be employment enough to watch the progress of the seasons?

I thought about how Thoreau found a source of abundance in the solitude of nature, a place to think and reflect. I removed myself from my problems and tried to think of only the glory and beauty in front of me. I felt infinitely less tense. The serenity of my present surroundings grounded me into submission to their glory.

Every part of nature teaches that the passing away of one life is the making room for another, Thoreau wrote.

When my children were young and saddened over their father's stroke and ultimate death, I tried to instill self-confidence with positive affirmations. I would have them repeat, "I am strong. I am beautiful. I am brave. I can do anything."

I moved back and forth in the rocking chair, a glass of merlot on one side and chocolate chip cookies on the other. I attested, "I am Andrea Lynne Parker. I am brave, I am brave, I am brave."

There was so much in my life to be grateful for. Turning the agency over to Nathan and Josh was a monumental step for me. I was surrounded by the love and devotion of my family and friends. We would be celebrating Andrew's 4th birthday soon. It was those moments when I felt the most blessed, surrounded by my family's laughter and bonding.

Even amidst the agony of my faltering marriage, small things also brought me joy, like the look on Josh's face when he pointed to my nameplate on the office door. Or the look in Kendall's eyes as she fed me cotton candy. The brief look exchanged with Niko, a stranger, in front of the café.

I watched the trees move in rhythm with the wind and the angelic sounds of nature surrounding me. I repeated to myself, "I am brave, I am brave, I am brave." I felt ready to go home. I looked up at the night sky with gratitude, folded the blanket, and took my empty glass inside.

The next morning, before I started the car, I leaned my head against the headrest and closed my eyes, and I willed myself to take the serenity of the past few days with me. I bid adieu to the lake with gratitude for its gift.

Then, I sent a brief text to my family and Ellen.

I'm on my way home. I wrote the same text to Jed but did not include him in the group message.

Jed's short reply came back within seconds. *I will have dinner ready.*

When I turned the key in the ignition, "50 Ways to Leave Your Lover" was playing on the radio. I laughed heartily and enjoyed the beginning of the drive. But halfway home, I became apprehensive, losing the calm of the past few days. I considered turning around and returning to the lake, but I forced myself to fall back into the serenity of my time there.

Arriving home was cathartic as I relished the memory of all that summer scenery and thought of Thoreau's deliberate lifestyle.

Jed was in the kitchen, moving a pot of boiling water to the back burner.

I wanted to make only insignificant small talk, so I asked

THE GOLDEN YEARS GLITCH

about the cat. "How is Coco?"

"She's good, annoying as usual. Did you have a nice time at the lake?"

Just as I thought, Jed must have talked with Josh. "I did. It was peaceful."

Jed replaced the water to resume its boil. He grabbed a box of linguine and took out the Chicken Francese he had warming in the oven.

He looked ruddy and handsome with a tea towel swung over his shoulder. He was the kind of man who commanded attention whatever he was doing. His deep-set blue eyes and his oddly formed intriguing lips invited you closer. He was aging well, my dear husband. His sandy blonde hair had long turned to a slick silver with just that small circle of baldness protruding in the back.

Sure, he moved more slowly, his eyebrows had thinned, and his neck sported a layer of new wrinkles, but Jed was still attractive. It would be easy to see Renee's attraction towards my husband, along with all the other women I didn't know about. I firmly believed there were others, probably many. Was it just flirtation he shared with Renee and any others?

There was also the less appealing side to Jed, like his narcissistic ego-demanding traits. Jed sought attention and made it clear I wasn't giving him enough.

As he handed me plates and utensils for the table, Jed sent an encouraging smile my way.

"Jed, please know that nothing has changed. I'm still hurt and agonizing over what to do. I still want to know the truth. You've lied so much to me in the past. I think you have become accustomed to your lies."

"What are you talking about, Andi? Geez, I think sometimes you conjure up things in your head to encourage your anger."

"How can we be together when I don't trust you? How do I know there isn't anything going on with Renee? How do I know there aren't or won't be others?"

Jed approached the table where I was now sitting and placed both hands firmly on the surface. He looked me in the eyes.

"Andi, how can you give up on our 25-year marriage so easily? Can we just have a nice evening and maybe watch TV together after dinner?"

Exhausted from the drive and the immediate confrontation, I slowly nodded yes.

Finished with Jed's delicious dinner, I rose from the table and said, "Thank you for cooking. I need to take a shower." I wasn't going to offer to help Jed clean up.

After lingering in the shower and dealing with the ever-present conflict, I was ready to release myself to a hopeful, dreamless sleep. I needed to recapture the peacefulness of my time at the lake.

The TV was on in the bedroom, turned to our favorite streaming channel for binge-watching. Jed had dimmed the lights and placed a glass of wine on my nightstand. He hadn't waited for an invitation.

I realized I must look a mess in contrast to his compelling sexiness. My hair was frizzy and still damp from the shower after I'd barely run a brush through it. I was sans make-up with visible torment in my eyes.

Jed grabbed my arm, and I shrugged away. I lost my balance and some of my nerve as I fell into his arms. My shoulders lifted, and I clung to him with the possibility of being "us" again.

"I want you, Andi. You have to trust and believe me for this to work out."

I tightened my arms around him, dropped my shoulders, and released a long-held breath. My anger deflated temporarily, which of course allowed my breasts to inflate with want and desire. And control. Jed's features warmed when he saw me relax.

Jed bent to press his lips to mine. I pushed them away slowly as I reminded him without words that my mouth was deemed forbidden territory. My hands pressed against his chest. I could feel his heart pounding in anticipation as I pushed him onto the bed. His hands gripped my hips as he waited for further instructions from me. The sound of his wanting echoed in my head as I delighted in my control and the effects of his little blue pill. My desire for power was more profound and more potent this time.

I could feel the heaviness of his heart against mine, reminding me of the thousands of times after lovemaking with our legs intertwined, not knowing where I began and he ended. Back when I felt like we were one.

Murmuring my name over and over again, his eyes winced in excitement. My pleasure heightened the more he tried to kiss me.

Not wanting to lay next to him afterward, I disentangled myself, freed from his perspiration and satisfaction. With one quick movement, I tossed aside the crumpled sheets and headed for the shower once more to purge away any remnants of our encounter.

I ran the water in the shower hot, washing away the dirtiness, and then I slowly turned the dial to cold to punish myself.

When I emerged, Jed was watching 30 for 30 on the sports network.

He watched me as I put on my nightgown. "Andi, I'm so fucking confused. You want me, and then you can't get away fast enough."

"I told you, Jed. This isn't make-up sex. It's just sex, and it doesn't change anything."

"Sex for sex? What's gotten into you?" Confused, he shook his head, "Sometimes I think we are back together and everything is fine. Other times, you barely talk to me, and then suddenly, we have phenomenal lovemaking."

"Everything is so uncertain. I move from day to day, unsure of how I feel. I can't promise that I want you to stay."

"But, can you promise that you will give us time?" Jed wanted to know.

He grew quiet in the darkness, unlike his typical prideful emotions after sex. He was less boastful this time.

"Can I at least stay here in OUR bed? I've missed this, Andi. I miss the special times we used to spend together. I miss us. I don't want us to drift further apart."

I gave Jed a light nod of affirmation and watched as he

walked to the bathroom.

With a smirk and an idea, I opened his nightstand and pulled out his little blue pill bottle. Putting it into the pocket of my robe, I walked out. I told Jed I had to get something from my car. With a bizarre sense of satisfaction, I placed the pill bottle next to the hidden golf club.

Ellen was going to love this.

When I returned to the bedroom, everything was quiet, with the exception of Jed's light purring. The torment of satisfaction versus sadness took over. I feared another sleep-deprived evening. I lifted myself out of bed and reached for a sleep aid, and my mouthguard for my tightening jaw.

CHAPTER TEN

"ANDI, WAKE UP. You're having a bad dream." I heard Jed's intent voice stirring me from my deep sleep due to the sleeping pill I had taken just a few hours before. I had somehow removed the mouth guard from my mouth, and it was now lying near my feet, where I must have tossed it during the darkness of my nightmare.

"What were you dreaming about?" Jed asked with genuine concern. "You are still shaking."

I picked up my mouthguard and hurled myself out of bed. "I don't remember." But I did remember. Staring at myself in the bathroom mirror, my nightmare came into focus. It was an altered version of the canyon dream again. I was dangling in the center, unable to propel myself to either side. Off in the distance, I could see the serenity of the nirvana side, but this time, a brown bear was lying in a field of sunflowers. I wasn't sure if I should be afraid of the imposing animal.

The dream was fading from memory. I shook it off, hearing the sounds of the TV, surprised that Jed had not returned to sleep. Looking at his nightstand, I smirked to myself in remembrance of my theft last night.

In the morning, I decided I needed to resume normalcy, so I texted Jeannie and Melanie. *Can Gail and Bonnie handle things at the shop so we can meet for lunch?* While working at Sweet Repeats, and between customers and consignment sellers, the three of us rarely had time to discuss the status of the shop and our future plans. I needed something to focus on, and I needed to be productive.

Melanie's response came quickly. *Absolutely, let's go to Becky's.*

I ARRIVED FIRST. The charming older gentleman was right behind me as I opened the door to the café. I reached for the door when his long arm extended over mine. "That's my job, young lady," he said. I ducked slightly under his arm and thanked him for the kind gesture.

"How nice to see you again," he said. "I hope you have a very lovely day. Enjoy your lunch."

"You, too, thank you." I turned towards a table and smiled sincerely at the café gentleman. He was tall, a bit shaky, and had a weathered face full of kindness and wisdom. I watched him while I was waiting for Melanie and Jeannie. Niko and his father shared the same dark-colored eyes and olive skin.

Near the cash register was a small display on three shelves titled "Lending Library – Take a book or leave a book." I watched as Niko's father reached into his inner coat pocket and placed a small book among the others.

A lovely young lady came up behind him and squeezed him gently and sincerely. I assumed she was his granddaughter, Becky. As he turned around, his face lit up brightly, and he swayed her back and forth in his unsteady arms.

He returned to the bookshelf, pulled out a different book this time, and sat at a small table in the front. I had an irresistible urge to join him at the table just as Melanie and Jeannie walked in.

Melanie wore one of her colorful ensembles. Red and black-checked capris with a scarlet red, frilled blouse and immense black, peace-signed earrings.

In contrast, Jeannie resembled a creamsicle in her light orange pants and matching blouse fringed in lace, topped with a long, two-stranded set of pearls. She tended to dress like fruit: in monotones of peach, tangerine, strawberry, and lemon. Always pastel, always perfect. She was so divinely put together, with her hair looking like she had just had a blowout.

Jeannie motioned to the older gentleman as she sat down. "Isn't he adorable? I met him here last month."

The words slipped out of my mouth before I could stop myself. "You should see his son."

Melanie let out a hefty laugh. "You go, Andi."

I avoided any further conversation about Niko, and I certainly didn't want to talk about Jed. "You know, I never anticipated to have so much success with the shop. I had hoped, but this surpassed my expectations."

Jeannie was in immediate agreement. "I think we need to add salespeople. Perhaps one full-time and another part-time. I've looked through the financials, and we can afford both."

I sat up straight, happy to talk about the shop. "That's great. It would enable us to spend less time at the store ourselves. I know I haven't contributed much the past two weeks."

Melanie looked at me with a sideways glance. "Are you serious, Andi? I'm amazed you are at the shop at all with everything that has happened in your life recently."

Jeannie placed her hand on my arm. "Please don't feel like you have to be there. Take all the time you need. Everything is running smoothly."

"I want to come back," I said. "I need to keep busy. I was thinking of some other ways to make the shop run smoother. We also need to reprint more promotional material. I want to make some changes before we make copies."

"Are you sure?" Jeannie asked.

I took a long, labored breath and let out my standard phrase. "I'm doing fine, really. Melanie, are you in favor of hiring two new people?"

Melanie tossed her erratic red hair affirmatively. "I think it's a great idea. I can make up a flyer to put in the shop," she said.

"If we had more space, we could include more items and accessories. I think we need to seriously look and see what is available," I said enthusiastically. "Do you know the old Craft Barn on the other side of town? I heard they were selling the property. I don't know if they would sell just the barn, but I thought I would drive by and check it out."

"Yes, I heard about it recently, too. The couple who own the building has decided to retire. They live in the manor home on the property and plan to move to Florida," Jeannie told us. "Actually, it was Lyla who told me about it. She has a jewelry display booth at the Craft Barn and is looking for other options since they will be closing."

Melanie laughed. "Who would have ever thought we would be thinking of expanding the shop already?"

Jeannie squirmed in her seat for a few moments before speaking again. "Last week, I went on a dating site."

I clapped my hands in approval, and Melanie reached over to Jeannie and gave her hand a tight squeeze.

"We need details," Melanie said.

Jeannie folded her hands in front of her. "It's a senior dating site. It took me hours to set up my profile. As soon as I set it up, I canceled it and then changed my mind again."

"So, have you met anyone yet?" I asked her.

"I've corresponded with a few men, but no one who interests me."

"Give it time. I'm excited for you," Melanie said.

I looked at Jeannie with delight. "That's fabulous, be patient. Oh, and don't forget we are meeting at Ellen's tomorrow at noon."

When our bubbly waitress arrived, I ordered only the Seafood Caesar Salad and lightly sweetened iced tea, in keeping with my newly suppressed appetite.

As we were finishing up, Bonnie called from the shop, unable to answer a customer question. Jeannie and Melanie rushed back to help her, leaving me to linger with my tea and thoughts.

I thought about my continuing love-hate relationship with Jed. I wanted him. I despised him. What I wanted and needed most was for him to realize the depth of my hurt. I also thought of Jeannie and the dating site. It must be so difficult to start all over again. Life would be much easier if I stayed with Jed and resumed my marriage.

Lost in my thoughts, drained and weary, I dropped my head, exhaling a louder-than-intended breath.

"Are you okay, young lady?" came the words from the elderly gentlemen.

I careened my head and looked up to his aging-wise eyes. "Yes, I'm just a little tired."

"Is there anything I can do to brighten your day?"

I stifled a laugh. "You just did, thank you." I asked him with a lilt, "Would you like to join me for a moment?"

"Nothing would give me more pleasure," Alex said as he took the chair beside me instead of across from me.

Becky came from behind the counter to our table, smiled at me, and with a wink, asked her grandfather, "Pa-Pou, can I bring you some tea?"

"Ah yes, Rebecca, that would be lovely. And I would like to introduce you to Andi."

"It's a pleasure to meet you, Andi," Becky said with the same smile and dark eyes as her grandfather and father. "May I get you a refill on your iced tea?"

I touched the top of my glass. "No, thank you kindly."

Alex and I fell into an easy conversation. His frailty was masked by his authoritative voice and strong mannerisms.

"Why does your granddaughter call you Pa-Pou?" I asked. "Is that a nickname from her childhood?"

"No, Pa-Pou is Greek for Grandfather. I am a first-generation American and very proud of my Greek heritage."

Hmmm, that explains their olive complexions and deep-colored eyes.

"Your granddaughter obviously adores you. Do you come to the café often?"

Alex shuffled his feet while sitting and rubbed the tops of his thighs. "I come here a few days a week. I live at Calvert Towers, a few miles away, and my son brings me here. I moved into the assisted living community when I turned 93 last year. I had been living with my son until then, and while he insisted we continue with the living arrangements, I did not want to burden him."

"Do you like living there?"

"I do, but I also like to keep active, and being around Becky keeps me young."

Alex pointed to the book stand. "I started the small lending library here at the café, which brings me great joy."

I turned around to look at the group of books again. "I'm sure they are appreciated."

A genuine smile appeared on Alex's face. "I like having things to do."

"Do you have other children and grandchildren?"

"No, it is just my son, Niko, Becky, and her two children. Niko's wife, Victoria, died two years ago from COVID. Victoria was a beautiful soul. Her loss was heartbreaking for both Niko and Becky. I lost my wife, Cecelia, 40 years ago, just months before Becky was born."

Alex didn't elaborate further on the loss of his wife, and I resisted the temptation to ask for any further details about her or his son.

"What was your career, Alex?"

"I was a high school history teacher for decades right here in town at the same school Niko and Becky attended. When I retired, I became involved with the town's historical society and helped restore the original town library on Cape Drive."

Becky looked at us several times with a generous smile.

"What about you, Andi? Are you retired?" he asked.

I told Alex about Sweet Repeats, my children, grandchildren, and the Parker Group. I did not include my marital status, although I had removed my wedding ring on the day I'd learned about Jed's Facebook debacle.

When I mentioned to Alex that I (not we) lived at the Villas of Walden's Pond, he exclaimed, "I know the community builder. He was from Concord, Massachusetts, the same town where Henry David Thoreau resided. He was a fan and follower of Thoreau's existential beliefs, and that is why he named the community after him."

"That's so interesting," I said. " I can't wait to tell the other residents the backstory of The Pond." Hearing the sound of three texts and one missed call, I told Alex, "I really have to go, but it has been so nice speaking with you."

"It's time for me to leave as well." Looking at an old pocket watch, Alex said, "My son will be here to pick me up in just a few minutes."

After sweet hugs and kisses to Becky, Alex tucked my arm into his as we walked out the door.

"My car is just at the corner," I said, pointing at my Mercedes.

"Let me walk you over."

We strolled the short walk to my car in the warming air as I secretly glanced for signs of his son's black Jaguar.

Alex gently directed me to the inside of the sidewalk and exclaimed that a gentleman should walk on the outside to protect a lady from both splashing cars and impending danger.

"You are a delight, Alex, and I look forward to seeing you again."

"As do I, my dear."

In front of me, the Jag pulled up alongside the older gentleman. Niko looked distinguished in his smooth, freshly ironed beige pants and blue polo shirt and called out to his father. "Hey Pop, you ready to go?"

When Niko looked over and realized I was on the other side of his father, he looked at me with a broad smile, as he asked his father, "Have you been having a good day, Dad?"

"Yes, I have. I had a wonderful afternoon with a lovely new friend."

Niko continued looking at me. "Lucky you, I'm envious."

"Thank you, Niko," I said, then realized I hadn't been introduced to him. "Your father told me your name."

"I can ask him for your name, or you can tell me yourself."

I smiled back and tried to think of something cute and sparkling. "Andi. It's nice to meet you."

Niko helped his father into the front seat and looked at me as he closed the passenger door.

"It's very nice to meet you, Andi. See you again soon, hopefully."

CHAPTER ELEVEN

"A Mud Run? Mom, are you serious? You need to go back to work or find more things to occupy your time." My daughter, Nicole, had called me after responding to the text I sent to the women of my family, including my older granddaughters. *I'm sending you a link for a Mud Run. I think we should do this together.*

"Yes, Nicole, it's a three-mile run with obstacles and inflatables for women's empowerment."

"In the mud?"

"Nicole, read the link I sent you."

"I did, Mom, and I saw pictures of women rolling in mud, going down big slides, and hurling their way over rope walls. IN THE MUD."

I was getting ready for the tea party at Ellen's house and putting the finishing touches on my makeup as I talked to Nicole. "Oh, sweetheart, it's something I want to do. I want to challenge myself. There are several different levels depending on your skills. For my age group, it's only one mile with fewer challenges. You don't have to do all the obstacles. It's a bonding experience."

"Why does it have to be in the damn mud?"

"You don't have to go if you don't want to. I already got a text from Brooke, Kelli, and Emily, and they are in. Madison is coming, too."

I could hear Nicole's exasperated voice on the other end of the call. "Why can't you take up knitting or play canasta? Or how about pickleball. Isn't that all the rage now with seniors?"

"I will do those things, too, but right now, I want to experience life to its fullest. I'm trying to figure this retirement thing out."

"And what better way to experience life and bond with your family than rolling around in the mud. Are you going to be skydiving next? Is this what you think you are supposed to do when you retire?"

I laughed at Nicole's description while putting on my shoes. "Maybe."

"There is no way Lisa would do this, and I seriously doubt Josh would want her to play in the mud with her mother-in-law."

"Do you want to do this or not?" I asked.

"I'm going to do it just to get pictures of you face down in mud. Perfect for our Christmas card."

"Good, I will send you the details. I have to go now. I'm going to a tea party, and then I'm going to look at an old barn."

"Mom, what the hell is going on with you?"

"Goodbye darling, have a nice day."

I pulled into Ellen's driveway just as Melanie and Jeannie entered the front door. Apparently, Melanie decided to dress in tea party mode. She wore a white flowered hat with a lace veil that covered her face.

Melanie did several twirls to show us her ensemble. "I bought this at Sweet Repeats. Isn't it awesome?"

"We have quite a nice selection of vintage clothing and accessories. We would be able to carry more if we had the space." Jeannie said.

I glanced at Jeannie's contrasting attire. She was wearing periwinkle polka dot capris with a matching top. She completed her outfit with pearls on her neck, arm, and ears.

"I'm going to drive by the Craft Barn this afternoon. I know it's not practical and more space than we need, but I thought I would check it out." I told them.

Ellen escorted us into her dining room.

Jeannie looked around the room in amazement. "Unbelievable, this looks beautiful."

Ellen's dining room table was set with an eclectic selection of mismatched teapots, teacups, and plates. A white tablecloth and delicate white embroidered napkins adorned the table.

Melanie picked up one of the teacups. "Ellen, are these all vintage?"

"Yes, I've been collecting pieces for several years," Ellen said with delight. "Have a seat while I bring out lunch."

Melanie tossed her fake boa over her shoulder. "Oh my gosh," she said as Ellen set a three-tiered doily-lined tray in the center of the table. "This is incredible. I can't believe you did all this."

Ellen pointed to the triangle sandwiches. "There are four different sandwiches, including avocado and quail egg, salmon watercress, cucumber dill, and ham and mango chutney."

I looked at Ellen and pointed at the sandwiches. "You made all these?"

Obviously pleased with our reaction, Ellen said, "Yes, and I will be right back with the scones and tea cakes."

Ellen placed another large tiered tray on the table. "And, here, we have three different scones. They are apricot with almond glaze, blueberry with lemon butter, and lavender cream."

Melanie took a blueberry scone and slathered it with clotted cream. "Oh my gosh, this is incredible. I am in awe of your talent."

Jeannie dabbed at her lips as she tasted her scone. "Ellen, this lemon curd is wonderful on the lavender scone."

Ellen gave us each a selection of tea with sugar cubes, cream, and honey sticks. It felt like we were at The Plaza in New York. All that was left was white gloves and fancy hats.

Melanie lifted up her teacup in a toast. "Pinkies up, ladies."

After we were sufficiently full of the delicate little sandwiches, delectable scones, and unfathomably mouth-watering petit fours, we enthusiastically offered to help Ellen find a place for a tearoom.

Ellen looked pleased and flattered with our numerous compliments. "Do you really think I can do this?"

"Yes," we answered in unison. "You *have* to do this."

BUT THEN ELLEN CALLED early the following day, just as I turned on Jed's fancy latte machine. "Tell me honestly, do you think the tearoom is a good idea?"

As I moved away from the grinding sound, I told her, "Yes, the shop would do so well. Your food is amazing."

"We didn't get a chance to talk yesterday about Jed. Do you

want to come over for dinner tonight? I have two grandkids coming, but we can still find time to talk."

"If you're cooking, I will be there."

Very soon, I was opening Ellen's front door, and without knocking, I stepped out of the path of her grandchildren, who were chasing each other with silly string.

"Hello there, Avery and Logan. How are you guys?"

"We're good," Avery called over her shoulder, resuming the chase after Logan, with their dog, Tyson, following behind.

Ellen removed her apron with one quick tug. "Oh good, you're here. Tim said he would take over with the kids while we went into the bedroom so we could talk. I gave Tim strict instructions to allow us at least 30 minutes of quiet time."

I followed Ellen into her Victorian-wallpapered bedroom. Every inch of Ellen's house was homey and inviting. In comparison, my house was monochromatic with shades of gray and blue. I don't have a separate playroom for my grandkids with lots of storage for toys and games. Nor do I have a play kitchen for Kendall and Andrew. Sometimes, I feel intimidated by Ellen's grandmotherly skills.

Ellen swished the door closed, and sat on the edge of the bed while she pointed to a white wicker chair with a hand-crocheted blanket. "What's the latest?"

I pulled the chair closer to her as she exhaled loudly, waiting for my response.

"He's still living at the house, but we are living separate lives."

"Why are you waiting to kick him out?" Her voice was terse and cynical. "Do you want him to stay? If you do, I promise I will find a way to be supportive."

"I don't know." I leaned forward in the chair. "I'm hurt and confused. I know I shouldn't, but part of me feels like I should believe that he was flirting and nothing more."

Ellen took a sip of the wine she had brought up with her. "Obviously, you need proof before you can move forward. It's hard for me to believe that Jed's messages to Renee were not proof enough for you. What we need is evidence."

"Actually, I was suspicious earlier today. Jed said he was going to Steve's tomorrow to put in a garbage disposal, and I felt he was over-explaining everything. It made me think that maybe he was going to see Renee."

"C'mon, Andi, I don't believe anything he says. Let's follow him and see where he goes."

"What?" I asked with part disbelief and part delight.

Ellen set her wine glass on an antique white hand-sewn lace dresser scarf and turned to me with wide eyes. "Do you know what time he is going to Steve's?"

I knew what she was thinking. "No, but I can ask him later."

Ellen wriggled her finger at me. "Okay, here's the plan. When you know the time Jed is leaving, you leave first and come to my car, which I will have parked around the corner. When we see Jed's car, we will follow him. Maybe he is going to Steve's, but I suspect not." Ellen's voice was full of mischievousness and excitement. "And we will take Tim's car because he would probably recognize mine."

By the time we left Ellen's bedroom, Tim was in the kitchen, wiping up spilled chocolate milk, pleadingly looking at Ellen.

As Ellen gathered the sticky, sweaty little ones to the table, she spooned large portions of spaghetti and meatballs.

Tim leaned into me and handed me a glass of chianti, "How is everything, Andi? I sure am sorry to hear about you and Jed."

"Thank you, Tim. Your wife has been a huge comfort."

Ellen patted Tim's hand and added, "Honey, I need your car tomorrow. It's best if you don't ask any questions."

Tim turned to Ellen and then to me with dismay but also affection, "Uh oh, this doesn't sound good." Tim had quickly and correctly ascertained the request for his car, and he added, "Would you like fake noses, dark glasses, and hats, too?"

Ellen wrinkled her nose in mock annoyance. Tim released a small chuckle and kissed the top of her head.

Interrupted by another spill, this time from Tyson, Ellen and I shared a mutual smirk confirming Tim's accusations.

When I returned home, I found Jed sitting at the kitchen counter, head bowed, fingers interlaced around his precious drink. "Did you have a nice night?" he asked, looking up at me.

I wasn't in the mood for obligatory polite conversation, "Yes, I'm just tired."

Jed stood up, reached for my hand, and looked at me hopefully, "Let's find something to watch on Netflix."

"Okay. By the way, what time are you going to Steve's tomorrow?"

Jed widened his blue eyes. "I will probably leave around 5:30. I'm going to Home Depot first to pick up his garbage disposal. It will be late by the time I install it—you know how Steve is. He can't do any household repairs and depends on me. Why?"

"No reason."

CHAPTER TWELVE

"I CAN'T DUCK DOWN ANY FURTHER. Jed can't see us anyway." I looked over at Ellen from the passenger seat of Tim's car, ready for our evening of surveillance. "This isn't the way to Steve's," I added angrily. "It's also not the way to Renee's house."

Ellen grimaced. She lifted her sunglasses that we had donned along with baseball hats for our surveillance. "And, just how do you know where Renee lives?"

"I did a little bit of spying on her Facebook page, found out her last name, and where she lives."

Ellen pursed her lips together with a hmmm sound. "And, what else did you find out?"

"She has big boobs, two children, works at the restaurant where Jed golfs and is eleven years younger than me. Did I mention she has big boobs? Wait, he's pulling into that shopping center."

Ellen drove closer to Jed's car. "Look, he's parking in front of an Italian Restaurant off to the side. And I bet he's meeting Renee there."

"Well, we can't exactly go inside to check it out, and have him see us."

Ellen removed her baseball hat and let down her long auburn hair that held only a few streaks of gray. "We will just sit in the car and wait for him to come out with her."

Since Ellen and I could talk endlessly about any subject, two hours quickly passed until Jed finally came out of the restaurant. Alone.

We waited a few minutes, looking to see if Renee or any other woman had come out of the restaurant alone.

"I really thought we would catch him with her." Ellen's voice radiated her disappointment.

"I don't know whether I am happy or not. Why would Jed have dinner alone on the other side of town?"

"Let's keep following him and see where he goes."

Ellen put the car in reverse, and after we caught up to Jed's car, we followed from a safe distance.

Forty-five minutes later, he was pulling into the entrance of The Pond while we stayed several car lengths away.

I waited ten minutes in Ellen's car.

"Time for me to go in and cleverly ask him about his evening," I said. "Hopefully, Jed will tell me he met Steve at the restaurant for dinner."

"I seriously doubt it, but this was fun."

I found Jed in the house, already changed as he walked out of the master bedroom. "There you are. Your car is here, so I thought you were home."

"Ellen picked me up, and we went out for a bit."

"It took me longer than expected at Steve's to install the garbage disposal," Jed volunteered before I could ask him.

I looked at Jed and wondered how he would answer my questions. "You must be hungry. You didn't eat before you left the house."

"Steve made me a sandwich. Thank you, though."

I raced with many thoughts as I tried to comprehend Jed leaving the restaurant alone. He was lying, but about what?

Jed followed me into the master bedroom and turned on the TV. I didn't object as I performed my nightly routine of getting ready for what I assumed would be another night tormented without much rest.

As I lay in bed next to Jed, he reached over and held my hand. I didn't move away and listened to his light nasal sounds, envious of how quickly he descended into sleep.

IN THE MORNING, I pulled a short-sleeved, blue and green Lily Pulitzer maxi dress from my closet and looked in the full-length mirror. Then, I plastered a smile on my face in approval. I wasn't about to spend the day sulking in bed, wondering what my husband had been doing.

Jed arched an eyebrow as I walked into the kitchen. "You look nice. Are you going into the shop?"

I poured myself a cup of coffee that Jed had made and took my spot at our kitchen table. "I have some errands." I left it short and simple, with no need for detailed explanations.

Jed sipped from his Pop Pop mug and gave me a hopeful, ever-present, playful look. "Can I make you some breakfast?"

How long did he think his boyish charm would mask his true self? "No, thank you."

I didn't think I could get through a simple breakfast without asking him where he had been last night.

Our open-concept home suddenly felt claustrophobic, and it became impossible to sit still. I rushed a good-bye to Jed and hurried to my car.

After arriving downtown, I walked past Becky's Café, hoping to see Niko through the window. I'm unsure what I would have done if I had seen him, but he wasn't there, so I continued to the shop.

Jeannie assisted a customer while Claire and Suzanne, our new employees and residents of The Pond, went through clothing and separated it into appropriate piles.

Claire was a shy, unassuming woman who seemed to light up at the shop. She engaged well with customers, and I was shocked to find out she hadn't worked for nearly 50 years.

Suzanne was vibrant and bubbly and always came to the shop dressed professionally with perfect makeup, hair, and attire.

Claire, carrying an armful of Talbot's clothing and scarves, walked over to a rack and sorted them by color.

After receiving a warm embrace from Melanie, I put my things down and immediately started helping.

"I haven't seen you in quite a while, Andi." Suzanne's voice quivered slightly, and I assumed she had heard the gossip. "How have you been?"

I tried to sound optimistic. "I'm good. How is Curtis? I love the flowers on your front porch."

After a few mundane pleasantries, I picked up the steamer and grabbed items from our "keep" pile.

It felt good to be productive. Actually, it felt amazing.

Jeannie poked her head into the backroom and winked at me with a smile generated from her heart.

Later on, Jeannie, Melanie, and I sat at the backroom table when the store had quieted while Claire and Suzanne took over the front. We discussed the shop and reviewed details before next week's accountant meeting.

My eyes fell on a comparison of Melanie and Jeannie's hands. Melanie's hands were strong and robust like her. They were artist hands, not bothering with manicuring. In contrast, Jeannie's hands were soft and delicate, well-shaped, and had a fresh frosty cream nail color showing off the radiant oval-cut diamond ring she still wears faithfully.

I tugged at my pink and yellow "Sweet Repeats" tee shirt that we often wore in the shop. "It's time to put these away. I think we should make a more professional appearance and dress with more panache."

Melanie let out a haughty sound. "I don't think I can pull off panache."

"No, I want you to dress like you," I told her. "In your own style. I love your colorful expressiveness, and it invites individuality in our customers." Melanie expresses herself with fashion—or, more correctly, her lack of fashion sense in her bohemian style. And that's what makes her so endearing.

Melanie tugged at the fabric a little too snug around her ample bosom.

Jeannie said, "I agree, it's a great idea."

"The shop is doing so well," Melanie said, smiling. "If we decide not to move, I wish we could have more room to expand." Melanie continued with thoughts on how we could rearrange the front section of the shop to allow for a display of boots, scarves, and sweaters for the upcoming fall season.

Jeannie stood up from the table and retrieved a silver bag from a counter. "A lovely woman, Mary Jo, came by to inquire about selling her scarves at Sweet Repeats. She brought a sample. She paints the scarves on silk by hand."

Rubbing the material through her fingers, Melanie exclaimed, "This is incredible, and the rainbow design is amazing."

I was in awe at the hand-stitched hem and brilliant colors. "These would sell so well with our clientele. They wouldn't take up much room. What do you think about telling Mary Jo we would give them a test trial until the end of the year?"

"We can display a few of them in the front window and drape some over tops and dresses," Jeannie said. "She mentioned that she had been selling them at the Craft Barn but was looking for another location since it will be closing."

It was comfortable to be in a work environment again, releasing my mind from thoughts of my marriage. Melanie, Jeannie, and I were ideal business partners. With my business acumen, Jeannie's actuary career, and Melanie's artistic talent, which she spreads throughout the shop, we blended well together.

Melanie's esoteric lifestyle and flair were visible in many ways at Sweet Repeats. She brought in a bowl of fake fruit for our sorting area, following the rules of Feng Shui. "The apples are signs of harmony, the grapes are abundance, and the oranges represent good luck," she'd told us.

Once, while we were sorting through a bag of donated linens and after I had tossed a stained vintage violet embossed tablecloth, Melanie picked it up and examined it thoroughly. She said she had an idea and would take it home. The following day, she had turned the tablecloth into a small curtain, which she skirted around our pedal stool sink in our lavender-painted customer bathroom.

Suzanne stepped into the backroom. "Do you know Phyllis from The Pond? She just came in with a pile of clothing she wanted to donate. I thought you might like to see the clothes and say hello."

I remembered seeing her at the pool and presumed she wanted a better look at the scorned woman in the neighborhood. I sighed, got up from my seat, and followed Suzanne to the front counter, where Phyllis stood with a broad smile, enveloping me in her perfumed cloud.

"Oh, Andi, this store is incredible," she said sincerely. "I've heard so many wonderful comments about the shop. I have some items I would like to donate. I heard you give much of the proceeds to local agencies, and I wanted to contribute."

"That is so kind of you," I told her politely as she lifted two heavy Nordstrom-labeled bags on the counter. I raised a few items: Chico's, Gucci, and Hermes. "These are gorgeous."

"Unfortunately, the styles and sizes were for a 20-year younger me," Phyllis said.

"I don't know how to thank you for your generous donations."

"You are doing such a wonderful thing for the community."

I recognized Phyllis' sincerity and regretted my previous assumption of her personality. I looked at her with sincere gratitude. "Phyllis, we appreciate your kindness."

"My pleasure. I look forward to seeing you around The Pond."

I brought the two bags to the backroom for preparation. All donated items are marked with a special tag so that we know the proceeds go to charity.

Melanie gasped as she held a vintage Farinae cocktail dress. The ivory silk evening wear had a lace bodice and hemline with a matching bolero jacket. "I wish this was my size. I would buy it now."

"Some of these will be difficult to price," Jeannie commented. "I can start researching the brands later this week."

"I feel terrible. I totally misjudged Phyllis," I said. "What a lovely woman."

Melanie gave Jeannie a conspiratorial glance. "Tell Andi about your date this Saturday, Jeannie."

I looked at Jeannie with a smile. "What? Tell me."

Jeannie's mannerisms were shy as she spoke. "I met him through the Senior Singles dating site. His name is Chuck, and he seems very kind. We've been emailing and talking on the phone, and I agreed to meet him at The Lighthouse Inn this Saturday. I am so nervous, and I have been thinking about canceling."

Melanie reached her hand and held Jeannie's perfect little

palm. "No, you have to do this."

Jeannie looked at both of us with moisture welling up in her eyes. "I know it's been two years since Wayne passed away, but it still feels like yesterday."

I asked Jeannie how much she knew about Chuck.

"He seems very sincere and has shared pictures of his home and family. His wife died more than five years ago, and he recently went on Senior Singles."

Jeannie showed us several pictures Chuck had sent to her. He had a serene smile and lively, deep brown and hazel-flecked eyes. But she looked conflicted. "I really don't know him. What if he isn't anything like his pictures? What if I have been conned? You hear stories about older women being taken advantage of all the time."

As she tightened Jeannie's hand, Melanie reassured her. "I have an idea. Would you be more comfortable if you weren't alone on your date?"

With a laugh, Jeannie looked at Melanie and said, "I think I'm a little bit too old to have a chaperone."

I interjected, "What a great idea. Melanie, you and I could go to The Lighthouse on Saturday if you are available. Jeannie, you wouldn't have to look at us. You would just know that we were there."

Melanie removed a rust brown hat from the box of Phyllis's donations and placed it on Jeannie's head. "Seriously, Jeannie, you need to get out and go somewhere other than here. Andi and I will be nearby for emotional support."

Jeannie seemed more comfortable with our assurances that we would offer support nearby. "Okay, but are you sure this doesn't seem like we are in junior high school?"

Melanie added a faux fur wrap from the bag and put it around Jeannie's shoulders. "That's exactly what it seems like, and that's wonderful. It will feel good recapturing our youth."

Jeannie let out a laugh, her freckles looking like sprinkles on a vanilla cupcake, and agreed. "Okay, thank you both so much."

We heard the jingle of the front door and finished our meeting.

I put my hands on my hips and shared my upcoming adventure. "I won't be able to come in tomorrow. I'm going on a mud run," I told Melanie and Jeannie.

Jeannie returned the hat and boa to the donation box. "Did you just say a mud run?"

I stifled a laugh. "Yes, I'm going with Nicole, Emily, Lisa, Brooke, Kelli, and Madison. It will be an interesting *and dirty* bonding experience. I still can't believe Lisa is coming with us."

"Make sure you get pictures for us," Jeannie said.

"I will be in all day Thursday, so I want both of you to take the day off," I told them.

"Actually, we have sufficient staff, so I think we can seriously reduce our hours," Jeannie said.

Melanie was pulling out more clothing pieces from Phyllis's bag with delight. "Let's create a schedule for our employees, especially since we have become so busy."

I stepped outside the shop towards my car and noticed Alex walking out of the café.

"Hello, Andi," he called out to me.

Delighted to see him, I quickly walked over to him and grabbed his elbow as his knee quivered. "Alex, I'm so happy to see you again."

Alex smiled broadly. "I wish we had time to talk more, but my son is waiting for me," he said, pointing to the jaguar that had just pulled up. "Will you be around this week? I have a Thoreau book for you. Perhaps we can get to know each other better if you have time."

"I will be at Sweet Repeats all day on Thursday. Would you like to see the shop? I will have time to sit together and chat." I guessed I would spend all day at Sweet Repeats even though Melanie said it wasn't necessary.

"It's a date," Alex said.

Niko was just getting out of his car to help his father. With a quick tugging of my Sweet Repeats tee shirt, I stepped a few feet closer to him. "Hi, Niko."

"It's nice to see you again, Andi," Niko said sweetly, tipping an imaginary hat on his head.

"Andi and I just made plans for Thursday. If you have time, perhaps you can join us," Alex said, turning to Niko.

"I have plans until 2:00," Niko said. "Can I meet both of you at the Cafe?"

"That would be lovely," I said.

LATER THAT EVENING, I was thinking of Niko while enjoying Honey Glazed Salmon with Jed. Well, I was enjoying the salmon, not Jed.

Just as I was lingering in the quiet of my thoughts, my phone rang.

I put my finger to my lips. "It's Nicole. I don't want her to know you are here." I put her on speakerphone so I could eat while talking to her. "Good evening, darling. How are you?"

"You sound perky, Mom. Planning any more insane outings?"

"I will let you know when I do."

"What do I need to bring tomorrow for this crazy mud run?"

"Lots of water, gloves, knee and elbow pads if you have them," I told her. "And, of course, an extra set of clothes and shoes. I will bring towels and soap. They will supply us with everything else we might need."

"Like the mud?"

I knew she couldn't see the smile on my face, but I was grinning from ear to ear. "Yes, dear."

"I can't believe we are doing this. Bye, Mom, see you tomorrow."

"Have a good night, honey."

Jed's mouth and eyes were wide open. He hadn't touched anything on his plate.

"Elbow pads, soap, and mud? What in the hell are you doing?"

"Going on a mud run," I said as casually as if I said we were going to the mall.

My phone rang again, and Jed continued to stare at me in total confusion. I put the phone on speaker again while I enjoyed my delicious dinner.

"GMOM, can Kelli and I bring two friends tomorrow?" Brooke's voice was bright and lively through the phone. She had adopted the name GMOM for me when she was two and had strongly requested that the other grandchildren not use the personal reference.

"Of course."

"This is going to be so amazing."

CHAPTER THIRTEEN

"BROOKE, LOOK," Kelli said as she pointed to the sign for Muddy Mamas in Washington County. Underneath the logo was their slogan, "Go All in and Get Muddy."

"Oh my gosh, I didn't know it would be like this," Lisa, my very timid daughter-in-law, commented. "Why are there tents everywhere?"

"That's where our team registers," I said.

Brooke looked at me and then at her sister, "What team? GMOM?" Brooke said.

I reached into my duffel bag and handed everyone a tee shirt. "We are participating as a team. Look at these cool shirts I had made for the event."

"Mudaholics? Are you serious?" Emily, my less timid daughter-in-law, said while lifting up the shirt to show the others.

Madison tentatively leaned into me, "Grandma, what's a Mudddahollowick?"

Nicole held the shirt up to her shoulders. "You want us to wear a shirt saying we are Mudaholics? Mom, have you lost your mind?" she asked disparagingly.

"Stop it, all of you. Our team is called the Mudaholics, and we are going to have a good time," I told them with a slight tone of aggravation. "Put on your tee shirts, and let's go register."

Lisa stopped a cheery woman in her 20s wearing a *Muddy Mamas* shirt. "Where do we shower when we are done?"

"There aren't any showers. On the last obstacle, you slide into a large vat of water to rinse off some of the mud," the amused young woman said.

Lisa's face saddened with an increased look of skepticism. "But where do we get changed?"

"Honey, everyone gets changed in the parking lot," the woman said, clearly enjoying this discord.

Madison was ready to cry and run back into the car by now. She clung to her mother's leg with fear. "Mommy, will we get hit by a car while we are naked?"

"Mom, why couldn't we have bonded somewhere nice and clean? Like a spa?" Nicole said. "Holy crap, did you see this poster?"

A large poster outlined the obstacle course with photos:

Hay Lady: Women climb over eight feet of stacked barrels of hay.

Hot Flash Splash: A large wet slip and slide where you go into, you guessed it, a pile of mud.

Hot Mess Express: Women come out of large steel pipes into, yup, more mud.

Does This Make My Butt Look Big: A large pink pyramid for climbing from one side to the other.

Just Roll With It: A sizeable mud-soaked spiral coil hung from a large wooden swing set.

Fishnet Stockings: Swinging rope climbing.

Light At The End of The Tunnel is the last obstacle, where you crawl through a large tube and come out in a pile of mud, then go through another tube and end in a pool of water.

There was a total of 25 obstacles. You could choose just a few or all of them. Each obstacle began and ended with mud. Maybe I didn't think this through carefully.

Nicole stood still, lifting her shoulders up and down. "Let me get this straight. First, we run for a mile, and then we roll around in the mud?"

I flashed a smile, trying to inspire confidence, but silently wished it was a spa, too. "Yes, Nicole, I told you it's a MUD run. You run in mud."

A charming, non-mud-clad young lady with a swinging blonde ponytail led us to the side. "Next group over here."

"This is not a race; this is for fun. Put on your tee shirts, put a smile on your face, and get muddy." I told my disgruntled Mudaholic team.

As we were heading out of the tent, I could see other teams with names on their shirts: Muddy Divas, Band of Mudders, The Dirtier the Merrier, Pretty Lil' Mudders, Mudwisers, and my personal favorite: Dirty Naughty Babes.

I took Madison's hand and stood with her off to the side. "You girls, go over to the three-mile run, and Madison and I will walk the one mile. We will meet you at the obstacle course."

Nicole shook her head, "Uh no, Mom, you said it was just one mile."

Brooke and Kelli each took one of their mother's arms and walked her to the start of the three-mile race.

"Unless you think you can't make it through and need to go on the one-mile walk with the grandmothers and little kids," Brooke said.

Brooke and Kelli's two friends were greatly pleased while listening to our heated discussion. And very proudly wearing their Mudaholics tee shirts.

Madison and I leisurely strolled the one-mile walk and waited for the rest of our group.

I GATHERED MY TEAMMATES together in a circle. "Okay, ladies, are you ready for the real fun?"

Only Brooke, Kelli, and their friends showed any enthusiasm. But I wasn't going to give up. We were going to bond and have a good time, one way or another.

I quickly changed my mind after the first obstacle, "*If mud ain't flying, you ain't trying.*" We had to hop in burlap sacks across a muddy field. The mud flew into my hair and face with each jump. I jumped so deeply at one point I couldn't move forward.

"Oh my God, Grandma is stuck," Kelli said, stifling her laughter.

When my teammates finally stopped laughing, they helped me to continue.

The next obstacle wasn't any easier. The *Net Crawl* was certainly not meant for a woman my age or my size, but I refused to acknowledge my apprehension. I looked up at the wire just inches from my face, laid on my back, and tried to shimmy through. Now, granted, the wire was covered with plenty of tape, but still, it was wire, and I was stuck.

Lisa's face looked like it had drained white as she tried to delicately help me through the wire. "Andi, you have to turn over and crawl low."

Madison ran over to me and pushed my right side, thinking she could flip me over. "Grandma, it's okay. You can do this."

After seeing her face, I knew I had to turn myself over and heroically make my way through.

"What's next?" I asked.

Emily read the sign. "It's called *Cat Gility*. We weave ourselves through the ropes."

We watched a team before us, and they seemed to have no trouble. However, their group looked more cat-agile than we were.

Brooke came over with her hands on her hips and looked very authoritative. "Look, guys, we can do this as a team. GMOM, you're super tall, and you can lift those giant legs of yours over each wrung."

Lisa stood next to Brooke. "She's right, we can do this to-gether. Madison, you can slide through the bottom row without any issues. Let's go."

Whoa, I thought to myself. Lisa is really getting into this.

And just like that, we wiggled our somewhat agile bodies through.

I must admit that two other teams zoomed past us while we were only halfway through. It was not a race, though, re-member that.

We stood in a row looking at eight-foot-high bundles of hay.

This time, Emily took charge, "Andi, we can use your height for this one, too. You stand in front and lift Madison up to the top of the hay. And then, when the rest of us get up top, we can help you up."

That made sense, didn't it? Not exactly.

I looked up at my team. Each had made it successfully to the top of the hay bundles. "So, what part of your plan involved getting me up top?"

Emily, our self-imposed leader for this particular obstacle, lay on the hay and reached down her arm for me. I dug my feet into the hay and plopped indelicately on top. I made it.

Oh boy, here comes the mud. Our next obstacle was a giant mud pit. Just mud in a pit.

I looked at my team. "Ladies, we've got this. We simply have to walk slowly through the mud."

Madison pointed to the people in the mud pit. "But Grandma, why are they crawling through the mud instead of walking through it?"

None of us knew how to answer her since we doubted we would get through without some or all of us falling knee-deep in the mud.

One down, two down, three down, and then four more. All of my team was down in the mud. But not me.

I looked at my team with a triumphant smile. "I guess these giant legs are good for something."

Yes, I was the only one on my team, including two other groups that were with us in the mud pit, who made it through without falling. But I had flaunted my success too soon. The rest of the afternoon went downhill for me.

We made it through the other obstacles after several falls, bumps, bruises, with mud caked everywhere on our bodies, and more laughter than I have ever experienced. We were a triumphant group of Mudaholics.

"Mom, this was fantastic," Nicole said as she ran to me so hard we both face-planted into the mud.

After we ended up in the pool of water, we headed to the parking lot, where we stripped off our clothes while hiding behind strategically placed towels and did our best to remove as much remaining mud as possible.

From the looks on the faces of my fellow teammates, the day was a success. There was animated chatter all the way home.

"Mommy, can I do muddy runs at home?" Madison asked, wiping her eyes with exhaustion.

"No, but did you have a good time today?" Emily asked her daughter.

Madison was bursting with excitement. "It was the best time ever. I want to do it again,"

Emily's exhausted face lit up, holding Madison's hand as

they walked towards their van. "Maybe in a few more years," Emily told her.

Julia, Brooke's friend, smiled ear to ear, passing around her phone to show everyone the pictures she had taken. "We gotta do this every year." Julia reached over to retrieve her phone. "Wait, I've got to send these pictures to ...."

Brooke cut her off and said, "Let me see all the pictures before you send them to anyone."

"Fine, fine," Julia mumbled.

"Kelli, we should put together two different teams, and we could do one of the competitive runs," Brooke said enthusiastically.

"That would be so much fun," Kelli responded.

The four teenagers headed into their vehicle while the rest of us climbed wearily into Nicole's van. It took less than five minutes for me to slump into the seat and close my eyes.

"I'm going to send you guys the pictures I took," Nicole said. "Wait till you see the one of Mom with her face down in the mud after she fell off the swing. Oh wow, look at this one of her when her feet got stuck on the ropes, and her shoe came off," Nicole turned to look at me. "I hope you don't mind, Mom, but I'm going to post these on Facebook."

Madison yawned sweetly, "Shh, I think Grandma is sleeping."

Emily passed her phone around. "Look at this picture I got of Brooke and Kelli when they got into a mud fight. I'm sending these to Nathan right now."

I pretended I was sleeping as I listened to their uplifted voices. I put my hand over my mouth so they couldn't see my smile.

I SOAKED IN A TUB of Epsom salt for two hours after the mud run. I will deny it to everyone, but I was exhausted, sore, and still getting mud out of places where mud should never be. Getting out of my soaking tub was challenging with my uncooperative throbbing legs. Even after thoroughly drying off, I could still feel specks of mud in my hair.

As requested, Jed was sleeping in the guest room and I was never so happy to see my cozy and comfortable bed. I could feel it reaching out to me, beckoning me into the pillow-top mattress. I was incorrect in expecting immediate sleep. I was too wired. I grabbed my iPod on my nightstand and turned it on to my favorite playlist. I wondered if Jed had left his earbuds; those expensive LG Tone Wireless Bluetooth Earbuds he claimed were the best.

I didn't have the strength to get up and search his night-stand, so I rolled over twice until I could stretch my arm into the drawer. I tossed aside papers and other gadgets until I felt the earbud case. At first, I thought I would add this to my "Jed's Stolen Items" pile in the garage, but then I decided to keep them for myself.

Phil Collins' "In The Air Tonight" was the first song in my playlist. I put in the earbuds, turned up the sound, and sang along with the lyrics, heavy on the *TA TA TA TA TA*, which was my version of the five-second drum solo that you can't help air-drum to.

I awoke after I had slept nine straight hours. I haven't slept so well in over 50 years. My muscles were still aching, and I submitted to their request for another few hours of lounging in bed.

I texted Melanie, Jeannie, and Ellen pictures of the mud run.

We have to put together a mud run team for us. It was an amazing bonding experience.

Melanie was quick to respond with a team name. *Mud-tastic Women*

But nothing could top the email I had just received from Brooke:

Hi GMOM,
I don't know how to thank you for such a remarkable day. I have a creative writing assignment for school, and I wanted you to see part of it.
I Love you,
Brooke

WHAT I LEARNED FROM PLAYING IN THE MUD
WITH MY GRANDMOTHER
By Brooke Stanley

As a girly girl, I doubt I ever played in the mud as a child. But there I was at 19, going through many obstacle courses covered in mud with my team, which consisted of my grandmother, sister, mother, eight-year-old cousin, two friends, and two aunts. Initially, none of us wanted to go on the mud run, but Grandma coerced us into it. So, the nine of us became the "Mudaholics" and started our dirty journey.

My highlight was the final mud mountain. Grandma, who is 69, could not make it over the massive pile of mud, but she kept trying. She would get close to the top and slide right back down to the bottom.

After twenty minutes of seeing Grandma's determination and frustration, the rest of our team, including my young cousin, climbed the other side of the mud mountain to the top. We all held onto each other while grabbing Grandma's hands and pulling her over to the other side.

You could hear the cheers from other women who had been watching us. The Mudaholics jumped up and down with Grandma in celebration of her accomplishment.

It wasn't just Grandma who had accomplished something; it was all of us, including the other women, at the mud run. I learned firsthand how determination, willpower, and support from others could get you to the top of any mountain, full of mud, disappointment, or anything. We worked together, pulled each other through the obstacles, and shared in the celebration.

And, as my grandmother said, "Empowered women empower women."

CHAPTER FOURTEEN

I AWOKE TO ANOTHER SWELTERING late August day and a lingering storm threat. I dressed quickly, looking forward to time at the shop and seeing Alex and, hopefully, Niko.

Jed greeted me in the kitchen, once again getting up earlier than usual, and handed me a Frappuccino he had made with the expensive espresso machine I gave him last Christmas. He wore his Ravens boxers with a loose muscle shirt, looking appealing and in excellent shape for a 74-year-old man.

"You mentioned you were going into the shop early. Will you be there all day?" Jed seemed to want to say more but stopped himself.

"I'm not sure, honey," I said, surprising myself. Why am I being so nice when I know he has lied to me?

Annoyed, I turned to the coat closet and grabbed an umbrella. "Gotta go, see you later."

Jed remained still and unsure what to say. "Okay, have a good day. Can I take care of anything around the house for you? I don't have any plans today."

"No, thank you. I'll see you later."

Jed continued to watch me as I walked out the door into the garage. As I pulled down the driveway, I could see Jed as he looked through the window, blowing me a kiss with a wink. Some type of odd, guilty behavior, I assumed.

BY MID-AFTERNOON at Sweet Repeats, I was pleased to see the young woman who came last month looking for an outfit for her job interview. "Delia, it's so wonderful to see you."

Delia did a little dance in front of the counter. "I got the job, and I need some more clothes. You guys were right—the staff wears a combination of funky and casual clothing."

I clapped my hands in pleasure. "That's fantastic. I'm so happy for you."

Delia started looking through a nearby rack of Chico's tops when she turned around and asked me. "By any chance, is Melanie available?"

I giggled, knowing she preferred Melanie's style. "No, so sorry."

Right then, Alex walked in, struggling to close the door behind him from the increasing wind. While I was helping Delia, he introduced himself to Claire, who had become a valuable part-time employee. I overheard him saying, "I'm a friend of Andi's, paying her a visit."

Claire flashed him a sincere smile while she straightened hangers on various racks. When two new customers walked in, she greeted them with complimentary punch and cookies.

After I checked Delia out, I walked over to Alex. I was about to extend my hand when he hugged me gently and familiarly. I gave him a tour of the shop and the background of how and why Melanie, Jeannie, and I had opened the store.

I took Alex's arm and led him through the store. "Let's go sit in the backroom. I'll go grab us some punch." We walked through the racks separated by color and name brands and skimmed past two tables of jewelry displays of Swarovski earrings and vintage brooches. Jewelry had become a popular item at Sweet Repeats. We had expanded Lyla's collection to a case near the counter.

"What a wonderful place. My wife would have loved this shop. I am so proud of you." Alex said this as if he had known me for many years.

"The shop has been a blessing to my partners and me in many ways," I tell him. "We give much of the profits to women in need."

With that, Alex grabbed my hand for steadiness. "I hope I am not keeping you from your work."

"No, I've been looking forward to seeing you today."

With slow movements, Alex maneuvered himself into a seat. "Sometimes things as simple as sitting down take me quite a while, but I get there eventually."

As I handed Alex the punch, he smiled. "Thank you, this is

so delightful. As promised, I brought you a book by Henry David Thoreau. There are many books by and about Thoreau, but I thought we would start with this one. *Where I Lived, And What I Lived For."*

"You are so kind, Alex. I don't know much about Thoreau. I read a little about him recently."

"He lived his life in solitude and self-sufficiently, and urged his fellow man to abandon their materialism for simplicity. I encourage you to read more about his beliefs."

I stood and offered Alex some of the cookies Ellen had dropped off that morning.

A languid smile stretched across his mouth. "Let me share one of my favorite Thoreau quotes with you," he went on. "'It's not what you look at that matters; it's what you see.'"

I watched Alex with sincere curiosity. "What are some of the things you have seen?" I leaned closer to him, anxious to obtain his wisdom.

Alex paused for an uncomfortable amount of time before proceeding. "I had," he said, stopping at the word 'had,' "I had a beautiful, loving daughter, Corrina. She was a lively, talented, and endearing soul. Corrina was much like my wife, Cecelia. Corrina's gentle kindness was a blessing to everyone. She had just finished nursing school and was engaged to a wonderful young man in his last year of medical school. My wife and Corrina were busy planning the wedding, which was set to take place in a few months."

Alex took several minutes, his chest heaving rapidly as if trying to catch his breath.

Then, he continued very slowly. "Corrina was driving to work, her very first day in the pediatric ward of St. Luke's Hospital. A gentleman in a black Cadillac was driving himself to St Luke's with signs of a heart attack. They were both pulling into the hospital when he lost control, hitting Corrina's car and sending her into a pole that went through her windshield."

I nearly gasped. "Oh, Alex, I am so very sorry."

"The gentleman did, in fact, have a heart attack. He survived, and we became friends. And that friendship continued for many years. He felt tremendous guilt. I didn't want him to carry that with him."

"Wow, what an incredible person you are."

Alex paused, and I stood up and touched his shoulder. His tragedy made all the uncertainty in my life seem insignificant.

Alex and I remained silent for several minutes. I wasn't sure whether to sit or continue to touch his shoulder. I refilled his punch and sat down across from him.

He thanked me and held the glass tightly. "You remind me of Corrina. You have some of the same mannerisms, and your eyes are the same deep cornflower blue. She was tall and carried herself, emphasizing her height, just like you. Being with you takes away some of the sting. I can imagine myself talking to her. I hope that doesn't make you uncomfortable."

"I'm honored, Alex." Unable to sit or stand still, I walked behind our table to the two tiny windows that looked out on a dumpster and a broken air conditioner. We had been hoping to convince the landlord to make more parking spaces available. Melanie had put together strands of crystals and beads over the windows to obstruct the unattractive view. Her little touches made such a difference to the shop. She'd added tapestries and posters of influential women to adorn the walls.

I walked back to my seat. Looking at Alex's eyes, now clearing up, I wanted to ask him more questions about his daughter and his life. "I'd love to hear more about your wife, Alex."

"My Cecelia was a beautiful woman with sparkling green eyes and beautiful deep brown hair with streaks of gold. She wore her hair in a long braid. She soaked up knowledge wherever she could. Cecelia was a political advocate long before it was acceptable for women. In the '60s, she attended rallies with Gloria Steinem and Betty Friedan. She was a beautiful, free spirit and devoted mother. We loved each other dearly and had many, many incredible times together. We had all the promises of a beautiful marriage that would last a lifetime, but ..." Alex paused before he continued. "Cecelia lost her soul when Corrina died. She stopped living and went into a deep depression. She couldn't remove herself from the depths of her loss.

For years, we lived in agony, barely speaking to each other. She left her career as a guidance counselor and became neglectful of Niko. Our marriage became estranged. Niko was married when Corrina passed and was busy living his life. All passion left Cecelia, and she spent her remaining years in darkness. Cecelia died of a broken heart when she was 62, just two months before Becky was born."

The depth of Alex's pain covered his face.

"That must have been such a difficult time for you," I said.

"Yes, it was. I lost myself until I started living more for others and less for myself."

I let out a long breath and looked at Alex with compassion. "How did you accomplish that?"

"I've tried earnestly to live my life in the manner of Thoreau: deliberately."

"That couldn't have been easy."

"It turned out it was easier than being angry. I spent too many years of my life in anger. I was furious at God and the world. How could a benevolent God take my Corrina, someone so special? I was also angry that Cecelia had left me and Niko. She had left us long before she died."

I was at a loss for what to say and waited for Alex to continue.

"Sadly, Niko lost his wife two years ago."

Alex leaned back in his chair and drew a huge inhale. He reached into his breast pocket for a freshly laundered and folded handkerchief and dabbed his eyes. The corner of his handkerchief was initialed AMC, prompting me to ask, "Alex, what does the C stand for?"

"Alexander Milos Cirillo. My mother told me she chose Alexander because it means defender of men. My Greek surname Cirillo means masterful, and Milos means soldier. So, I am the masterful soldier and defender of men."

I smiled at Alex, sensing his pride. "It's perfect for you."

"It's a lot to live up to. Niko's full name is Nikolai, which means people of victory."

Nikolai, I thought to myself, *what a beautiful name.*

Another treasured hour was spent obtaining more information about this remarkable man. I learned that Alex read ferociously, played the Bouzouki (a musical instrument played in Greece), has an affinity for opera and orchids, cherishes his son, granddaughter, and two great-grandchildren, and has never traveled beyond the contiguous states.

Alex took out his pocket watch, "Niko should be at the cafe soon. Shall we head over there?"

I smiled at Alex, grateful for my enjoyable time with him.

Alex composed and collected himself for a few moments before standing.

Then Alex and I slowly made our way to the front door after he said a lengthy goodbye to Claire and the remaining customers.

The wind was intensifying just as Niko was walking into Becky's Café. Seeing us, Niko reached for his father's arm. Niko wore beige khaki shorts and a white polo. He looked dressy, even in casual clothes, and I noticed a scent of musk and wood as he stepped closer. "How was your visit, Dad?"

"It was lovely. I'm a little tired, and I think I will ask Becky to drive me home."

"Dad, if Becky is busy, let me take you home. I don't want you to tire yourself out."

Becky walked over. "I can take you, Pa-Pou," she said, kissing her grandfather.

"Looks like it's just you and me, Andi," Niko said while escorting me to a bright table by the front window.

"Your father is truly fascinating," I said. "I enjoyed talking with him. And I'm so sorry to hear about the loss of your wife." I felt my head tilt in sympathy.

He nodded in agreement, "Yes, it was very devastating and happened so quickly."

As Niko dropped his eyes in remembrance, I noticed his lashes were longer than mine. I tried to force myself to concentrate on his words, not the waviness of his hair or the appealing scent drawing me closer.

My turn to say something. Damn, no words were getting into my

*head other than what I was saying to myself. Whew, the waitress was
coming over with glasses of water.*

"Your daughter's café is adorable," I said.

"Becky works very hard. She was recently divorced, and it's
been difficult for her."

I looked up to see the waitress still standing at our table,
apparently waiting for us to respond.

"Andi, would you like something to eat?" Niko asked.

I resisted touching my growling stomach. *Oh, what I would
give for a double cheeseburger and onion rings. I could have acted dainty
and ordered a small salad with dressing on the side. I couldn't imagine
trying to talk to Niko and eat simultaneously.* "No, thank you, I'm
good."

"How about some nachos?"

I shook my head, unable to say anything coherent. *Sure,
Niko, I will indulge in nachos and have stringy cheese fall from my
mouth while we talk.* Instead, I simply said, "Sounds good."

"So, tell me something about you, Andi. All I know about
you is the shop."

I hesitated, not sure how to answer his question. "Well, I
have three lovely children and five wonderful grandchildren. I
owned a marketing agency for more than 35 years that my two
sons now operate." I also wanted to say that I keep putting my
hands up to my neck because I am trying to hide the turkey
wattle I noticed this morning.

Niko leaned in, and I felt his sincere interest, making me
more comfortable. "Tell me more about your family."

*Family. Should I let him know that I am married? Should I tell him
my husband has lied to me and was probably unfaithful?* I opted to
exclude any mention of Jed.

"My sons, Nathan and Josh, are polar opposites. Nathan is
ambitious and outgoing, while Josh is gentle and timid. My
daughter, Nicole, is a combination of the two boys: sweet and
affable but tough. I have four granddaughters and one grandson. They are absolutely spectacular." I let out a laugh, and Niko
looked confused, so I clarified. "My family is indeed spectacular,
but just like every family, we have our issues," I said smiling.

Niko's face warmed. "Oh, now, that sounds interesting. Go on."

I took in a deep breath which made his eyebrows rise in curiosity. "Well, like I said, Nathan is tough, but that toughness can intimidate Josh, and I worry that maybe they shouldn't work together. Sometimes, I think they took the easy way and joined my company. And with Josh's passivity, I think his wife, Lisa, controls him and their lives." I paused as Niko leaned in closer.

"Don't stop now," he said.

As I became more comfortable, I continued. "Nicole is a wonderful mother and daughter. I often wonder if she would have preferred a mother who had worked less and had been more attentive at home."

Niko shook his head in understanding. "I'm sure you were a wonderful role model."

I was concerned Niko would ask me about my marital status, which I had so conveniently left out. "Tell me about your family. Do you have other children besides Becky?"

"No, it's just Becky and my two grandchildren. I'm very fortunate that they live close to me. We have a wonderful relationship."

Niko didn't elaborate further, and I couldn't think of another word to say. It was easy when I was talking about my family. Soon, an uncomfortable silence fell between us.

I was really struggling to keep this conversation going. *What the hell was wrong with me?* I wiped my sweaty hands together and waited for Niko to say something else.

"What do you like to do, Andi?"

"Um, I like to spend time with my family and friends." *Why did I start my answer with Um, and why did I sound so stupid? There's more to me than my family and friends, right? Oh, I know. I will tell him about the mud run. That will make me seem more interesting.*

"I just went on a women's mud run with my family."

Niko's eyes widened. "A mud run? That sounds incredible. Did you actually run in mud?"

"I did! You go through several obstacles in the mud." *Why*

do I sound so idiotic? I needed to tell him more about it. But no, I just squirmed in my seat.

Niko let out a little laugh with his adoring smile. "I knew you were different."

Different? Does he mean different good? Different weird?

I crossed my legs, uncrossed them, folded my arms, unfolded them, and then picked up my glass and set it down, forgetting to take a drink. *Why am I so uncomfortable talking with Niko?* I thought of Jed's Facebook messages to Renee and how easily he wrote to her.

The waitress returned quickly with a pile of nachos, and I requested another glass of water. *I wish they served wine or bourbon.* I changed my mind about drinking more water. I had already downed two full glasses. If I continued to fill my bladder and I had to laugh, I just might not make it to the bathroom.

I accomplished putting a small amount of olives and sour cream on a chip to avoid opening my mouth too wide. Niko ate so comfortably. I watched him bring the food to his mouth, his lips moving up and down. *Oh, good grief, I think he can tell I am staring at his mouth.*

I managed a few more comprehensible sentences before I was interrupted by the sound of my phone. I let it go to voicemail, and shortly after, the dings continued with incoming text messages.

"Please, check your phone. It seems like someone is trying to reach you."

From Melanie: *Jeannie is having a crisis. She's trying to decide what to wear for her date tomorrow and threatening to cancel. Can you call her?*

From Jed: *What time will you be home? What do you want for dinner?*

From Ellen: *I have another plan for catching Jed. It's probably illegal, but that's okay.*

Niko must have noticed the disgruntled look on my face after I read the messages. "I hope everything is okay."

Oh, yeah, my husband just wants to know when I will be home. I must have neglected to tell you I was married. And my best friend wants to do something illegal to catch my husband being unfaithful.

"Everything is fine," I said out loud. "But I really should be leaving. It was nice to see you again, Niko."

"You too, Andi. I look forward to the next time. May I have your phone number? You know, just in case my dad wants to get in touch with you," he said in a teasing voice.

I wrote my number on a napkin, handed it to him without looking at his face, then walked out.

Having almost forgotten the Thoreau book from Alex, I rushed to Sweet Repeats to retrieve it. I picked it up from the table and opened it randomly to this quote: *Rather than love, than money, than fame, give me truth.*

CHAPTER FIFTEEN

"I DON'T THINK I'VE EVER seen that dress before," Jed said as I walked into the family room in a veil of my favorite gardenia perfume I had just sprayed on. "It looks amazing on you."

I did a little twirl and grabbed my purse. "I purchased it from the shop. I'll be out for a few hours."

Jed shifted his feet and continued to look at my dress. "Can I ask where you are going?"

I responded with only a quick glance at his face. "I'm having dinner with Melanie and Jeannie."

As if knowing my objection to kissing him on the mouth, Jed leaned over, placing his lips on my cheek, lingering longer than I liked. "Well, enjoy. I'm meeting some of the guys from the golf league, but I shouldn't be out long."

With quick goodbyes, we were on our separate ways.

Just two hours earlier, Jeannie had called with a quivering voice, "I don't think I can go through with my date."

With an unusual sternness, I told her, "It wouldn't be fair to Chuck to cancel this late. Melanie and I will be there for emotional support. I promise it will be fine."

Melanie and I had agreed to arrive at the restaurant after Jeannie and Chuck. We would work it out to be near them but not too close.

"Wow, you look great," Melanie said as we met in the lobby at The Lighthouse Inn.

"You do, too. I love your style." I pointed to Melanie's flat ballet slippers decorated with faux jewels and baubles that she collected of broken jewelry from pieces donated to the shop that could not be sold.

I could see Jeannie and Chuck were seated by a window in the enclosed sunroom off to the side.

"May we have a table in the sunroom?" I asked the woman with an impeccably styled chignon and wearing a much sexier version of my black dress.

"Certainly," she said, escorting us to a table with a slight view of Jeannie and Chuck.

"Oh, he's so cute," I said to Melanie.

Melanie stood up and walked over to my side of the table. "I don't want to make it obvious, but I want to get a look at him, too. It's so sweet how they are leaning into each other."

Within minutes, our waiter arrived for our orders.

I texted Jeannie. *Enjoy your date. We are here if you need us.*

"I hope the evening goes well for Jeannie," I said. "She is such a beautiful, amazing woman. She deserves to find happiness with someone again."

Melanie looked at me with concern. "I can only imagine how difficult it must be to start over again."

I gave Melanie a slight smile, knowing she was aware of my uncertainty.

I scanned the menu quickly and ordered the Chicken Milanese. As the waiter turned to Melanie, I added, "I will also have a Cosmopolitan." It was the drink that always made me feel chic and sophisticated. Damn, I looked at my fingernails and regretted that I didn't have a manicure. When a woman drinks a Cosmopolitan, she should have lacquered red nails. I suddenly wished I knew how to do a chignon or French twist to my hair.

Melanie placed her order, "I will have the Chilean Sea Bass Acqua Pazza and a club soda with lime."

When the waiter returned with our drinks, I recalled how Melanie chose sparkling water whenever we were out or toasting our success. "Do you not drink alcohol?"

As she twisted the lime into her club soda, Melanie said, "I haven't shared this with either you or Jeannie, but I am a recovering alcoholic. I have been sober for 21 years. It nearly destroyed my marriage and has caused some, hopefully, not irreparable, damage to my relationship with my son, Scott. We are still struggling to work on re-establishing our relationship." As she lifted her hand for a sip, her arm, heavily laden with silver bangles, jingled like little bells.

"Melanie, I had no idea."

Melanie took a deep breath and steadied herself. "I started drinking in college and became quite the party girl. I didn't take my studies seriously, and it took me an extra two years to graduate. When Jack came into my life, I was able to quit drinking. Jack is the yin to my yang: quiet, reserved, unwavering, and solid. When we settled into married life, I was content and began teaching art at the high school. Life was running smoothly, and we had Scott after a few miscarriages."

Melanie shook her head in remembrance, her long earrings caught in her unruly hair. She tugged them free and continued. "When Scott was around 10, I was invited to a retirement celebration for one of my fellow teachers. I had a drink, and then another, and then another." Melanie's voice trailed off in distraught remembrance.

We both sat back in our seats while the waiter delivered our meals.

Melanie's eyes grew wide behind her huge round red glasses. "Within days, I started hiding alcohol around the house. I became a controlled drunk and would wait until I came home from work to start drinking. When I drank, I was nasty and confrontational to Scott and Jack." She could see the surprise on my face. "It's true. I was abusive, loud, and unkind."

I couldn't fathom Melanie drunk. I could see her smoking pot and indulging in a somewhat reckless lifestyle during her youth. But nothing like this. "I can't believe you went through that. How did you get sober?"

"Jack gave me an ultimatum and put me in rehab. It worked for over a year. Jack threatened to leave me and take Scott with him. But that wasn't enough to make me stop drinking for long."

"What caused you to finally get sober?"

"I hit rock bottom. I stopped at a bar coming home from work one day, convincing myself it would be okay. I had too many gin and tonics and had a car accident. Thankfully, no one was injured, but it was enough to scare me. So, I went back to rehab, and that time, it was successful."

I looked at Melanie in awe of her struggles and successful battle. "That couldn't have been easy."

Melanie collected herself briefly. "I found strength through prayers. Addiction is a daily struggle, and for me, prayer is needed every day." She shared more details between bites of our meals, and we were soon both filled with tears. "Andi, I know you are going through a challenging time. My only advice is to live your best life. If your marriage is worth fighting for, fight hard, but if it is poisoning your soul, walk away. I am still working on my relationship with Scott. He hasn't forgiven me for the heartache I caused him and his father."

"How are things with you and Jack? Did *he* forgive you?"

"Things were strained between us for many years after I became sober. But we worked together and went to therapy. AA and ALANON helped both of us." Melanie placed her fork down, and sat back into the cushion of her seat. "I don't drink anymore but I am 'California sober.'"

By the questionable look on my face, Melanie realized I was unfamiliar with the term.

"While I don't drink alcohol, I do smoke pot occasionally which helps ease the wanting of a drink."

"How often do you see Scott?" I asked next. "Does he have a family?"

"I only see him about twice a year, with little conversations between. His wife, Allison, is very understanding and sends me pictures and updates on my two grandchildren."

I reached across the table for her hand. "Thank you for sharing such an intimate part of your life."

Melanie's eyes widened as she looked at me intently. "Andi, we all have backstories, heartaches, and pain. You will get through this difficult time. Just know that your family and friends love you dearly and will support whatever decision you make."

"My one son and daughter don't feel that way. They are insistent that Jed and I split up."

"It's your life, Andi, not theirs. Live it for yourself with whatever decision you choose."

I realized we hadn't bothered to check on Jeannie. I sat up tall and looked at Jeannie's table, where she and Chuck were engrossed in each other. I relaxed and gave Melanie a big thumbs-up. "They are so cute, looks like they are deep in conversation, and both seem very engaged," I said.

"I hope it goes well for Jeannie. She is such a treasure."

We'd just finished our meals when Jeannie texted us:

Chuck is leaving shortly. I will walk out with him, and after he pulls away in his car, I will meet you in the lobby.

Melanie and I were seated on the rose velvet bench in the lobby when Jeannie walked in, and with one look at her, it was apparent things had gone well with Chuck. She had chosen a form-fitting black pencil skirt and an off-the-shoulder white silk top with pearl buttons. Her skin was glowing, and her hair was perfectly coiffed, as if she had just stepped out of a salon. Her ruby-red lips and shadowed eyes would have certainly captured Chuck's attention.

Jeannie sat with us, crossed her legs, and leaned against the padded velvet cushions. She squeezed her eyes shut while telling us, "It was wonderful. I genuinely like Chuck. He's gentle and kind, and we made plans to get together next weekend. I won't be needing a chaperone anymore."

Melanie and I nearly squealed in delight. The three of us giggled like teenagers as we walked out of the restaurant. The hostess spoke as we were leaving. "Hope you enjoyed everything."

Jeannie smiled broadly back at her and said, "It was fabulous."

As I OPENED MY FRONT DOOR, even before we exchanged greetings, Ellen handed me a plate of vanilla and caramel teacakes. "I have a new plan for catching Jed in the act."

I took one of the teacakes oozing with icing. "Does it involve deceit and disguises?"

"No disguises and not really deceit, but I'm pretty sure it's illegal."

"Go on, I'm intrigued."

"We are going to break into his email and Facebook accounts."

I looked at her and giggled. "Ellen, we can't do that. Even if I wanted to, I don't know his passwords."

"I realize that, but my brother is a software genius, and he said he can figure it out."

"You told Doug?"

Our eyes widened as we scanned my taupe and cobalt blue kitchen as if looking for someone listening to the conversation. We knew no one else was home, but the pretense made Ellen's deviant plan more exciting.

I put the teacakes and a bottle of Chardonnay on the table.

The plan was quite simple, actually. Ellen took out her cell phone with its bedazzled case, compliments of her youngest granddaughter, and called her brother.

Doug answered jovially, already knowing why we were calling. "Let's start the easy way first. Do you have any joint streaming accounts in Jed's name and email account?"

"Yes, Netflix and Amazon Prime," I said.

"Great, tell Jed you have to access the Netflix account because you want to add your laptop as another device and that you need the password. Chances are, he uses the same password for everything. Most people our age don't realize that we should have several varying passwords and change them often."

I put his suggestion on my mental to-do list.

"What if he did use a different password?" I asked Doug.

"Then we have to go another route. Let's hope we don't have to do that because that would involve breaking a few laws."

I looked at Ellen with a raised eyebrow. "Your sister seems anxious to get us arrested, so I would prefer not to resort to anything else."

"We will get in one way or another," Doug said. "By the way, I never liked your husband."

I said goodbye and a sincere thank you to Doug and ignored his last comment.

Ellen clapped her hands in delight, "This is going to work. I know it."

But I realized this could backfire, and Jed would have cause to accuse me of devious behavior. "This could end very badly. Won't Jed know that someone accessed his accounts? He often comments that I have to trust him," I said, scratching my head.

Ellen crossed her hands in front of me. "If there is anything deceitful, and I'm sure there will be, would he have the balls to accuse you?"

Later that evening, over a dinner of linguine and clams a la Jed, I casually asked him for the Netflix password, which he gave without question.

Let the investigation begin.

After a lengthy text exchange with Ellen, I questioned the inappropriate behavior that had occurred while Jed lay right beside me.

Jed gave me the Netflix password.

Great. When do you want to try to break in?

Stop saying it like we are doing a breaking and entering crime.

Well, we kind of are. But you need evidence. Besides, this might not work. When do you want do this?

Sometime next week after Labor Day, okay? I have to prepare myself before I become a criminal. It's possible we will crack the code for his accounts, and there will be no evidence of him cheating.

I doubt that.

Texting my secret messages to Ellen with Jed right next to me was so easy. Did he do the same with Renee? With others? Doesn't this make me as culpable as him?

As I put the phone on my nightstand, Jed reached over, pulling down the light blanket and fingered my satin nightgown. "If you are cold, I can keep you warm," he said.

This was Jed's first attempted physical contact since my sexual-controlling maneuvers. This could be the last time we have sex if I find evidence of his betrayal. Or, it could, of course, be the beginning of trusting him again. I was willing to take the chance. Without words, I removed my sleepwear and let him crawl on top of me.

This time, I didn't need to take control. I already had it.

CHAPTER SIXTEEN

"MOM, I'M NOT COMING to your house for the Labor Day party if Jed will be there," Nathan had told me earlier that day. "I don't care if you are just roommates or whatever you guys are doing. I won't be around him."

Jed's birthday was the end of August, and mine was the 1st of September, so we'd always had a large party on Labor Day for the multiple celebrations. In addition to our children and grandchildren, much of our extended family also attended.

I always look forward to my birthday. As one of seven children, birthdays were the one time when we received extra attention. My mother would cook our favorite meal for dinner, and we could invite a few friends for cake and ice cream. Purple was my favorite color, and my parents put purple balloons in my bedroom while I slept. I would wake up to the sea of purple and be anxious for the best day of the year.

Sometimes, my birthday would fall on Labor Day, and I would pretend the country observance was just for me. Having Jed's birthday a few days before mine was a double celebration.

Nathan's words roared through me until I finally spoke to Jed.

We were both getting ready to begin our mornings. "Labor Day is next weekend. I think it would be best if you spent it with Chloe and her family. It would be too uncomfortable for my children."

Jed put down his toothbrush. "Really? Well, sure, Andi. You call the shots."

I followed Jed into the bathroom, explaining, "Jed, nothing has changed. I'm trying to become comfortable trusting you again. I want to, I really do. Just ...."

Jed tightened his mouth. "I know, Andi, just give you time. I should be grateful that you let me stay in the house, right?

Who's coming this year?" Jed's protesting tone was beginning to heighten.

"Everyone is coming, including Greg and his family."

Jed unparted his lips just enough to let out a small sigh. "We've always celebrated our birthdays together. It feels wrong. Will it be this way for every family event?"

"I don't know, Jed. This isn't easy for me, either."

Jed's face reddened, and I was anxious to stop the conversation. "What am I supposed to say to my daughters?"

I almost laughed at the way Jed spoke with disgust.

"Tell them we are still figuring things out, and you want to celebrate your birthday with them. Or, tell them the truth."

Jed looked at me with a smirk. "The truth? That you screw me physically one day, and the next day you screw with my mind."

I have to admit, that was an impressive statement. And true.

He walked out of the bedroom without waiting for my reply.

Jed and I always worked as a team for family functions. Each of us took responsibility for making the events as seamless as possible. We would be exhausted yet elated after each celebration. This year, I would face it alone for the first time since we'd been together.

I followed Jed into the kitchen. I didn't want to leave the conversation with his clever retort. "Please try to understand."

Reluctantly, Jed agreed to separate celebrations. "I get it, Andi, but this is so difficult. I feel displaced. But okay, I will get in touch with Chloe. I think Rachel will be coming home, too."

Rachel, Jed's other daughter, was not one of my favorite people. I would not miss her sarcasm or snootiness. Even Jed had little patience for his moody, sullen daughter. When Rachel married Jeffrey, a wealthy, equally temperamental personality, she became pretentious and arrogant. When speaking about Jeffrey, Rachel would draw out his name haughtily, saying Jahffreee, as if he deserved a higher recognition like royalty.

She flaunted their wealth flamboyantly. Jeffrey and Rachel had been living off his inheritance, had made foolish investments, and overextended themselves. They had started and failed several businesses. The family's money was dwindling, and they found themselves financially strapped.

When this happened, Rachel quickly ran to her *daddy*, seeking assistance.

Jed, in turn, had asked me, "Do you think we could loan Rachel and Jeffrey some money until they get back on their feet? Kathleen has offered to help a little, and I thought we could contribute."

Without even considering her request, I had said, "No, absolutely not." I also seriously doubted that his ex-wife, Kathleen, could or would offer monetary assistance. When Jed and I married, she tried to get more alimony from him, knowing his financial situation had increased.

Kathleen was always included in our birthday/Labor Day celebrations. We felt it was a special moment for their grandchildren to see us all together in a healthy environment. She always brought her infamous homemade potato salad.

Jed would always thank Kathleen graciously for her food contribution.

"Well, I know how much you've always liked my potato salad, Jed. I brought you some melon, too, just the way you like."

I remember saying to Kathleen, "I already have melon here."

"Yes, but Jed prefers his melon cut into small balls."

I nearly choked on her comment. From then on, I would let her deal with Jed's small ball preference.

Kathleen continues to ask Jed to come over and repair miscellaneous items in what she still calls "our" house. Whenever she called, he went running—perhaps out of guilt. Jed was at Kathleen's home at least once a week. It appeared that she was incapable of doing even simple home repairs.

At least this year, I wouldn't have to deal with her, their daughters, her potato salad, or her small-balled melons.

Jed understood why I didn't want to help his daughter, but I sensed some resentment when I gifted Nicole and Eric a substantial amount when they purchased their first home. I'd wanted to make things equal with Nicole since Nathan and Josh were reaping the rewards of taking over the agency.

Jed never brought it up again. Rachel and Jeffrey managed to downsize but continued to live above their means.

"NATHAN, IF YOU ARE GOING TO be in my way, can you at least help me?" I asked my son. "You're following me around the kitchen while I'm trying to prepare everything for the party. Everyone will be here shortly, and I still have so much to do. I appreciate you coming early, but please stop asking me so many questions."

"Well, at least HE'S not here."

I turned to Nathan while handing him a pot of boiled potatoes, "Peel these. It wasn't easy telling Jed he wasn't welcome to the party, especially since it was also his birthday celebration. He was always such a help, and I miss that."

"You miss his help, or do you miss him? And how can you miss him when he still lives here? Why are you making potato salad anyway?" Nathan snapped while dropping peels on the counter. "Oh yeah, that's right, Kathleen won't be here to bring her specialty. Isn't there a better way to peel these?"

"Yes, but I wanted to see you struggle a little bit," I said while patting him on the nose and handing him a plate of onions and celery. "Do you think you could manage to dice these? I never realized how much Jed took care of when we had parties."

Nathan picked up a knife and started chopping an onion without peeling it first. "I think I can manage to chop these, Mom. Jed might have been helpful in the kitchen, but he's been a lousy husband."

I reached over and showed Nathan how to peel the onions. "Just chop and try not to cut yourself. You and Josh will have to do the grilling. I don't even know how to turn it on."

"Chill, Mom. I have experience putting hot dogs and hamburgers on a grill."

"Thank you, my darling," I said, blowing Nathan a kiss and making him smile.

Nathan still didn't want to let things go. He turned around with the knife in his hand. "Mom, it's hard to understand why you are hesitating to throw Jed out on his ass. He's always sat back, lived his easy life, while you struggled through long hours at work."

I continued wincing with authority at my eldest son. "I know, Nathan. Let me handle this on my own." I was accustomed to Jed doing the shopping and prepping the night before. He made it seem effortless. He would hold attentive conversations with our guests while flipping burgers and grilling corn.

I welcomed the sight of Nicole, Eric, Brooke, and Kelli, along with Nathan's wife, Emily, and their children as they walked into the kitchen.

Nathan's eyes were watering from the onion. "Ladies, come help Mom finish before everyone else arrives. She seems to think she can't do this without Jed's help."

I snapped my towel at Nathan. "I didn't say that."

Emily grabbed the condiments and started to interrogate me immediately, never one to shy away from expressing her opinions. "Andi, why is Jed still living here? I thought you threw him out?"

Nicole didn't give me a chance to respond. As she retrieved the punch glasses, she added her opinion. "I don't know why you are letting him stay here. While you worked, he always sat back and lived his easy life. And you continue to make it easy for him."

I quietly continued preparing the rest of the food, not wanting to discuss the status of my marriage with my children.

Emily added the chopped vegetables to the potatoes and stirred the dressing mix I had previously made. After tasting the dressing, she added more salt, pepper, and vinegar. "I'm going to miss Kathleen's potato salad," she said, ducking as I threw a pot holder her way.

I reached out to grab her arm and tell her to stop adding salt, but I retreated and let her over-season the potatoes.

I swallowed back my annoyance when Eric, my typical reserved and non-judgmental son-in-law, and husband to Nicole, walked into the kitchen and taste-tested every item. "I don't know why you are hesitating to throw Jed out. How can you let him live here knowing he cheated on you?"

The rest of my clan laughed at the unexpected harshness coming from Eric.

"Et tu, Eric?" I asked.

As Nathan, Emily, Eric, and Nicole continued berating my choices, I looked from one to the other waiting for an opportunity to speak. I'd wanted to remind them I was the matriarch of this family. I remembered Melanie's words about living my life for myself and not for my adult children. I didn't have a chance to change the subject before Brooke and Kelli, who had been assigned the job of setting up the croquet in the small patch of lawn in front of the patio, walked into the kitchen.

My granddaughters wore ridiculously short skirts and midriff-exposing tank tops, adding their own opinions on my marital status.

"GMOM, how can you be with someone who humiliated you on social media?" Brooke wanted to know.

As the eldest grandchild, Brooke had assumed the role of boss to Kelli and her cousins, with much authority. She was abrupt and ambitious, traits I didn't adopt until I was well into adulthood. Nicole never showed an interest in the Parker Group, but I could see a place in the company one day for Brooke. They would probably sync well if she could adjust to Nathan's controlling tendencies.

I turned to my eldest granddaughter and handed her a bowl of berries. "Brooke, I was just getting ready to remind everyone that I am the head of this family and do not appreciate being scolded. I thank you for your concern, but please trust me to make the right choices for my life. Go, make the punch, but don't add the sherbet too soon."

Brooke made a fruit, ginger ale, and sherbet punch for every family event. I had a large cut glass punch bowl that had been my grandmother's, and I loved telling my family how it had been used for over a hundred years. Brooke was always the one who appreciated stories of her ancestors.

Kelli, who was busy gathering plastic tablecloths and napkins for the folding tables I had set up on the patio, walked in and hugged me, "I love you, Grandma."

I looked at Brooke with a twisted smile. "And that's why you are my favorite, Kelli."

As Josh and the rest of the family arrived, I winced at Nathan just as he was about to utter more complaints.

My brother, Greg, and his family arrived shortly after, and we scrambled to get everything onto the tables. Nathan made a disaster with the potato salad, which Emily had definitely over-seasoned. And Brooke put the sherbet in too soon, and it melted quickly in the sun. Josh and Nathan handed over the barbecue tools and gave the grilling job to Eric.

But as we sat down and I looked at my wonderful family, their criticisms and all, I was filled with love. I was surrounded by my well-meaning, loving children and grandchildren. I was very blessed indeed.

There wasn't enough room to squeeze in on the patio, and we had to alter the event into an indoor/outdoor party. I was accustomed to the large backyard in our previous home with plenty of room for the grandkids to play.

Nicole suggested, and I am considering, that future large family functions be held at her house. I would probably enjoy being a guest instead of a host anyway. I had been able to run a business more easily than I could cook and plan a large family celebration.

A few hours later, as I was putting away toys from my younger grandchildren, disposing of the plates with unfinished potato salad, and starting on a second dishwasher run, Josh came into the kitchen and asked me to join everyone outside.

I walked out to a large sheet of birthday cake with purple icing and white lettering: *Happy Birthday, Mom*. As I blew out the 70 candles, I realized it was the first time in 25 years that it didn't say *Happy Birthday Mom and Jed*. The cake was always half chocolate for Jed and half vanilla for me.

Sitting next to the cake was my birthday box. About 10 years ago, I requested the kids and grandkids to stop giving me birthday, Mother's Day, and Christmas gifts. I had everything

I needed and didn't want anything. What I wanted most of all was cherished family memories. I bought three large decorated boxes from Home Goods, one for each Holiday. I asked the family, in lieu of gifts, to write a letter, draw a picture, or create something small that could go in the boxes. I didn't want the letters or drawings to be about me. I wanted them to be letters about their lives and things that represent who they were individually.

The boxes had become my most treasured belongings and had multiplied through the years. I'd read and reread the letters and watched the growth of my children and their families. I learned a great deal about the other sides of my children that I wasn't aware of. Many years ago, Josh wrote a letter about his concerns about joining the company. He expressed his apprehension to work so closely with Nathan. He had only ever expressed those feelings in his letter. Last year, Brooke's letter included the reason she chose a college nearby so she could live at home. Despite Brooke's bold and outgoing personality, she wasn't ready to live away from her parents and sister.

It was an unspoken agreement that the letters were to remain private and not to be discussed. It was a means for everyone to share things that had happened in their lives in the past year. Some good, some bad, some ugly.

While the younger grandchildren were waiting for the cake to be cut, Jed's car pulled up earlier than I had expected.

Jed parked his Corvette in the garage and came to the patio with flowers and a smile. He looked adorable in his dry-cleaned and pressed pastel blue shirt, turned back at the cuffs. His year-round tan made him look more robust and healthier than he really was. His AFIB issues, high blood pressure, asthma, and chronic bronchitis often resulted in consecutive days of bed rest and inactivity. This was one of the reasons I would never have imagined Jed pursuing other women. He fought aging, though, and he fought it well.

Jed immediately walked over to Josh, giving him a fatherly hug. "It's good to see you, buddy," Jed said warmly to my younger son while looking at Nathan.

"Hi, Grandpa Jed," Andrew said, wrapping his arms around Jed next to his father.

Jed picked up Andrew, "I've missed you, buddy."

Greg greeted him with a handshake. "Hey, Jed."

"Let me know if you would like to get together for a golf game sometime," Jed told Greg.

Nathan's two young daughters, Madison and Kendall, ran over to extend their hugs to Jed.

"I've missed you guys," he said. "How have you been?"

Nathan didn't wait for the kids to respond and stepped forward. "Mom said you would be at Chloe's today," Nathan spoke with a severe undertone, leaving no doubt that he resented his presence.

I gave Nathan and the rest of my family a warning glance, silently pleading with them not to start an argument.

We all noticed Jed looking at the birthday cake with his missing name. "That's right, Jed, we are celebrating GMOM's birthday," Brooke said, making her point sarcastically by not calling him Grandpa Jed.

I felt a twinge of sadness for him. "Would you like some cake?"

"No thanks, I had some at Chloe's. I'm going to take a shower and lie down."

Without saying anything further, he walked into the house.

After devouring the vanilla, sans chocolate cake, everyone said their goodbyes. As the first big event without Jed's help, I thought things had gone well. I was sitting at the kitchen counter, looking at the remaining mess, and enjoying a glass of chardonnay when Jed walked in freshly showered, his wet hair combed back. He had changed into his boxer shorts and stood shirtless before me.

"I hope everyone had a good time."

"It was very nice, but I'm exhausted."

"Do you want some help cleaning up?"

"No, it's all good," I said unconvincingly, hoping Jed would help me finish so I didn't have to do it alone. But then, why should he clean up at a party he was uninvited to?

CHAPTER SEVENTEEN

"HAPPY BIRTHDAY TO YOU, Happy Birthday to You," Ellen sang while walking into my house, holding a large purple bag with pink, white, and purple tissue paper. I love Ellen's birthday gifts. She knows me better than anyone. I opened the bag, thrilled to see lotions, perfume spray, sachets, and soaps in my favorite scent, gardenia.

"Thank you so much, Ellen. This is wonderful," I said, hugging her tightly.

"How was your birthday party?"

I escorted Ellen into the kitchen. "It was good, and I enjoyed having everyone here. Truthfully, I really missed having Jed around. He's a much better cook than me and cleans up while he goes along compared to my process with just as much food splattered on the floor and everywhere."

"Was Jed gone the whole time everyone was at your house?"

"He came just as we were getting ready to have the birthday cake. You should have seen his forlorn face when he looked at the cake with only *Happy Birthday Mom*. He didn't mention it later, but I know he must have been hurt." I brought the leftover birthday cake to the table and cut a hefty piece for each of us. "Let me get you a piece of MY cake."

"Well, at least you didn't have to see Kathleen."

We tapped our forks together in agreement.

Ellen looked at me with raised eyebrows. "Are you ready to log into Jed's accounts now?"

"No, not now. Jed should be back any minute."

"Okay, but don't keep putting it off. You need to get on with your life one way or another."

"I will, I promise."

Ellen put her finished plate in the sink. "I don't want to be here when Jed comes home. Call me tomorrow."

"I will call you when I get back from fishing," I told Ellen.

"Fishing? Seriously?"

"Yes, you never know what I might catch."

BROOKE LOOKED AT ME INCREDULOUSLY. "Deep sea fishing? GMOM, are you crazy? Why are we doing this, and why do you want to go on a smelly boat with a bunch of old men?"

"First of all, it's not all old men who go deep-sea fishing," I told her. "And, it's important for women to expand their interests and be well-rounded."

Brooke and Kelli helped me pack the van we borrowed from Nicole with a cooler full of water and snacks.

"What is with you and all these ridiculous ideas now? Aren't you supposed to play Scrabble and pickleball when you retire?" Brooke said.

"Well, I do intend to play Scrabble and pickleball, amongst other things, *including* deep sea fishing," I told her.

"Why do we have to leave in the middle of the night?" Brooke continued.

"It's 6:00 a.m., and that's hardly in the middle of the night, Brooke," I spoke to her with a slight edge of annoyance but also amusement.

Kelli ushered Madison into the van. "I don't mind going, Grandma, but why does it have to be on a full moon?"

Brooke shared a smile with Kelli. "She's going to have us howl at the moon when we are on the boat. She wants us to become one with the ocean."

"Fish are more active during a full moon, and we will be more apt to catch some." I turned to make sure my granddaughters were all buckled in. I second-guessed myself about bringing Madison. She was so enthusiastic about being included with her older cousins that whatever we were doing didn't matter to her.

Madison's eyes were drooping from getting up early. "Grandma, will there be mud again?"

I tucked her seat belt tightly around her. "No, darling, we'll be out in the ocean."

Was I wrong to think this would be a wonderful bonding experience with three of my granddaughters?

"Promise we don't have to listen to 60s music on the ride," Brooke said while putting her earbuds in.

I allowed all three girls to doze off during the hour-long drive to the Chesapeake Bay while I did, in fact, listen to my 60s music.

"Wow, THAT'S A BIG BOAT," Madison said as we stood before Captain Ron's Charter.

"Good morning, ladies," Captain Ron said as he and the staff helped us aboard the boat along with 65 other hopeful anglers.

The captain and the staff members were delighted to see Madison, who appeared to be the youngest participant.

Madison was pleased with the attention and began to ask numerous questions.

"Do you have a bathroom?"

"Do I have to touch the worms?"

"How deep is the ocean?"

"My dad said I might throw up. Do you think I will?"

The captain was a heavily tanned, weathered, amazingly sexy man. "She's just excited," I told him with a tilt of my head. "Is the weather going to be okay? It looks a little cloudy."

"It will be just fine, ma'am."

Ma'am? What the hell. No one likes to be called ma'am.

Brooke tilted her head and looked at me. "Really, GMOM, are you seriously flirting with the captain who looks like he's 90? He really shouldn't be driving a boat at his age."

I turned closer to Brooke so Kelli and Madison couldn't hear me. "I wasn't flirting, and he's not 90, and cut the shit, Brooke." I can't imagine ever talking to my other grandchildren the way I talk to her. Being my first grandchild, Brooke and I have always had a special bond and ease with each other.

Within minutes, both Brooke and Kelli were engaged in a lively conversation with two boys, and suddenly, the trip became much more enjoyable for them.

The two teenage boys, Tyler and Cole, introduced themselves to me with toothy smiles and wide eyes.

I handed Brooke and Kelli their hoodies, telling them to cover their shoulders to avoid sunburn. Truthfully, I wanted them to cover their over-exposed chests, barely covered by their bikini tops.

Cole reached over and took hold of Brooke's fishing pole. "I can help you throw out your line," he told her.

"I *bet* you could help me with that," I heard Brooke reply sarcastically, and I realized that my granddaughter had inherited this trait of mine and, at times, my inappropriate wit. It either came to her naturally, or I was a terrible influence. Either way, it pleased me.

"Madison, I want you to set up between the girls and those boys and ask them if they could help you with your pole," I said.

I watched Madison move between the two groups as I positioned myself next to Kelli. Brooke looked over at me, and I gave her a quick wink before I turned back to stare as the horizon grew further in the distance.

Brooke, Kelli, and their young male counterparts giggled over crossed pole lines and dropped reels. I heard one of the boys claim he was "an expert angler." Fortunately, Brooke did not reply sarcastically.

Tyler caught a fluke fish, too small to keep. We heard laughter and applause as others caught sizable and keepable fish. Our little group wasn't having any luck. Two of the mates threw out plenty of chub into the water near Madison's pole to entice the fish, but nothing was biting.

An hour into our excursion, the waters became choppy and uncomfortable. The sky ahead had darkened quickly, and the seas became increasingly rough. One of the mates came around offering Dramamine for seasickness. Brooke and Kelli gladly accepted the pills as their nausea became evident. I gave Madison half a pill but declined the Dramamine for myself, claiming I don't get seasick.

"If you feel seasick, sit facing forward and look at the horizon," the captain told everyone. "Don't go below, and be sure to take slow breaths."

His words gave little comfort as vomiting set in quickly with many passengers. Cole, the other young man captivated by my granddaughters, tried to make it to the side of the boat and ended up throwing up on the deck floor, narrowly missing Brooke's feet.

A few mates were handing out buckets, and others were hosing the floor. The aroma and gagging of others hit me like a bullet as I ran toward an unoccupied bucket. I arrived just in time to release my breakfast and much of last night's dinner.

"Grandma's puking!" I heard Madison say with more excitement than concern.

As Madison walked towards me, I waved her away and told her to stay with Brooke and Kelli. And as the captain had ordered, I stared at the horizon until the entire content of my stomach was removed.

"Sorry folks," the captain's voice came on the loudspeaker, "We have to head back now. The water is too choppy to continue."

As we disembarked the vessel, the staff gave free vouchers for a return trip. "Sorry about the weather, but I hope you enjoyed the first part of the trip, ma'am," the captain said, looking at me directly.

"It was fine, sir."

AS WE SETTLED IN FOR THE DRIVE HOME, I checked my phone before we headed out and anxiously replied to a message from Niko.

Would you like to get together for coffee tomorrow?

Yes, that sounds nice.

Or how about a casual lunch?

Lunch sounds great, and casual sounds even better. I have to stop at the shop tomorrow.

Hope you are having a nice day.

Yes, I'm just getting ready to leave the Bay. I took my three grand-daughters deep sea fishing.

Wow, you really are different.

By different, I take it you mean intriguing.

That's precisely what I meant.

Well, I will do my best to intrigue you.

So, apparently, I have no trouble being charming when I'm not speaking to Niko. Perhaps our relationship can be strictly via text.

Was it fun?

It was a blast ... for my stomach.

I wondered if the girls could see the smile planted on my face as we headed home. The deep-sea adventure was successful despite the choppy waves and my expulsion. I heard the girls talking animatedly while we drove home. "That was so cool," Kelli said. "When can we go back again?"

"You want to do it again?" I asked in amazement.

"Yes, it was so much fun," Brooke added.

"And we got to see Grandma throw up," Madison said. "I can't wait to tell everyone at school all about it."

So, it wasn't so bad, and now I have an afternoon to look forward to with Niko.

I FOUND MYSELF, once again, with another what-to-wear co-nundrum. I wanted to call Ellen for her opinion, but I hadn't mentioned Niko's name to her before. Ellen would be support-ive but would also give me her opinion and proclaim it was too soon. It was, but I could keep this under control. Besides, wasn't I possibly on the way to being a single woman?

Niko said it would be a casual lunch. Are jeans too casual? Should I show some cleavage? I wanted to send the proper sig-nal, whatever that might be. I held up two options until I finally settled on my go-to black leggings and a flowy white blouse. Simple, understated, no cleavage, nothing suggestive or obvi-ous. Should I wear the three-inch boots that I know elongate my already sufficiently lengthened legs? Probably not. Niko was only about two inches taller than me, but that doesn't mean I have to settle for flats. Oh, the pressure. I finally decided on my two-inch sandals.

CHAPTER EIGHTEEN

MONDAY, MONDAY. The Mamas & The Papas song came to mind as I woke with anticipation of lunch with Niko.

I arrived early and waited outside Sweet Repeats for 10 minutes before Niko's expected noon arrival. I hesitated about having him come into the shop to pick me up amongst questioning eyes. I recognized his black jaguar as it turned onto our street. My hands began to sweat, and I quickly wiped them on my leggings. Will he shake my hand hello or lean in for a more affectionate kiss? No, definitely not a kiss on the cheek. Way too soon.

As it turned out, Niko pulled up to the curb, jumped out to open my door, and gently held my arm as I climbed into the passenger seat.

"Wow, you really were deep-sea fishing. Your face is full of color. You look great," Niko said. "You play in the mud and catch fish. It's a pretty cool combination. No knitting and bingo for you?"

Why does everyone continually give me options for how to spend my time? I wondered if Niko played pickleball.

I raised my eyebrows ever so slightly and stared straight ahead as we drove to the restaurant. I was hoping I wouldn't become awkward again. "Now that I'm no longer working full-time, I'm trying to be more adventurous." *Whoa, that sounds a bit suggestive. I wonder if I could just sit silently and stare at Niko.*

Looking over at him, I could see his eyes open wide. "So, did you catch anything?"

Okay, back to being serious. "We had a few mishaps, but it was a wonderful time." I chose not to divulge my uncontrollable vomiting on the boat.

"Thank you for agreeing to lunch. To be honest, I was nervous about asking you. I didn't want to seem presumptuous, but I enjoy your company. I'd like to get to know you better." Niko spoke with genuineness.

"Thank you for inviting me," I said, unable to think of anything witty or charming.

Thirty minutes later, we arrived at Maggiano's Italian Restaurant.

Niko placed his hand on the small of my back as we entered the restaurant. I could feel his touch all the way to my cheeks.

Maggiano's was a genuine Italian restaurant, evident with the exposed brick oven and the "ciao signor e signora" from the hostess who greeted us.

We had a few uncomfortable minutes before the waiter came to take our order. I fidgeted nervously on the upholstered seat, my black leggings causing me to slide forward on the plastic. Niko leaned back in his chair as I stared at the form of his chest through his short-sleeved, Oxford, button-down shirt. I hadn't noticed the depth of his collarbone before. I had the urge to run my fingers from one side to the other.

It was also the first time I realized that Niko had a tattoo. I could only see a part of it under the hem of his shirt sleeve. I wanted to ask him about the design, but it somehow seemed inappropriate.

But then, it only took me a few minutes before I decided it wasn't inappropriate after all. "What is the tattoo on your arm?"

Niko lifted his shirt sleeve, exposing most of the tattoo. "It's Achilles, the Greek Warrior. Achilles was the greatest warrior in ancient Greek mythology. He stands as a symbol of courage, strength, and patience."

Then Niko pulled his sleeve up further exposing his forearm and showing Achilles' helmet touching the top of his shoulder. I had a near-irresistible urge to kiss Achilles from his feet to his helmet. But, this time, I would control my inappropriate impulses.

"Buon appetito," the waiter said as he set down our Pizza Margherita and a bottle of their house wine.

"Grazie mille," Niko said to the waiter.

"You speak Italian?" I asked him.

"Solo un po'"

Hmmm, I would like him to *Solo* on my body. *Concentrate*, I told myself. *Get a grip.*

Between bites, I found myself staring into Niko's dark, inviting eyes that grew even darker as he spoke.

"You're a cheap date," Niko said with an adorable grin while putting a third slice of pizza in his mouth.

I wasn't sure what to say about being a cheap date, so I let out a sound that was a mixture of a giggle and a snort. "This place is great. I've never been here before."

Niko set his pizza onto his plate. "I thought casual would be best for our first, um, date."

He said "date" like it was a question mark.

Whew, I'm not the only one acting like a pubescent teenager.

I did my best to act nonchalant like I had lunch with men I hardly knew all the time. "So, are you retired?"

"Yes, I retired five years ago when I turned sixty-five. I was a principal at Prince Frederck High School for thirty-five years. Sometimes, I wish I hadn't retired yet, but I keep busy. I try to help Becky out with the grandkids and spend time with Dad. I also do a little day-trading and golfing."

Do you need a nine-iron? I have an extra one hiding in my garage.

I could feel my shoulders' tension lessen. "That's wonderful. Did you find being a principal to be more challenging or rewarding?"

"A little of both. I miss it, though."

"Tell me about Becky and your grandchildren."

With a huge sigh, Niko's eyes closed briefly. He looked at me before speaking. "Becky has been through a great deal. As you already know, she lost her mother two years ago, and then shortly after, she and her husband divorced. She is raising Noah, 9, and Aubrey, 11, alone. The café is getting busier, but it's still new. It was difficult for her and the kids during the divorce. I never cared for Adam, her husband."

I took a sip of wine and put down my slice of pizza. "I'm so sorry to hear that Becky has had a difficult time. Hopefully, life will be easier for her soon. She's lucky to have your support, and obviously, her grandfather adores her, too." I was on a roll.

I had put three sentences together at once. So, I decided to continue. "When did you meet your wife?" I asked.

"We met in college. Victoria was an affable, strong-minded, beautiful woman. She could carry on long conversations with anyone. She was empathetic and worked as a hospice nurse, a perfect occupation for someone with her kind heart. She brought comfort to everyone who had the honor of knowing her."

His face softened when he talked about Victoria with love that came from deep within his heart.

"She sounds lovely. I'm so sorry you lost her."

Niko's discomfort was noticeable as he shifted in his seat. "It was difficult for me and nearly crushed Becky. Dad, Becky, and I became very close and devoted to each other. Victoria had COVID in the earliest stage of the pandemic and passed away within a month."

I was overwhelmed by his evident devotion and love for his wife. It made me appreciate him even more. Then I realized he was going to ask me about my family. Could I just say I was a widow and not get into the last twenty-five years of my life?

Niko seemed to want to change the subject as he asked me, "Are you close to your children and their spouses?"

I took a deep breath before I gave him a brief description of my family. "I was delighted when my daughter Nicole and Eric got together. They are kind to each other and have created a beautiful family. Nicole and Eric have always set aside time for just the two of them. I admire their honest communication and commitment to each other. Their daughters, Brooke and Kelli, are uniquely talented and quite beautiful. Kelli has her mother's gentle ways, and Brooke gets her feistiness from me. I get along very well with Emily, Nathan's wife. She is very strong-minded, and I have learned to accept and embrace her boldness." *Whoa, I'm really getting the hang of this.* I lifted my shoulders in a large shrug before I continued. "Things haven't been quite as easy with Josh's wife, Lisa. We still struggle to find a comfortable place for our undefined relationship. She is refined and subdued, and I guess the correct word to describe her is *proper*."

Niko moved his hand almost as if he would reach over and touch mine. "And you're not proper?" His chuckle was hardly stifled.

I twisted my lips and contorted my face. I'm sure that was a rather unattractive look. As I gathered myself, I cleared my throat. "I'm not *improper*, but I am not as stringent as Lisa would probably prefer." I finished the last of my wine, and as soon as I put it down, Niko poured another glass.

Between bites and light banter, I imagined touching the barely visible chest hairs peering through Niko's shirt. I needed to focus on something else to keep my mind off his body parts. "Tell me about your father. He is so charming."

"He was a fabulous dad, active at school and with the community. When my sister died, our family dynamic was crushed. My mother shut down and never emerged from the grief that took over her like an untreatable disease."

I could tell it wasn't easy for Niko to talk about his mother.

Niko took a heavy swallow of his wine before continuing. "She turned away from both my father and me. She could no longer express her love for either of us and removed herself from our lives. We became a very dysfunctional family."

I wanted to know everything about Niko: his body, mind, past, future plans, and very essence. He seemed to genuinely want to know about me and my back story as well.

Niko sat upright in his chair and leaned toward me with folded arms. "Shall we learn more about each other?"

I was resuming my lack of witty repertoire. "Uh, okay, I suppose."

"Okay, you start. As me five questions."

I did a little movement of my shoulders and rubbed my hands together. I started with my questions to him:

Religious or spiritual?

Spiritual.

What superpower would you like to have?

Breathe underwater.

Interestingly, most people choose flying.

Do you have a favorite book?

Moby Dick. I've read it so many times the book has become frayed.

Ahab's mad obsession with killing the whale shows the obsessions we all have. It shows how many people don't see the price they pay for their desire or others that they hurt in their pursuit. Ahab's obsession ultimately led to his destruction and only caused him suffering.

I made a mental note to myself to re-read Moby Dick.

What song do you like to play loudly?

Born to be Wild.

Okay, Steppenwolf, good choice.

If you could spend an evening with anyone, alive or deceased, who would that be?

I would want to be right here where I am.

Be still my heart; I'm sinking fast. I was aware that a blush immediately arose on my sunburned cheeks.

Niko smiled and looked at me. "How did I do?"

"You did quite well."

I ignored the curve of his mouth as he took the last bite of his pizza.

Niko looked at me with an adorable, sheepish grin. "Okay, it's my turn. Get ready." He placed his hands on the table and leaned in toward me. His proximity made it hard to concentrate on the words coming out of his mouth.

I took a deep breath and prepared myself for his questions:

What is your favorite music?

Ragtime piano. His eyes lifted with curiosity.

Favorite movie?

Casablanca

Favorite flower?

Yellow roses

Favorite song?

Fly Me To The Moon.

Do you have any hidden talents?

I could probably beat Michael Jordan in a free-throw contest.

I didn't say that to be cute. It's true. My claim to fame is shooting baskets from the foul line.

Niko clapped his hands. "Basketball player, huh?"

"Nope, just free throws."

"I have one more question," Niko said. "This will help me in the future when choosing another restaurant for us. What is your favorite food?"

"I can't imagine anything better than this pizza," I told him.

Oh my, did that come across as weird?

He sat back smiling, stretching his shoulders, Achilles now showing part of his legs.

Favorite sexual position?

No, I didn't ask him that, but my mind definitely wandered in that direction.

I saw the animated waiter coming towards us with the check. I tried telepathically to have the man turn around but to no avail. Breaking eye contact with Niko was challenging when the waiter inquired about our meal. As Niko took the check and thanked the waiter, I watched his solid and uncalloused hands. I could feel my smile widen and my imagination deepen.

Niko's chin rested on his right hand as if he was posing for a dating profile. "This has been such an amazing afternoon. I have a sudden urge to install a basketball hoop in my driveway and listen to ragtime piano. I will keep a list of more things to ask you next time."

When we left the restaurant, Niko put his right hand on my shoulder and gave me a mesmerizing look. "Remind me to thank my father."

I moved my body ever so slightly and leaned into him.

Both of Niko's hands cupped my face while looking into my eyes. With that, he reached my parted lips. His lips were smooth and warm, his scent delicious. The kiss was so sweet, and the heat so immediate. I think I floated to the car.

Later that evening, as I lay beside my husband, I thought of the incredible hours I had spent with Niko. *I am now no better than Jed. He must lie in bed with thoughts of Renee while he is next to me.*

As I rolled away from Jed, I noticed my laptop on my nightstand. I realized I should be able to find more information about Niko through some searching, and I wouldn't be doing anything illegal. I waited until I heard the familiar sound of Jed's mouth breathing, which I was now beginning to detest.

Nikolai Cirillo. Several articles and photographs popped up regarding his thirty-five years as principal at Prince Frederick High School:

Mr. Cirillo was accompanied by his wife, Victoria, daughter, Becky, his father, Alexander, and his two young grandchildren at his retirement ceremony.

There were several pages and links to comments about his principalship:

Mr. Cirillo has gone above and beyond to help our school bring about positive changes.

He seems to know the name of every student.

He always takes the time to help with any issues.

Mr. Cirillo is a principal with amazing principles.

His dedication and commitment to the students and teachers are above reproach.

There were numerous photos of Niko in a suit and tie at the high school. I've always felt that not all men look good in formal attire, but that was not true with Niko. His suit jackets emphasized his well-formed shoulders, and I'm sure his dazzling smile and sex appeal did not go unnoticed by the female staff and students. There were a couple of comments about "hot" Mr. Cirillo. There were also photos of him wearing school sweatshirts and throwing a ball with the players at sporting events.

Niko was obviously well-regarded in education and through his community involvement. His comments during interviews were never braggadocious, only gracious gratitude.

The photo of him at his retirement ceremony showed his lovely wife dressed conservatively in an Ann Taylor, blue, belted dress, perfectly suited for her small stature. She looked elated and sophisticated, holding hands with her husband with pride. Victoria was a beautiful woman who seemed genuinely kind.

After further scrolling, I found Niko's Facebook page. I could feel his aura as I looked through his page. There were numerous photos of Alex, Becky, and his grandchildren. There were photos of Victoria showing a life full of fun, hope, love, and golden memories. They were a family bonded together by genuine affection, with mutual admiration evident. There were photos of their last anniversary and further signs of passion, compassion, and respect. It was a slide show of his enviable marriage.

CHAPTER NINETEEN

THERE ARE CERTAIN PHRASES THAT IRRITATE ME:

Half a dozen of one.

It is what it is.

I'm allowed to feel whatever I want to feel.

I'm just being honest.

At the end of the day.

With all due respect.

Just sayin'.

Yolo.

Ellen used almost every one of these annoying phrases on our way to the Starbucks in town with several quiet, separate rooms.

"You've got to have faith that this is right," Ellen said, trying to calm my nerves.

"Right? I don't see how invading another person's privacy is right. I'm not sure I want to go through with this. I don't feel it's fair to Jed. It affirms his belief that I don't trust him. I was awake most of the night, debating whether I had the right to break into Jed's private conversations. Doesn't everyone deserve privacy?"

"You've got to know one way or another so you can move on."

"Well, I might not have to move. I may be able to stay where I am."

Ellen narrowed her eyes in skepticism. "I'm just saying ...."

Our behavior felt wildly inappropriate, not to mention illegal. I was also mildly amused by the internal conflicting thrill this was stirring. I went back and forth in my mind on whether to continue.

Ellen and I ordered lattes and croissants. We found a private room and hoped no one else would come and use the remaining four chairs.

JUDY SMITH

We sat huddled next to each other as I tapped my laptop.

I took a few deep breaths, trying to quell the mounting anxiety. "This could end very badly. Won't Jed know that someone accessed his account?"

Ellen held a devious glare. "If there is anything accusatory, and I'm sure there will be, would he have the guts to accuse you? Now, it's time to be detectives."

"Before we resort to hacking, I want to tell you about Niko," I said.

"Is that your octogenarian friend?"

"Actually, Alex is 93, and Niko is his son," I explained. "He's gentle and warm and intelligent. He's passionate about life, and he listens."

Ellen folded her arms across her chest and looked at me. "Sounds like he has made quite an impact on you."

"Ellen, he really has, and I'm anxious to see him again."

"Okay, I'm happy for you, but open your laptop and see if we can crack this case. Let's deal with one man at a time."

I took my frustration out on the croissant, now lying in pieces on my napkin.

Then I opened the laptop and set it up using Starbucks' WIFI password. Within minutes, I'd opened the Facebook app to log in. I looked at Ellen before proceeding, our eyes wide as we scanned the room for listening voices.

I went onto the Facebook login page, took a deep breath signed in as Jed, and tried *chloerachel515* as the password. Exhaling with disbelief, I was in his account. I nervously played with the plastic lid on my latte cup, deciding if I wanted to continue.

Ellen seemed giddy. She squinted and urged me to continue. "Go to the top right and click on messenger."

I gave Ellen a stern look and put my hand on hers, bracing myself. I hesitated and was ready to close the laptop when Ellen reached over and opened Messenger.

Before reading any of the messages, I scrolled through, scouring the list of women's names: Renee, Liz, Kathleen, Billie, Susan, and so on.

The first message was to Renee. It was dated on the night we followed Jed to the restaurant. I swallowed hard repeatedly as I read his words.

JED: *It was wonderful to see you tonight.*

RENEE: *You looked so sexy. You look great in yellow.*

JED: *I will have to buy some yellow underwear.*

RENEE: *Lol. I'm sorry I had to work. I was hoping to get off earlier.*

JED: *No problem. Just seeing you made my day. I'll see you tomorrow afternoon.*

RENEE: *Goodnight, sexy.*

JED: *Goodnight, babe.*

So, Renee also works at the Italian restaurant where we had followed Jed. That explains him going in and coming out alone. My head was spinning as I continued to read more messages, including some to Jed's ex-wife Kathleen. Apparently, they had been getting together as sex buddies.

Thank you for the extra special birthday gift, LOL, was Jed's message to Kathleen. Kathleen responded with *Happy Birthday, Baby.*

Jed had obviously enjoyed more than her potato salad and balled melons during our marriage.

And to Liz: *I will be at your place when you get home. I'll have linguini and clams waiting for you.*

He apparently made the same dish for Billie and Susan, too.

From Barbara: *Thank you for the sailing day. The sea air and champagne did wonders for me. Hope to see you soon.*

I could hear repeated "Oh, my God" gasps coming from Ellen until I finally closed the top of my laptop. There was a dull pain in my stomach and bile threatening to rise in my throat. My mind went dull. My throat was constricting, and my chest tightened as I clenched my eyes to forbid tears. It felt like an out-of-body experience. I was floating in the air, looking down at Ellen, reading the despicable words on my laptop. I was the spectator, not the villain in the story.

I surmised that Jed used Messenger instead of texting to avoid my being able to access his phone.

I put my head on the table, closed my eyes, and sobbed.

An employee came over to clear the table, and Ellen shook her head and whispered, "Can we just sit here for a while?"

"Of course, we aren't busy," she said. "Stay as long as you want."

After I composed myself, I logged onto Gmail and put in Jed's email address and the same password. Voila, it worked again.

There were emails showing he had joined "Senior Singles" and "Our Time." There were also promotions for Penile Enhancement. I didn't bother reading any further. I packed the laptop into my bag and told Ellen I was ready to leave. I gripped her arm for support as we walked out with my head bowed, hiding my liquid-filled eyes.

Ellen held my hand and tried to steady me. "I'm so sorry, Andi. At least, now you know," she said with tears in her eyes as well. "I can't believe Jed did this to you. I was angry at him before I knew he was involved with so many women, but now I want to destroy him. Will he stop his affairs when he's 80 and finally grow up?"

Ellen's voice trailed off, and I knew she had more to say, but I fell silent and nodded wordlessly. I knew she was right.

"Ellen, I've got to get out of here." I held her hand tightly, barely able to put one foot in front of the other. When we reached her car, I stopped and didn't open the passenger door to get in. "I want to walk home. Alone."

As Ellen started with her objections, she stopped herself and embraced me. I held her close for several minutes, as if she were an anchor, and I needed her to keep me steady. All these years, I should have known. This really shouldn't have been a shock. But it was, and I felt it to my core.

Ellen's voice cracked with deep sympathy. "Andi, I wanted you to know for sure, but I didn't know it would be this bad."

"I will be okay, I promise." I hugged her again and told her softly, "*It is what it is.*"

I walked in the brisk air filled with light rain for nearly an hour. I didn't stroll. I walked fervently, anxious to reach my destination. But there was no finish line or cheering crowds awaiting me. My throat was aching with the taste of rain and the saltiness of my tears.

I reached for my front door knob and steadied myself with my other hand on the frame. Jed opened the door at the same time as I was pushing it in, and I nearly fell on my face. Jed grabbed me under my shoulder, preventing my fall. "You're shaking. What happened?"

Unable to look him in the eye, I wiped non-existent raindrops from my jacket. "I wanted to walk home from the restaurant. I didn't realize it was supposed to rain."

All I wanted was to take a sleeping pill and tuck myself into my 1,000-count Egyptian sheets. I could hear Bob Dylan's "Make You Feel My Love," one of my favorite songs, playing in the background and saw a bouquet of fresh flowers on the dining room table. Jed's ironic timing at seduction nauseated me.

Jed stepped closer to me than I was comfortable. "I miss you, baby."

I wasn't prepared for the inevitable confrontation just yet. "Jed, I've had an exhausting day. I'm going to bed."

Jed looked confused and put his hands in his pockets.

My hands were curled into tight fists. "I'm just drained, Jed," I said.

I walked into the bedroom, directly into Jed's closet, and took out his yellow sweater. Not every man can pull off wearing yellow like Jed. I held it close for a few minutes, letting my tears fall onto it, rubbing my runny nose on it, crumbling it up, and putting it under the bed. Tomorrow, I would put it with the golf club and the bottle of little blue pills.

CHAPTER TWENTY

"ARE YOU OKAY?" Ellen's voice was hesitant when she called early the following morning.

I pulled the comforter away from my body with the intention of getting up, but then I changed my mind and pulled it even tighter to my chin.

It amazed me that I could sleep soundly for seven straight hours next to Jed, without the assistance of alcohol or sleep aids, after the many confirmations of his betrayals. He had left earlier to help his sister, Eve, install a new dishwasher. I lingered in bed, numb and frozen with my new reality. The world was spinning around me, and I was trying to figure out where to stop.

"I'm not as angry as I thought," I told Ellen.

"Are you kidding me? Please don't tell me you are staying with him. What did he say when you got home?"

The heat from the comforter was radiating through me. I tossed it aside and sat on the edge of the bed as I talked to Ellen. "He must have been preparing for a romantic evening with flowers and music. He accepted that I was tired."

"I can't believe you didn't attack him and kick him out," Ellen said.

"I will throw him out, without a doubt. I'm struggling to make peace with it. Listen, I love you, and you are the best friend anyone could ever have, but I need a few days to deal with this. Don't worry about me. I will call you soon."

"I'm here for you, day or night. Love you."

I flung myself back into bed, watching the ceiling fan whirl above me as I contemplated my next step. The rhythmic beating spinning from the fan seemed furious and felt like it would spin out of control at any moment, mirroring my emotions. Other than Ellen, I didn't want anyone to know about Jed's other indiscretions. I certainly did not want to add any fuel to Nathan's anger about what Jed had posted for all the world to see. I did not need a confrontation between them. Nathan and Nicole would be pleased enough to know Jed was out of the house.

Jed had believed he was invincible and irresistible. He was discreet, had kept up appearances, and remained attentive to me. He was so egotistical that he thought his charisma would carry him through his indiscretions, but then he got sloppy. The images of the messages on Facebook continued to bring forth the painful realization of his infidelities. But, in a way, I had needed this incontrovertible written proof. Yet it also became the death of my dreams, the death of what I thought I knew, the death of a love I thought I had. I had held such high expectations for this next chapter of our lives. I was irritated with my naivety and the farce of what I thought had been a happy marriage.

As the fog was beginning to lift, one thing was clear. I had to put aside my anger and hurt. I had people in my life who needed me. I reminded myself of the wise words from Alex:

Treasure and be grateful for what you have today. Life changes quickly.

WHEN I FELT STURDY ENOUGH, I showered and took excessive time to prepare. Once again, I wanted to look good when I confronted Jed. Most importantly, I wanted to feel and portray strength. I put on my favorite pair of jeans, an off-the-shoulder white sweater, and some of Lyla's jewelry.

Standing tall, I held my head high, allowing the adrenaline to pump through my blood. A rush of emotions assaulted me as I went from one thought to another. I walked in a circle, not knowing what to do first.

I decided to take and hide one last item of Jed's. Opening his closet door, I grabbed the white button-down shirt that I found irresistible. Then I spied the golf rain jacket that Nicole had given him for Christmas last year. I decided to take both items along with his yellow sweater hidden under the bed. I contemplated packing and throwing all his belongings into the garage, but I finally decided he wasn't worth expelling the effort.

I had just one more thing to do. I entered my quiet kitchen and opened the pantry where, for some unknown reason, I had saved and stored the cracked vase. I grabbed the vase, walked back out to the garage, threw it into Jed's golf bag, and smashed it with one of his golf clubs until it finally broke into pieces.

I tucked the shirt, sweater, and rain jacket into my secret hiding place.

With each action, I felt stronger but couldn't control my erratic breathing. I went to the front door, hoping to suck air into my lungs. There was a briskness in the fall air and a deep ink-filled sky. I swallowed heavily with gratitude instead of anger for finally knowing the truth.

Feeling the redemption, I walked back into the kitchen with legs that felt like lead and gently closed the door. I opened the antique white cabinet door above the refrigerator and retrieved a bottle of Don Perignon. The champagne was a birthday present from Jed's daughter, Rachel, to both of us.

I took out a Waterford fluted glass and sat at the kitchen table.

Then, I texted Jed. *When will you be home?*

He responded immediately. *I should be home within the hour.*

I was jolted into reality by the loud pop as I opened the champagne. I poured a full glass, took a sip, and prepared myself. Rather than rehearse what I would say, I took deep breaths, raising my shoulders higher each time in confirmation. My breath became stuck between inhales, and my pulse raced rapidly. I was on sensory overload: cold, flashes of warmth, anger, and confidence. I closed my eyes and filtered out the external noises: the ice maker, the heater, and Coco Chanel's meows. I exhaled a low "ommm" and waited.

I took one last cleansing breath when I heard the garage door open.

As Jed entered the kitchen with his long-legged stride, he cheerfully sang, "Pretty Woman." He stopped when he saw the opened bottle of champagne.

Jed's voice sounded hopeful. "Hey babe, what are we celebrating?"

"The truth."

"The truth about what?"

Jed immediately turned around and poured himself a drink.

I looked at Jed and simply said. "Sit down, please."

"Honey, are you feeling okay? Are the kids okay?"

"Everyone is fine. Including me, because now I know."

Jed squirmed in his seat, and I suspected he realized he was caught doing something else he shouldn't have done. "What does that mean?"

"Renee, Kathleen, Liz, Billie, Susan, and so many more." I held my breath as I waited to see how he would respond.

"What are you talking about?"

I took a few minutes, watching Jed's handsome face contort as he conjured up lies to dispel the truth. Some primordial part of me took over, my calm words quelling my despair. I forced myself to look directly into his eyes and not be fooled by his charm. As confident as I was that I wanted him to leave, there remained that little bit of uncertainty. Was there something wrong with me that made him want so many other women? I remained steadfast in what I knew I had to do.

Jed's posture stiffened as he looked down at his shoes, shifting his weight from side to side as if contemplating his next move. "Those women are acquaintances, that's all."

His lie radiated toward me, and the rattled expression on his face increased.

I wasn't about to reduce the conversation to a screaming match. Just state the facts, I reminded myself. Stay calm and focused.

But within seconds, my temper resurfaced. "You can't possibly think that I believe your bullshit. Not anymore. And Jed, Kathleen? Have you been sleeping with her since your divorce? Were you fucking her when we were all together for birthdays and graduations?" I wondered if this was retribution for my affair with Jed when they were married. No, it wasn't the same. Jed told me they were separated but living in the same house because of the children. Of course, none of that was true. Maybe I deserved this. "There's nothing you can say, Jed. It's over."

"Andi." Jed said it with such fervor it startled me into reality. "You have to believe me. I love you. I don't know what you heard or how, but I love you. Yes, I flirt, and maybe I'm overly friendly, but that's how I am, and you know that."

Jed turned his back on me as he walked toward the window, deliberately avoiding eye contact.

"Stop minimalizing what you did." I waited for his eyes to lock on mine before I continued. "I don't want this to get ugly. Nothing will change my mind. I want and need you to leave. Today." I was swinging to the bright side of the canyon with all my might. I kept my voice firm and unwavering. "Your idiotic excuses to try and validate your affairs are laughable."

Jed could read the severity on my face and downed his drink while turning away from me. Guilt was flooded all over him, from head to toe.

"You know, Andi, I hate that you call all the shots. You tell me something, and I immediately obey. The way you have been acting these past few weeks confuses the hell out of me. And you were always so busy, and even now, you don't have time for me. Maybe I flirted with other women because I felt low on the Andi list of things to do."

I poured myself another bubbly glass. "I will not sit here and listen while you try to justify sleeping with other women. Grab some of your things and leave now." Hearing the distinct edge to my voice, Jed looked at me, empty drink in his hand, and shook his head slowly while he released a deep breath.

Jed continued to take long breaths. "This is my house, too. You don't have the right to kick me out of *our* home."

"We will work out the unpleasant details later. I will contact a lawyer tomorrow." I put my hand up to stop him from launching into a narcissistic monologue.

I wanted to leave while Jed packed, but after two glasses of champagne and with a heart full of despair, I knew it was best to stay put.

Jed's expression sobered. "Once again, it's whatever you want, isn't it?" His lips pressed together so tightly they appeared glued shut. "Can't you let me stay here until I have a chance to find a place? Can't you have some compassion?"

"No, Jed, you've been doing whatever you wanted through-out our entire marriage. Nothing you say can convince me to change my mind. I'm disgusted by your behavior. It's pathetic that I didn't realize it sooner. I've put up with your *flirtations* for too long."

A tear slipped from the corner of Jed's eye, followed by an-other. "I love you, Andi. Can you honestly tell me you don't love me anymore?"

I paced from room to room until I finally planted my feet in front of Jed. "I love you. I always have. I always will. But I've devoted too many years of my life to you. Years that were filled with golden memories that I will always cherish. But years that were enveloped in disloyalty and deception. If I stay with you, I will disappear. I will become lost in your needs and your lies. We were never right for each other. You need someone willing to devote their every existence to your needs. I can't live in the same house with you for one more day." I took a few steps back from Jed when I saw the increased rage in his eyes.

Jed came closer to my face with a surprisingly direct look. "You will regret this," he said.

I looked at Jed deeply, so deeply I was afraid I might get sucked into the safety of a life full of lies, but it was a life I knew how to exist in.

With suddenly strong legs and conviction, I stood up and walked upstairs to the loft, leaving him to gather some things.

THE NEXT MORNING, I welcomed the sun streaming into the window. I lay in bed, feeling the warmth radiate through me. I texted my family and Ellen.

Jed has moved out of the house. I'm fine, honestly.

When strength returned, I stood up and glanced around the bedroom I had been sharing with Jed. There were good memories mixed in with the bad. There had been nightmares along with sweet dreams. I stripped off the bedsheets and com-forter and all the annoying decorative nautical pillows. Time to get new bedding. Time to move on.

Sweat sprang to my palms as I removed the sheets and continued into the sunroom. I turned the light on in the room that had become Jed's den. Nothing in the room was mine. There was the 55-inch TV that I had bought him when we moved to The Pond. The stream of the sun highlighted Jed's trophies and pictures. I stood back and stared at the large photo of Jed's semi-pro baseball team. He was carrying the same teasing smile and a twinkle in his eyes that he had 50 years later.

What do I do with the room now? Do I stay at The Pond, or do I start all over? It wasn't like I would change the space into an exercise gym or sewing room. Would he want his recliner and TV to move into Kathleen's house? Then it occurred to me that Jed's den could now be a playroom for the grandchildren.

Pushing away my random thoughts, I read my text messages:

Nathan: *It's about time! Do you need help getting his shit out?*

Nicole: *What happens now, Mom? Are you filing for divorce?*

Josh: *Can I do anything for you?*

Ellen: *You go, girl.*

And one unexpected text.

Niko: *Would you like to get together for a walk sometime this week? Or a hike, since you seem like the adventurous type? LOL*

Sure, I replied to Niko. *That sounds nice.*

CHAPTER TWENTY-ONE

"JEANNIE, THANK YOU SO MUCH for having us over," I said, looking at the lovely charcuterie board she had put together.

Seeing Jeannie's sparkling non-alcoholic white grape drink on her kitchen island next to the appetizers, Melanie said to her. "You can have alcohol around me. It doesn't bother me." Then she turned to me. "I told Jeannie about my past and that I am a recovered alcoholic."

"We are so proud of you, Melanie," Jeannie added cheerfully.

"To us," I said as we clinked glasses and sat around Jeannie's counter on plush navy-blue high-backed chairs.

Jeannie was dressed in one of her fruity ensembles. Deep plum palazzo pants, matching bolero jacket over a lighter plum camisole. Slim silver ballet shoes and a long silver pendant completed her outfit. I felt underdressed in my black leggings and white Bruce Springsteen tee shirt. I looked down at my feet and realized my short alligator boots would be more suited for a rodeo. Then there was Melanie in her rhinestone knee-high western boots, also looking out of place with her torn black jeans and some kind of cowl neck sweater longer on one side than the other.

Jeannie fidgeted before she spoke. "I want to talk with you about something I am struggling with."

Melanie and I looked at each other, sensing it had something to do with Sweet Repeats. "Whatever it is, Jeannie, we are here for you," I told her.

Jeannie heightened herself on the chair, "Chuck and I have seen each other a few more times since our original dinner. We become closer each time we get together, and the relationship deepens." Her expression turned thoughtful as she raised her shoulders. "He's easy to talk with, and I enjoy being around him."

"That sounds wonderful," Melanie said. "What's the issue?"

Jeannie's naturally peach cheeks turned a bright shade. "Sex."

While I held my composure, Melanie forcefully touched the counter with her wrists, rattling the glasses. "Do you mean you had sex, or are you thinking about having sex?"

I raised my index finger, motioning for the conversation to be put on hold while I reached for the bottle of wine.

"Tell us more," I said, topping off Jeannie's glass.

"We haven't slept together yet," she clarified. "I haven't been with anyone since Wayne died two years ago. I don't even know how to flirt and have forgotten how to be sensual with a man. I can sense that Chuck wants to be more intimate. I'm accustomed to how sex was with Wayne. I'm used to the touch of his hand and how his lips felt on mine. How do I replace that with someone else without feeling unfair to Wayne? Before he passed, we hadn't made love in nearly a year. We just stopped. Wayne had prostate cancer three years before he died, and, oh God, I can't believe I'm going to say this, but he had difficulty obtaining and keeping an erection." Jeannie lifted her glass to her mouth, enjoyed a hefty helping of Cabernet, and looked at Melanie. "Are you sure you don't mind that we are drinking in front of you?"

"Of course not," Melanie said. "I will have another glass of my sparking grape cider."

Jeannie removed her jacket while fanning herself for a few minutes before she continued. The sweet breeze of her perfume filled the air. "We tried medication and even devices, and while it worked temporarily, Wayne's frustration continued until he ultimately lost the desire. I accepted it and assumed it was the end of my sex life. I never lost my desire, though. Just thinking about being intimate with Chuck makes me so nervous."

Melanie sent a smile over to Jeannie. "I'm sure it's just like riding a bike; you hop back on it and enjoy the ride," she said with hopeful levity.

Jeannie stood up, went to her kitchen sink, turned on the faucet, and dabbed her napkin in the water and onto her forehead and neck. "I've never talked to any of my friends about sex, so this is all new to me. My body has added new wrinkles, creases, and cellulite since the last time I was intimate. I can't imagine exposing myself and my body to another man."

I stood up and put my hands on my black leggings, "Are you serious? Jeannie, you are a gorgeous woman with a rocking body. Why would you be insecure about showing it off? Don't you think Wayne would want you to move on and live your life to the fullest?" I looked down at Jeannie's adorable freckled nose and blushed cheeks as she uncomfortably talked to us.

"Wouldn't you be nervous about someone new seeing your naked body?" Jeannie asked.

"Yes, to be honest, I would," I told her. "But don't you think a man would be equally nervous, especially since most men our age have erectile issues? Start off your relationship with Chuck with honest communication and tell him how you feel. It will undoubtedly help him with any concerns he may have."

As I sat back down, Melanie stood and lifted her massive hair and twisted it very adeptly into a bun. "This conversation has certainly taken an unexpected turn. Jack and I have always had a decent sex life. In the past few years, it has decreased to every few months. We both love each other very much, but sex just became less important. Talking about it makes me realize how much I have missed the lovemaking." Melanie said all this while she walked around the kitchen and tossed her arms dramatically.

None of us shied away from the privateness of the conversation. I felt comfortable as I told them about my marriage. "With my first husband, Daniel, lovemaking felt programmed with synchronized touching and movements. There was mutual caring and love, but we lacked pizazz in our sex life. I was too timid to talk with him. In fact, we never discussed our intimacy. Daniel seemed happy with our lovemaking, so I assumed I should be, also. On the other hand, I had a fabulous sex life with Jed."

I took a deep breath before I continued. I hadn't even told Melanie and Jeannie that Jed was no longer living in the house.

"Jed and I knew all the sweet spots for each other and never had a problem with my drive or his. But apparently, while I only needed Jed, he needed other women. *Many* other women," I said to both of them easily. "I worry that it will be difficult to live without sex now that Jed is gone. I am used to having sex whenever I want and with a man who knows his way around my body."

Melanie reached over to touch my hand. "I didn't realize Jed had moved out."

"Yes, it was my decision." I looked at Jeannie now. "I know how you feel, I really do. I have scars from two cesareans and a burst appendix, and breasts that have nursed three children for a total of five years. My middle has a middle, and my thighs seem to have track marks. So yes, I'm concerned about showing a man my imperfections. But I'm counting on him having some imperfections, too."

Melanie and Jeannie both smiled.

I took this as an encouragement to continue. "If a woman feels sexy, it gives her power. Own your power. Wear something scintillating that makes you feel sensual."

"I don't have any lingerie that would be considered sexy. My nighttime wear consists of Grannie Gowns and fully-covered pajamas," Jeannie said timidly. "I even have a pair of footed pajamas."

Melanie sat back down, hungrily investigating the forgotten charcuterie board. "I could use a pick-me-up to help Jack with his pick-me-up. Let's go shopping this week. A little present to ourselves. There is a lingerie store in Annapolis. We can make a day trip out of it."

"I'm in," said Jeannie.

"I don't have anyone to shop for, but I'm in, too!" I told them while secretly thinking about Niko. Would there come a time when Niko and I would see each other's naked bodies? Perhaps I could start doing stomach crunches now. Suddenly ravenous, we all picked at the charcuterie board and dismantled the perfect display Jeannie had created.

Jeannie took her place back on her chair again with more

composure. "While I have appreciated the sex talk, I also wanted to speak with the two of you about Sweet Repeats. We've had more success than we could have ever imagined. The Women's Shelter is incredibly grateful for our donations. But I think there is more that we can do. We've had such an abundance of donations that our storage room is now maxed out. I had to turn down donations yesterday. We should either find a larger location or accept fewer items."

"What percentage are donations vs. consignment?" I asked Melanie since this was primarily her responsibility.

"The donations have slowed down a bit, so it is probably 50/50."

"I can store some of the donations in Jed's closet," I said wryly. 'I'm serious; once he removes his belongings, we will have enough space in his closet and the garage."

"That could work," Jeannie said. "We definitely want to keep all the consignments because they help women looking to sell their clothes and other items."

Melanie grabbed her purse and retrieved a flyer. "I've looked around and asked our real estate agent about other opportunities for a larger building, and nothing has come up in town. But the agent gave me the promotional sales flyer for the Craft Barn."

"I drove by it last week. Doesn't it seem too large for our needs?" I asked.

"Are we talking about sex again?" Melanie asked wryly.

Jeannie stood up, heading to the refrigerator. "I think we need something stronger." She took out a carton of Caramel Cookie Crunch ice cream, three bowls and spoons, and a large scooper.

"Do you have any whipped cream?" Melanie asked.

Jeannie smiled, "As a matter of fact, I do."

CHAPTER TWENTY-TWO

"HOW OFTEN DO YOU AND TIM MAKE LOVE?" I asked Ellen while we were taking our monthly walk along our small boardwalk. The ritual started as a weekly event and dwindled quickly to once a month, barring excessive heat, wind, rain, snow, or cold. The elements had to be nearly perfect for us to walk outdoors.

"I think we should sit to have this conversation. You've become very bold lately. May I ask why you need to know about my sex life?"

Once we reached the gazebo, we sat down out of breath, reaching for our Yeti water bottles.

"I was talking with Melanie and Jeannie, and I was surprised with how infrequently they have sex," I said.

"Okay, this is a new topic for us."

"We talk about everything else. Why not this?"

"Well, sure, there's nothing like old women talking about sex. Tim and I have always enjoyed a good sexual relationship. I wouldn't call any of it bad, but our desires changed once we reached our mid-sixties, and it became less important. First, I developed some issues during menopause, and then Tim had erection problems, but Viagra and estrogen helped. Even though we have more time now, we don't seem to take the time for each other. Care to know anything else about the intimate private things in my life?"

"But you and Tim are together a lot."

"Usually it's because we are watching the grandkids together. Other times, even when we are alone in the house, he does his thing, and I do mine. It's easier to crawl into bed together and watch TV than to go through the process of making love."

I stood up and walked in place for a few minutes. "That sounds a bit harsh."

"It's true, though. Mostly, I feel like I don't need it anymore.

Now we have sex on our birthdays or other celebrations. Maybe a few times a year."

I continued to move back and forth while Ellen sat on the bench. "I'm astonished. Are you okay with it?"

Ellen stood up and grabbed my arms. "Stop moving around. Can you please sit down? This is uncomfortable enough without watching you shifting back and forth."

I gave in and sat on the bench again with Ellen. "Seriously, don't you want to have sex more often?"

"I hadn't thought about it until you brought it up. Now I'm horny and will certainly shock the shit out of Tim when I get home. I'm sure you and Jed had a wild sex life. Is that why you brought it up? Are you worried that you won't have it anymore?" Ellen's voice raised.

"Shhh, I think that guy on the bike heard you say you were horny."

"What did he look like?'

"Young, very young." I got up from the bench and grabbed Ellen's arm. "Can we please walk some more?"

Ellen shrugged her shoulders, and we continued on our walk. "Go on, tell me about your wild sex life with Jed."

"Not wild, but yes, a very mutual, strong sex drive. As you know, mine was exclusive. Jed's was not."

"How is the philandering son of a bitch?"

I would have preferred to enjoy neutral conversation amid our brilliant surroundings and the crispness in the air. On dreary days, my mind immediately turns to flowing thoughts and anger towards Jed. But on days like today, when there is a slight breeze from the heavenly blue skies, I prefer non-confrontational communication.

"I saw him a few times last week when he came to retrieve more of his stuff. He's bitter and can't comprehend why I don't understand his loneliness. He tries to make me responsible for his behavior. He's coming back tomorrow evening to get more of his belongings. He asked me to be home so we could talk about logistics."

"What kind of logistics?"

"I assume he wants me to help him financially. I don't even know where he is staying."

Ellen grabbed my arm and forced me to look at her. "Have you at least talked to a lawyer?"

I concentrated on a stray falling leaf before answering her.

"I haven't spoken to a lawyer yet, but I'm sure I will have to pay Jed for half of the house and give him half of our savings. It doesn't matter that I contributed the most financially. We were married, and he is entitled to half of everything."

"Do you really think you owe him monetary support?"

I let out a substantial sigh. "I just want to be fair."

"I'd rather talk about sex than about Jed. Are you ready to go? I have a sudden urge to get home to Tim."

I had walked several feet ahead of Ellen, and she reached up to pull me back towards her. "Can you slow down? When did our walks become marathon events?"

I lifted the sleeves to my Jimmy Buffet Parrot Flip Flop sweatshirt and increased the intensity of my steps.

"I'm just trying to get in shape."

"What are you talking about? You're in great shape."

I put my hands on my hips and continued to walk. "I have to get in better shape by tomorrow."

"What's going on tomorrow?"

I looped my arm through Ellen's as we walked to my car. "I'm going hiking tomorrow. With Niko."

"Hiking? Niko? I talk with you daily, and I'm just hearing about you going on a hike?"

I opened the car door and slid into the seat. My calves were already aching from walking. How was I going to make it through an actual hike?

Ellen fanned herself and finished her water bottle as she sat down in the passenger side. I started my car, and within a few minutes, Ellen complained about the heat. "Do you seriously have the damn seat warmer on? That's another thing that interfered with our sex life. Hot flashes. They are less now than during menopause, but I still get them. I can't even get too close to Tim when we are in bed together."

I turned off the seat warmer and started to pull away just as the sexy, young bicyclist was lifting his bike onto the roof of his car parked next to us. We both turned our heads and watched his flexing muscles as he effortlessly hoisted it to the rack.

I relaxed in my seat and prepared myself for the short drive home. "Do you want to hear about Niko?"

"Yes, please. That has to be more interesting than my sex life."

"He's amazing. He's so interesting, and he listens. Jed never really listened to me. I was accustomed to the majority of our conversations being centered around him. Niko is interested in what I say and how I feel."

Ellen continued to fan herself, faking a hot flash. "Just how far has this gone?"

"Not that far. It's much too soon. I'm still legally married and dealing with the fallout of everything that happened. But I want to get to know him better. He's fun to be around. He took me to lunch, and we stayed for hours. I didn't want it to end."

"I'm so happy to see the heavy weight removed from your face. You deserve to be with someone who will be honest and treasure you."

"Thanks, but now, back to sex, why don't you come to a lingerie shop with Melanie, Jeannie, and me tomorrow. It will be fun."

I dropped Ellen off at her split-level house just as Tim pulled into the driveway. "Don't tell Tim about lingerie shopping. Surprise him tomorrow night."

I drove away singing, "Let's talk about sex, baby."

WOULDN'T YOU THINK SOMEONE who has gone deep-sea fishing and mud running would have a pair of hiking shoes?

I looked at the pile of shoes on my closet floor and hoped to find something suitable for hiking. I had many boots, including brown, black, and even purple Uggs. There were red suede boots with three-inch heels along with black and brown knee-high boots and plenty of dress boots. But, alas, nothing suitable for hiking. I pulled out the same pair of tennis shoes that I wore deep-sea fishing. *These will have to do.* I hoped there wasn't any lingering vomit smell on the shoes.

I arrived at Calvert Park first and imitated the other hikers as they stretched their arms and legs. I wore stretch pants, a Girl Power tee shirt, and a Ravens sweatshirt tied around my waist. It looked cute when I put it on this morning until I saw other women wearing appropriately matched jogging outfits.

I looked at my phone, hoping I had sufficient time to go home and change. Just as I put the phone back into my pocket, Niko pulled up. I was relieved to see he was wearing jeans, a high school hoodie, *and* tennis shoes.

We greeted each other warmly and set out on our hike.

Niko took my hand as we followed a trail in the park. "Have you parachuted or bungee jumped since I last saw you?" He asked with a smile.

"No, things have been quiet lately." Oh, what a lie that was. But I couldn't very well tell him that I illegally broke into my husband's email accounts and found out he was a serial cheater. I also couldn't tell him that my friends and I have had intense conversations about sex recently. *I'll just stick with withholding some of the truth.* "How is your father?" I asked with a nice, quick change from the events in my life.

"He's doing relatively well. He likes to keep busy, which is good. His unsteadiness is getting worse, and I am concerned about him falling. I'm trying to get him to use a cane all the time, but he can be stubborn."

I nudged Niko on his side. "Is that a trait you share with him?"

Niko smiled and nudged me back. "I guess you will have to wait and see."

"Perhaps that's part of the Greek personality?" I suggested.

Niko put his arm around my shoulder. "I do have some of the Greek stereotypes. I can be loud, like to dance, play backgammon, and enjoy good food."

I reached my hand over and placed it on Niko's tattoo. "Are you a strong warrior like Achilles?"

"That's another thing you will have to wait and find out on your own. I can't divulge everything at once. However, you should know that Achilles was known to be immortal and impervious to all wounds except his heel. When Achilles was a baby, his mother dipped him by his heel into the river to make him immortal. Since she held him by his heel, that was the only part of him that became vulnerable. During the Trojan War, he was shot in the heel with an arrow and killed. Thus, the phrase 'Achille's heel.'"

Feeling a little flirtatious, I said, "I will have to make sure I am gentle with your heel." As soon as the words came out, I wanted to take them back. Flirtation was Jed's thing, not mine.

But Niko seemed very pleased and stopped walking. He pulled me close to him in a warm, quiet hug. So far, the hike was going quite well. Until.

Shortly after we resumed walking, I stopped again. "I think I stepped in dog shit. I mean, poop, I stepped in dog poop."

Niko laughed heartily, too heartily. "That's okay, you can say shit."

I tried wiping the mess off with leaves and sticks, which resulted in getting some of it on my hands.

While he continued to laugh, Niko turned me around, and we headed back to our cars. "Let's get you cleaned up," he said.

Niko had paper towels in his car, and we found a water fountain. We sat on a bench and proceeded to remove the offending waste from my shoe.

"I'm not exactly Aphrodite, am I?" I said with the dirty paper towels in my hand.

Niko's fingers tightened around mine. "I don't know about that. I think you could pull off being the Goddess of beauty and sexuality."

CHAPTER TWENTY-THREE

JEANNIE LOOKED AT MELANIE, Ellen, and me with embarrassment. "What if someone we know sees us walking into Lacy Silhouette's Lingerie?"

"They will be envious that we have a reason to walk into this store," Melanie said.

The display window of Lacy Silhouettes gave us no indication of what we found inside the store. At first, we were comfortable looking at the tasteful bras and underwear. The lingerie sets were cute and flirty in white, pink, red, and black. But the further we went into the store, we began to see the barely covering teddies, tear-away underwear, and ultra-shaping bodysuits with strategically placed cut-outs.

A young woman with heavy black-lined eyes and a short skirt approached us. "May I assist you?"

Melanie stood very confidently. "We are looking to spice up our love lives."

"You've come to the right place. Follow me, ladies." She said this without a flinch, but I guessed she heard this all day long. Why else would you go to a sexy lingerie store?

She took us to a small section of the shop with a display of beautiful peignoir sets, tasteful lacy nightgowns, and sexy but not overly skimpy undergarments. "Take your time, and let me know if you have any questions."

Melanie picked out a pink satin short gown with delicate white lace trim and held it up to Jeannie. "This is perfect for you."

Jeannie took it and held it against herself. "What do you think?"

"You will look like a sexy angel. It's perfect," I said.

Melanie chose a fiery red short gown with a matching robe that would look incredible with her emerald green eyes and expressive red hair. She also bravely selected a pair of crotchless underwear.

Ellen held up her purchases: a black lacy bra and a pair of edible panties.

I selected several pairs of underwear, much more appealing than my typical grannie panties, lacy but full-coverage bras, and two strappy, cleavage-exposing gowns.

"I'm sure you will be happy with your purchases," said an older, attractive, and sophisticated woman behind the counter. She lifted her eyebrows. "Have fun and come back again."

We thanked our kind saleswoman and giggled all the way to lunch while we tightly held our packages.

SITTING IN A LEATHER BOOTH, our shopping bags by our sides, we laughed through our seafood salads and French onion soup.

"I feel sexy just thinking about Tim's reaction," Ellen said proudly.

"But edible underwear? Have you ever tried it before?" I asked her.

"Many, many years ago. I will leave it at that."

Jeannie twisted her head around to ensure no one was listening. "It's amazing how clothes, lingerie or not, can make you feel younger and sexier," she said softly.

"I realize now that I assumed my sexuality would fade as I aged," Ellen said. "I also assumed that proper old ladies don't openly talk about sex."

Melanie exited the booth and did a catwalk before us with her hands on her hips. "They will never say, *What a sweet old lady* when I get old. They'll say, *What on earth is that crazy old woman up to now*? I don't see myself in a rocking chair with an afghan draped over my lap and a cup of tea by my side. Sure, I may do some of that, but I would like to think I will still be saying inappropriate things while wearing inappropriate clothing. I've always been odd and quirky. Why would I change now? I'm in the seventh decade of my life, a life full of tremendous joy and what once seemed like insurmountable sadness."

Melanie returned to her seat, lifted her head, shaking it

from side to side with a broad smile as she continued. "Sometimes I look at myself in the mirror and wonder when I started looking like my mother. Don't get me wrong, my mother was beautiful, and I'm blessed to have inherited some of her genes. But at what point did I start to age like her? My body shows the unmistakable signs of senior age: my legs have lost their tone, and my skin hangs more softly over muscles that are not as strong as years past. My breasts have lost their fight with gravity, and the battle has begun for the correct-fitting bra."

With our honest conversation, we started moving closer to each other as if plotting a major coup.

As we huddled together, I discussed how my mother viewed aging. "My mother never showed signs of being someone other than a wife and a mother. From her June Cleaver hairstyle to her ill-fitting sense of style, she never seemed to embrace being a woman. I don't want to be like my grandmother, either. She always wore a housedress with her bra strap sliding down her arm wrapped with the flab I obviously inherited. I don't suspect that either of them ever wore sexy lingerie."

"I could never imagine my mother as a sexual being," Ellen said. "Nor did I see any physical contact or attraction between my parents. It took many years of marriage to realize that I actually enjoyed being sexual."

I squirmed in my seat as I thought of my relationship with Niko, which was just beginning. "That's why we shouldn't stop now. We shouldn't deny ourselves the pleasure." I was convincing myself, as well as my friends. "Ladies, new opportunities are available to us. Just look at what we have accomplished in such a short time with Sweet Repeats."

Melanie reached into her bag and held up her short flirty nightgown. "I agree with Andi. We are vital and strong and embracing our empowerment. We can't defy the laws of gravity, but we can fight against the emotional downfalls of aging."

We ended our shopping trip and two-hour lunch with confident highs. Packages in hand, we hugged each other dearly and said our goodbyes.

Walking into my home, I was greeted by the contented purring of Coco Chanel.

I HAD NEARLY FORGOTTEN that Jed was coming over when I heard the garage door open. He walked in with his sexy "haven't shaved in three days" look, a hint of his Aramis cologne, and a long-sleeved button-down yellow shirt. I never should have told him my affinity for button-down shirts or how much I (and Renee) liked him in yellow.

Jed had texted earlier that day. *I need to get some more things from the house. Can we talk? I should be there around 4:00.*

It was inevitable that I would see Jed often as we discussed the details of our current situation. I needed to keep the conversations brief, whether in person or via text. *Okay.*

Jed walked in through the front door instead of the garage since he wouldn't be staying. Walking towards the bedroom, he barely looked at me. "I need to get some things from my nightstand, and then can we talk?"

Looking for those little blue pills? I thought to myself.

"That's fine. I need to take the cushions off the patio chairs; it looks like rain is coming."

I heard Jed's voice from the bedroom rise as I was heading outside. "Wow!"

When I entered the bedroom, I found Jed holding up the Lacy Silhouette bag I had forgotten to put away.

"Wow," Jed said again as he reached into the bag and held up one of the low plunging gowns. "I hope these are for my benefit."

"No, Jed. They are for me, not you. You lost that right when you decided to be with other women."

"Babe, please listen to me. I realize I have a problem, and I'm going to get help. I will do anything to get you back. Anything." Jed sat on the bed, still holding the gown. "I can't bear the thought of you wearing this for another man."

"How do you think I feel knowing you're fucking other women?"

"What has happened to you? Your language, your provocativeness, and this," he said while reaching into the bag and bringing out the lacy bra. "It worries me. It also excites me," he said, pointing to his crotch.

I reached down to touch Jed's engorgement and, well, let's just say his reaction to my lingerie purchases gave the right effect. I didn't even have to put them on. But it wasn't meant for him.

I didn't want to. I swear I didn't want to.

This time, I definitely wasn't going to tell Ellen.

CHAPTER TWENTY-FOUR

I HAD AN APPOINTMENT to check out the Craft Barn, so I ignored a few texts coming in until I settled into my Mercedes. Before starting my car, I read through my text messages:

Jed: *Thanks for last night. It was beyond amazing. Can we talk tonight?*

Stephanie, the real estate agent: *I will meet you at the Craft Barn at 11:00.*

Ellen: *I won't go into details, but my husband is probably out buying me a special gift.*

This was too interesting not to call her.

"Do you mean the lingerie was a success?"

"It sure was, and I wouldn't be surprised if he's at the jewelry store right now."

I could hear Avery, Logan, and Tyson running around the house as she talked. "Tim even offered to watch the kids by himself today. I just walked by him, and he pinched my ass. If I had known it would be that easy to rekindle a fire, I would have purchased the correct fire starters long ago."

"How was the edible underwear?"

"We never made it that far."

"That's wonderful. I'm heading over to check out a possible new building for Sweet Repeats. I will call you later." Before I could hang up, I could hear Tim come towards Ellen singing, "My Girl."

As I started the car, I looked at a container in the corner of the garage containing some of Jed's favorite things. I immediately got out of the car and opened the top. I pushed aside trophies and albums until I found a box of photographs mostly of him, Kathleen, and their children. I took the box and placed it with the other stolen items. If I keep this up, I will have to rent a storage locker.

I was running early to meet the real estate agent, so I

stopped at Hemlock Green Garden Center and purchased mum plants for Nicole, my two daughters-in-law, and for Sweet Repeats. The bright orange, yellow, and burgundy colors exploded in my back seat. I was ready for a new season, and Fall was my favorite. Days had already turned cooler, and the pumpkin spice scents were everywhere. Before starting the car, I went back inside and purchased one more plant for Becky.

On my way to the Craft Barn, I passed Maggiano's, the restaurant where Niko and I shared pizza and laughter. I immediately pulled in front of the restaurant with an idea.

"May I purchase just a pizza box from you?" I asked the very handsome man at the counter.

"No pizza? Just the box?" he said with a thick Italian accent.

"Yes, I just need the box. But something thicker than a standard box."

The confused young man handed me an empty, wider box with a large Maggiano logo. "No charge, Signora."

I dropped $20 in the tip jar and thanked him enthusiastically. I knew exactly what I wanted to do with the box. I just had to wait until the time was right.

At precisely 11:00 a.m., I pulled alongside the real estate agent standing outside her mini-van with two car seats in the back. "You must be Andi. It's so nice to meet you. I'm Stephanie."

Stephanie was dressed in fall attire, wearing knee-length boots over brown pants and a brown cowl neck sweater. She looked harried and overwhelmed. I could relate to those challenging years of working and raising children.

Now that I no longer had to wear appropriate business clothes to work, I had enjoyed transforming my look. I wore a silk blouse with flowing sleeves that made me want to twirl my arms.

"I remember those days," I said, pointing to the car seats.

"Tell me it will get easier as they get older."

I touched Stephanie's arm in sympathy. "It doesn't get easier; it just gets different."

Stephanie and I walked closer to the buildings, and she gave me the background of the property.

"The barn was part of the Thompson Estate. The original manor house was destroyed over 50 years ago due to fire. The barn, the guesthouse, and the two outbuildings are included in the sale. The owners live in the two-bedroom, 1,500-square-foot guesthouse, and the two outbuildings are unused. The original barn was restored 22 years ago with a third floor added, and the entire barn was expanded."

As I followed Stephanie toward the barn, I stopped in amazement at the large stone rustic exterior, an homage to local farmhouses in Calvert County. The barn was shadowed by three giant hundred-year-old trees and rose bushes severely in need of pruning. Weeds popped up in neglected flower beds, and a wide porch badly needed cleaning. The barn and the acre it sat on had a rural-country feel next to suburban neighborhoods.

We entered through a distressed sliding door. I stepped into a remarkably welcoming modern interior. With an open feeling, there were individual kiosk-looking sections. Many display tables were made from repurposed material, looking fabulous among the revamped interior.

Just like the exterior, the interior required updating. Walking through the three floors, various vendor booths displayed their wares of jewelry, scarves, unique pottery, blown glass, hand-painted kimonos and kaftans, and boho dresses. There were wooden toys, leather goods, and so much more. The third floor was full of vintage and antique items. I estimated the barn to be 50% occupied.

"What do you think of the building?" Stephanie asked as I descended the stairs, which needed a few nails and had boards that needed to be replaced in several spots.

"It's amazing! I would like to reach out to my partners and see if they are available to come by."

"I don't have to pick up my children until 3:00."

"Great, I will get back to you shortly."

Stephanie started to walk towards a section of wooden toys. "Take your time. I am going to do some early Christmas shopping."

I stepped outside and sent a text to Melanie and Jeannie:

I'm at the Craft Barn. The place is incredible. Would you be able to come over?

Jeannie responded first: *I'm home and can leave in a few minutes.*

Melanie: *Jeannie, pick me up, and we will go together.*

I SAT ON A CREAKING ROCKING CHAIR on the barn's patio, trying to get a feel for the atmosphere. While waiting for Melanie and Jeannie, I researched the Craft Barn's website to check its visibility.

When they arrived, I told them what I had found out online. "It looks like the website has stayed the same for years. There are no notices of upcoming events or featured vendors. They have a Facebook page, but entries are only once a month. Other than a Christmas and Spring Bazaar, there aren't any other significant activities. There is small signage out front that is not visible from the road. We could do massive promotions and advertising. The place obviously needs more visibility."

Melanie walked around the barn and surveyed the building. "Can you imagine if we incorporated color in some of the vendor spots? We could display some merchandise by the front counter for more visibility. On weather-permitting days, we could arrange tables on the porch for additional displays."

Melanie and Jeannie were just as enthusiastic as I was.

As Melanie and I talked, Jeannie was jotting down notes. I'd never seen her so casually dressed in jeans and a plain white tee shirt covered by a non-descript beige sweater. Other than a hint of peach gloss, she was sans makeup. Fully coiffed or not, she was adorable.

"Obviously, we have to review the financial aspects in great detail," Jeannie said. "It would be helpful if we could find a way to rent out the outbuildings. I have many questions: zoning issues, taxes, insurance liability, utility expenses, vendor fees, and obtaining a loan."

After giving us some privacy, Stephanie walked over to us. "Do you have any questions?"

"Do you know why other vendors don't fully occupy the building?" I asked Stephanie.

"I don't think the owners put much effort into growing the business. They are both in their 80s now," Stephanie said while looking at her watch.

We told Stephanie we would be in touch with her shortly.

"We can do this, ladies," Melanie exclaimed.

Jeannie bit her lower lip. "Once we get all the particulars, we can decide."

My first instinct was to run home and tell Jed about the barn. He could estimate the renovation cost and do much of it himself. My second thought was Niko.

On the way home, I called Jed. "Jed, can you replace the dining room chandelier bulb when you come by later? I wasn't able to screw the bulb in place."

"Is this a code for something else?"

"No, you ass. It's only the light that needs screwing."

"I love it when you talk to me like this. I will be there in about an hour."

I looked at the phone with part humor and part annoyance. I had expected to regret sleeping with Jed. I didn't. Once again, I had control.

When Jed walked through the door, looking pleased with himself and carrying another bouquet of flowers, I was tempted to ask him to leave. But then again, I still needed the lightbulb replaced, didn't I?

"Don't look smug," I said. "Last night didn't change any-thing. It was just sex, however satisfying it may have been."

"It was rather obvious you were satisfied."

I planted my feet and leveled a straight look into his eyes, my voice amped up with anger. "Are you waiting for me to have an epiphany and claim this was a mistake and that I want you back in my life? That's not happening, Jed, not now, not ever."

Jed dutifully took a seat and looked at me with a rueful grin. "Can we just sit and talk for a few minutes? I've been trying to tell you I need help, and I have made an appointment with a therapist. Can you stop pacing around?"

Unable to stand still, I handed Jed the lightbulb as I entered the dining room.

Jed pointed to one of the dining room's heavy white padded walnut chairs. "Can you just sit down? I'll fix it. Just let me talk to you first."

I turned on the chandelier and pointed to the missing bulb before I sat down.

The muscles on Jed's face tightened. "Andi, I love you, and I've made a horrible mess out of things, but I will do anything to get you back. I hope a therapist can help me understand why I have done this to you. I solemnly vow that I will never be unfaithful to you again. You know how good we are together."

"Jed, there was a time when I believed that you and I were a perfect team," I told him. "But when I look back, I also see that I overlooked many red flags. There were many questionable times when you were at your so-called estimates or golf outings. And, by the way, how long have you been sleeping with Kathleen?"

Jed got up and pushed his chair back. I knew he was heading to the kitchen to make himself a drink. "Bring me a glass of wine," I called after him. If we were going to have this conversation, I was ready.

I hoped my mellowed tone and relaxed shoulders showed him the importance of his honesty. I knew I would never go back to Jed. But there remained this need to understand why he would betray me repeatedly. "Before you start defending yourself or making excuses, just be honest with yourself and me."

With his drink in one hand, Jed ran his other hand through his hair, unsure how much to divulge. "Kathleen and I always remained friends. I admit that sometimes I would see Kathleen when you were so busy at work and with the kids. She always had time for me, and we had our children in common."

"When you said you remained friends, you meant you continued to sleep together, right? So while I was out working long hours to support us, you were lonely and turned to Kathleen?"

"How many times are you going to bring up that you supported us? That's why I felt insecure around you. You made me feel less of a man. You were tough and strong but I felt like you constantly threw it in my face that you made more money. So yes, Kathleen filled a void."

"There were other women, too, Jed. How much of a void did you have?" I resisted the temptation to scream at Jed and throw him out immediately. I couldn't stop from letting my feelings out further. "I can just imagine the conversations between you and Kathleen about how lonely you were and how hard you tried to make my life easier by taking care of things around the house. That's the same bullshit you fed *me*. Poor Jed, you had to help around the house while I supported you. By the way, Kathleen reaped the benefits of my working so much, too. How many times did we give her money to help her? Yes, that's right, WE gave her money. Did you two discuss that when you were sleeping together?"

Jed stood up and started to walk into the kitchen to make another White Russian. I watched as the heavy cream was less than before, making the drink stronger. He poured the last of the thick liquid over two ice cubes.

While he stirred the drink, Jed returned to meet my gaze. "I know this will take an incredible amount of trust, but it will be worth it, and we can become stronger than before. In the past, I compensated for my lack of self-worth with you by getting attention from other women. I was wrong, and I should have told you how I felt, but it was never easy to talk with you." He turned around with glimpses of tears in his eyes. "You made the income, and I sincerely tried to do my part. I felt unimportant and taken for granted like I was one of your employees."

I was momentarily taken aback. Jed had tapped into a sensitive spot for me. I had always struggled with the impossible balance of career and motherhood.

"Jed, I'm sorry if I made you feel that way. It was never my intention. I appreciate everything you have ever done for me, for us. I wish you had come to me and talked about your feelings." My tears began to match his. I swiped them away with impatience. "Regardless of how you felt, it doesn't take away from the fact that you cheated multiple times." At that moment, I realized Jed had never asked me how I found out about the other women.

Putting his head into his hands, Jed heaved with deep breaths. "Please, please, believe me. I will do everything to make this up to you."

"How can I expect you to be honest?" I immediately regretted asking the question and attempted to take my words back. I didn't want to give him the mistaken impression that there was a chance for us. "Lying is second nature to you. I don't want to be tempted to believe you."

"Just think about it. I am getting help. Don't give up on us. I'm living in Eve's basement, and she has me fixing her house instead of paying her rent. At least let me move back in until I can find a place." Jed spoke with reverence and hope that sounded sincere.

"I can't, Jed. I need to move on with my life. I finally have time to discover who I am. To find the me that I was meant to be." I took the drink from his hand and poured it down the drain. "Please leave now while you are sober."

CHAPTER TWENTY-FIVE

I LOVED WAKING UP to a text from Niko:

Hi Aphrodite, I know this is short notice, but I was wondering if you would like to attend an event at Dad's community. Calvert Towers is having its semi-annual family and friends gathering on Sunday. I will be there, but Becky and my grandchildren are unable to attend.

Hi Achilles, I would be delighted to attend.

Dad will be thrilled. Do you want me to pick you up?

I have to stop at the shop earlier, so I can meet you at the community.

Lie.

I wondered how many things I would continue to withhold from Niko. Like the fact that I'm still married and never know when my husband will stop by the house?

ON SUNDAY MORNING, I was cheery and anxious about my afternoon with Alex and Niko. I wasn't sure what to expect. After trying several clothing options, I finally settled on dark tan leggings and a fashionable long-sleeved "Free People" white sweater. With the cooler October air, it felt good not to worry about profuse sweating. I added short, brown, leopard-print boots and a long strand of pearls. With slight makeup and a dash of gardenia perfume, I walked into the living room, where Jed sat, looking at his phone.

"Jed, you've got to tell me when you are coming over."

Jed stood up, looked at my outfit, and said, "I didn't realize you were going out, and I didn't know I needed an invitation to enter *our* home. We still have details we need to figure out. I'm working on Eve's house and came to get some tools out of the garage."

Jed sat back down, returning to his phone, and I walked out the door without saying anything further.

It was barely a 10-minute drive to Calvert Towers. A large sign out front of the building stated, "Welcome, Family and Friends."

I saw Alex immediately as I walked into the lobby. He looked so dignified in his tweed sports jacket and pocket square.

He seemed genuinely excited to see me. "Andi, you look positively divine this afternoon."

I squeezed into the arm he held up high for me and kissed him on the cheek. We were greeted by other residents and staff as we walked into an impressively large dining room. Alex was obviously well-liked by everyone as they greeted us.

We were stopped by several people with the same question, which Alex answered with much pleasure.

"Is this your daughter?" they asked.

"No, we've actually just recently become acquainted," he'd say each time.

Alex and I walked arm in arm to the table where Alfred, one of his community friends, was sitting, along with Alfred's son, daughter-in-law, and two grandchildren.

I was delighted when I saw Niko walk in. He looked so casually handsome and sensual in his dark khaki pants and brown vee-neck sweater. He placed a gentle kiss on my cheek. "Thank you for coming," and took the seat beside me. "Hello everyone, I'm sorry if I'm late. I was talking with Mr. Remington and his son."

The room had been decorated with mums, pumpkins, and garlands of leaves. It was a brilliant display of orange and yellow. Each table held a large bowl of water with floating Gerber daisies. Calvert Towers took great pride in their community and their residents' well-being.

The room became quiet as piano music could be heard nearby.

Niko stood up. "Excuse me," he said and approached the piano player.

I watched as he walked over to the older gentleman playing the piano. He leaned in and whispered something to him before returning to the table.

Shortly, the piano player looked over at Niko and winked at him. "I have a special request," he said.

Then I heard the piano player sing, "Fly Me To The Moon," the song I love dearly.

I felt Niko's hand on my shoulders. I resisted my desire to lean into him. "You remembered my favorite song. I can't believe it."

I had difficulty containing the tears welling up as I told him the story of the song. "It was my father's favorite song, and he would play it often. He would offer his hand to my mother and they would dance in perfect unison, with his hand placed gently on the small of her back and their eyes locked at each other. It brings such wonderfully warm memories."

Niko reached for my hand. I leaned over and gave him a kiss on the cheek. I noticed the smile on Alex's face as he witnessed the tender moment between us.

After another two hours of delightful conversation, the music stopped, and the staff began to clear the tables. I didn't want my time with Alex and Niko to end, and just as if he was reading my mind, Niko asked me if I would like a tour of the community.

I noticed that most residents were in wheelchairs or used walkers or canes. The way Alex had held onto my arm unsteadily, I understood why Niko wanted his father to use a cane. The community was lovely, with several small gathering rooms for games, playing cards, and social events.

Niko tucked my hand into his arm as we walked through the hallways. "Dad is very comfortable here, and the staff is very accommodating. His room is down this corridor."

The door to Alex's room was decorated with an earth-toned fall wreath. A picture of him and his name was pinned underneath it.

I looked around at the tidy room, which was filled with books on both walls. A comfortable brown leather sofa sat across from a matching recliner. Another comfortable plaid chair was positioned to gaze out a large window overlooking a courtyard with a brightly lit gazebo in the center.

Off to the side of his room, I could see a decent-sized bedroom with framed pictures of his family and the town.

"This is really nice," I said to Niko.

"At first, feeling like I was putting Dad into a home was difficult. But there is a comfort level knowing he is being cared for and is still so close by."

Hearing the door open, we saw Alex accompanied by an aide.

Alex patted his son affectionately on the back. "I'm glad Niko showed you around."

"It's time for your father's medication, and he seems a bit tired," the kind aide said to Niko. "And, thank you for the chocolates. You're spoiling us."

Niko looked at the aide sincerely. "Thank you for all the special care you give my father."

Alex took a seat in his recliner and looked tired but content. "Andi, thank you so much for coming."

"Thank you, Alex, for a lovely afternoon. I enjoyed it very much," I said as I bent down to kiss him.

Niko reached down for his father's hand and held it briefly. "Take your medicine and get some sleep, Dad. I will talk to you tomorrow."

"They are a cute couple, Mr. Cirillo," I overheard the aide say to Alex.

"Yes, they are," Alex said as we were leaving.

Niko took my arm in a proprietary way as if it was common for us to be together. I reveled in the comfort of walking so close to him as we said our goodbyes to the staff.

"My car is over there," I said as I turned to its location.

Niko turned around to face me. "Would you like to take a little walk?"

I hesitated before answering him. "As long as it isn't a five-mile hike and we avoid dog poop. But yes, that would be nice."

Niko once again tucked my hand into the crook of his elbow. I wanted the walk to go on forever.

"Andi, obviously, I am developing feelings for you," he began. "I don't want to complicate anything in your life, and I certainly don't want to be involved with a married woman. I had assumed you weren't married, but Becky mentioned to me yesterday that she had seen your husband at your shop before. At least, she assumed it was your husband."

"No, we are most emphatically not together anymore," I told him. "It was a good marriage until it wasn't. I was deceived and blind the entire time. It ended up being a relief to know the truth about what I had chosen not to see." I neglected to mention to Niko that it was just last week that I officially asked Jed to leave.

"Andi, I'm sorry if you are going through a difficult time," he said. "Yet selfishly, I'm delighted if it means I can spend more time with you."

I looked directly into Niko's eyes for emphasis. "My marriage is over, and the damage is irreparable. But there is still so much that needs to be settled. Niko, I obviously have feelings for you, also. That's why I should probably return to the car and go home."

With that, I tightened my hand on his arm as he moved closer. We walked in rhythmic silence to my car, with thoughts of "Fly Me To The Moon."

CHAPTER TWENTY-SIX

THE FOLLOWING DAY, as I was getting out of the shower, I thought it was Coco Chanel running around the house. Instead, I found Jed on the step ladder, replacing the bulb.

"I forgot to change the lightbulb," Jed said.

"Maybe you could call next time. You startled me," I said, closing my robe tighter as Jed's eyes lingered on the open space. "And, what's that smell?"

"I'm making you breakfast. Eggs Benedict and spinach, your favorite. Now, excuse me while I stir the hollandaise sauce. Go get changed; it will be ready in twenty minutes." Jed turned around with a wink.

Walking back to the bedroom, I tried not to let my heart fill with the wrong emotions. I quickly dried and styled my hair. Without much thought, I put on jeans and an oversized white sweater over a white tank top. I added long silver hoops and grabbed my leopard-print short boots. At the last minute, I grabbed a matching leopard cape.

"Who is Niko?" Jed said, holding out my phone. "He wants to know how you are."

I glared at Jed while taking my phone from his hand. "You have no right to look at my phone."

"I didn't snoop. I heard the text and picked up your phone. I was going to bring it to you."

"Well, you had no right to look at my messages."

"Really, Andi?" Jed's face turned into an upturned smile. "So, only you can invade someone's privacy?"

So, he did realize I had cracked into his Facebook and emails. I didn't bother to respond to Jed.

I texted Niko. *Hi, I'm doing well. How are things with you?*

I'm good. Dad had a little setback. He is in the hospital with pneumonia. The doctor said he was relatively strong for his age and should be fine.

Oh no. I'm so sorry. Can Alex have visitors?

Yes, I will be there all afternoon. Stop by if you can. Dad is in St. Luke's, Room 332. It will be good to see you.

I can be there around 3:00.

Jed observed me while I texted Niko without asking any more questions.

As Jed put the eggs Benedict on the table, my phone rang. "Hey, Melanie."

"Hi, I will bring a tape measure today to get the size of the rooms. We should also bring boots so we can check out the other two buildings. I wonder if they are safe. And, by the way, Jack liked the crotchless underwear."

I could feel the curious look on Jed's face as he tried to comprehend the odd conversation I was having. "I'm anxious to hear all about it. I have to be somewhere at 3:00, so let's meet at the Craft Barn early. Can you be there by 10:00?"

"Yes, not a problem. I will let Jeannie know. See you soon."

As I stood up, Jed grabbed my arm, put his hands on my shoulders, and pushed me back onto the chair. "What the hell is going on with you? Mud, crotchless underwear, and unsafe buildings? I don't know who you are anymore."

"I'm just finding out, too." I got up again and impulsively kissed Jed on his cheek. I thanked him for breakfast and grabbed my things. "I've got a lot to do today. I will talk to you later," I said while dramatically swinging the cape around my shoulders.

"You are putting up this huge barrier between us."

"I'm aware of that, Jed, and the barrier is going to stay there."

I ARRIVED AT THE CRAFT BARN before Jeannie, Melanie, or Stephanie. I sat on the grass in front of the barn and visualized the changes we could make. A large, colorful sign with a new logo that Melanie could create would bring more awareness to the business. We could repaint the white columns and trim a deep rustic red. I pictured strings of lights, vintage bicycles with baskets full of artificial flowers, and steel buckets full of reeds and lavender. The place could look magical for holidays.

I took out my phone and started taking pictures when I heard the sound of two cars coming up the path. I walked towards Jeannie's Prius, anxious to show them more.

Stephanie looked more rested today, leading us to the small house behind the barn. "I told the owners of your interest, and they would be happy to meet you and answer any questions you may have."

Edward and Peggy Koontz were a sweet couple who were anxious to talk with us. We sat around their retro yellow kitchen table while Peggy fed us lemon bars and apple cider. I put my glass down carefully on the vintage blue tablecloth with red flowers and yellow fruit. My grandmother had the exact same tablecloth, which evoked magical childhood memories of many meals shared on her table. I would anxiously await one of Grandma's homemade pies she baked nearly every day.

Peggy spoke first. "My parents bought the property in the early 1900s. Edward and I moved into the manor house after my parents passed, and we lived there until the fire. We moved into the guest house with our young son and have lived here ever since. Edward used the barn for his furniture refinishing business for many years. Our son, Donald, had the idea for creating the Craft Barn. Edward sold many of his pieces in the barn."

Edward squeezed his wife's hand tightly in return. "Our son is retiring soon and wants to move to South Carolina if we agree to move with him and his family."

"For the past ten years, we have left the Craft Barn to run itself with the help of our manager, who is also ready to retire," Peggy said. "We've had some interest from builders who intended to build a couple of homes and get rid of the properties on the land. Obviously, we would prefer to keep the buildings intact."

Melanie looked out the window. "We would like to walk through all the buildings today if that is okay with you."

Edward stood up and shook hands with us. "Of course, let us know if you have any questions."

Before going outside and checking out the rest of the property, we toured the spotless guest home. It needed updating but no major renovations.

"We could use part of the house for our offices and clothing storage," Melanie said. "I'm sure we could find a use for the rest of the house."

Stephanie spoke as we walked to the first building. "I don't want to rush you ladies, but a builder has expressed great interest. He has been talking with the town council regarding any historical restrictions. They were surveying the land yesterday."

The smallest of the two outbuildings definitely required renovations. The floorboards were loose, and the door, roof, and windows needed replacing.

The second building fared much better and could be useful for vendors. In the larger building, we found several old tables, one on top of the other, and mismatched collections of vintage dishes in several boxes. The outside of both buildings was choked with weeds.

"Let's walk through the barn again," Melanie said. "I want to take some measurements."

Stephanie opened the door to the barn. "Feel free to talk with the vendors. They are most anxious to see what will happen to the business."

A young woman behind the front counter was sorting through tickets. She was wearing one of the kaftans I noticed yesterday. She looked hopeful as she asked, "Are you thinking about buying the place?"

Jeannie walked over to the front counter. "There is much to consider, but we are interested. Do customers pay here at the counter for their purchases?"

She held up a box of tickets. "Yes, all items have these tickets with the price and a vendor code," the young woman said. "The shop gets 20% of all sales, and we charge a monthly fee for the space. The cost is based on the size and placement in the barn. I can ask our manager, Marilyn, for the details."

"That would be wonderful," I said.

"I will let you ladies wander around the store," Stephanie

said as she walked toward a kiosk with handmade scarves. "Let me know if you have any questions."

Jeannie took out her notepad and jotted down notes and comments while Melanie took measurements and I took pictures.

"Shall we go to lunch and talk about this more?" I asked Melanie and Jeannie.

Melanie closed her tape measure and handed Jeannie the measurements she had made. "Sounds great."

"I have clothes in my car that I've been storing for the shop," Jeannie said. "Would you mind if we went to Becky's Café so I could drop these off at Sweet Repeats?"

"That would be perfect," I said. I had put Becky's mums in my car before I left, intending to stop by the café anyway.

"ANDI, IT'S SO GOOD TO SEE YOU," Becky said, giving me an unexpected embrace when we arrived. "Dad said you were going to see Pa-Pou at the hospital today. I saw him last night. He was in good spirits but looked very weak and pale. Dad has been at the hospital with him the whole time. He hopes to meet with the doctor today for more information. I'm sure your visit will cheer him up."

I handed her the pot of mums. "I'm looking forward to seeing him."

"You are so sweet, thank you." Becky walked us over to a quiet table near the back of the café and then greeted another group arriving.

"Who is Pa-Pou?" Melanie asked with a controlled laugh.

"Alex, the elderly gentleman who visited me at Sweet Repeats," I explained. "He is her grandfather."

"That's very considerate of you to go and see him at the hospital. Will his son be there?" Melanie asked with a raised eyebrow.

I sat down very quickly and tried to change the subject. "Yes, he will. Let's either talk about the shop or your crotchless underwear."

"Did I miss something?" asked Jeannie as the waitress came by to take our order.

"We will save the underwear conversation for a later time," Melanie said, giggling like a teenager. "What do you think about the Craft Barn?"

I inhaled and exhaled deeply. "I have so many ideas on adding more vendors to make it more profitable. We could host events and extensive promotions and advertising to create more business. Melanie, you could revise the website and social media to bring in traffic. Jeannie, it will all come down to you at this point." I looked at Jeannie, seeing the apprehension on her face.

Jeannie looked at us quizzically. "All up to me?"

Between bites of my tuna salad, I told Jeannie, "We need you to tell us the financial feasibility. Once we have that, we will know if we should proceed."

Melanie smiled brightly at Jeannie and me. "I have a good feeling about this."

I raised my finger instantly. "You know, it just occurred to me that we could use some of the space for Ellen's tea room."

"Oh my gosh, do you think she would be interested?" Jeannie asked.

I reached for my phone and texted Ellen: *If you are serious about opening the tearoom, I have THE perfect opportunity.*

I put my hands together, "We will find out soon, I just texted Ellen. Enough shop talk. Jeannie, how are things with Chuck?'

Jeannie's face turned a brighter shade every time she spoke of her new boyfriend. "It's going very well."

"Well, details, please," Melanie requested from Jeannie.

Jeannie batted her perfect eyelashes, "We haven't been intimate yet, but I really enjoy being around him."

I smiled at Jeannie with sincere affection. "Don't be hesitant to follow your heart. Live your life to its fullest extent." I looked at the time on my cell phone. "I have to be somewhere at 3:00. I need to get going. But seriously, Jeannie, enjoy this time of your life."

ON MY DRIVE TO THE HOSPITAL, I fluttered from subject to subject, like a movie playing through my mind. I thought of the challenging time ahead with Jed, the opportunity to purchase The Craft Barn and relocate Sweet Repeats, Jeannie's newfound happiness, and, of course, Niko.

Peeking into his hospital room, I saw Alex with eyes closed and light, murmuring snores. He looked pale, just as Becky had said. Niko was sitting in the chair next to him. His frameless glasses were on the tip of his nose while he read a magazine. He wore khaki dress pants, an oxford shirt, and an Irish wool cardigan. Put a pipe in his mouth, and he would look every bit like the adored principal he was. Niko looked so inviting I wanted to plop myself onto his lap.

"How long have you been standing there?" Niko asked with a distinct smile.

I took a few quiet steps into the room, not wanting to disturb Alex from his slumber. "I just got here. How is your dad?"

"Let's take a walk down the hall." Niko took my hand and led me to a waiting room.

There were a few visitors aimlessly watching a talk show on the TV. We found two chairs off to the side.

"I spoke to the doctor last night. He said Dad is stable, but his lungs are inflamed. They are treating him with IV fluid, oxygen, steroids, and antibiotics. He will be in the hospital for at least a week." Niko looked down at his shoes while he spoke. "Thank you for coming. It's really good to see you. How is everything?"

I put my head on his shoulder and felt his warmth as he tilted toward me. "Everything is good."

We sat silently for several minutes, our heads touching and an invisible thread linking us.

"The nurse thought you might be in here," a calm-looking man with his hands in his pocket said to Niko.

We stood in hopeful anticipation of good news.

"Dr. Gordon, this is Andi," Niko said, placing a warm arm around my waist.

"It's nice to meet you, Andi. I've just come from your father-in-law's room."

Neither Niko nor I corrected Dr. Gordon on his assumption.

"Let's sit down and discuss your father's condition."

Niko and I sat in our chairs while Dr. Gordon pulled another chair out and turned it to face us.

"The inflammation in your father's lungs has not subsided. His pulse oximetry level remains low, and he has not responded to the antibiotics."

Niko looked Dr. Gordon directly in the eyes. "Are you anticipating the pneumonia will get worse?"

"Not necessarily, but it is a concern given your father's advanced age. We will continue the same treatment of IV fluids, oxygen, medication, and obviously rest. Let's take this day by day. I will be back tomorrow afternoon."

Niko and I stood, thanked the doctor, and retreated to our seats.

"I know Dad is 93, and I've been lucky to have my father around for this long, but I can't imagine my life without him."

I touched Niko's arm, unsure of what to do. "Is there anything you need? Perhaps I can get you something other than cafeteria food for dinner?"

Niko gave me a weary smile before reaching for my hand. "No, just seeing you helps a great deal."

We sat in contemplative silence for a few minutes.

"I'm going to leave the two of you alone," I told him. "Can you text me tomorrow and let me know how Alex is doing?"

"I will. Let me walk you to the elevator."

Before the elevator doors opened, Niko turned me around and gently kissed me on the cheek. Just then, Dr. Gordon walked by with a warm smile directed at us.

CHAPTER TWENTY-SEVEN

WHEN YOU IMAGINE FOUR OLDER WOMEN, bundled in afghans, rocking away on a country porch, you might envision them talking about their children, grandchildren, and aches and pains. Perhaps they would be knitting and sipping on hot cocoa. Not our group. This is how *our* trip unfolded.

MELANIE HAD SIPPED her pumpkin spice latte on our drive to Greg's lake house. "This is a fabulous idea."

"I'm so glad you came, Ellen," Jeannie had said.

Meanwhile, Ellen sat in the front passenger seat, turned, and smiled at Melanie and Jeannie. "Me, too. I've been up here with Andi before, but never at this time of the year. Thank you for including me."

When Jeannie told us she had prepared all the financial information we needed to buy The Craft Barn, and we were discussing where to meet, I'd thought of the lake house. It was only two hours away and had spectacular views. We'd decided to stay for the weekend and define how and if we would purchase the buildings. Jeannie had the financial details, Melanie had the layout conceptualization, and I had pages of promotional ideas.

"If you decide to buy the Craft Barn, I am totally onboard for running the tearoom there," Ellen said. "It's such a fabulous opportunity for me, and I would love to be a part of the project."

We knew we had much to discuss before making our final decision on whether to proceed.

After arriving, we'd quickly unpacked our bags, provisions, and several bottles of wine and settled into those four chairs on the back porch facing the amazing lake—not at all looking grandmotherly. Late boaters were cruising along, enjoying the chill of the fall air before the arrival of winter. Soon, the boats would be set on the docks for nearly half the year before spring came around again.

The four of us took deep, cleansing breaths and swallowed them with intensity. We, too, wanted to capture the feel of the season as much as possible. The nights had turned cooler, and the pumpkin spice scents were everywhere.

When Jeannie's phone rang, she excused herself. We heard her say, "Hi, Chuck," as she walked back into the house.

After several minutes, Jeannie joined us outside. "How is everything with Chuck?" I asked her.

Her smile was as broad and clear as the lake in our view. "It's wonderful. I've wanted to talk with you about my evolving relationship with Chuck." Jeannie cleared her throat and gathered the nerve to talk with us. She wrapped her arms around herself as if it was a protection against the words she was about to say. "We were intimate last Saturday evening. You know, *that* kind of intimate. I was initially nervous, and so was Chuck, but we quickly became comfortable with each other, and it was lovely." The sight of Jeannie talking about sex was just as adorable as her slight figure with feet that barely touched the ground as she sat in the chair.

Melanie smirked, her silver bangles catching the light from the falling sun. "Lovely? Can sex ever be lovely? I would rather hear you say it was raw and dirty."

"I've never had raw and dirty sex," Jeannie said sheepishly. "Even with Wayne, sex was always pleasant and a bit programmed, and I was okay with that. It was nice with Chuck. He was kind and gentle and he understood my apprehension." Jeannie blushed and paused momentarily as her eyelashes fluttered on her cheeks. "It's been a long time for him, too. I actually researched online about sex for women in their 60s and 70s."

"You've been missing out, Jeannie. It can be lovely, sweet, and tender sometimes. But it can also be adventurous and daring," I told her.

Ellen lifted herself higher in her chair, preparing for her own self-realization. "I was worried this would be boring business conversations all weekend. I see we are going to dive right into this. Jeannie, I was never, as Andi put it, *adventurous,* and I feel like I missed out on exploring more of my hidden sexuality. Tim and I have been enjoying sex more since our lingerie-buying trip. In fact, I want to go back to the shop for more items. We've been together for nearly 50 years, and yet we never went beyond casual exploring."

Ellen poured herself another glass of wine and looked at the lake with a new passion before continuing. "I've never been with anyone other than Tim. And he's never been with anyone other than me. Or, so he says. Unless you were with him, Andi." Ellen looked at me, half smiling and half inquisitive.

"No, Ellen, Tim and I were never intimate. We never had a relationship, just a few uneventful dates, until I realized he was more a match for you than me."

Melanie pointed at me. "Whoa, you were with her husband?"

"It was NO big deal. I can't believe you even thought that," I said, turning to Ellen.

"Well, you weren't exactly virginal, Andi."

"I wasn't *exactly* a slut either," I said, half miffed at her accusation. "You make me sound like I slept with the football team. Ellen, I was with two guys before Daniel. TWO guys. If you thought Tim and I had slept together, you should have asked me, or you should have asked Tim. We both would have been honest with you."

"It's just that you've had more experiences than me," she said.

I stood up, grabbed the wine bottle, and refilled my glass to the rim. "I'm glad I was with more than one man, and I'm glad that Tim was the only man for you."

Ellen turned around again and looked at me.

At this point, Jeannie walked to the edge of the porch to give us some privacy while Melanie did the opposite and turned her chair to face us.

"Andi, please don't be upset." With controlled effort, Ellen relaxed her shoulders and looked at me with sincerity. "It's just that you've had more experiences than I. I wish I had your flair, confidence, *and* sensuality. I was always envious of you. You have always been so strong and self-assured. You raised three wonderful children and had a successful business that you started on your own."

"And I wish I was more like you," I told Ellen. "I would have liked just one man I could have been married to for fifty years. You have a husband who loves you and will always protect and cherish you." I took a deep breath and continued. "My husband was secretly screwing his ex-wife and many others while we were married. So, don't be envious of me."

Ellen came over to me and offered a hug, which I returned gratefully, and then excused myself as I walked into the kitchen.

I grabbed four bowls, two pints of ice cream, and four spoons.

I put the items on the table in front of our chairs. "Jeannie, come over here. I think we all need some comfort food."

"Anyone interested in my sex life?" Melanie said.

We were all grateful for the levity.

The four of us hungrily spooned ice cream into our bowls.

Jeannie looked at her full bowl of Rocky Road and held her finger up at us as she walked into the house.

Jeannie returned with a smile and held up a bag of M&M's. "I saw this in the cabinet earlier when I put things away."

I started to laugh and reached for the bag. "I left them here last time."

"You were going to tell us about your sex life, Melanie. I hope it's been more exciting than mine," Jeannie said meekly.

"I've had a few partners before Jack," Melanie said, glancing at Ellen. "During my drinking years and when Jack and I were married, I had sex with another teacher. It happened only once, and it took Jack years to forgive me. Once I became sober, truly sober, Jack and I worked on building our relationship. We went to therapy, and we shared our anger and our frustrations. I had a lot of things from my childhood to work through, and I was blessed to have Jack's compassion. But it wasn't easy. Those years were a difficult and painful time in my life. But I survived, and more importantly, Jack and I survived."

Jeannie shocked all of us by saying, "Holy shit."

Melanie looked lost in her thoughts before she spoke again. "Sex with Jack was intense in the beginning, less frequent after Scott was born, and nonexistent when I drank. When I sobered up, sex became part of our life again. But we had ups and downs as age and circumstances changed us."

Ellen placed a spoonful of M&Ms in Melanie's bowl and patted her shoulder. "I can't imagine how difficult and painful this must have been for you."

While Ellen stood before her, Melanie took the spoon and added even more M&Ms into her bowl. "I had, and still have, much sadness over my relationship with my son, Scott. I will always wish for another chance to be the mother he deserved. My behavior brought much stress into our marriage." Melanie's face dropped as she wiped away tears that came so easily to her. "I can't remember the last time Scott hugged me with feeling. But I am his mother, and I will do everything in my power to repair the damage I have done."

I reached for the candy bag and waited to see if Melanie wanted to continue speaking.

Melanie spoke with continued raw honesty. "And there was menopause, which did exactly that: it paused our sex life. I was sweaty, my vagina was dry, and the effort didn't seem worth it. When that changed, Jack developed erection problems. I stopped feeling sexual, and I became okay with that. Gratefully, things have changed again recently."

I blew out a long breath of air. "I think there's a stigma for women as they age. We aren't supposed to be interested in sex. Our bodies are flabby, we have hormonal issues, and our hips and knees ache. We are expected to leave our sexual lives behind us. Grandmas aren't supposed to enjoy sex. No one wants to visualize that. We are supposed to bake cookies and talk about our arthritis."

"I'm learning rather late in life that it doesn't have to get less adventurous. I feel bolder now," Melanie said. "Hold on, I'll be right back."

"Whoa," Ellen said while we waited for Melanie to return.

"This has become really interesting. Thank you again for inviting me."

When Melanie returned to her designated chair, she pulled out a joint and a lighter from her pocket. Tipping down her eyeglasses, aqua blue trimmed this time, she passed the joint around.

"I don't drink, but on occasion, I get high," Melanie said nonchalantly with a smirk.

Two of us joined Melanie. I will leave it at that.

(But I will say this – it wasn't who you would expect.)

"I've never had an orgasm," Jeannie said.

(And now you know which other one of us shared the joint with Melanie.)

"You've never had an orgasm?" I spat out.

"You've *really* never had an orgasm?" Melanie repeated, taking a heavy hit and passing the joint.

Jeannie made an indeterminable sound, halfway between a laugh and a cry.

Ellen gave Jeannie the compassion Melanie and I were currently lacking. "I think you should be open and honest with Chuck about that," Ellen said. "Perhaps the two of you could work on it together. I didn't have an orgasm with Tim until we had been married for three years. I had faked it, and when I finally told him, we watched videos together."

"But, won't it be harder at this age?" Jeannie said her comments directly to only Ellen.

"The harder part may be true," Melanie said, continuing her amusement.

Ellen reached over and put her hand on Melanie's mouth.

I knew Jeannie had more to say as her cheeks flushed, her eyes widened, and her mouth prepared to release more well-stored emotions. The first of those, the one that poked through the surface, was the most difficult. We all listened intently as Jeannie spoke, her voice barely above a whisper.

"I did what was expected of me as a child and an adult." Jeannie stood and walked to the edge of the porch. She placed her hands in her pockets and pulled down her cashmere sweater, looking uncomfortable. "Wayne was a good man with a hearty laugh and a zest for life. He explored the world through travel and books. He could quote philosophers as easily as he could blindly name all the blends in a bottle of wine. We loved each other with tenderness and compassion. We explored life's glories and shared a life of comfort. Wayne sought out our excursions, and I tended to the details."

"It sounds wonderful," I said.

"It was. But it was lacking in passion for each other. Wayne never had a deep interest in sex. I don't think he had any serious relationships before me, and we met when we were both in our late 30s. It was Wayne's decision not to have children. I was initially indifferent, and by the time I had changed my mind, it was too late. I tried not to resent Wayne for it, but I did so internally."

"I'm so sorry, Jeannie," Ellen said. "You shouldn't have lived your life in silence and not speaking up for yourself. But it's good that you are doing it now. Release all those emotions you have been holding in so tightly."

Jeannie lowered her gaze before she spoke again. "I want all of my youth back. I want to wake up again in my pink and green gingham bedroom in my canopy bed. My sister in the room next to me, and my parents down the hall. I was safe. I want the smell of my mother cooking breakfast and kissing us off to school. I want the life I had before my sister died."

We all shifted in our seats and waited to see if Jeannie wanted to share more as she wiped the tears from her eyes.

"My mother and father became so protective of me that I had little chance to spread my wings or experience life beyond the walls of home or school. My father, a first-generation Irish immigrant, pushed me into mathematics in college. I did as I was told. I mastered in Actuary Sciences. I never liked what I did, but I was good at it. I was a good child, a good employee, and a good wife. But something was missing. Me, it was *me* that was missing."

Jeannie blew out an extended breath and wiped the edges of her eyes.

"It was hard to get ahead in a man's world, to be taken seriously. Men don't like taking orders from a barely five-foot woman in a male-dominated field. There is no *Actuary Barbie* to emulate."

"Especially since you are so gorgeous," Melanie said.

Jeannie smiled briefly and looked away. "How do I start now? How do I become a new woman? A sexual woman?" She turned back and looked at each of us, hoping for answers.

"Actually, this is the best time to start," I told her. "In ten years, I will be 80. I will lose some elasticity and mobility. I want to enjoy it as much as possible before real physical problems start, but I never want to stop enjoying sex."

"Are you and Jed still having sex?" Ellen asked me, sensing that Jeannie wanted less focus on her.

"Jed is the most sexual man on the planet," I admitted. "Yes, we've had sex a few times, even though we are separated. I've even considered using Jed as a sex buddy when needed, just like his ex-wife, Kathleen, has obviously done. I know how to have sex with Jed, and he knows what I want. I get it, Jeannie. I really do. How do you have sex with someone new?"

My heart pounded as I thought about Niko and wondered what sex would be like with him. I imagined him being tender and gentle. I could tell from the few kisses we shared that I loved the feel of his lips on mine. It would be easy for me to guide him through my desires. I impulsively picked up my phone and sent a text to Niko. *I'm at the lake with some friends. I'm sitting on the porch and thinking of you.*

Melanie exhaled deeply and reached over to retrieve the joint in a foggy haze. "My gyno dismissed me."

"What the hell are you talking about?" I asked, unsure if I wanted the answer.

"My gynecologist said I didn't need to continue my annual visits. She said *at this age,* and since I had a hysterectomy, there wasn't much left to examine."

"So, your vagina is too old?" Jeannie said, looking serious. "One time, my gynecologist told me my vagina had atrophied and that I would lose it if I didn't use it."

Ellen released an energized rush of air. "I think my vagina is getting younger now that I am using it more."

We all laughed and ate more ice cream.

Jeannie got up and started for the door.

"Where are you going?" Ellen asked her.

She turned and glanced over her shoulder. "I'm going to see if there are cookies."

With that, we all became breathless from the laughter.

"We never talked about the Craft Barn," I told Jeannie.

"Yes, the finances look good. We should do it," Jeannie said with her eyes closed. "I researched the property and found the taxes are reasonable, the zoning is up to code, and the location offers sufficient parking."

"Works for me," I said.

"I think we should change the name to just The Barn," Melanie offered.

SO, FOUR OLD LADIES SAT on a porch with golden autumn winds blowing around them. We looked at the lake, smoked a joint, and talked about our vaginas.

And that's how four old ladies expanded their business.

CHAPTER TWENTY-EIGHT

I FINISHED MY WORDLE in the last attempt. Thirty-nine consecutive guesses—a new record for me. I often lost my patience after four lines and gave up. I looked at the time on the phone: 8:30. Usually, I would have been up, dressed, fed, and out the door by now. But I had come to enjoy my lingering time in the morning. The many years of being at the office by 7:30 were long behind me, and I was living the reward now. Through the window, I could see the first dog walk of the day begin. I watched as Dixie, Muffin, Ginger, and Harley rambled by. Each one marked their territory on my little patch of ground.

Fall had been kind this year. The windows were open, allowing the morning air to find its way to me as I lay in comfort and solitude. The copper sun outside my window signaled the promise of a beautiful day.

I sat back on my new bedding, sans sailboats and anchors, and reflected on the status of my life. All in all, things were going well—better than expected, actually. The bank approved our business proposal with a sizable loan. Next month, Melanie, Jeannie, and I would take ownership of The Barn.

Jed had been going to therapy and proclaimed that he was changing. We'd started our divorce proceedings and even reached a financial agreement, much to Jed's delight. I was more than generous. I had to let go of my anger to allow myself to move on. And I'd seen Niko a few times this past month. He was busy caring for Alex, who was back at Calvert Towers, where they'd moved him to the assisted living section. I'd had only two short visits with Niko's father. Alex was always pleased to see me, but I was concerned that I tired him out quickly.

It was always good when I could say that my children and grandchildren were all well. And, right now, they were. Nathan and Josh were awarded the Breslin proposal. Nicole and Eric were busy with their never-ending renovations to the house.

All five grandchildren were coming over tomorrow for pumpkin carving. So, you see, all was right in my world.

After a few more minutes of basking in the drift of the sun, I forced myself out of the comfort of my bed. I pushed away the comforter, noticing my feet and that I was badly in need of a pedicure. I put that on my list of things to do today.

I heard the arrival of a text, jarring me out of my self-congratulatory mood. I was delighted to see that it came from Niko.

Good morning. Do you have time to get together today? I've missed you.

Yes, I would like that. I've missed you, too. I'm so sorry, but I've been busy preparing everything for the new building.

As long as you aren't avoiding me.

Not at all. Would you like to come to my house later?

Yes, sounds wonderful. Does 3:00 work for you?

Perfect, see you then.

This would be Niko's first time at my home. I realized I had to clean the house and make it look more organized. Hmmm, I didn't really have time for a pedicure, but it wasn't like he would be seeing my feet, right?

"WHAT ARE YOU DOING?" Ellen asked when she called me. "It sounds noisy."

"I'm getting a pedicure."

"So nice. Tim and I are shopping for things I need for the tearoom. I was surprised when he agreed to go with me. Of course, ever since I started wearing lingerie, he agrees with everything I want."

"That's awesome on both accounts. By the way, Niko is coming to the house this afternoon."

"Is that why you are getting a pedicure?"

"No, we aren't anywhere near the exposed toe part of our relationship. But we are enjoying an interesting flirtation. Niko's very sensual, and he makes me feel alive."

Ellen sighed loudly. "Anything that keeps you away from Jed is a good thing. Enjoy. Talk to you later. And, by the way, go with lipstick red for your toe color."

I nervously walked several times from the bedroom to the dining room and then to the living room, waiting for Niko. I started pacing at 2:30 and didn't stop until I saw his car pull into the driveway at 3:05. I gave him a little leeway for being 5 minutes past his expected arrival time.

Niko handed me a spectacular bouquet of yellow roses. "It's so good to see you. Hmmm, you smell delicious."

"These are gorgeous, thank you so much. I can't believe you remembered."

"Of course, when we were at Maggiano's, you said they were your favorite flower."

I inhaled the flowers deeply, taking in their essence and delight that Niko remembered. I arranged them in my favorite vase and set them on the kitchen table. Then I pointed to the kitchen table. "Please sit."

"Andi, your home is lovely."

"Thank you. It's nice to have you here. How is Alex?"

"I know he's unhappy being in assisted living, but he doesn't complain. It's unlikely that he will be able to return to independent living."

Character lines formed from the crease of Niko's deep chocolate eyes, which now showed signs of weariness. I reached for his hand and held it tightly.

"Would you like to see the rest of the house?" I asked Niko, still holding his hand and leading him up to the loft first. I noticed him looking, with disdain, at some of Jed's things which still remained in the house. In particular, the montage of photos on the stair wall as we ascended to the loft. There were pictures of my children and grandchildren, some without Jed but many with him. I had removed the wedding photo on my dresser the day Jed moved out, but I hadn't thought about the photographs elsewhere.

I had also removed the wretched portrait of our blended family from the den. You could see the disdain between the two groups. It was like the Senate House with Republicans and Democrats on opposite sides of the aisle. We were never a happy bunch. Some tolerance, some acceptance, but never happy. It's a wonder Kathleen wasn't in the family photo, flanked by Jed. My sweet, loving, and accepting Josh was the only family member who got along with everyone.

As Niko and I walked downstairs, I heard the garage door opening.

"Oh shit." I was unsure if I'd said that loud enough for Niko to hear. I held my breath, hoping it was one of the kids, even though they'd never used the garage entrance.

Niko and I had just reached the bottom of the stairs when Jed walked in with a bouquet of flowers. Really oh shit, this time.

Jed looked at me, then at Niko.

He gestured with the flowers to Niko. "Hello, I'm Jed, Andi's husband." Jed looked pale and thin.

"I'm Niko. Nice to meet you, Jed." Niko said to Jed with more than slight gravel in his voice.

"Jed, what are you doing here?" I asked him.

"Besides bringing you flowers, I brought some salt for the water softener. I noticed it was low the last time I was here." Jed reached into the cabinet for another vase for the flowers he had brought. "Yellow roses, good guess, Nick, they are her favorite," Jed said, intentionally calling him Nick instead of Niko as he set the vase next to the roses.

"Andi told me they were her favorite flowers on our first date."

"First date?" Jed said with a loud inhale.

I motioned my head towards Jed. "Can we talk in the other room?" I knew I had to derail this conversation before things got worse.

Just then, Niko sat at the kitchen table, staking his ground and making it known he wasn't about to leave. That would have been fine, except that he sat in Jed's seat.

I'd had enough of this dick-measuring, chest-puffing bullshit.

I suddenly wished I was back in bed when I was reveling in the status of my personal life. I was unnerved by having both Jed and Niko in the kitchen. I grabbed Jed's arm and led him into the bedroom.

Jed shrugged my hand off his arm once I'd closed the door. "Just how long have you been dating this guy? When was your *first* date?" The cold edge in his voice made me uncomfortable. I could see his arms were shaking a little under his hoodie with the sleeves pushed to his elbows.

"How dare you! You are such an arrogant, narcissistic, controlling bastard. You have no right to question anything I do. It is none of your business where I'm going, what I'm doing, and with whom I am doing it."

"I would prefer you not have another man in OUR home while we are still married."

"And I would have preferred that you hadn't slept with other women while WE were married!"

"So, this is retaliation?"

The depth of Jed's anger can be frightening, so I tried to restrain him gently by putting a soft touch on his arm. "No, this is me living my life without you." My pulse beat hard and thick as I tried to usher Jed out of the bedroom, biting my tongue and trying not to say more. I knew Jed was reaching his anger limit. I didn't want him to raise his voice more and I wasn't sure if Niko was out of listening range.

Regardless of the horrible things Jed had done to me, I still felt a sting of sadness for him as he looked at another man in the house that he had shared with me. The same man who was sitting in the chair that once was his.

Niko stood up as Jed and I entered the kitchen. Jed moved closer to Niko. He stretched himself taller, as he always did when he tried to intimidate someone, with his height. But the four inches made little difference, with Niko holding his stance, firmly looking Jed in his eyes.

As I watched their macho competitiveness, I nearly burst into laughter. I tried to compose myself and escorted Jed to the door.

"Are you ready to go to dinner, Andi?" Niko asked with a light touch on my shoulder.

Dinner? I thought to myself, we had no plans for dinner, and it was 3:30.

I regarded Jed and Niko with an expression that indicated I wasn't entirely pleased with their interaction.

"Yes, I just have to grab a jacket." Then, I realized I didn't want to leave them alone. "Never mind, I don't think I will need anything."

Puzzled, Jed shuffled his feet and reluctantly headed out the door.

I attempted to quell our discomfort once we were settled in Niko's car.

"I'm sorry, I wasn't expecting Jed to stop by."

"Does he do that often? With flowers?"

"No, not often. Our divorce will be finalized soon."

"I noticed he still has a lot of things in the house."

I started to feel annoyed that Niko had so much to say about my relationship with Jed. We hadn't even established our own relationship. Niko's face lost his perpetually easy-going smile as he waited for my answer.

"I know Jed, and it is best to let him move at his pace. He becomes angry and vindictive easily, and it's best not to provoke him. Please trust me."

"You're not the one I don't trust."

We both had settled uncomfortably in his car. "Where are we going? It's kind of early for dinner," I observed to Niko. "And, unplanned."

"Let's just drive for a bit and stop somewhere. Okay, with you?"

"Why don't we visit with your father first since we have time."

Niko nodded his head in agreement but, unfortunately, wanted to continue talking about Jed. "Andi, it seems as though Jed has the freedom to come and go in your home. It was a little unsettling to me."

"I know it was uncomfortable for all of us. Jed still feels responsible for the well-being of our home, and I'm trying to make this as comfortable as possible until the divorce is final."

"Our home?"

"After being married for 25 years, it's an adjustment to

living there alone. Jed took care of everything in the home, and I'm sure he's trying to be considerate."

"I've never been divorced, so I can't completely understand. But, if you have any thoughts of staying together with Jed, let me know so I can step aside."

I reached over for his hand in reassurance. "Niko, I have no desire to stay married. I am happily moving on."

He looked momentarily relieved by what I was saying, but then an unsettled expression was on his face. "I seriously doubt that Jed is moving on. He obviously loves you and is still hoping for a reconciliation."

"I can't control what Jed does or feels. I never could. But I know how I feel."

As we pulled up to Calvert Towers, I was relieved to not have to continue the conversation.

Walking to Alex's room, it was readily apparent that Niko was a regular visitor, and the staff greeted him warmly and with much familiarity.

"Mr. Cirillo, you have visitors," the attending nurse said while propping Alex on the pillows.

"Nikolai and Andrea, what a lovely surprise." Alex was weak-voiced and pale. His face was without his typical expressive Greek eyes. His use of our full names was endearing.

"Alex, it's good to see you," I said, kissing him on his cheek and squeezing his hand.

"Hi, Dad. You're looking good this afternoon," Niko said, turning to the nurse for any indication of his father's progress.

"Your father is doing well today," she said, winking at Alex. "He's our favorite patient."

Alex's eyes were glossy from the heavy medication. "I've been thinking about your mother today. One of my favorite things was watching her brush her long chestnut hair while sitting at her vanity. There were all kinds of lotions and creams on the top. I used to tell her she was so beautiful that no magical creams could make her more ravishing and ..." Alex's voice trailed off.

"Dad, we are going to let you rest," Niko said.

"Thank you for coming to visit. It is so good to see you both."

THE CAPTAIN'S TABLE is a charming Calvert County hotel/restaurant, a favorite among tourists. As we pulled up to the restaurant, the outside was aglow with twinkling autumn lights. The framed doorstep was impeccably decorated with purple, burnt orange, and yellow mums.

When Niko opened the door and stepped aside so that I could enter first, I walked into a room delightfully decorated for fall. The smell of pumpkin and spice wafted through the welcoming air. The stairs to the second floor were aligned with candle-lit pumpkins of varying shapes and sizes on each step. The main room was also tastefully set with monochromatic white pumpkins, gourds, and mums. Autumnal taper holders made of real pumpkins and gourds held white candles. It was Halloween on steroids, and I loved it.

The waitress seated us by the picturesque dining room window, which offered a magical view of the Patuxent River. The outdoor patio included rows of seating topped with orange throw blankets and pillows. It was a perfect romantic setting for a Hallmark movie. I hoped it would remove traces of the tension from earlier.

I looked down at my tan-checked pants and sweater and wished I had grabbed my fur-lined cream vest to add style. "I feel so underdressed."

"You look lovely, as always."

I pointed to the walk-in fireplace on the side of the main room, lined with more white twinkling lights, varying-sized lit candles, and white pumpkins. "The only fall decoration I have in my house is a single lonely mum plant."

Niko put his head back in laughter. "I know, when I get home, I'm going to see if I have any Halloween decorations. What was your favorite Halloween costume when you were a child?"

I rested my hand on my cheek and tried to recall my favorite costume. "Oh, I know. I must have been around 10 or 11, wearing my older cousin Marielle's cheerleading outfit. I had high aspirations of being a cheerleader just like her."

"And, did you become a cheerleader?"

I let out a sigh. "No, I was too tall, awkward, and gangly. So I played basketball instead."

Niko smiled and leaned forward. "Ahh yes, the infamous foul shooter."

I bowed my head slightly in recognition. "And, what was your favorite costume?"

"That's easy. My best friend, sister, and I dressed as Wizard of Oz characters. My sister was Dorothy, my friend was the Tin Man, and I was the Cowardly Lion. My mother went into great detail making the costumes for us, and everyone was envious. We stood out when all the other kids were ghosts and pirates."

Our waitress, Alana, was a lovely woman dressed in a tuxedo-style pantsuit, her hair in an elegant French twist. She suggested a Spicey Pomegranate Martini, to which we agreed.

We clinked glasses, and Niko said "Yamas," which I now know is Greek for Cheers. I watched as his sensual lips touched the glass and let my mind wander for a sweet minute.

I moved aside the centerpiece of faux autumn aspen tree branches in thick stone canisters to get a full view of Niko.

Niko's tongue touched his bottom lip, removing a drip of the orange liquid. I took a sip of my own drink. When I sat my drink down, it looked like Niko was staring at the lipstick smudge I had left on the rim of the hand-cut glass. This was getting too heavy, too soon. I almost asked the waitress for ice cubes.

Snapping myself back to the moment, I tilted my drink to him. "Well, I'm in the holiday mood now."

"Tell me about your favorite Christmas memory as a child," Niko said, still holding his Martini.

I collected myself and wiped away the invading images of Niko's mouth. "It was the year my youngest brother, Michael, got a bike for Christmas. My family had seven children, so there were plenty of hand-me-downs, especially for Michael. By the time a bicycle was given to him, it had already been used by his three older brothers and was in pretty bad shape. He always asked for a new bike, and when he was nine, he was given one for Christmas."

"So, your favorite memory was when your brother got a gift he always wanted?"

"Yes, no gift has ever made me happier. I can still recall the excited look on Michael's face and his tears of joy. Tell me about your favorite Christmas."

"In Greece, boats symbolize moving towards a new life. On the islands, many people decorate their boats for Christmas like we decorate trees here. Every year, my father would give Corrina and me model boats, and we would decorate them with fabrics, little shells, and anything we could find."

"Did you continue this tradition with Becky?"

"We did, and now I decorate them with my grandchildren, Noah and Aubrey." Niko sat back, ever so the proud grandfather.

"That sounds so amazing." I was enjoying seeing this softer side of Niko: the son, the father, the grandfather, the principal, and my date.

Alana came over with a smile and our first course, acorn squash soup served in pumpkin stoneware-lidded bowls.

There was no conversation between us as we watched each other spoon smooth puree into our mouths. I wonder if neighboring diners were watching the two senior citizens and their attempt at seduction.

When we finished our soups, Alana quickly brought over our entrees.

I tried to delicately cut my braised chicken thighs with butternut and spinach. I instantly regretted my order. The chicken was heavy with garlic, and the spinach was instantly stuck between the tiny gap in my bottom teeth.

I let go of my nervousness when Niko leaned over the table to feed me a forkful of his Scallops Genovese. The simple gesture of Niko giving me a taste of his dinner seemed so personal and sensual. I handed him several forkfuls of my chicken so we would be equally garlicked up.

Niko spotted the waitress, and with a smile, he pointed to our empty martinis for two more glasses. I put my hand up to decline another drink but changed my mind with a slight gig-gle.

I stood up to use the restroom, and as I walked, I slowed, hoping Niko was watching. I couldn't resist looking back. There he was, indeed, watching my every move.

While the afternoon may have been uncomfortable, our evening was perfect, from the spirit of the historical inn to the magnificence of the food and my companion.

Once we returned to my house, I invited Niko in, where we settled comfortably on my suede beige sectional.

"Jed won't be stopping in tonight, will he?"

"No, definitely not."

I stared at his face for a long moment before tentatively reaching out my fingers to touch his face. With the utmost re-serve, I only touched his cheek.

Niko reached his hand to cover my fingers. "I had a fabulous evening, Andi," Niko spoke evenly with his words measured. "I really like spending time with you. I have to admit I have reser-vations knowing you are still married and your husband's attachment to you."

I allowed the smile on my face to grow larger. "So did I. It was perfect. And please don't worry about Jed. There are just a few things we have to work out."

I felt simultaneously bold and shy. The need to feel his touch blossomed deep everywhere within me. His eyes told me he was going to kiss me. I tried to convey to him my desire for the same.

I moved my head closer just as Niko did. I felt the warmth immediately from his soft, subtle lips. I turned around and set-tled myself against the billowy couch cushion so we could face each other. Niko's smiling eyes met mine and I easily sunk into his warmth.

"You look tired. Let me rub your feet."

I removed my socks and shoes and put my feet on Niko's lap. Boy, was I glad I had gotten a pedicure with lipstick red polish.

CHAPTER TWENTY-NINE

"It's okay, Kendall, just stick your hands inside the pumpkin and pull out all the gunk," I said to my youngest granddaughter.

"But my hands will get really dirty."

Madison pulled out piles of pulp and seeds from her pumpkin with aggression. "This isn't anything compared to mud." She'd had a new kind of toughness since the mud run and our fishing excursion.

Kelli placed a towel under her very apprehensive young cousin's pumpkin. "Kendall, I'm going to carve your pumpkin with moon and stars, and then you can paint on it."

Lisa stepped forward to supervise her young son amongst all the women. "Andrew, we aren't going to carve your pumpkin. We are going to paint it with all kinds of colors."

Andrew looked disappointed and reached his hands into Madison's pumpkin.

Brooke held out a gift bag to me while she glanced at Kelli, who presented me with a huge smile. "Hey, I've got something for you, GMOM."

I opened the bag and took out a purple sweatshirt with *BEST EFFIN' GRANDMA* in white lettering on the front.

I hugged Brooke. "This is fantastic," I said. I slipped it on and showed it to Lisa, who didn't seem to find it amusing at all.

"What's an effin, Grandma?" Kendall asked Brooke.

"It means she's a funny grandmother," Brooke said, barely able to contain her laughter.

I took the sweatshirt off and put it back in the bag. "I love it," I quietly said to Brooke and Kelli.

"Brooke, did you tell Grandma about the Sisterhood of the Moon Festival?" Kelli asked.

Brooke touched my arm, "GMOM, we have to do this! It's next spring at a campground in Cape May. It's a four-day festival for women."

Kelli twirled in circles and waved a towel through the air. "There will be ritual ceremonies, yoga, dance, divination, shamanic healing, and moon howling. We will be staying in tents, but it's called glamping with running water and real beds."

Brooke nudged my shoulder. "Think of it as a slumber party with soul in the spirit of sisterhood. It's your kind of thing, GMOM."

Kendall came over to me and hugged my legs. "Can I go glamp at the moon, too, Grandma?"

Lisa looked at Brooke, Kelli, and me and shook her head. "Kendall, I don't think your mother will let you go away for four days, especially not to a Wicca Festival."

Not able to control her annoyance, Brooke corrected Lisa. "Aunt Lisa, the festival has nothing to do with witchcraft. It's about women bonding and sharing experiences."

Madison looked over at her aunt with a smirk. "I'll be allowed to go. I do everything with the grownups now."

Lisa's signs of disapproval had both Brooke and Kelli rolling their eyes. I gave the girls a stern look, hoping they would exhibit more kindness to their aunt.

"Madison, your mom is invited, too. It's for all females, any age," Brooke said without looking at Lisa.

"Of course, I will go," I said. "It sounds fabulous. What did your mom say?"

Kelli looked at me with a smile. "That's the best part. She's the one who told us to ask you."

Ellen impatiently waved a brochure in our faces. "We've got to go to this seminar."

Per Ellen's persistent request, Melanie, Jeannie, and I met her at Harvest for lunch. I'd noticed a change in Ellen recently. Her typical black wardrobe had been replaced with shades of purple and red. Today, she wore a bright orange sweater over orange and brown leggings.

"I like the necklaces," I said, pointing to the multiple strands of silver in varying lengths around her neck.

"I just bought them," Ellen said. "At Sweet Repeats, as a matter of fact."

"Your sex life still going strong?" I asked her with a lilt to my voice.

Ellen looked at me smugly. "No complaints from me and certainly none from Tim."

The headline for the brochure Ellen was so anxious to show us read: **WILD AND WISE OLD WOMEN**

Melanie scanned the rest of the text. "Listen to this," she read out loud. "Join us for a gathering of wild, wonderful, wise old women, filled with positive, uplifting, and inspiring energy. Regardless of your age, be a woman who flies directly into the face of ageism and sexism. Do not walk meekly on the road to old age."

Melanie lifted her eyes in approval. "This actually looks really interesting."

"Apparently, three older women offer a seminar with classes and events of interest to older women like us," Ellen said. "Look at the class titles."

WOMB WALK & TALK

CHANNEL YOUR INNER CHILD

SPIRITUAL EMPOWERMENT

BE A CRONE GODDESS

"I think we should go," I said. "I could wear my Best Effin' Grandma sweatshirt. Brooke and Kelli were just telling me about a Sisterhood Festival next year. Seems like something is in the air. Or were all these events available before, and I was too busy to notice?"

Ellen looked at me with her newfound empowerment. "Sometimes things don't make themselves available until we are ready."

I looked at Ellen with amazement. "Whoa, Dalai Lama, when did you become so spiritual? Did the lingerie change you that much?"

Ellen tilted her head. "In some ways, yes. Let's just say I feel more liberated."

Melanie enthusiastically read from the brochure. "Oh, I

like this: 'Wild Women Can Never Be Changed. Love every age of your life, and don't fear passing through any of them. Every stage has its own magic.'"

Melanie looked over at Ellen as she returned the brochure to her. "Where did you get this?"

Ellen put the Wild and Wise Woman brochure in her purse. "Well, I guess no one else filled out the customer form at Lacy Silhouettes."

"What does the lingerie store have to do with this?" I asked.

"On the customer form, along with other information, it asks for your age. Perhaps they sponsor it or know the people putting on the event."

Jeannie gently folded her hands in front of her. "They obviously have targeted the correct demographic and psychographic audience."

And that was how we ended up becoming Wiser and Wilder Older Women.

TEN DAYS LATER, Melanie, Jeannie, Ellen, and I drove the hour and half-long ride to Baltimore for the Wild and Wise Woman Seminar. The event was held at a banquet hall in a first-class, charming hotel in the center of town.

As we walked into the hotel and followed the signs for the seminar, we saw many similar-aged women heading in the same direction.

Melanie opened the door and entered the ballroom first. "Whoa, look at the attendance. There must be more than 200 women here."

Through the sea of predominately gray hair, I saw women ranging in age from around 60 to 95. Once we signed in, we sat in one of the many rows of seats.

Three women sat on the stage in front of us and introduced themselves.

A woman with zebra-striped pants, a red beret, and a sassy smile went first. "Hello, my name is Eleanor and I am 90. We are here to impart wisdom to our fellow sisters that we have learned through our journeys." Eleanor paused momentarily, took several deep breaths, crossed her zebra legs, and sat up straighter. "It's time to stop trying to please everyone. It's now time for just you." She swept her arms around the room. "At our age, we have lost our fertility, much of our external beauty, and physical activity, too. We have lost some of our eyesight and hearing and are now faced with a body that does not obey us. But what we do have is wisdom. The wisdom we have gathered on this journey is of tremendous value to others and ourselves. We hope you will enjoy the four classes we have put together for you." She put her hands together, bowed her head slightly, and said, *"Namaste."*

The next woman stepped down the three stairs from the stage, wearing a tomato-red jumpsuit. Her lipstick and blush matched the ensemble. She topped it off with flowered platform sneakers. "My name is Harriet, and I am 83," she began. Her hands shook as she held the microphone. "Ladies, I want you to remember one thing: it's a grand life if you don't weaken. I was diagnosed with Parkinson's ten years ago. At first, I resigned myself to a bleak future that would end all the activities I enjoy." Harriet turned and pointed to Eleanor. "Until I met Eleanor, and she changed my life. She encouraged me to look my Parkinson's in the eye and do everything in my power to prevent it from weakening me. I take boxing and line dance classes and am quite good at ping pong." Harriet motioned to the third and younger woman on the stage, who helped Harriet up the stairs to return to her seat.

Harriet handed the microphone to the younger woman, who was impeccably outfitted in a magnificent mid-length, belted Christian Dior shirt dress. The signature piece of her ensemble was an eight-strand white resin set of pearls with a gold and mirrored clasp. She had long, gray, braided hair that nearly touched her waist. She was beyond gorgeous; she was magnificent. I had an immediate reverence for each of the women.

"Welcome, my name is Lydia, and I am 74," she said. "Once we realize that no matter what age we are, we are still vital beings with life experiences to share with others, we can be less consumed with what others think of us and more aware of who we are. One of my favorite inspirational sayings is, *What would you do if you knew you could not fail*? Think about that, ladies; what is something you are too afraid to do that would bring you happiness?" She put both hands on the belt of her magnificent dress and did a little shimmy.

Laughter came from the audience as we each thought of the things we had always wanted to try. You could hear the women in the audience whispering their secret desires.

Jeannie leaned over and said to us. "I always wanted to try scuba diving."

Melanie giggled. "I want to go bungee jumping."

Ellen sat up with pride. "I want to try every position in the Kama Sutra."

I was concerned that our giggling would upset the seminar leaders, but Lydia looked at the four of us with a wink.

Lydia walked closer to Ellen and said soft and low. "I recommend the *Blossoming Position.*"

Without hesitation, I said, "I've always wanted to go to a nude beach."

As Lydia walked back upstage, she handed the microphone to Eleanor. "If I was going to give my younger self advice, I would say, be authentic. Love deeply and often, show your love to the people in your life, and do so authentically. Never stop being who you are to please someone else. Rid your life of toxic people and things," she said.

Eleanor clapped her hands. "There is just one more thing," she said, pointing to the room's entrance. "You may have noticed the empty pail by the door. This is called our *Fuck It Bucket.*" Eleanor waited for the light laughter and chatter to stop before she continued. "Next to the bucket are sheets of paper with the following words: *I now release all that no longer serves me for total healing, purification, and transmutation for the best and highest good.* When you leave, I want each of you to take one, and below the sentence, I want you to write something that has been preventing you from living your best life."

The audience was eerily quiet as we listened to Eleanor.

"After you have written down whatever has been causing you darkness, I want you to tear up the paper and put it in the Fuck It Bucket. Feel the lightness as you release what has been suffocating you."

Everyone smiled and applauded while we thought of what was hampering us.

Lydia stood up and put her hands together. "Each class runs for 30 minutes. Please enjoy."

AT THE END OF THE DAY as we left the seminar, Melanie said, "Well, my womb is full from walking and talking."

Jeannie stopped us. "I liked how Lydia talked about being in charge of our own happiness. I know it's true, but it's something I have to keep reminding myself."

"I'm so glad we went," a very excited Ellen said. "These are things we weren't taught while growing up. I wish someone had told me about tapping into my Divine Feminine Energy when I was younger. I'm being serious. I've never been comfortable talking about my femininity and sensuality. It's such a major part of our essence, yet we don't honor it."

I stopped walking and asked Melanie. "What are you doing?"

She was waving her arms in the air with her head held high and eyes closed.

"I'm communicating with my body through ecstatic dance," Melanie continued to twirl around the parking lot. "C'mon, join me."

And so, we did. The four of us danced to the music playing in our heads and moved to the individual beats. Soon, many women of all ages joined us, moving in their own rhythm throughout the parking lot. I felt a uniting of mind and spirit within myself and the merging of energies from other women.

Afterward, I slid into the passenger seat of Jeannie's incredibly immaculate beige Prius. "I'm anxious to get rid of anything in my life that I don't need or that doesn't bring me joy. We should find a way to integrate some of these lessons into The Barn."

On the drive home, we sat taller in our seats and felt the bond of our little Sisterhood group.

I thought of the paper I had put in the Fuck It Bucket—I released my uncertainty.

CHAPTER THIRTY

"MOM, I DON'T UNDERSTAND why you are meeting Kathleen," Nicole said. "She's Jed's ex. Are you forming a club of his exes? I'm sure there are others."

Oh if she only knew about all the others.

I was talking to Nicole on speakerphone while getting ready to go out. "Because she asked me to come over, and I'm curious about what she wants to discuss."

"I want to talk with you about something else. Lisa called me after the pumpkin carving at your house. She thinks you are pushing the girls into inappropriate conversations and activities."

I nearly tumbled over as I put one leg into my jeans while talking to Nicole. "They aren't *her* daughters. Is she worried I will corrupt Andrew?"

"I just wanted to tell you what she said. Maybe tone it down when she is around."

"Should I get one of those grandma sweatshirts? You know, like a tree with five apples with each grandchild's name, and *I PICKED THE BEST.*"

"I'm sure she would think it's more appropriate than Best Effing Grandma."

"That was a gift from YOUR daughters, and I love it." I realized that I was getting upset unnecessarily. Had I learned nothing from the Wild and Wise Woman Seminar? *Do not allow anyone to try and change you.* "It's okay, Nicole. Lisa is a wonderful mother and wife. She's entitled to her opinions."

"I've got to say, Mom, I don't know if it's due to your retirement or Jed being out of your life, but I like the new you. I'm glad Brooke and Kelli have you as a role model."

"Ahh, thanks, darling. I've got to go now and meet Kathleen. Love you."

Kathleen lived in the same house she and Jed had shared for many years. I pulled up to the Cape Cod home decorated with pumpkins and hay stalks. Skeletons and spider webs greeted me at the front door. Before I could ring the bell, Kathleen answered.

Kathleen greeted me with a half hug. "Thanks, Andi, for coming. It's good to see you." I received her hug with mutual acknowledgment.

I almost laughed at the imprint on her sweatshirt: *Grandma's little pumpkins.* Each pumpkin was personalized with her grandchildren's names. Kathleen is an attractive woman with perfectly bobbed mocha-colored hair, an athletic body, and always expertly applied makeup. She was a retired preschool teacher with sweet patience and kindness. She didn't deserve to have a husband who cheated on her. In many ways, I felt inferior to her. Kathleen always had time to make cupcakes for school birthday parties and events. She made Halloween costumes that usually won awards. She was involved in the PTA, knitted blankets for every new baby, and, of course, made the best potato salad. She also knew how to make perfect little melon balls for Jed.

After a few mundane pleasantries, the real conversation started.

"I assume you want to talk about Jed?" I asked her.

Kathleen walked me into their den, a dark but comfortable room with wallpaper resembling wood paneling. Four plastic pumpkins sat on the fireplace hearth, one for each grandchild. Two pillows on the couch said *Best Grandmom* and *Best Pop Pop* on either side.

I watched as Kathleen flitted around the room, wiping away invisible dust off the sofa cushion. She folded and refolded a warm-colored crocheted blanket. It was a house well-lived in with good bones and strong memories.

Kathleen pointed at the couch for me to sit. I sat uncomfortably next to Jed's Pop Pop pillow. She gave me a nervous smile before sitting beside her own personal pillow.

"Andi, you and I have never been friends, but we have always managed to be kind and to respect each other. I wanted you to know that Jed is living here now."

I held up the pillow as evidence. "I see." Might as well get everything out in the open right away. "Were you with my husband during my entire marriage?"

Kathleen cleared her throat and took a deep breath. "Yes, off and on. Just like you were with Jed when he was *my* husband."

"Kathleen, when I met Jed, he told me you were separated but still living together."

"He kind of said the same thing to me about you."

"And you believed him?" I looked at her incredulously. "Did you think we were separated for 25 years?" I wanted to punch the pillow right in the *Pop Pop*.

"We both know that Jed has been unfaithful. We also know he's wonderful in many other ways."

I looked at Kathleen harshly. "Do you think Jed will stop being unfaithful now that he's living with you? He doesn't exactly have the best track record."

"I know, Andi. But I believe him this time. He has promised me, and he realizes that, at his age, he needs to settle down. We've had several conversations about his infidelities. He's been going to therapy to work on his issues. He's promised to be faithful to me, and I believe him. We've even started couples' therapy."

I nodded wordlessly. I knew how much Kathleen wanted to believe Jed. I gave her a hesitant smile and stared uncomfortably at the plastic pumpkins.

Feeling more relaxed with the direction of the conversation, Kathleen stood up and walked into the connecting kitchen. "I'll be right back. I'll get us something to drink."

I looked around the room while she was in the kitchen. Pictures of Kathleen and Jed with their daughters when they were younger and pictures with their grandchildren were on the walls and the mantel. I picked up one of the photos and realized, by the age of their youngest grandson, that it had to have been taken last year. If Jed was going to be faithful to anyone, it would be Kathleen. They had a stronger history and a family bond that Jed and I never shared.

"Have some mulled cider," Kathleen said, placing the mule copper glasses on the coffee table in front of the couch. She set a bottle of whiskey next to the glasses. "I brought this, too, in case you wanted to make it a bit stronger." She excused herself and returned from the kitchen with a plate of pumpkin bars that I'm sure she had made earlier in the day for my visit. She really was perfect.

I sipped the warm, delicious bronze liquid, picked up the whiskey bottle, and added some to my drink. I held up the whiskey to Kathleen. She nodded affirmatively, and I passed the bottle to her.

Kathleen held her glass in both hands, curled her legs beneath her, and took a long swallow. I could easily picture her and Jed on their respective sides of the sofa, holding their cocktails while watching America's Got Talent. I tortured myself with thoughts of the two of them together during the time Jed and I were married. Did he complain to Kathleen about me? Or did they never discuss me the way that Jed and I rarely talked about Kathleen?

Kathleen's neatly glossed lips pursed together as she spoke. I never realized just how lovely she really is. "Jed and I are a family, and it means a great deal to me when we are all together. I never wanted the divorce, but he wanted you."

"And, now he wants you."

"Andi, I'm sorry if you feel that I took Jed away from you. Honestly, I never got over him leaving me for you. To me, he never stopped being my husband. I know most women would never have accepted what he did, but I loved him then and now." She took a long, controlled breath before continuing. "Unlike with you, Jed is the father of my children, and I've been able to forgive him more easily."

I lifted my glass in the air to her with a sincere smile. "I hope Jed remains faithful to you, Kathleen. I really do."

"I have to believe that Jed realizes he is not the hot young super stud he once was. I think he's ready to settle down and be faithful."

"I hope so, Kathleen."

Kathleen looked at me with a mixture of understanding and resolution.

I wondered if I should have told her about Renee and the others. But, by the look on her face, I think she already suspected.

A silver charm bracelet laden with varying trinkets clanged as she took a generous sip from her drink. I couldn't take my eyes off the colorful array of charms. There was an Eiffel Tower where I knew she and Jed had honeymooned, valentine hearts, and varying birthstones that must have represented her grandchildren. I might not have sweet reminders of my grandchildren on my clothes, pillows, and jewelry, but my grandchildren still think I'm the Best Effin' Grandmother!

I sat against the offending pillow, sipped my drink, and felt complete. It's hard to explain, but I was happy for Kathleen. I hoped Jed could see what a wonderful woman she is.

We chatted amicably for a few more moments about our children and grandchildren. Being with her like this was easy as I mentally passed Jed back into her arms.

I smiled as I walked out the door of the house that had once belonged to my ex-husband and his ex-wife and had now been returned to them.

I TOOK NOTE ABOUT THE GROWTH I'd achieved after my conversations this morning with Nicole about my daughter-in-law and then with Kathleen. According to the Wise, Wild Women, *growth never stops*; it's an everyday occurrence. The last two days have been about women's empowerment, but now I was ready for some time with Niko. I was delighted to receive his text.

Any chance I could see you today?

Sounds lovely.

Want to meet at my house? Around 5:00? I'll make us dinner.

Perfect.

Wow, how lucky was I? Another man who liked to cook. If I was meeting Melanie and Jeannie at The Barn, I didn't have time to change. I looked down at my jeans, dark blue sweater, and the short beige boots I love and decided it was sufficient.

Melanie and Jeannie were already at The Barn when I arrived.

Jeannie waved her arms around the room. "Can you believe this will be ours in two weeks?"

Jeannie's fruity ensemble for today was apparently pumpkin with her burnt orange corduroy pants and matching sweater.

"My granddaughter suggested we offer rental and sales of used prom dresses. Kelli said that many girls get dresses from Rent the Runway, which is still expensive. We could do bridal and formal wear, too," I said.

"I love the idea. Wouldn't it be great if we could offer some Women's Empowerment events here? Follow me." Jeannie led us to the second floor. "This entire section is used for vendor inventory and miscellaneous boxes of things we probably don't need. We could set up chairs and offer small classes of 25 people."

We walked up to the third floor, and I bent down and held my knee, cursing my boots that had made me feel so good an hour earlier. "That's fabulous, and it brings more people into The Barn, which helps with sales. We should put the prom dresses upstairs. The young girls won't be affected by walking up three flights."

Jeannie looped one arm around mine and the other around Melanie. "We really are doing this, aren't we? I never felt this excited before in my actuary career. It was a job, I was good at it, but it was a job. This is a labor of love for a good cause. With Sweet Repeats, The Barn, and Chuck, I don't remember ever having so much to look forward to."

I tightened my grip on Jeannie's arm. "Does that mean everything is going well with Chuck?"

"*When you find love, cherish it with your entire being,*" Jeannie repeated the words from one of the classes we had attended at the seminar.

Melanie looked over at Jeannie. "Love?"

Jeannie nodded at Melanie and then at me. "Yes, I am falling in love with Chuck, and it's amazing. I am myself around him, and simple things like walking with him are magical."

Melanie and I each embraced our fellow Wild Woman, rejoicing in her happiness.

WALKING INTO NIKO'S HOME was like entering the movie of his life.

Niko directed me to the family room, where we sat on his navy microfiber sofa with plaid cushions and a near perfectly matched throw rug on walnut hardwood floors.

I looked around the room with an overwhelming sense of comfort. "This is such a relaxing and inviting room."

"It's all Victoria," Niko said. "She was the designer and domesticator of our home. We've lived in this house since Becky was born. Sometimes I think it's time to move on, but the thought of packing and moving becomes daunting."

Niko showed me around, the signs of Victoria evident in each room with its carefully selected wallpaper and accoutrements. She obviously had impeccable taste.

Niko led me out of the kitchen's sliding glass doors. "The backyard of the house was my present to myself. I had a koi pond installed ten years ago. I've always been lured in by the tranquility of ponds." It was easy to imagine Niko sitting by the pond, introspective, with his dark, intense eyes.

"Niko, this is spectacular." The twenty-foot kidney-shaped pond had a slopping slate waterfall and colorful fish of all sizes.

"Maintaining the pond is a lot of work, but I find it therapeutic. We can sit on the patio and have dinner if it's not too cold. It should be done now."

Niko excused himself, leaving me on the patio while he checked on dinner. I picked up a small blanket on the patio chair and wrapped it around my arms.

I had never seen Niko in jeans before. His J.Crew light blue shirt was opened just enough for me to see the strength of his collarbone, and I wondered what it would feel like against my lips. I shook off these thoughts and walked closer to the pond.

I listened to the sound of the waterfall and transported myself to another dimension. I envisioned myself in this life. A quieter, more refined life with calm dinners and perfect evenings. And, like Jeannie said, I wanted to let myself enjoy life's simple things.

Niko set the platter of sweet-smelling tomato sauce and spices on the table, removing me from my visions. "This is Moussaka, a traditional Greek dish made with eggplant. I have fundamental culinary skills."

"This is more than basic skills," I said. "This is fabulous. I didn't realize I was so hungry. The only thing I've eaten all day is a pumpkin bar at Kathleen's."

"Is Kathleen one of your business partners at the shop?"

"No, actually, she is Jed's ex-wife. This is delicious," I said, trying to veer the conversation away from Jed.

"Why were you with her? Are the two of you friends?"

"She's really lovely and wanted to talk with me about Jed. They had been seeing each other throughout our marriage, and now they are back together."

Niko turned his chair to face me directly, showing a slight view of his tattoo and perfectly formed forearms. "Wow, were you aware of that?"

I would have preferred to end this conversation, sit with his arm around me, listen to the waterfall, and lose myself in his life for the rest of the evening. "All the signs were there, but I chose to ignore them. Jed is a very skilled and charming manipulator. I was happy in our marriage and assumed he was, too." I was not ready to discuss the intimate details of my marriage to Jed with Niko. I stood up and walked closer to the pond again. "I want to put it in the past and move on."

The darker intensity of Niko's eyes was making me uncomfortable. "It doesn't seem like Jed is moving on," he said.

I returned to my chair and took a sharp breath in. "I've asked Jed not to come to the house unannounced."

"I'm sorry. I am trying to establish where I fit in. You have so much in your life with your business and your family, including your ex. I don't like the guy, and he's very territorial around you. And I don't know where things stand with you and me."

I looked at Niko with a large smile. "I thought it was obvious how I feel about you. Yes, my life is more hectic now than I expected once I retired, but that doesn't mean I don't have the time or desire to be with you. I've had a lot of changes in my life the past few months, and I'm still in the process of putting everything together."

I needed a few minutes of silence between us to reestablish a comfort level. Gratefully, Niko sensed my hesitancy to continue the conversation.

Niko stood up, bent down to kiss me, took my hand, and offered me a smile. The darkness of his eyes had lightened. "It's getting chilly, let's go inside. I have baklava for dessert."

We sat in his family room, with the essence of Victoria in every nook. I felt like I was invading her space, the place where she lived and loved her husband. I understood how Niko felt in my home with traces of Jed and our shared life.

I pointed to a vintage secretary's desk with two stacks of perfectly organized files. "You have some really lovely pieces in your home." Everything in there was meticulous and pristine. Not a virtue of mine. I told myself I needed to tidy up before he came to my home again. He would be horrified if he looked inside any of my closets.

"Victoria and I enjoyed antiquing together. Some of these pieces were from my father when he downsized and moved to Calvert Towers."

I walked towards a floor-to-ceiling bookcase, admiring his collection of the classics, which were interspersed with photos of Victoria, Becky, and their life together. This is where Niko had belonged, just as Jed belonged to Kathleen. I didn't have that now. The thought temporarily made me feel lonely and sad. But then, I realized the fullness that I do have in my life.

I held up a photo from their wedding day. "Your wife was beautiful."

"Yes, she was, and we had a wonderful life together. I loved Victoria dearly and Andi, I know that she would want me to move on with my life. I have no problem discussing Victoria, but I want to get to know *you* better."

I ran my hand over the spines of books and touched the photographs of his life.

"Niko, I'm 70 and still finding out about myself. I am more comfortable now than I probably have ever been." I pointed to another picture of Niko, Victoria, and Becky together with their grandchildren. "Even though I have been married twice, I never felt this kind of marital devotion that I see in your pictures." I paced around his room, unsure if I wanted to sit and talk more or run out of the room and cry. "After Daniel died, it was a struggle. I had to work hard, very hard, to provide for my children. It wasn't easy; none of it was easy. Even with Jed, I was the provider. I felt pressure to succeed more, and soon we were living a lifestyle that wouldn't let me slow down."

Niko walked over and guided me to the couch. "Look at everything you have accomplished. Andi, you're an amazing woman. You should be proud of yourself and your accomplishments. Not just the success you created with your business but the strength of your family. That's all you, Andi. You did it all."

I couldn't stop the tears flowing from my eyes. "I know, but I was tired all the time. I'm trying to act so strong right now, but all my life, I had to be strong. I had to take care of everything for everyone." I tried to stand up, wanting to walk away from my unsteadiness.

Niko took my left hand and rubbed the spot that had held my wedding ring for 25 years. Then his hands pressed deeper into mine as we locked eyes. "It's okay, Andi. Don't stop the tears. Let them flow. It's okay to be vulnerable."

I wasn't able to control either the tears or my words. "Even as a child, I had to be strong. I was the oldest and helped care for my siblings. I never learned what it would be like to be taken care of, to not have to make things better for everyone around me."

It felt cathartic to speak the truth. "I'm strong, but it's a different form of strength. I falter easily when I feel attacked. I've always hid it, but I hurt easily. I'm a consummate people pleaser."

"You don't have to do that anymore."

My breathing had stopped being normal, and I couldn't control the irregular beating of my heart. "It's all I know."

Niko pulled me closer into his embrace. I allowed his arms around me to be the only thing I felt in the world. It felt so natural and comfortable to lean into him.

For that space in time, there was no tension, no anger, or sadness. Only a peaceful pause to my ever-changing life.

THE FOLLOWING DAY, I felt relaxed and energized, as if I had returned from a week-long vacation. An umbrella of calm covered me with tender memories of my evening with Niko. I had an urge to find order within myself and my surroundings. I started gathering numerous items I no longer needed and quickly filled two bags. As I was heaving the bags into the trunk of my car, I spied the hiding spot where I'd kept the stolen items from Jed. I couldn't help but smile as I added the white shirt, yellow sweater, and favorite jacket to the donation bags and then happily tossed those blue pills into the trash. There, now I'm making progress!

CHAPTER THIRTY-ONE

I WAS FRUSTRATED with the sounds gurgling in the pipes throughout the house. I called Jed out of habit. "Jed, I just woke up, and the water softener is making a lot of noise. I don't remember this ever happening before. Can I turn it off?"

"No, you can't just shut it down. I will be over in 15 minutes."

I looked at the time on the phone. "I've got so much to do today. We are meeting with an electrician at The Barn to deal with some wiring issues, and the contractor never showed up yesterday, so we have to deal with that. On top of that, Thanksgiving is in three days, and I haven't even started the shopping."

"I'll be right there, babe," he said and hung up.

I was irritated that Jed called me *babe,* but I appreciated that he could take care of the water softener.

I hurriedly dressed in jeans and one of Jed's old gray contractor sweatshirts. After hundreds of washings, his *Prime Remodeling* logo was barely visible.

I made my list for Thanksgiving while I waited for Jed.

AS THE DOOR OPENED, I caught the scent of Jed's Aramis cologne.

I moved away as Jed started walking towards me. "I'm sorry I had to call you," I told him.

Sensing my distance, Jed walked into the laundry room, opened the cabinet above the water softener, and removed a new filter. "When the blue light goes on, you need to change the filter. It's pretty easy. Just remember to turn off the water first. You take the filter off with the filter wrench and release the pressure ... are you listening to me?"

"None of that seems easy."

Jed winked at me with his *I'll take care of you, little lady* condescending look. "It only has to be changed every few months.

I can take care of it."

"No, Jed, I can do this. Next time it has to be changed, I will video you while you change it so I know how to do it."

As he put the tools away, Jed looked at me with sincerity mixed with sadness. "How about if you let me take care of it for you? I like doing things for you. I always have."

Jed pointed to the imprinted words running across my chest. "My logo looks damn good on you, Andi."

Jed opened another cabinet. "The heater filter needs to be changed, too." Jed unwrapped the cellophane and removed the filter. I'll take care of it since I won't be here to keep you warm."

I tried to look grateful as I closed the cabinet. "Jed, I appreciate everything you do for me, but I need to start taking care of things on my own. I can and I will."

He put the filter down and placed his arm around my shoulder. "It's hard to hear you say that. I don't ever want to stop doing things for you."

I took the empty filter box and put it in the trash can. Jed followed me and turned me around to face him. "Andi, I understand you and Kathleen had milk and cookies together."

"I don't know if pumpkin bars and whiskey are the same as milk and cookies. But yes, we had a rather pleasant conversation. Does that worry you?"

"It doesn't worry me, but it is odd, don't you think?"

"Kathleen wanted me to know that you are back together."

"I would rather be here with you. I never wanted to leave. You threw me out."

I looked at Jed incredulously. "Do you really want to go there again? Wouldn't it be wonderful for you to continue to go back and forth between Kathleen and me? You want it all, not just Kathleen. You also want other women, but it's time to settle down and be faithful to one woman only."

I couldn't stop pacing as a thousand words wanted to come out all at the same time. "Jed, you destroyed our life together. A life that I enjoyed and a marriage that I thought was successful. You took it all away."

I put my hand up to stop Jed from talking. He didn't deserve to justify his actions or express his feelings. I'd heard enough of his never-ending asinine immaturity.

Jed followed me from room to room as I attempted to gather the fortitude to not explode.

Jed grabbed my arm and tried to steady my movements. "We could have worked it out."

I shrugged off Jed's arm as I walked into the kitchen with him following me. "Jed, be with Kathleen, be happy. And try to be loyal to her. She loves and believes in you."

Jed straightened his posture and took a step closer to me. "Andi, I'm sorry, truly sorry."

The sound of my phone going off in the kitchen pulled me away from a conversation I didn't want to have again.

The text was from Melanie: *The contractor called, and he won't be able to come out until after Thanksgiving.*

"Shit."

"What's wrong?" Jed asked.

"It's the contractor for The Barn. He can't come out until next week. Look, thank you for taking care of the water softener and the filter for the heater. I truly appreciate it."

I grabbed my coat and purse and led Jed out of the kitchen. I instinctively leaned into him and kissed him on the cheek. Realizing I may have sent the wrong signal, I hurried to my car, and headed out.

JEANNIE AND MELANIE were already inside the barn when I walked in.

"We aren't officially opening until the first of the year, so we have time," Jeannie said unconvincingly.

"I was hoping the vendors could start setting up soon," I told Melanie and Jeannie. "And we need to take care of the front porch before it gets too cold."

Melanie put her hands on her hips. "Maybe we could fix the patio boards ourselves. Jack hurt his back and won't be able to help right now."

I looked at Melanie and took on her confidence. "Let's go

take a look. Maybe they just need to be nailed down. Do we have any tools?"

As we were walking outside, we heard the sound of a car pulling into the gravel driveway. I looked up and immediately recognized Jed's White Ford 150 Pickup. I walked over to his truck in confusion.

"What are you doing here?" I asked him.

Jed stepped out of his truck and grabbed his tool belt and box. "You seemed stressed about your contractor delay. Andi, just let me help you."

Before I could respond, Jed walked closer to the barn entrance.

He stood, legs slightly apart, taking in the exterior. He shook his head in approval. "Well done, Andi, this place is amazing."

Jed was always supportive of my business. He encouraged me to expand the agency, and he often had endless conversations with me about the direction of my company.

He walked over to the front porch where Melanie and Jeannie were standing. "Hello, ladies. It looks like you have a few floorboards that need mending."

Melanie and Jeannie exchanged confused but grateful glances.

I touched Jed's arm as he strapped his tool belt around his waist. "Jed, you really don't have to help." For many years, the gesture of Jed putting on his tool belt snugly on his hips caused an intense and immediate reaction for me.

Jed turned back towards me. "Andi, can you get the level out of the truck bed?"

I walked over to the truck to retrieve the level. While Jeannie showed Jed the loose panels, Melanie followed me to the truck.

Melanie sensed my apparent misgivings. "He owes you. Let him help out."

"It's just that I don't want to feel indebted to him."

"Don't overthink it. Jed's helping out, that's it."

I heard the phone ring in my back pocket. I handed the level to Melanie and answered the call. Knowing it was Niko, my mood immediately improved.

"Hi, how are you?" I said to him, smiling to myself.

"I'm good, thinking of you. How is everything?"

"Right now, I'm stressed. I'm at The Barn, and we've had a few issues with the contractor. Okay, if I call you later?"

"Of course. Want to get together this evening?"

"That sounds fabulous."

I hoped Niko didn't sense I was rushing him on the phone, but I was worried he would hear Jed's voice in the background. His concerns about Jed in my life were evident, and I wanted to remove any lingering issues he may have.

I heard the pounding of the hammer and the soft giggles of Jeannie, and I knew Jed was the reason.

I watched Jeannie as she nearly swooned over Jed. "Andi, isn't it wonderful? Jed has already fixed the floorboards and is going to look at the stairs now." Her five-foot little body adoringly looked up at Jed's six-foot-five frame. "I don't know what we would have done without you, Jed."

I noticed Jed widen his grin and flex his arms while hammering the boards sturdily into place. He glanced over his shoulder to make sure the women were witnessing his male prowess. I wondered how many women he had flirted and ultimately slept with during his contracting days.

I was tempted to tell Jeannie about Jed's multiple indiscretions. It was upsetting to see her nearly fawning over Jed.

Even Melanie, who had more of a bullshit meter than Jeannie, was falling victim to his charm.

Melanie looked at me with a slight nod to silence any of my objections. "Jed, could you help me hang this sign?"

She was correct. We needed the help, and I should be grateful to Jed. I tried to ignore the cute smiles and winks he threw my way while he assisted Melanie and Jeannie. When the electrician arrived, I showed him the outbuilding where we needed lighting installed.

No sooner had I finished explaining to the electrician where we needed the outlets and ceiling fan, when I heard the heightened sound of two male voices.

"I stopped by in case you needed any help, but I see that

you had already called someone," Niko said as he pointed to Jed, loud enough for everyone to hear.

"When I was at the house earlier this morning, Andi mentioned her contractor was delayed, so I came to help her," Jed said to Niko. "No worries, buddy, I could use an extra hand. Do you know how to use a Sawzall?"

"I think I can manage it, *buddy*," Niko said to Jed while looking at me. Niko heaved a sigh of discontent.

Niko looked at Jed and then at me, going back and forth three times. I knew he was assembling a puzzle with pieces that didn't fit and wouldn't see it correctly. He would only follow the wrong signs to his ultimate conclusion.

I stepped closer to him and touched his arm to show him solidarity. His eyes were almost accusatory and darkened in disappointment.

Melanie and Jeannie stood in place, not knowing what to say or do.

Niko took my arm. "Hey honey, I've never seen the guest house before." He glared angrily over his shoulder at Jed as we walked toward the house.

Not only has Niko never called me *honey*, but he has also never been to The Barn. Shit, this was not going well. I could not stifle my annoyance with both Niko and Jed, and I huffed loudly towards the house.

Once inside, I turned to Niko and put my arms around him. I wanted to make him less tense and assure him that there was no alternative motive for Jed to help out.

"He was at your house this morning?"

"Yes," I responded hastily, annoyed to feel his unfounded judgment.

Niko's typically warm, kind expression had turned dark with furrowed eyebrows and tight lips. "Andi, is something going on with the two of you? Are you still in love with Jed? Oh geez, are you sleeping with him?" His arms rose above his head in frustration. "That's not what I meant. It came out wrong." Niko's handsome face had broken into a scowl.

I watched Niko remove his jacket and roll his sleeves as if

preparing for a fight.

I focused my eyes on his with steady and slow breaths.

For a few short moments, I couldn't find my voice. "Niko, I don't feel I should have to explain anything to you, but I will. I called Jed this morning because the water softener at the house wasn't working. He heard me talking to Melanie about the contractor, but I did NOT ask him to come here. I did NOT ask for his help. I am grateful for his help, though, and I'm grateful you came by to help, too."

Niko dropped his head in frustration. "Look, Andi, I really care about you and enjoy our time together. You obviously have a lot going on in your life right now, and you are still in some kind of relationship with your ex-husband." Niko's voice grew husky. "Impulsivity isn't easy for me, and being with another woman wasn't part of my plan. But you came along, and I feel we have started a relationship. I can't do this with your husband lingering in your life."

I wanted to reassure Niko, but I also wanted him to trust my actions. Despite my nerves, I managed to keep my voice even. "Jed is my soon-to-be ex-husband, and our only relationship is two people who were married for 25 years." Each breath I took seemed labored and intensified. "I am neither romantically involved with Jed nor want to be. But just like you, I have a past."

Niko let out short, harsh breaths, and my words didn't seem to calm him. "But your past is still part of your present. I've been trying to establish a relationship with you, and Jed is always in the background. I want to do this, Andi. But I can't be a part of this when I feel like you are still holding onto Jed."

I wasn't prepared for this conversation, and my feelings were conflicted. I wanted to wrap my arms around Niko and beg him to understand. I wanted to tell him I was enjoying our relationship. But I was angry with him for not allowing me to explain the situation. I needed to be strong and not fall victim anymore. Why did I need to apologize? "Niko, I am not holding onto Jed, and we are not getting back together."

Niko took a few steps closer to me, and I thought he would

apologize for overreacting. But I was wrong. I wasn't expecting the words he said. "I think we shouldn't see each other anymore until you have figured out what you want and when you have more time for us. I can accept that your time is limited with your new project and your family, but I can't accept that your life is still so deeply involved with Jed's." Niko's mouth hardened as if he wanted to retract his words, and then he turned around, retrieved his jacket, and walked towards the door.

I blinked twice in disbelief. How could this be happening? How could I lose something that was just starting to blossom into something wonderful?

I resisted the temptation to follow him and beg him to stay. I stood silently while I digested his unexpected words.

JED, MELANIE, JEANNIE, and I worked diligently for the next four hours. I tried to keep my mind on the necessary tasks and off Niko. It was difficult, but I didn't want to wallow in sadness and the uncertainty that I had released into the Fuck It Bucket. I had spent too much time the past few months trying to escape devastation and pain.

Melanie approached me as I retrieved Jed's drill from his truck. "Do you want to talk? Are you okay?"

I looked at her with gratitude for her concern. "Hopefully, it was all an unfortunate misunderstanding. I'm sure Niko will call me later." I wasn't sure, but the hopeful part was correct.

Soon, Melanie's playlist of 60s music drifted through The Barn, allowing me to lose myself in the familiar songs.

Later that evening, sitting on the edge of my bed, exhausted from the draining day, I debated whether to call Niko. Instead, I chose to sulk over a bowl of rum-raisin ice cream and choco-late cookies.

I am a Wild and Wise Woman. I am strong, I am strong, I am strong.

CHAPTER THIRTY-TWO

THE HOUSE WAS CROWDED AND CHAOTIC. I watched the dynamics of my very different children and grandchildren as we gathered for Thanksgiving. I was so accustomed to Jed handling most of the preparations for family celebrations that I didn't realize all the effort he put into brining, prepping, and basting the turkey.

Jed and I celebrated and hosted the holidays in our home every year of our married life, especially Christmas. It was an open house for the days before and following Christmas. Jed created a unique Christmas cocktail every year, and I set out our special holiday dishes and crystal. I did all the shopping for gifts, and he did all the wrapping. Piles of packages adorned our tree, candles were in the windows, and holiday music filled the rooms in our home from Thanksgiving to New Year's.

Nathan came into the kitchen and rolled up his sleeves. "Okay, bird, I'm coming in."

I handed Nathan the carving knife and kissed him on his cheek.

When I put the serving platter on the table, Josh started to laugh. "Did Andrew carve the turkey?"

Lisa inspected the side dishes on the table. "I hope there aren't nuts in any of the food. I think Andrew may be allergic."

"No nuts, Lisa," I assured my daughter-in-law. "Who wants a roll?"

Everyone has their traditions on holidays; for me, one of our traditions was passing dinner rolls. I don't pass them. I throw them. This year, even Lisa showed less chagrin as I tossed her a roll. Perhaps she's coming around.

Josh clicked his glass and called attention. "Is everyone ready? Which two NFL teams have played a game on Thanksgiving Day since 1966?" he asked the group as part of his traditional holiday trivia.

"That's too easy, dude," Nathan said. "It's the Detroit Lions and Dallas Cowboys."

Josh held up the bowl of cranberry sauce. "How many ridges are there in a 14-ounce can of Cranberry Sauce?"

"17!" Brooke shouted. "You asked that one last year."

Kelli let out a cough. "And, why was the cranberry sad?"

Everyone looked at Kelli without an answer.

Kelli snickered, "I got you this time, Uncle Josh. It's because it was actually a *blue*berry."

I was prepared for Josh's annual trivia and did some online searching myself. "I have one," I said. "What do sweet potatoes wear to bed?"

Nicole rolled her eyes. "Oh, Mom, they wear yammies."

Kendall raised her hand excitedly. "Hey, Uncle Josh, why did the turkey cross the road?"

Before Josh could answer, Kendall shouted, "He wanted people to think he was a chicken."

Josh stood up and went over to his young niece. "Okay, Kendall, how do little pumpkins cross the road?"

Kendall looked at her parents and tapped her finger on her cheek. "I give up," she said.

Josh laughed, "I got you now. They do it with a crossing gourd."

The conversations were just as bubbly and fulfilling as the food and drink. Any mention of Jed remained off the table.

Long after everyone had left and the last dish was clean, I sat in the family room and thought of my many blessings. My children and grandchildren were all healthy and happy. I had a new, exciting venture with The Barn and many dear friends. I'd let go of my anger with Jed and wished him well. And, I had what I thought was the beginning of a new relationship.

I resisted the temptation all day to text Niko. I missed him so much. I missed what I thought we had started. Perhaps he was right, though. He wasn't right about my still wanting a relationship with Jed, but maybe I needed some time to adjust to my life alone. Yet, I couldn't stop the images floating in my mind of Niko sitting on the red Adirondack chair, watching his koi fish with a glass of merlot by his side. I wanted to be on the other side of him, talking about our day or just enjoying the soothing sounds of the pond and our light breathing.

I WAS FEELING FESTIVE, and on Friday, I sent a text to Nicole, Emily, Lisa, Brooke, and Kelli:

I've decided I want a real Christmas tree this year. I'm going to a farm tomorrow where you can chop down your own tree. You are taken on a hayride and select the tree you want. I think all the grandchildren would really enjoy the process. Who wants to go with me?

Nicole: *Seriously Mom? Since when did you become Paula Bunyan? After you chop down the tree, do you get dragged into a mud pile? I'll go just to take pictures!*

Lisa: *No, thank you, Andi. I would prefer Andrew not to be around saws.*

Emily: *I will come with Madison and Kendall.*

Brooke: *I'm in.*

Kelli: *Sounds great. I'm in, too.*

I had to laugh at Lisa's response. Did she think I was going to hand Andrew his own saw?

"CHOP! CHOP!" was the name of the Christmas tree farm, and we were armed and ready for the excursion. The twinkling lights strung around the rows of trees and the holiday songs played from the speakers were only surpassed by the hot chocolate and roasted chestnuts offered. I was certain this was going to be another positive female bonding experience.

It was a spectacular end-of-November afternoon with the sun warming the chilled air. There we were—seven women of varying ages, setting out to tackle a "man's" job.

We sang Christmas carols as we were pulled along on the hayride through rows of trees just waiting to be selected. Madison and Kendall sang loudly, pointing at me, when "Grandma Got Run Over By A Reindeer" came on the music loop. Everyone on the hayride looked at me with pleasure at the adoration of my grandchildren. Even Brooke and Kelli joined in the caroling. We were a picture-perfect family with our red and white Santa hats and giant smiles.

"There," Kendall called out as she pointed to a tree. "That one in the second row, it's perfect. Mommy, can we get that one?"

"Let's go check it out," Emily said, leading the way off the hayride.

"No, I want this one," Madison said, running to the end of a row, pointing at a bare pine.

Brooke and Kelli each picked their choice. None of us agreed on the right tree.

We finally took a vote and selected a six-foot Douglas Fir.

I held the saw in my hand and looked at the tree.

"Mom, do you know how to cut down a tree?" Nicole asked.

I looked at Nicole and the rest of my group. "It can't possibly be that hard."

Kendall twisted and turned in a circle. "I'm cold. I think I peed my pants," she said in a very unhappy voice.

Madison nudged her little sister in annoyance. "You think? You can't tell if you peed?"

My amusement continued as I listened to my little group.

"You spilled your damn cocoa on my legs, and I can feel it on my feet," Kelli said to Brooke while looking at the damp evidence.

"You're the idiot who wore Crocs to cut down a tree," Brooke said.

"That's not how you use a saw, Mom," said Nicole as she held up her phone. "Stay just like that so I can get a picture."

I looked at Nicole unamused as I fell against the tree just as she snapped the photo.

"Did you just fall in horse shit?" Brooke said, looking at me.

"Don't talk like that in front of the little ones," Emily said with apparent regret for being part of our dysfunctional group.

Emily looked at her shoeless child. "Kendall, why are you only wearing only one boot? Where is the other one?"

"I think she left it on the hayride," Madison said matter-of-factly.

"And you didn't think maybe you should pick it up for her?"

"No, but I really have to pee now, too."

"We're in the woods, go pee behind the tree," Brooke told Madison.

"Mommy, Brookie said I have to pee outside."

I looked over just in time to see Nicole taking pictures. "Mom, you look ridiculous. Can we just ask someone to cut it down for us?"

"Here, ladies, we can saw the tree for you," said two boys from Chop Chop whose interests were clearly in Brooke and Kelli and not in our tree. It seemed like a pair of boys were always around my granddaughters.

I handed them my saw. "Go for it," I said.

Within a few minutes, the boys cut and dragged the tree to the parking lot while intensely conversing with Brooke and Kelli.

"Thank you for your help," I told the helpful tree draggers. "We can take it from here."

After the two young men went on their way, I realized I'd dismissed them too soon. I looked at the tree and then at Emily's soccer-mom minivan. We somehow had to get the tree up on top.

"Mom," Nicole said, clearly exhausted from our tree excursion. "They will hopefully have someone here to tie the tree to the car for us."

"I'm sure Robby and Ethan can help. I'll go ask them," Brooke said, winking at Kelli.

"No, they've helped enough," Nicole responded with an edge of annoyance.

"Well, it looks like they are busy helping other people," I said to my dismayed little group. "We can wait."

Emily bent down to her two young daughters. "Can we just try and tie it ourselves? Kendall and Madison are muddy and tired, and I never found Kendall's boot."

Kelli nearly ran to the string bale. "Hold on, I can get some string." Kelli returned with a large spool of string along with Robby and Ethan.

The boys quickly hoisted the tree on top of the van.

While we sat in the car, I held the large spool of string and handed it to Nicole in the front passenger seat. She then tossed it to Robby, who passed it to Ethan and then back to me. I instructed Nicole to open the windows so we could secure the tree firmly to the minivan roof. We ran the string many times through and out of the vehicle, securing it tightly under the doors. All the while, the boys seemed more interested in talking with Brooke and Kelli and paid little attention to our task. Robby and Ethan closed the doors tightly, but not before slipping their phone numbers to my granddaughters.

An hour later, we were headed home. It was a quiet ride without the gaiety of Christmas music or the amusing chatter we had enjoyed when we embarked on the journey.

"You didn't realize we couldn't get out of the car when you tied the tree on the roof?" Emily said as the seven of us pondered how to get out of the minivan.

"I wasn't the only one who tied the string around the doors," I told Emily. "We did this together."

"Are we stuck in the car forever?" Kendall asked in tears.

"Oh, stop it, Kendall," Brooke said with annoyance.

"Stop yelling at me, Brookie," Kendall said in full-blown tears.

With an edgy laugh, Nicole said, "Mom, we can't just sit in your driveway forever. Can you call a neighbor and ask someone to bring a knife and cut us out of the car?"

"Stop exaggerating. None of us realized we were tying the string to the doors," I said.

"I called Nathan. He will be here in ten minutes," Emily said.

"WELL, LADIES, it looks like you have a bit of a predicament here," Nathan said through the open window.

"Stop taking pictures and get us OUT of here," I said loudly to Nathan.

Nathan folded his arms in front of the car and laughed. "Not just yet. I called Josh and Eric. I'm waiting for them to see this."

Still no word from Niko.

CHAPTER THIRTY-THREE

WHEN I OPENED THE FRONT DOOR to Sweet Repeats after a long Thanksgiving weekend and failed tree excursion, I was greeted with a blast of cinnamon, pine, and Christmas music.

"Chuck and I are talking about living together," Jeannie said as we decorated the shop for Christmas. A brilliant smile rocked her face. "Not right away, perhaps sometime next year."

Melanie nearly gasped on her mug of hot chocolate. "What?"

"Things have been going so well, and I want to enjoy every minute together. I'm shocked, too, but why not?" Jeannie bit her bottom lip in girlish excitement.

Our friend had fallen in love, and we couldn't be happier for her. I looked at Jeannie in her green Rudolph sweater with miniature red bells on the antlers and nose. I couldn't figure out if she was intentionally going for an Ugly Christmas Sweater look.

Then there was Melanie in red jeans and red and white candy cane leg warmers. I was no fashionista today, either. There was no apparent excuse for my pair of navy pants two inches too short with my sneakers that had previously been in vomit and dog shit and my pink Sweet Repeats sweatshirt. At least it was Monday, the store was closed, and we were out of view. We were decorating the shop for the holiday, but soon, we would be packing everything up and moving it to The Barn.

I pulled down my sweatshirt and wished I looked more festive. "Jeannie, I think it's fabulous. If we learned anything from our Wild Women Seminar, it's carpe diem. Seize the day." It wasn't just words I was saying. I meant them sincerely.

Jeannie took a deep breath. "I want to step out of the widow role I've been carrying around. When Wayne passed, I assumed my life would be on a continual hold pattern. Before Sweet Repeats and The Barn, my days were empty, and my nights lonely. I realize how much I've regretted not having children."

Jeannie put down the garland she was untangling for the window decoration. "I've never done anything impulsive in my life. I've followed a straight white line and did what was expected of me."

I looked at Jeannie with sheer delight. "I'm so happy for you." The spark in Jeannie's eyes was all that was needed to know this was right for her.

"I never thought I would find love again," Jeannie said with a smile that beamed from her face.

Melanie decorated the front window with red and green ornaments hanging from gold ribbons. "What about you, Andi? How is your *friendship* with Niko?"

I attempted to ease the tightness in the back of my eyes. "We aren't seeing each other right now. Niko was annoyed when he saw Jed helping at The Barn and assumed we were still together." I blinked away a lone tear. "I miss him. I was really falling for him."

Melanie set the ornaments down and focused on me. "Don't you think you can work things out?"

"I don't know. I haven't reached out to Niko. I don't know what to say."

"What Would a Wise Wild Woman Do?" Melanie asked.

"I don't know, I really don't."

SINCE JED LEFT, it had become a ritual for Nicole and me to talk on the phone every morning. "Mom, are you sure you want to have Christmas Eve at your house?"

"Yes, everyone will be together this year."

"But Thanksgiving seemed to be stressful for you."

"It was an adjustment doing a big Holiday without Jed's help, but things are different now."

"You sound so much happier now that Jed is gone."

"I am, Nicole. I truly am."

After my conversation with my daughter, I realized I had only two weeks to prepare everything for Christmas Eve. Somehow, I had accomplished almost all of the shopping for my children and grandchildren. I sat at the kitchen table and made a to-do list for today with all the remaining things that needed to be done, including some last-minute gift shopping.

1. Order food from Colonial Farms.
2. Finish wrapping.
3. Set up the train set around the tree for Andrew.
4. Cucumbers for Madison, who insisted on cucumber tea sandwiches for Christmas Eve.
5. Get Josh's chocolate-covered cherries, his personal favorite.
6. Stocking stuffers for Lisa, who I had somehow forgotten.
7. Taylor Swift pajamas for Madison—a last-minute request.
8. Amaryllis plants for Melanie, Jeannie, and Ellen.

Nothing on my list had anything to do with Jed, and it felt good. I stood up and assessed the house for anything else I might be missing. The depressed-looking tree was still standing tall, thanks to Nathan. It was missing several branches due to the over-extensive string wrapping on the car. I knew this tree would remain one of my favorite Christmas memories ever.

It was my first Christmas in more than twenty-five years without Jed. Our long-held traditions were now gone. We would typically take my three youngest grandchildren and his two youngest to Santa's Village, followed by hot chocolate and candy canes. I took them alone last week and wondered if I would run into Jed and Kathleen.

Signs of Jed's absence were evident throughout the house during the holidays. The Christmas tree looked empty without the sentimental ornaments from our life together. We wouldn't be hosting our annual party or attending any celebrations together. Jed would be with Kathleen and their family. I was without Jed, and I was without Niko. But I wasn't alone, and I was okay.

I texted my Grandchildren and their mothers: *Brooke, Kelli, Madison, Kendall, and Andrew: There is a gingerbread decorating contest at Becky's Café and we are going to participate. Let me know when you are available this weekend.* I didn't want to give them an option to not participate.

Nicole: *Mom, I think you retired too soon. Aren't you busy with The Barn?*

Kelli: *How about this Sunday?*

Brooke: *Sunday afternoon around 2:00 works for me.*

Lisa: *I won't be available on Sunday, but I'll check with Josh to see if he can bring Andrew.*

Obviously, Lisa still preferred Andrew to have extra supervision.

Emily: *Sunday would be perfect. It would allow me to finish shopping while the girls are with you.*

I was determined to do one grandmotherly thing this Christmas.

JOSH SETTLED HIS SON on a kitchen chair. "Andrew, have fun with Grandma and your cousins." Then, looking at me, he said, "Mom, don't let him choke on anything, don't give him any candy, and don't let him get too dirty: instructions from Lisa."

I hugged Josh with promises to protect his son.

Josh retreated into the family room to watch football, trusting me to not harm Andrew.

"Are we making this from scratch?" Brooke asked with an incredulous look on her face. "Don't they have kits for this?"

Kelli looked only a tad less confused than Brooke. "When we were little, we just put the sides and roof on and stuck candy on the outside."

I looked down at the flour, spices, butter, eggs, rolling pin, mixer, and pastry bag I had assembled. I immediately questioned my decision to make the gingerbread house from scratch. Pastry bag? I didn't even know such a thing existed before.

I put on my glasses and looked at a printout of the recipe. "We are making it from scratch because this makes it more challenging. Okay, first, everyone put on an apron." I handed each grandchild the Christmas aprons and pastry bags I had purchased for this occasion.

Brooke looked at the red apron with Snowmen dancing in various positions. "Uh, no."

Kelli looked wide-eyed at her Twelve Days of Christmas apron. "Don't you have any plain aprons?"

"Oh, just put them on. Madison and Kendall don't seem to mind," I said. "Do you think some boys will stop by and see you in your aprons?"

Brooke pointed to her three little cousins. "Madison and Kendall put theirs on backwards, and Andrew put his apron on his head."

I went to each child and tied on their festive aprons properly. "Okay, let's get started."

I read the printed instructions: "Measure six cups of flour, fluffing it up from the container."

Kelli pushed her apron around her hips. "Do you have any idea what fluffing it up means?"

"Not a clue. Kendall, you put the flour in the bowl, and Kelli, you help Madison fluff," I said, trying to take control.

Kendall and Brooke put the measured cups of flour in the bowl. Kelli and Madison put their hands directly into the flour, raising it up and down with their fingers.

"Perfect, I think it's sufficiently fluffed," I told my sous chefs.

"Andrew just dumped out the bag of flour," Kendall said, pleased to get her cousin in trouble.

"Oh shit," I said, not as quietly as I should have.

"Grandma said the S word," Kendall said, laughing.

"Mom, what's going on?" For a few moments, I had forgotten that Josh was in the other room within hearing range. He looked at Andrew sitting on the floor, hitting the flour with a rolling pin. "Oh my gosh."

I motioned for Josh to leave the kitchen. "Josh, it's all under control. Go watch your football game."

I removed the flour from the floor, sat Andrew on the counter chair, and while I wiped up the mess, I asked Kelli to read the rest of the recipe.

"The next part is easy," Kelli said. "We add the baking powder, ginger, cinnamon, cloves, and salt. I will add the spices, and Madison, you fluff again."

"Okay, very good," I said, hoping we could get through the next step without incident.

Kelli looked around the counter for a stand mixer. "The recipe calls for a stand mixer to beat the butter, brown sugar, eggs, molasses, and water."

"I only have a hand mixer, but it will be fine. I'll put in the ingredients, and Brooke, you mix it up," I said happily that things were progressing.

"I have to pee," said Kendall.

"Why does she have to pee so much?" Brooke asked.

"Do you want me to pee on the floor, Brookie?" Kendall said, knowing how much her cousin disliked being called Brookie.

Andrew touched my leg to tell me something just as I had started the mixer. It startled me, and I lifted the mixer attachments up. Soon, the gooey mess flew out onto his clothes and cheek.

"I didn't make it to the bathroom in time. I told you so, Brookie." Kendall said, wearing only her apron and sweater.

"Brooke, can you take her to the guest room and get her changed? I keep extra clothes in the dresser."

Brooke looked at me with annoyance. "I bet she peed herself on purpose."

Andrew took a bag of candy and started putting several pieces in his mouth. "I like baking with you, Grandma."

"Kelli, can you just finish the gingerbread house?"

I turned my attention back to the recipe, "Put the flour and molasses mixture together and make a cohesive dough."

Kelli looked at me with confusion. "Cohesive?"

"Oh, just give it a shot. Put it on the floured board and knead it, but not too much. It says we can add more flour if needed."

"It's kind of sticky. Maybe we should add more flour," Kelli said. She took the bag of flour and patted some into the bowl, releasing too much. We both laughed and attempted to remove the overflow of flour. Our attempt created more of a mess until we finally settled on a sufficient texture.

Returning to the printed recipe, Kelli looked at me and said, "Now it goes in the refrigerator for two hours or up to three days. Did you realize that?"

"No, put it in the refrigerator. We'll just leave it for an hour and then take it out. It's going to take an hour to clean up this mess."

A side note: When a recipe says to refrigerate for two hours or more, you really should.

Precisely an hour later, we set the unfinished gingerbread mess on cardboard and began decorating with candy and icing.

Kelli surveyed the odd-looking house. "You know, it's really not that bad," she said, sticking a gumdrop in her mouth.

Brooke started taking pictures. "Are you kidding me? I had to prop up the sides with pretzel sticks. It looks ridiculous."

"Josh, Andrew is a mess," I told my son. "He has icing in his hair. I will give him a bath so you don't have to take him home looking like this."

"Good idea, Mom," Josh yelled from the family room.

I still hadn't heard from Niko.

CHAPTER THIRTY-FOUR

GRANDMA GOT RUN OVER BY A REINDEER.

Why does that song play more often than any other Christmas song?

Every year, I have the grandchildren over to put the final touches on the Christmas tree. Unlike most grandmothers on the planet, it is the only time of the year that I bake cookies.

I sat on my plush light gray carpet and picked up bits of popcorn and cranberries when I heard Kendall's voice rising.

"Grandma, I need you now. Grandma, hurry."

Brooke looked over at me and rolled her eyes. "Why does she have to be so needy?"

I decided to ignore Brooke's impatience with her younger cousin and put my arm around her shoulder.

I rushed into the kitchen, where Kendall, Madison, and Andrew were baking cookies. "Where's Kelli?" I said, looking at Andrew sitting on the floor with a bag of chocolate chips. "She's supposed to be baking with you."

Madison moved her hips back and forth. She pointed to the laundry room. "She's talking to a boy."

Hearing the noise, Kelli came out of the laundry room. "Oh no, what happened?"

Kendall looked at Kelli. "You were making kissy faces on the phone and not watching us."

I walked over to Kelli, gave her a hug, and pointed to the three little ones. "Obviously, we can't leave them alone."

I heard the sound of the front door open and hoped it wasn't Lisa. "Hurry, Kelli and clean up Andrew." Kelli scooped up Andrew and rushed him into the bathroom, knowing the importance of returning a clean, unharmed child to his mother.

Once I heard the gravelly masculine voice, I knew who it was.

"Ho, Ho, Ho, Merry Christmas."

I walked into the living room to see Jed holding a large, beautifully wrapped Christmas present. "Looks like you are having quite the party."

Madison and Kendall ran into the room and hugged Jed's legs. They had become adjusted to Jed not being around all the time. "Pop Pop," the girls said in unison.

Jed placed the present under the tree and then hugged the girls. "It's so good to see you. I've missed you both so much."

Brooke and Kelli walked in with Andrew and looked at Jed.

"Why are you here, Jed?" Brooke said.

Jed held hands with Madison and Kendall. "I stopped in to see your grandmother. It's good to see both of you."

Kelli took a few steps towards Jed and looked back at Brooke to see how she was reacting.

As Brooke folded her arms tightly around herself, she looked at me and then at Jed with obvious disdain.

I was shocked that Kelli continued toward Jed and hugged him. As she typically emulates Brooke's behavior, I was pleased that she was responding to her own feelings.

I could see the wetness forming in Jed's eyes as he gratefully accepted and returned Kelli's affection. Jed held a special affinity for Kelli. He was the patriarch of the family and their only grandfather. Jed had taught Kelli how to play chess when she was very young. Whenever they were together, she would retrieve the chess set, and they would retreat to a quiet room and play for hours. Jed had attended dance recitals, soccer games, and school events for every grandchild.

Jed was a wonderful and endearing grandfather. In so many ways, he was also a perfect husband. With just that one huge flaw.

Brooke looked appalled at the warmth shared by Jed and Kelli. "Does your girlfriend know where you are?"

I put my arm around Brooke. "It's okay, sweetheart. Could you and Kelli take the kids upstairs?"

Without another word, Kelli escorted Madison, Kendall, and Andrew to the loft while Brooke stood grounded in her stance.

I gently walked her towards the stairs. "Brooke, I understand your anger towards Jed, but please don't be rude. He has been a good grandfather to you and loves you dearly."

Brooke looked at me with rage and confusion. "How can you say anything nice about him after what he did to you?"

I embraced her tenderly and looked her in the eyes. "Honey, what Jed did to me and ultimately to our family was horrific. But I have put down my anger and moved on with my life. I can't forget what he did to our marriage, but I forgive him. I know he is repentant and continually apologizes for his behavior."

Brooke was unable to accept my words. "That's bullshit, GMOM. Please tell me you aren't taking him back."

"No, never. I am extremely happy in my life. I have an amazing, beautiful, loving, crazy family and phenomenal friends. My life is very full and rewarding. This experience has made me stronger and eager to explore the next chapter of my life. Now, you need to do yourself a favor and let it go."

Brooke held on to me before she started towards the stairs. "I don't understand how you can be so forgiving."

"By forgiving, I am no longer the victim."

Jed sighed heavily, bent his head down, and closed his eyes. "Ahh, that hurts." He lifted his head and looked at me. "I miss those kids, Andi." Jed tried his wide-eyed, sensual look on me to no avail. His mood was raw, his face was reddened with evidence of heavier drinking, and he had lost more weight.

I felt saddened for Jed and put my hand on his arm. "Why are you here?"

Jed put his hands in his pockets. "I saw my lawyer yesterday and signed the divorce papers." There was regret in his voice and eyes. "Thank you for the generous settlement."

I gave Jed a slight hug. "I wish you well. I really do." I could feel a slight tremble and hesitation from him. "Take good care of yourself, Jed."

Jed backed away from me and kept his head down. "You, too. If you ever need anything, please call me. Merry Christmas, Andi."

"Merry Christmas, Jed. Give my best to Kathleen and your family."

I watched Jed turn away and walk out the door. There was nothing further that needed to be said. And, with that, my life for 25 years was officially over.

I would miss Jed. I would miss the partner I had become so accustomed to having in my life, as well as the sex and the companionship. It really had been a good marriage until it wasn't. It may have been riddled with lies and unfaithfulness, but there were also many cherished moments.

I had recently had a few homeowner's mishaps without Jed here, and I was sure I'd continue to have more. I didn't realize I had to shut the water off outside and nearly froze the pipes. I'd never had to take or bring in the trashcans before, with the exception of when Jed had a knee replacement. Jed put gas in my car when needed and scheduled oil changes. I didn't know where to find the appliance manuals and warranties, and I supposed I'd have to learn how to do minor repairs. Perhaps I should also get a standing mixer. And a cookbook. I could start baking. I already had a pastry bag.

But I would be fine, and I'd learn as I went along.

I was, after all, a very wise and very wild woman.

After the grandchildren left and the kitchen was restored, I sat on my favorite chair facing the tree with its barren branches. I gazed at the white lights and thought of my 70 Christmases. It had been a difficult and challenging year. I was now divorced and alone. And yet, this had been my favorite Christmas season. It took me a long time to get here. To get to the place where I felt authentic.

I looked with satisfaction at the presents I had put under the tree.

Except for the three youngest grandchildren, I decided to make this year's Christmas gifts "experiences." There was rock climbing, zip-lining, and an escape room for Brooke & Kelli. Scuba diving lessons for Nathan and Emily and a hot air balloon ride for Nicole and Eric. A getaway weekend, including babysitting, for Josh and Lisa.

As I was turning off the lights, I saw the present from Jed. I bent down to pick it up, and it was too heavy to lift without using both arms. I brought it into the kitchen and set it on the counter. I laughed heartily when I took off the bow, unwrapped the pretty wrapping paper, and saw a toolbox. It contained everything a "handywoman" would need. Something tells me Kathleen may have suggested and wrapped the gift.

I was still hoping for a relationship with Niko. Perhaps now, since the divorce was final, we could see each other again. I'd made a Christmas gift for Niko, too. I took the empty pizza box from Maggiano's, where we had gone for our first date. I remembered Niko saying that his Moby Dick book was torn, so I put a new copy in the box. It was wrapped and in my bedroom closet in hopes that someday, and hopefully soon, I would see him.

WE ALL GATHERED IN MY HOME on Christmas Eve. I was wearing a green velvet pantsuit I had purchased from Sweet Repeats.

Nicole grabbed my hand, "Mom, why are you crying?"

Everyone stopped opening gifts and turned to look at me. No matter how hard I tried, I couldn't stop the tears from flowing. I held the gift from Brooke and Kelli in my hand. "This is incredible. I love it so much."

Kelli came to my chair and hugged me, "Grandma, these last six months have been so much fun with you, and we wanted to show you how much we appreciate you."

I turned the picture around for everyone to see. It was a collage from our adventures this year. There was one of me on the last mud obstacle when I finally made it over the top. I was covered in mud, and the only thing showing was my vast smile of accomplishment. There were pictures of me with each grandchild, our faces aglow with love. One of the pictures was of Madison and me on the deep-sea fishing boat before the upturning of my stomach. I hadn't realized Brooke had taken a picture of our dilapidated Gingerbread House. My favorite was the photo of all of us in the car with the string wrapped around it before Nathan cut it away.

While I had specified no presents, Nicole sat beside me, putting a present in my arms.

"Mom, you are an inspiration to me and to all of us," she said, a few tears dripping down her cheeks.

I unwrapped the box and held up a sweatshirt with "One Tough Mudder" imprinted in bright purple lettering.

Just when I had a grip on my tears, Lisa handed me another gift.

She stood in front of me as I opened it and smiled.

I looked at her in disbelief, and the tears sprung again. "Oh my gosh, this is fantastic. I'm going to have another grandchild," I said, looking at the sonogram she had wrapped up in a pretty red box.

This was who I am, and these were my people. They were each unique and fabulous, and my blessings were many. I didn't know what the future held for me, but I knew I'd welcome new opportunities and tackle any obstacles with determination.

"Grandma, look, it's snowing," Andrew said as he took my hand to look out the window. "Can we go outside and watch the snow?"

I bent down and picked up my youngest grandchild. "Of course, we can. Let's go."

We gathered our coats, hats, and gloves and headed out the door.

"Wait, stop, we can't leave yet," Brooke said. "Kendall, go pee first."

CHAPTER THIRTY- FIVE

When I walked in, Ellen was smoothing a pink tablecloth on the last table.

I picked up one of the tea cups, sitting perfectly atop a white doily. "Every detail looks absolutely amazing," I told Ellen. "Looks like you are all set for the family and friends grand opening."

Ellen tugged her frilly apron off and smoothed her long skirt. "I feel like I'm in a fairy tale, and my dream has come true."

"Oh Ellen, this is so amazing and you are the princess in the story."

Ellen nervously looked at her watch, "I only have 20 more minutes before they arrive. I have to go check on the scones and sandwiches." She gave me a quick kiss on my cheek and dashed out of the room.

When Ellen left, I scanned the tearoom, taking over a quarter of the first floor in The Barn. Eight round tables were set with single red rose centerpieces and vintage teapots. The room was ready to host our family and vendors for the private preview of *Grandma Ellen's Tea Room*. In just a few days, a New Year would begin along with the opening of The Barn and Tea Room.

I turned toward the sound of heels to find Melanie dressed for the occasion. She wore a long plaid skirt, a white ruffled blouse, a green faux feather fascinator hat, and a matching green feather boa.

Jeannie followed Melanie inside. She looked absolutely stunning in a vintage red rose dress and white hat with delicate red carnations. As she entered the room, she held Chuck's arm, who wore a matching red tie.

With my black velvet, low-back dress and black fringed hat, we were quite the trio.

Chuck put his arm around Jeannie and smiled as if he had

won the lottery. "I'm so delighted to finally meet everyone. Jeannie talks about you all the time."

We directed Chuck to where Jack and Tim were sitting and introduced them to each other. The three men were soon engaged in a lively conversation. For a quick second, I allowed myself a twinge of sadness that Jed was not sitting with them.

I miss Jed often, especially at times like this. I missed him over the holidays and the cherished times of lengthy discussions about the events in our lives. Of course, I missed him the day after Thanksgiving when the garbage disposal broke. I suppose I will always grieve for the loss of our relationship, the loss of what I thought was honest. But I have become stronger and more grounded from the past traumatic months.

As I looked at the empty seat where Jed would have sat, I rejoiced in my new life and silently wished him well in his new life.

MELANIE, JEANNIE, AND I looked for Ellen to offer our assistance.

Jeannie picked up one of the dainty napkins, "Ellen really went all out. This is beautiful, I love it."

I watched Ellen enter the room with a silver tray laden with Royal Copenhagen teacups. "There's Grandma Ellen now," Melanie said, smiling at her.

Much of the china Ellen was using had been found in several boxes that were in the large outbuilding. She had also found two old rusted bicycles and several tables that Jack was able to restore. We had repurposed many of the items from the barn and the buildings, adding character and charm.

Ellen put the tray on a long side table and retied the red bows on each white slipcovered chair. "Ladies, can you believe this? I always dreamed of opening a tea shop, and here I am at 69, starting a new career, actually my first career."

The four of us sat at one of the tables, taking long breaths before everyone arrived.

Melanie and Ellen went to the guest house to retrieve the numerous platters as we heard the sound of cars pulling in.

Jeannie and I greeted our guests as they started to arrive.

Wearing matching pink party dresses and carrying little white patent leather purses, Kendall and Madison ran up to me with outstretched arms. "Grandma, this is a real tea party and not with plastic teapots," Kendall said. Madison took Kendall's arm and told her, "This is a grown-up party, and you have to act like a lady."

I bent down and wrapped them both in my arms. "You girls look so adorable."

Kendall and Madison ran to the first table to join Ellen's grandchildren.

Since fancy tea party attire was optional, Brooke and Kelli arrived in short black skirts and midriff-baring sweaters.

I pointed to the gold hat rack with hats and fascinators in varying colors and styles. "Would you girls like to find hats and scarves to wear with your *little* outfits?" I said to my teenage granddaughters.

I looked at Nicole, Emily, and Lisa with approval. To my delight, each of them dressed appropriately for the occasion.

Nicole scanned the room with wide-eyed approval. "Mom, the room looks amazing."

Lisa waved a white-gloved hand to me, "Andi, this is spectacular. I love tea parties."

I finally found an activity where Lisa willingly participated without judgment.

I kissed her gently, "Thank you, my dear."

Nicole ran up to Ellen, her Godmother, and hugged her. "Ellen, this reminds me of all the tea parties I used to have with you."

I was thrilled to see the last two guests had arrived. Becky and her 11-year-old daughter, Aubrey, had accepted my invitation. I had only seen Becky twice in the past two months since I had been avoiding the café. We hadn't entered our dilapidated gingerbread house and didn't attend the contest.

Wearing matching red and white polka dot dresses, white heels, and red feather hats strategically placed over their left eyes, they greeted me with genuine hugs. "Thank you so much for inviting us," Becky said, eyeing the room. "This place is spectacular. Have you thought about having birthday parties here?"

"No, we haven't, but what a fantastic idea," I said. "Thank you so much for coming. Our official grand opening is in a few weeks. This is our test run. We look forward to getting your opinions and any suggestions you may have."

As I walked Becky and Aubrey to a table, Becky leaned into me softly, "Dad misses you."

"I miss him, too. Very much."

GRANDMA ELLEN'S grand opening was a huge success. All the guests raved about the delicate triangles of deviled ham, egg salad, and cucumber sandwiches. And, of course, her multiple selections of scones with clotted cream and lemon curd were the favorites. I enlisted the help of Brooke and Kelli for clean-up so Ellen could go home for some much-deserved rest.

Ellen let out a long breath. "I don't know how to thank the three of you for making this happen."

I put my arm around my dear friend. "We should thank you. Grandma Ellen's tearoom will bring in many customers to The Barn."

The Barn was all set now. Our vendor spots were filled and ready for our Grand Opening at the beginning of the year.

Jeannie and Melanie said goodbye to Chuck and Jack, who had graciously offered to allow the three of us time for a private celebration.

After all the guests had left, Melanie, Jeannie, and I walked through The Barn for our final inspection. There were 32 vendor blocks with scarves, jewelry, pottery, clothing, and so much more, all on the first floor with Grandma Ellen's tea shop.

The second floor included vintage and antique items and a section of artwork by women from the art gallery in Mathews Island.

"Thank goodness we don't have to climb up the three flights of stairs often," Melanie said while holding onto the railing.

Jeannie walked through the rows of young evening wear on the top floor. "It's a perfect place for the prom and bridal dresses. Brooke and Kelli really did a great job with the setup."

We put on our coats and walked outside. First, we went into the guest house, which will now be the location for our Sweet Repeats shop. We had hired a moving company to transfer the merchandise from Sweet Repeats to the guest house.

I looked around the converted house where we used the bedrooms for varying clothing styles. "I'm so glad Mary Jo wants to manage Sweet Repeats. She has been a tremendous help ever since the day she brought in her handmade scarves."

We continued our walk outside and headed back to The Barn.

Melanie pointed to the largest outbuilding, "I am so excited about turning this building into an art studio."

Jeannie looked at me with concern. "Are you okay with Jed supervising the renovations?"

I took a heavy sigh. "I am. I appreciate Jed's help, and it's comforting knowing we can depend on his expertise. And, Jeannie, as long as you are the go-between person, it will be fine."

We walked over to the other building, which needed significant renovations. "I spoke to someone who does stain glass work and is looking for a place. It would be a wonderful addition, and I hope it works out," Melanie said.

We returned to The Barn to retrieve our things as we prepared to leave.

As we walked back into the main room, I looked around and said, "Looks like we are all set."

Jeannie smiled broadly. "And the best part is with our newly hired manager we won't have to be here every day. Chuck and I plan on doing some travelling."

Melanie raised her arms in delight. "Jeannie, I am so happy for you. You deserve all the best."

We sat down at one of the tables in the tearoom. I put my exhausted feet on one of the chairs. I looked at my dear friends with teary eyes and waved my arm around the room, "We did it—we did all of this. I am so honored to have accomplished this with you."

Jeannie looked at us with watery eyes, "I'm so proud of us."

The three of us held hands with a mixture of laughter and tears.

We sat for several minutes and rejoiced in our accomplishments.

Melanie stood up. "I better go before I fall asleep."

I hugged them both. "I will lock up the back, you two go ahead. It was a fantastic day."

Just as I finished locking up the back door, I heard the sound of a car on the gravel driveway. I assumed Melanie or Jeannie had forgotten something.

I opened the door, shocked to see the one person who had been in the back of my mind all day. Niko. In a black suit and tie. With yellow roses.

My mouth dropped open, my eyes widened, and I stumbled to get the words out, "Um, what, why, um, you look incredibly handsome. Why ...."

I backed up several feet and reached for the counter to lean on.

I inhaled the woodsy scent of Niko's cologne as he moved closer. He placed the flowers on the counter.

He finally spoke after several moments of silence. "I wanted to congratulate you on The Barn. Becky told me that the tea party this afternoon was amazing and Aubrey is already planning on having her birthday party here. They both told me how glamorous you looked, so I thought I should dress the part." Niko stepped even closer. "You do look fabulous, Andi."

I felt a tear travel down my face. "I've missed you, Niko. I'm sorry things were unsettled before, but ...."

Niko took out his phone and within seconds, "Fly Me To The Moon," began to play. He pulled me into his arms, "I was wondering. Would you be my date for New Year's Eve?"

CHAPTER THIRTY-SIX

The following April

I PUT MY BRAND-NEW Rose Gold Kenneth Cole luggage on the bed and prepared to pack up from my week at the Sisterhood Festival. As I started placing my belongings into the bags, I reflected on the amazing turn of events in my life this past year.

It had been a year of hurdles, as I suppose much of life is meant to be. But this year had been monumentally teeming with changes. I retired from my business and expanded another, was betrayed by my serial-cheating husband, discovered a wild woman had been living deep in my soul, and met a dark-eyed, loyal Greek man who brought much joy into my life amidst all the turmoil.

But alas, the hurdles, along with the pleasures, continue as life evolves. Jed was diagnosed with cirrhosis of the liver caused by excessive alcohol use. His weight loss has aged him considerably. Much to Niko's dismay, I had seen Jed a few times within the last few months. It's hard to remove him completely from my life as I worry about his health and well-being. It's difficult to dismiss someone who was such an instrumental part of my life for many years.

Niko and I are still finding our way around each other, and oh, what a pleasure that has been! For the most part. I don't think he will ever be comfortable until Jed is completely removed from my life.

I REALIZED I HAD neglected to return a call from Niko.

"Hi honey, I'm so glad to hear from you," Niko said when he answered my call.

"I'm sorry, sweetheart, I meant to call you earlier, but we were in classes all day. How is your dad?"

"He's about the same, charming the nurses and telling stories."

"And, how are you doing? I've missed you."

"I've missed you, too," he said. "Feels like you've been gone for months. I had lunch with Nathan yesterday, and we were laughing at the pictures from Nicole. I loved the shot of all of you in a drum circle."

"You should have seen the girls belly dancing."

"I would have preferred to have seen you belly dancing."

I laughed softly as I touched my not so tight middle. "Tonight is the final event. The Full Moon Goddess Ceremony is being held around a bonfire."

"I'm so glad you are having a good time. When will my wild Goddess be back?"

I sat back down on the bed and leaned against my luggage. "I should be home by early afternoon tomorrow, probably by 3:00. Do you want to meet me at my house, and I will show you my eight lunar phases?"

I heard the soft hmmmm from Niko's voice. "This should be interesting. Eight phases?"

I leaned further against my Kenneth Cole. "Yes, the moon can be full, waxing, and crescent."

I listened to the familiar sensual tone of Niko's voice. "Say no more; I'll take them all."

After we hung up, I envisioned showing Niko the ritual moon dance circles I had learned.

Just as my mind had turned to inviting Niko into my own sacred lunar space, I received a text from Jed:

My truck hitch is still in the garage. Okay if I stop by and pick it up?

Sure, I won't be home until later. You still have the garage opener, so just go in.

I heard movement from outside my cabin room. Brooke was standing in her typical impatience mode. "GMOM, are you ready?"

"Yes, I'll meet you down there. Are Emily and the girls ready?"

"I just saw them leave their cabin."

I was the last to arrive at the bonfire. I wanted to have a view of the beautiful women in my family before I joined them.

My eyes filled with tears of joy as I looked at Nicole, Brooke, Kelli, Emily, Madison, Kendall, and Lisa. Kendall was curled up on Kelli's lap, mesmerized by the brilliance of the flames.

"Do you think I will be a Goddess someday, too, Grandma?" Kendall said with her eyes still on the fire.

"I think you already are, my love," I told her.

"What does a Goddess mean?" Kendall asked me with wonder.

"It means you are free to be yourself and whatever you want," I told her.

Emily knelt down in front of her daughter. "Sweetheart, when you are in touch with yourself, nothing can stop you from reaching your goals. Like Grandma said, always be true to the real you."

Madison stood up and addressed all of us, taking a bow. "I am brave, I am kind, I am strong, I can do anything!"

Emily looked at her daughter with watery eyes. "Was that your final affirmation?"

Madison nodded and smiled with a beam brighter than the flames from the fire.

Earlier today, we were asked to write positive affirmations for ourselves and things we would like to remove from our lives.

Kendall curled up tighter on Kelli's lap. "I asked for the world not to have any more bullies," Kendall's sweet little voice murmured.

Kelli wrapped her arms around her young cousin. "That's perfect, Kendall." She took a deep breath and said, "I want to remove as much drama from my life as possible."

Nicole reached over and gave a tight squeeze to her younger daughter.

I remained standing lovingly looking at the beautiful women in my life. Brooke joined me and wrapped her oversized L.L. Bean plaid shirt around her shoulders. She faced us with her hands on her hips and looked serious. "I have learned to stop pressuring myself to be perfect. I've heard the word *authentic* so many times this week. And, that's what I want, to be true to myself and not the image of what I think others want me to be."

I heard Nicole's soft clearing of her voice as she got up and stood next to me.

Nicole reached for my hand before she spoke. "Mom, I've watched this past year as you have triumphed over a difficult time with courage and determination. You are stronger now than ever before, and from that, I have learned the greatest lesson."

I will forever cherish these moments when all was right with the world and the stars aligned perfectly. "Thank you all so much for coming on this journey with me."

"Andi," Lisa called out to me. "Come sit here," she patted the chair next to her. "Charlotte Andrea is moving quite a bit today," she said as she rubbed her swollen belly. "I can't believe I am doing this," she said with a glint of amusement.

"Doing what, Lisa?"

"This Sisterhood of the Moon Festival." Lisa tapped her six-month-old unborn child. "It really is different having a girl."

I didn't want to leave this spot. I wanted to stay for hours and capture this precious moment in my heart for eternity. These were my women, the young and the very young. And they were my Goddesses.

Life was good. Oh, so good.

I PULLED INTO MY PERFECTLY ARRANGED quad community with a smile on my face and warmth in my heart. Until.

I closed my eyes for a brief second, hoping it was a mirage. Two cars parked in my driveway: a black jaguar next to a Ford 150. It can't be. It just can't be. Oh Shit! I completely forgot that I had changed the garage code. Actually, that was Niko's idea, so Jed wouldn't have access to come and go whenever he pleased. Jed must have come for the hitch and couldn't get into the garage.

Since Jed and Niko had taken the two parking spots in my driveway, I parked in front of the house where I could see the two men, who shouldn't ever be together, sitting on my patio.

Talking. As I walked up the patio with trepidation and concern, neither one of them seemed agitated. No macho chest huffing, just two men talking about golf. And smiling.

While Niko retrieved the luggage from my car, Jed and I walked to the garage.

Jed's gait was slow, and his breathing was labored as he spoke. "He's a good man, Andi. I'm glad he's in your life."

After Jed left, Niko embraced me whole-heartedly in the driveway while I awaited the fallout from Jed's appearance at my home.

"Tell me all about your trip. I can't believe how much I have missed you."

What type of alternate universe had I just stepped into? No comment about Jed at all.

As we walked into the house, I turned to Niko, "I think I should get you a key."

TO MY GODDESSES:

As I look at each of you, my heart overflows with intense love and devotion. I am blessed and honored to have you in my life, and I cherish you with all my being.

It may have taken 70 years to find my authenticity, but this is my reward. Every moment of pain, sorrow, sadness, and uncertainty has led me to appreciate the depth of where I am now. And I'm not done. I am far from finished. You may not always understand my decisions and how I choose to live my life, just as others may not understand your choices as you travel on your own journey. That's okay; just make them **your** *choices.*

There will be moments when you will have all the confidence and belief in yourself to face the world head-on. You will have strength and convictions in your actions and be surrounded by unexpected joy and happiness. You will float so high on a silver cloud that you will feel in-vincible. But sometimes you will fall so hard, and the pain will seem unbearable, and you will think you will never get up again, and some of those times, you won't want to.

I wish I could shield you from those sad and challenging times, but those difficult moments will ultimately provide you with depth, under-standing, and compassion. I will always be your biggest cheerleader, and I will feel your pain, heartache, joys, and happiness as if they were my own.

Remember when your hands reached over the mud pile and helped me reach the top? The next time you feel yourself slipping back and un-able to reach the top, my hands will reach for you.

Spread your wings, take the world head-on, and be the incredible person you were meant to be. Explore the world with wide eyes and an open heart. Experience the highs and the lows with understanding and compassion. Never be afraid to step out of your comfort zone.

It is better to risk being criticized for being true to yourself than to be loved for what you are pretending to be. Rejoice in your individuality. No one else is exactly like you.

It truly is an incredible journey … enjoy.

ACKNOWLEDGEMENTS

A huge heartfelt thank you to my publisher, Nancy Cleary, Wyatt-MacKenzie. You have been a joy to work with, and I am deeply grateful to you for making this dream come true.

My editor, Donna Freitas, thank you for your guidance and encouragement. You are beyond fabulous!

Thank you to my wonderful sister, Peggy, and dear friend, Stefanie Rotter, for your feedback and editing.

To my friend and publicist, Lynn Oros, I treasure you and our friendship.

Gail Ross, for your friendship and "How's the book coming along?"

Helen Ippolito, my own "Grandma Ellen," for teaching me the grace and elegance of tea parties. You're a fabulous friend!

Thank you, Ellen Waldron, for believing in me. Always.

Of course, thank you to my goddesses: Jamie, Brooke, Erin, Magdalena, Kendall, and Robin. Each of you fabulous ladies bring me happiness beyond all measure. I love you so dearly.

We hope you enjoyed *The Golden Years Glitch* by Judy Smith.

It was selected for the "Book Club for One" Card Deck Collection!

Check out these engaging cards based on the book—with book club questions, inspiring golden quotes, *and so much more...*

Visit:
WyattMacKenzie**Books**and**Gifts**.com

Or scan:

We have promotional copies — request one for your Book Club!

You can also get a free pdf of the Book Club questions.

Use the Contact Page at the website above.